She was rich. Penny s̶̶̶̶̶̶̶̶̶̶̶̶̶̶̶̶̶̶̶̶̶̶̶ fact. It was all right for Fiona, she and Alastair had moved seamlessly into the echelons of the upper-middle classes. But wealth didn't go with Penny's self-image. Penny Green was an impecunious freelance journalist who lived from hand to mouth and didn't mind about it. Her idea of extravagance was fish and chips with curry sauce on the side. All this money – whatever would she do with it?

Money Talks

Sherry Ashworth

CORONET BOOKS
Hodder and Stoughton

First published in Great Britain in 1997 by
Hodder and Stoughton
First published in paperback in 1998 by Hodder and Stoughton
A division of Hodder Headline PLC
A Coronet Paperback

10 9 8 7 6 5 4 3 2 1

ISBN 0 340 68198 5

Printed and bound in Great Britain by
Clays Ltd, St Ives plc

Hodder and Stoughton
A division of Hodder Headline PLC
338 Euston Road
London NW1 3BH

For my sister, Rona

Thanks to Aunty Sylvie, for inspiration

Chapter One

Just for one moment, Penny let her concentration lapse. It was enough. A searing pain told her that she had stabbed herself in the eye with the mascara brush again. Immediately she screwed her eyes tight shut, and opened them to see two black, crescent moon-shaped black smears below her lashes. Then she said something unprintable.

As she licked at her finger and rubbed at the mascara stains she told herself that it was her mother's fault. Most things were your parents' fault, if you thought about it. On this occasion, the accident most definitely was her mother's fault because she shouldn't have told Penny that Aunty Lily had been matchmaking on her behalf.

Penny could only assume that both her mother and her aunt felt sorry for her because Fiona was getting married today and she was not. Preposterous! Even though Fiona was her younger sister, neither her mother, Rose, nor apparently Aunty Lily could get it into their heads that Penny had not the slightest inclination towards matrimony. Better dead than wed, that was her motto.

She squinted at herself in the mirror. All that rubbing had left her eyes red-rimmed. So she applied a little more foundation and resolutely picked up the mascara brush again. As she thickened and lengthened her lashes she tried not to think about the treachery of her aunt and mother, and the uncomfortable necessity of being rude to an unsuspecting male guest at Fiona and Alastair's wedding.

Penny rose and looked at herself in the full-length mirror on the back of the wardrobe. Yes, she was wearing far too much eye make-up. Excellent. Next she glanced down at the rest of her. The Tummy Trimmer Pantie Girdle was possibly a mistake as, one, it pushed a shelf of flesh above her waistline and, two, it hurt. But there was nothing she could do about it as she had no other underwear with her. She had consented to get ready for the wedding in her parents' house so that they could all leave for the register office together. Not for the first time that morning, Penny decided that had been a grave mistake. Independently, Penny, Fiona, their mother and their father were capable of being rational, sane and well-balanced individuals. Together, hysteria set in.

She struggled into her black camisole and considered the effect on her bust. It didn't flatten it as much as the lady in the dress shop had said it would. Perhaps she would have been better off with a steamroller. Then she stepped into the expensive grey satin trousers bought in honour of Fiona and Alastair. They hung well, even if they did make her look rather hippy. The matching jacket was generous enough to hide that fact, and the overall result, Penny thought, was ... well, it was OK. Then she mussed up her hair with her hands, in an attempt to look raffish.

She looked at herself and saw a fat, slightly garish woman, lacking her sister's natural elegance or her mother's compact neatness, and concluded she probably looked more like her father, which was a problem as he was a man. At that thought Penny smiled at herself and her face brightened, revealing lively dark brown eyes, a full, mobile mouth and an expression of frank good nature. Then she pursed her mouth and tried to appear sombre and thoughtful, parodying to herself the familiar head and shoulders photograph that accompanied her agony column in the *Manchester Post*: Penny Green, the Caring Face of Manchester. That was her too. But today she was donning another persona, that of the bride's sister, and everyone seemed to think that she wanted to be a bride too. Even her mother, who ought to know better.

'Penny!' called a voice from the next room.

It was Fiona. Being the bride, she had the benefit of a

professional beautician who was administering a traditional bridal make-up, presumably without accidents with the mascara brush.

'Penny! She's finished. Come and have a look!' Pleased to be able to think of someone else rather than herself, Penny made her way to Fiona. Her sister was seated on a straight-backed chair by the bedroom window, and the beautician was fussing around her.

'Well?' asked Fiona.

'Wow!'

Penny needed a moment or two to find an appropriate response. Fiona's soft beauty, her faintly freckled skin and pale eyelashes, had gone. Her fair hair was neither in a serviceable pony tail nor in the French plait that she wore for the office. Instead she looked as if she were auditioning for a cover shoot for a brides' magazine. Her hair was piled precariously on top of her head, except for some artfully arranged ringlets that fell at prescribed intervals, framing her heart-shaped face. Foundation had made her complexion flawless, a pencilled outline formed her lips into a perfect bow, and her eyes glittered with eyeshadow and excitement. Fiona's excitement was the only genuine thing about her, Penny decided. Rather her than me.

'Doesn't she look fabulous?' said the beautician.

'Fabulous,' echoed Penny.

'Thanks, Kimberley,' Fiona said.

'Ee, I think it's so romantic! To get married after only six months because you're sure he's Mr Right. It gives you hope, doesn't it?'

'It certainly does.'

The beautician looked up at Penny as she spoke, then stopped in her tracks.

'Don't I know you from somewhere?'

It was coming. Penny winced.

'You're not Penny Green, the Caring Face of Manchester?'

'She most certainly is,' said Fiona, smiling at Penny's discomfiture and her own immaculate face in the dressing-table mirror.

'Are you sisters?' Kimberley asked, delighted. 'Just fancy! I read your letters every week, Penny. I was thinking of writing to you. You give such good advice. You see, my boyfriend owes a lot of money, and me mam says I should give him the push, but I'm dead fond of him – in love, really – and I don't mind him not paying his way ... You don't mind me telling you all this, do you?'

Penny shot a quick glance at Fiona, who answered it with an impish smile. She wasn't going to help her sister out of this one.

'Not at all,' Penny said.

'Well, he bought this garage under the arches and he couldn't make it pay – that's why he owes money – only he can't get another job, and he's on the social. I give him an allowance for his beer so he can go out with his mates but me mam says he's using me and should give me a hand with the housework. But you can't ask your fella to hang out your undies, now can you?'

'You can't do that,' Fiona agreed.

'Me mam says I should give him his marching orders, but I love him to bits. I do, Penny. Now who's right, me or me mam?'

The last thing she wanted to do on her sister's wedding day was solve other people's problems. That was what she did for a living. And yet, if anything was going to restore her to a sense of normality, and more than that, a sense of potency, it was going to be solving other people's problems. Penny felt herself transformed from the bride's inadequate sister to the Caring Face of Manchester. Clark Kent had nothing on her.

'There is something in what your mother tells you. It's not a good idea to establish a relationship in which you provide everything, and he nothing. You're doing all the paying and all the loving. You need to ask yourself whether your choice of an impoverished boyfriend isn't a reflection of your own low self-esteem.'

'Oh. Right.' Kimberley looked disappointed. Penny immediately felt guilty. She was a hard-bitten old cynic. And it was Fiona's wedding after all.

'But if you really love him . . .'

'Oh, I do. I do, Penny.'

'If you really love him, I'm sure you can get through the hard times. Money isn't as important as some people think it is. If you can trust him, and if he's kind to you, that's all that matters.'

'Absolutely,' Fiona chimed in.

Privately, Penny was amused. What did Fiona know about money problems? The adorable, utterly perfect Alastair, that Braveheart among Scotsmen, was quite clearly loaded. He'd courted Fiona with surprise trips to London and Paris, and had even insisted on paying half the cost of the wedding. Not that their father, Harry, had been too pleased. Rose had been more ready to accept, however. But Penny wasn't going to to think about that now. There was no need. She'd made her parents promise that they would not argue today. And, surprisingly, they hadn't. So far.

'Ee, Penny, I do feel better. You've made my day. I feel like I'm getting married myself. Now I must be off, I've got another bride in Little Hulton. Cheery-bye!'

Kimberley snapped her make-up case shut and left the room. Penny and Fiona were alone.

'Nervous?' asked Penny.

'I don't know. I don't feel as if this is happening to me. I feel like I'm acting out my own wedding.'

'Perhaps because it's all so sudden?'

'No.' Fiona was emphatic. 'Even after two weeks, I felt as if I'd known Alastair all my life. I'm comfortable with him. After a time, it seemed strange that we weren't already married. I think it's just the rigmarole of the ceremony that seems artificial.'

'But you wanted it.'

'I know. Because I want to show everyone how much I love him.'

'Fiona, this is beginning to sound like a bad Hollywood movie.'

'You're just like Mum. Anti-romance. You think I'm too happy

– that I'm tempting fate. I think you've been reading too many problem page letters.'

'Did I tell you the one about the woman who's divorcing her husband because he won't give up chomping pickled onion corn snacks every evening?'

'I don't believe it!'

'You'd better. Or the man who can only make love to his wife when he knows other people are nearby?'

'An exhibitionist?'

'Sort of. But isn't a wedding like that? The whole point is that everyone knows you're going to have sex that night. Finally you have permission. I think that takes all the fun out of it. Hordes of relations cheering on your orgasms.'

'Penny!'

'It's not too late, Fiona.'

'Now stop it! And what was it Mum was saying about Aunty Lily wanting you to meet someone?'

'It's someone Kitty knows, apparently. This is something they've been cooking up between them for some time.'

'Has Lily changed her mind? Will she be at my wedding?'

'No. But Kitty's coming.'

Penny smiled to herself. Aunty Lily's outright refusal to attend Fiona's wedding was caused by the fact that her and Rose's brother Simon had been invited too. They hadn't spoken for fifteen years and had no intention of starting now. The *Guinness Book of Records* beckoned. Yet Penny wondered whether there might not be other reasons, too. Lily herself had never married; she, too, was the elder sister – the spinster – when Rose had married Harry. Would this wedding bring back uncomfortable memories? Penny was sad for a moment, then recalled with amusement that Lily had nevertheless insisted that her sidekick, Kitty, her partner in crime in the residential home where they both lived, should be invited. She would be able to find out exactly what went on afterwards.

'Penny, you do like Alastair?' Fiona asked.

'Yes, of course I do.'

'He likes you.'

Penny wondered about that. In fact she doubted whether Alastair had actually noticed her, besotted as he was with Fiona. The truth was, she hated nothing more than trying to communicate with a couple who were welded at the hip and she had vowed never to lose her identity in that way. Then the phone rang.

Both of them turned to look at the telephone, at the side of the double bed. It rang a couple of times, then stopped. Obviously Rose or Harry had picked it up. Fiona left her chair, brushed herself down, and moved towards her wedding dress which was hanging on the wardrobe door.

'Will you help me on with this?'

Then there was the sound of someone scurrying up the stairs, as if there were no time to lose. The girls stopped in their tracks.

Rose threw open the bedroom door. It was a shock to both of them to see their normally dowdy mother in an almost lurid emerald-green suit. She looked absolutely furious. Her eyes were small and hard and her mouth pursed tight.

'What's wrong?'

Penny correctly anticipated the two words that were coming next.

'Your father!'

'What's he done this time?'

'I don't know where to begin! But to cut a long story short, Fiona, you haven't got a photographer.'

Penny felt herself prepare for action again. In her anger at Harry, Rose was firing at random, upsetting Fiona when it wasn't necessary. If there was one role this bride's sister could fill, it was that of problem-solver.

'Sit down, Mum. Look, if I move this bouquet, there's room for you on the side of the bed. Just begin at the beginning.'

'You won't believe this! The photographer apparently rang last night to say that his wife had gone into labour, he had to be with her at the hospital, and his assistant was off with the 'flu. Your father took the call. And he didn't tell me!'

'He probably didn't want to worry you,' Penny suggested.

Rose's 'Huh!' was infinitely expressive, Shakespearian almost. It conveyed immeasurable contempt.

'So who was on the phone now?'

'The photographer, to say he's a proud father and he hopes we've fixed ourselves up with someone else. This time *I* took the call.'

'So did Dad find someone else?'

'What do you think?'

'I'm asking the questions.'

'No, your father didn't find somebody else. He didn't even try.'

Penny was puzzled. That was not the father she knew. Harry would do anything for his daughters, and would certainly kill to prevent Fiona's wedding being spoilt.

'We must have photographs,' Fiona said quietly. Both Penny and Rose turned to look at her and felt guilty.

'Oh, you'll have photographs all right. Your father's taking them,' Rose announced.

'Dad's taking the pictures?'

'He's only just told me.'

Penny laughed. 'But he always misses off the heads!'

'I *know* he always misses off the heads.'

'And his camera's at least twelve years old!'

'Well, young lady, that's where you're wrong. His camera is barely twelve hours old. He went into town last night to buy a Nikon. With the money I'd put aside for re-covering the settee!'

'And he didn't tell you in case you stopped him?'

Rose was silent. Penny had guessed the rest correctly.

'What are we going to do?' asked Fiona, fingering the lacy folds of her dress.

Penny bit her lip and thought. There was bound to be a solution, and she was conscious of her mother and Fiona waiting for her to come up with it. All part of being an Agony Aunt. Everyone expected you to have the answer to everything. A plumber at midnight ... your husband in bed with your best friend ... a new crisis in the Middle East? Just call Penny.

'I can get hold of a photographer,' she said. 'I'll ring round the freelances from the paper. Someone's bound to want an afternoon's work.'

'And Harry can take his Nikon straight back to Dixons.'

'No,' Penny cut in. 'Let him keep it, and he can take some pictures too. Then Fiona can have a choice. Please, Mum.' Rose looked implacable. 'Please?' Rose refused eye contact with her elder daughter, and Penny knew she was winning. 'For Fiona's sake?'

Rose emitted another theatrical sigh, preparatory to a major concession.

'Blow the rest of the settee money on yourself. Take a weekend break at a health farm.'

Fiona joined in. 'Get a new spring outfit.'

'Take a toy boy out for an evening.'

'Penny!' said Rose, shocked.

She smiled to herself. Her mother was ever the prude. Penny enjoyed teasing her.

'I was asked to write a piece on a male escort agency for older women. I was rather hoping you'd do my research. I'll fit you with a bugging device, of course, so you'll be quite safe. The men are absolutely dishy.'

'Penny, you're not serious, are you?'

Rose was not noted for her sense of humour.

'Absolutely. It's my revenge for you and Lily finding *me* an escort.'

Rose laughed now, more from embarrassment than anything else. 'It was Lily's idea. You know she's always looking out for you.'

There was a cautious tapping on the bedroom door.

'Come in, Dad.'

Harry appeared – a tall, greying, well-built man in his late-fifties. His bright multi-coloured embroidered waistcoat contrasted with his sheepish expression. Rose turned her head and would not look at him.

'Sorry,' he said.

She made a short, exasperated noise, something like 'Hurrumph!' Penny was satisfied. It meant her mother was coming round. Fiona's wedding would be a success after all.

The wedding cars had come on time and taken them to the register office where a dapper young man in a smartly tailored suit had ushered them into an imposing room with fleur-de-lys wallpaper. Here Fiona and Alastair were seated in the front row in the centre, there was a brief exchange of vows, a moment of surprise when everyone realised they were now actually married, and Penny found she had cried throughout the whole procedure and now had to contend with a persistent trickle of black mascara from the corners of her eyes.

In the wedding car that she shared with her parents and Alastair's mother, she was able to tidy herself up with a few Kleenex, and by the time they arrived at the Tavistock Suite she was almost presentable. Yet she had stopped caring about her appearance. It was such a relief that the ceremony was over, and now the celebrations could begin. Or, rather, now the alcohol could begin.

Rose placed a restraining hand on Penny as she made for the bar at the far corner of the hall.

'Not yet. We'll have to stay at the entrance and greet the guests.'

'Why me?'

'I think we should all be together,' her mother said grimly.

She made it sound as if receiving the guests would be an ordeal. Which, of course, it would be for her. Penny was highly sensitive to her mother's emotions, had been since a very small child. Reading round the subject had taught her that most elder daughters respond like that to their mothers. So Penny knew that her mother was loathing the thought of the rest of the family trooping in and sizing up the wedding banquet, the decorations in the hall, the clothes they were wearing, then pigeon-holing the Green family. What didn't help was that Harry's family was considerably wealthier than hers, and Rose's brother Simon a Professor of Geography at the university who tended to think of himself as God. His wife, Pearl, being female, naturally thought of herself as somewhat superior to God. Penny couldn't stand any of them.

Feeling a surge of solidarity with her mother, she put her arm in hers just as Harry came in, bringing Fiona and Alastair with him. Both wore beatific smiles and Penny despaired of them. She watched Alastair go over to his widowed mother who, suffering rather badly from arthritis, was seated on a chair near them. That was sad, Penny thought to herself. His father had died only a few weeks ago. It wasn't sudden; he had been very ill with something or other which had led to complications. Margaret, Alastair's mother, had insisted the wedding go ahead. Both she and Alastair had been very brave about it all.

Penny glanced into the body of the hall where round tables were laid with all the paraphernalia of a celebration dinner: artfully arranged serviettes, heavy silver cutlery, menu cards, ice buckets and sprays of flowers. There was a small stage, too, where the band was setting up its equipment, and a parquet dance floor in front of it. A large chandelier hung down from the ceiling.

'Everything looks great,' Penny whispered to her mother.

'I hope the caterers know what they're doing.'

'It's a shame Lily isn't coming.'

Rose allowed herself a small smile. 'Perhaps it's just as well.'

Penny smiled too. She knew what her mother meant. Lily, Rose's elder sister, wasn't exactly the black sheep of the family. On the contrary, she had made more money than the rest of them put together. The chain of dry cleaners she had built up had been remarkably successful. But the truth was, Lily could not be counted on to behave herself. Her raucous Cockney laugh, her habit of speaking her mind and a tendency to confuse home truths with insults had given her a certain reputation. Rose stood

11

by her with dogged family loyalty. Simon wouldn't speak to her. Penny adored her.

'If Lily were here,' she said archly to her mother, 'we wouldn't need an MC. She could do the job, and give a brief character assassination at the same time. "My brother Monty and his wife Sally. Good-natured enough but thick as two planks. Two fools – incapable of running their own lives. Simon and Pearlie . . . I haven't spoken to Simon for fifteen years. So what if I told the committee of his Rotary Club that he wet the bed when he was a boy? It was true, wasn't it? Airs and graces, he gives himself—"'

Rose dug Penny sharply in the ribs, and the pain halted her impression of Lily. Just in time, for Simon himself walked into the hall. Although not exactly slim, he seemed to have swelled with self-importance rather than self-indulgence. His lounge suit was immaculately if generously cut. He kissed everyone in turn as if conferring a favour.

His wife Pearl followed him.

'Penny!' she screamed as she greeted her. 'I read your page every week – I *love* it. I don't know how you think up all those different problems.'

'They're real, Aunty,' murmured Penny.

'Well, I never! Geraldine, did you know Penny's problems were real?'

Geraldine, Simon and Pearl's elder daughter, followed them. Penny found herself stiffening imperceptibly as she greeted her cousin. There was no love lost between them. They were close in age, and being members of the same family, friendship had been enforced upon them. As a child, Geraldine had attended elocution lessons, dancing lessons, piano lessons, and always coloured neatly between the lines. The young Penny had a Manchester accent, couldn't tell her right from her left, and had turned untidiness into an art form.

'Penny! You look lovely!' Geraldine sounded surprised.

'You too. It was a good photo of you in the paper last week.'

Geraldine gave a silvery laugh. 'I looked awful! I'd been dancing all night.'

With one of the Manchester United squad. Geraldine had connections in high places. Mind you, she had to. Geraldine Colman was an image consultant, and therefore whom she knew was more important than what she knew. Penny looked at her now, in a skimpy black dress intended to reveal tanned expanses of flesh. It was the sort of dress created to make other women feel inadequate.

'Montague and Sally Colman!' boomed the MC in a stentorian voice, over the clatter of dishes, the chatter of the guests and the clinking of glasses.

Aunty Sally got to Penny first.

'Penny! Haven't you grown? And doesn't Fiona look lovely? She always was the beauty of the family. And what a wonderful husband she's found herself! Except I couldn't understand a word he said to me. He sounds just like Sean Connery! Fancy Fiona falling in love with a Scotsman. I would have thought you'd have been the one to marry a Scotsman. You were born in Scotland. I remember when Harry rang me up from the hotel to say you'd arrived prematurely ... What a holiday present! Your poor mother! And now Fiona is a married woman. Doesn't time fly? Well, please God by you.'

Aunty Sally emitted conversation constantly, like a radio transmitter sending out programmes. Neither was dependent on an audience. Penny looked longingly at the bar where glasses of champagne and Buck's Fizz were lined up for the guests. How soon could she escape?

'Mum,' she said, 'I'm sure I'm not needed here. Six is too many for a reception line and it's not me everyone wants to see. Why don't I go and mingle with the guests, and make sure everyone's comfortable?'

'Harry, what do you think?'

'Good idea. Look – here's Bobby.'

Penny disengaged herself from the line and moved swiftly towards the bar, avoiding eye contact with anyone so that she would not be pulled into a conversation against her will. At last she reached the bar and helped herself to a glass of champagne. She had to restrain herself from drinking it down in one.

For a moment she yearned for the normality of her comfortable everyday life, her small rented house in Chorlton, her desk at the *Manchester Post*, the satisfaction of reading the letters of thanks she received when her advice had worked and the pleasure they gave her. She had discovered it was easier not to want things for yourself but instead to try to involve yourself with others. You risked less that way.

Something in her flinched from being on show like this at her sister's wedding. It wasn't that she was shy; she enjoyed company and took a real interest in other people. It was just that she was terrified of not living up to their expectations. She knew she wasn't a beauty, she'd failed to get a place at Oxford, and although she preferred to be single, it would have been nice for that to have been a matter of choice. So Penny made the best of a bad job – she had her defences. If you could make people laugh they liked you, and if you could help them so much the better. Thinking that cheered her and she prepared to enjoy the wedding celebrations. But why was it she felt slightly uneasy, just like a sparrow who had sensed, but not seen, the cat lurking in the bushes? Now why was that?

She drained her champagne and picked up another glass. As she did so, she noticed Kitty. Oh, hell, she thought to herself. That was why she felt uneasy. Kitty was planning to introduce her to that man. Apprehension diminished her pleasure at seeing Kitty. Quickly she tried to think of a way of wriggling out of the trap. Ought she to tell Kitty she'd recently started going out with someone? Or that she'd recently discovered she was gay?

To her relief, Penny saw that Kitty was alone. She made her way towards her, carrying a glass of champagne. As she reached Kitty, she kissed her soft cheek, complimented her on her appearance, and proffered the drink.

'Are you allowed champagne?' Penny asked. She wasn't sure if Kitty was on any medication.

'I like champagne.'

It was a politician's answer. Penny handed her the glass with some amusement.

'So, how are you?'

Kitty shook her head. 'I'm not at all well.'

Penny did not enquire further. Kitty, well into her seventies, looked pink with health, but not feeling well was de rigueur for the residents of Gladesmore. In fact Kitty had not gone to live there because of any particular incapacity, but out of loyalty to Lily. After Lily had had her stroke, her friend Kitty followed her, and Penny knew that Lily paid both women's fees.

'And how is Lily?'

'Doing very well. Now you mustn't worry about her, Penny.'

Immediately Penny began to worry.

'She told me to tell you – now, what could it have been? I should have written it down on a piece of paper – paper – that was it! She read a letter you answered in the paper. The one about the lady who wanted plastic surgery. Lily said to tell you you were wrong. She should have the plastic surgery, if that's what she wants.'

Penny smiled.

'Yes, but the woman in question had no income, and from what she wrote to me, I reckoned her problem was more in the mind. Low self-esteem.'

'Lily said she should have had plastic surgery,' Kitty repeated. To her Lily's word was law. 'And she said something else. She said I had to introduce you to—'

'No, it's all right, Kitty. I'll be very busy tonight. I have to look after Fiona.'

'No, I *have* to introduce you. Lily said so. He's a lovely boy. He's been working in America and met Mary Tyler Moore at her country house. He said she was very nice. And he's bought himself a house and had it all done up and Lily thinks he's ready to settle down. But I told her he was a guppy ...'

15

'Do you mean a yuppy?'

'Yes. And ever so good-looking. He came to see me at Gladesmore and Lily liked him straight away and she said to me, she said, "Kitty, he'll do nicely for Penny," and I agreed.'

This was getting worse by the minute. Penny had to stop her.

'I've given up men,' she said. 'Too many calories.'

Kitty looked bemused.

'Look, I'll take you over to Monty and Sally – you remember them? They've come up specially from London. I know they want to talk to you.'

Penny shepherded Kitty to the small table where her uncle and aunt were helping themselves to peanuts, and stayed with them for a while to get them all conversing. Then she rose and surveyed the room, searching, despite herself, for this good-looking acquaintance of Kitty's. Forewarned was forearmed.

It was because she was scanning the crowd that she saw Rick Goldstone before he saw her. She could hardly believe her eyes. How many years was it? Ten, twelve? Rick had been in her class at school, and had acted in drama club plays alongside her. He'd gone to Cambridge, hadn't he? Why was he here? Of course. Rick's mother, Brenda, was a schoolfriend of Rose's.

Penny made her way towards him immediately. An old friend would be most welcome right now.

'Hello, Rick.'

He turned suddenly, and his face filled with delight as he saw her.

'Penny!'

She almost averted her eyes. Rick Goldstone was as good-looking as ever. Not that it bothered her. One of the advantages of being out of the running so far as good-looking men were concerned was that it gave you *carte blanche* to talk to them like a normal human being. Her relationship with Rick had never been romantic. At school, when they'd appeared together in *The Rivals*, he was the handsome hero, Jack Absolute, while she was the dowager Mrs Malaprop. Yes, she was out of the running so far as Rick was concerned. Those laughing eyes and the way the firm lines of his face contrasted with a sensitive, boyish mouth had not affected her then, and they didn't affect her now.

In the moment or two she studied him, he studied her and saw with appreciation that Penny had grown into a woman. She still wore too much eye make-up, though. Looking at her, he felt as if the years had rolled back.

'You're the same,' she said to him, 'but not the same.'

Penny could tell Rick was paying close attention to her and that made her uncomfortable.

'I, however, am exactly the same, only there's more of me,' she said, patting her tummy. Best to get it in first. Show the world that you're perfectly well aware of your shortcomings.

'Posh,' Rick said, referring to her satin trousers.

'You too,' she said. Suddenly she realised that she had come across the ideal solution to the threat of Kitty's matchmaking. If Penny could persuade her that she was with Rick, Kitty would be so blinded by him as to give up her own scheme immediately. It was worth a try. The first step was to keep talking. 'Shall we go and get another drink?' she suggested.

'Same old Penny,' he said.

Spotting a passing waitress, Rick took two glasses of champagne and handed Penny one.

'Are you with your parents?' she asked him, shouting a little so her voice would rise above the noise in the hall. Most of the guests had arrived by now.

'That's right. When they told me about the wedding, I thought it was you who was getting married.'

'Me!' She laughed. 'Didn't you know? I'm the founder member of Celibates Anonymous.'

'Me too. That is, I'm still single.'

Penny was surprised but pleased as it made what she was going to ask him that little bit easier.

'And what are you doing now?' he continued.

'Journalist. Freelance, but I do the problem page for the *Manchester Post*, and a problem hour for Tune FM.'

'An Agony Aunt!'

'Would you have believed it?'

Rick paused and looked at her again, eyes narrowed, as if there was some clue in her appearance. His gaze travelled down her body. Then he looked her in the face and smiled.

'Yes,' he said. 'You always wanted to heal the world.'

'And you?' she asked, changing the subject.

I trained as an accountant. I'm a management consultant now.'

Quite, thought Penny to herself. Rick exuded an unmistakable air of affluence. He continued to smile at her without saying anything. Penny wondered what was amusing him. Had one of the buttons on her camisole popped? She glanced down to check. Everything seemed OK. She decided to move the conversation on, and come to the point.

'It's rather lucky you've turned up tonight. You can save me from a fate worse than death. Believe it or not, a friend of my aunt's has been matchmaking and is dead set on introducing me to a horrendous-sounding American social climber. Me! Can I pretend I'm with you?'

'Why pretend? You *are* with me.'

'Thanks, Rick. Look, here she is now.'

Kitty approached them. Penny gave an audible cough as a signal to Rick.

'Hello again, Kitty. Before you go on to say anything else, I want to introduce *you* to someone. This is Rick. We're engaged to be married.'

Kitty looked delighted.

'Lily will be pleased,' she said. 'It's what we both hoped for. Oh, I am having a lovely time!' And she wandered off again.

'Where's my ring?' Rick asked.

'Shut up. That worked a treat. I wonder where that good-looking American yuppy is?' Feeling safe now, Penny surveyed the guests.

'He's standing right beside you,' said Rick.

Penny turned to look at him.

18

'It was me Aunt Kitty wanted to introduce to you. Her nephew who's just come back from the States.'

'You?' Penny hooted with delight, all the more loudly because the champagne was drowning her inhibitions.

'But, remember, you've committed yourself now. Go back on your word and I'll sue you for breach of promise.'

Penny laughed again. Rick always had been a tease. It was one of the things the other girls liked about him.

'Dinner is served!' boomed the MC.

The waistband of Penny's trousers pressed uncomfortably against her skin. Surreptitiously, she eased it away from her to let her stomach expand. The meal had been every bit as good as she had hoped and marked a fitting end to her pre-wedding diet. She watched the band confer about the first number, saw the bandleader gesture to Harry who in turn spoke to Fiona and Alastair. The dancing was about to begin.

Penny was pleased. She had spent the duration of the meal making conversation with Alastair's mother Margaret on the top table. She was a quietly spoken woman who answered questions economically. By the end of the meal she had given away very little about herself, despite Penny's persistent interrogation. All she had discovered was that Alastair's father used to manage a distillery a very long time ago. Margaret seemed to do nothing now except take out books from the library, sew, and visit housebound villagers. Fiona was going to have fun, Penny thought to herself.

Now the dancing was beginning, she was free to leave the table. She excused herself and moved into the body of the hall. Rick waylaid her.

'Will you dance?' he asked her.

The band had just struck up 'Congratulations'.

'The question should be "Can you dance?" To which the answer is "no". But I'll sit this one out with you. On condition we're close to the bar.'

'Done.'

It occurred to Penny that Rick Goldstone's willingness to squire her this evening probably did have something to do with Kitty after all. No doubt he had been primed by the two aunts: on no account must Penny be allowed to feel left out on her sister's wedding day. But what the hell? He was good company, he knew her well, and she was under no illusions.

'This is fun,' she said, grinning at him. 'I was dreading having to make an effort with someone, and I'm just so relieved I won't have to with you. I'm afraid weddings bring out the cynic in me. Even my sister's.'

'Any particular reason?'

Penny wondered whether to give in to the temptation to bitch about Fiona. Well, perhaps just a little bit.

'All my life I've waited for Fiona to go off the rails, and it seems I'm going to be disappointed. After qualifying as a solicitor and landing a job immediately, she then gets swept off her feet by a dashing Scotsman who instantly proposes. And now she's a happily married woman.'

'What's wrong with that?'

Alcohol was making Penny candid. 'Oh, nothing, except I'm sure I'd like her more if she did something wrong. Or have more in common with her, maybe, Not that *I've* done anything wrong.'

'What a shame. I was hoping to tempt you.'

Penny looked at him and raised her eyebrows. It was a pity he felt obliged to flirt with her. He was over thirty now and should have passed that stage. She ignored his words and continued with her line of thought.

'Also, it's hard to believe that anyone could have such an idyllic existence as Fiona. Something's bound to go wrong, isn't it?'

'Not necessarily. Maybe you anticipate too many problems.'

'Everyone says that. Maybe. But listen to just how lucky Fiona is – Alastair is rolling in it – money, I mean – and not only that, but his mother is giving them her house to live in.'

'That's generous.'

'I'm not so sure. Alastair's father died recently, and I reckon his mother is lonely. The way I see it, by getting Fiona and Alastair to go and live in Scotland, she keeps a son and gains a daughter-in-law.'

'But Fiona wants to go?'

'She's delighted. Claims she's been unhappy in the office, and I guess what she really wants to do is get married and have lots and lots of babies. Real Aga Saga stuff. She'll throw herself into village life and be a wonderful wife and mother. Can you believe it?'

Rick shrugged. He knew Penny's question was rhetorical.

'What does Alastair do for a living?'

'Something to do with computers. Fiona did tell me but I didn't understand. He's on a contract for a firm in Trafford Park, which doesn't expire for six weeks yet. So Fiona's starting her married life alone.'

'Doesn't she want to stay in Manchester with him?'

'I'm sure she does. But Alastair's mother needs help moving out of the house, and Fiona wants to make everything perfect for her new husband.'

'Lucky Alastair.'

Penny threw Rick a contemptuous glance, meant to reprimand him for his political incorrectness. Once again she was disconcerted to see how closely he was watching her. And he still hadn't stopped smiling at her. Perhaps he was on Prozac.

'What do you think of your brother-in-law?' he continued.

Penny paused. She was feeling contrite after her earlier cynicism.

'He's very nice. I mean, I'm sure he's very nice but I don't really know him yet. The trouble is, nor does Fiona. She only met him six months ago.'

Her glance travelled over to Alastair, who was dancing with his new wife. He held her as if she were a precious, fragile object. Alastair was fair-haired, tending to red, rather cherubic in appearance. Penny thought how like Fiona he looked; both of them having an air of vulnerability, a soft beauty. It's all too perfect, she thought.

'So how did you become an Agony Aunt?' Rick continued.

'I'd been working freelance for the paper for some time, doing these personality quizzes – you know the sort of thing, check out the health of your marriage, do you have a roving eye – and at the same time I'd taken a couple of counselling courses and was working for the Samaritans. Then when the editor decided to start a problem page, they gave me first refusal.'

Penny and Rick became aware that they were being joined by a third person. Both looked up to see who it was. Geraldine.

'This is my cousin Geraldine, Rick. Geraldine, this is Rick, an old schoolfriend.'

'And her husband-to-be,' he added.

Geraldine looked puzzled.

'She's just proposed to me,' he told her.

'Don't listen to him, Geraldine. Come and join us.'

Geraldine arranged herself carefully on the chair, her dress riding up her thighs.

'Doesn't Fiona look gorgeous?' she said, looking down at the way her silky dress clung to her own svelte figure.

'Gorgeous,' Penny agreed.

'Whose is the wedding dress?'

'Hers,' said Penny, surprised. Surely Geraldine didn't think Fiona had borrowed it?

'Who is the designer?' she explained.

'Fiona didn't tell me.'

'Can I ask where they're going on honeymoon?'

'Scotland,' Penny said. 'Some big hotel.'

'Nice,' said Geraldine, in such a way as to insinuate it might not be nice enough. 'And you, Penny? How's work?'

'Busy. February is suicide month.'

Geraldine smiled, but directed it at Rick. Then she glanced at Penny again. 'I read your page sometimes. You must find it hard not to laugh at the some of the letters you get.'

'Unfortunately most of them are pretty serious reading.' Penny was growing irritated.

'You're actually quite famous now,' her cousin persisted. 'I heard you on the radio. I bet you're making a lot of money.'

'I'm off income support, if that's what you mean.'

Geraldine laughed and Rick cut in, 'But you're a freelance, Pen. Surely you could make as much money as you like?'

She sensed his loyalty to her, and appreciated it, but Rick had missed the point.

'I'm not into making a lot of money. One, I'm sure it doesn't bring happiness, and two, when most of the problems I deal with are caused by lack of money, it would be pretty hypocritical of me to profit from them. I couldn't do that.'

He looked interested.

'But surely you have the right to make a living from helping people? And the right to seek prosperity?'

'You sound like Thatcher,' Penny said acidly, almost spitting the name at him.

'There's nothing wrong with being rich.'

Geraldine agreed.

'There is.' Penny was adamant, and irritated too. 'By definition being rich means having more of any available resources, therefore the condition of being rich creates poverty. One state controls the other.'

'So what would you do if you were rich?' Rick persisted, enjoying seeing Penny ruffled. 'Say, if you won the lottery?'

'I don't play the lottery,' she said loftily.

'But if you did?'

'I'd give it away,' she said. Of course she would. Wealth was unthinkable; at least, unthinkable for her. Perhaps she would give her parents some money first, but then, certainly, she would give it all away. She was absolutely sure she was telling Rick the truth.

'Everyone claims they'd give their money away,' piped up Geraldine. 'But money is irresistible.'

'Not to me it ain't,' countered Penny.

'But I'm irresistible,' said Rick.

'That's why I came over,' Geraldine said demurely. 'I was hoping you'd ask me to dance.'

Penny was taken aback. Fancy nicking him from right under

her nose! Then she reminded herself that Rick didn't belong to her, and that really she had no objection to his dancing with someone else. If only that someone wasn't Geraldine! Perhaps he'd turn her down. Then the band struck up 'If I Were A Rich Man', and Rick rose to escort Geraldine on to the floor.

Penny watched them go feeling slightly betrayed. He was supposed to be her old friend. Yet he'd been picking arguments with her, and had gone off with Geraldine. She watched them move round the floor and noticed they were talking. Penny felt excluded.

Then she smiled to herself. What had she been thinking? It wasn't as if Rick had sought her company on his own initiative. Geraldine was probably much more his type. Penny was getting above herself, hankering after the likes of Rick Goldstone. Come on, Cinderella, it's twelve o' clock, she told herself.

So the Caring Face of Manchester prepared to think of something, or someone, else. Not herself. Instead Penny tried to pick out her parents on the dance floor, and sure enough there they were, her mother looking rather ill at ease in Harry's arms, and he beaming over her shoulder at the couples they passed. It was odd for Penny to see her parents in such close proximity to each other. They led such separate lives now. She supposed most marriages ended like that, once the momentum of having and rearing children had run its course.

She watched her father break away from her mother, who went back to her table to speak to Fiona, sitting this dance out. Harry, meanwhile, approached the party from his school. He taught music at the local comp and had insisted on inviting all the peripatetics. Penny knew this had been against Rose's wishes. She saw a rather bony woman in a plain black dress rise, and watched Harry take her on to the dance floor. She seemed to cling to him rather pathetically, Penny thought. And her father looked almost paternal as he danced.

It was sad that her parents argued so much. When she was younger Penny used to imagine impossibly dramatic reasons for their constant rowing. Now she knew it was a lot simpler than that: Rose saved money and Harry spent it. That was enough to make any two people miserable. Not having money shouldn't make you miserable, but it does, Penny thought, just like not having a man. That was true for most people, of course. But not her.

And then, naturally, she thought of Lily. Her aunt had money but no man. It was a shame Lily had missed the wedding through her own mulishness, and yet the time to worry would be when she lost that fighting spirit. Her first stroke had not dimmed it.

She was still the scourge of Gladesmore Residential Home. Only Kitty could put up with her. Penny smiled to herself at the thought of her aunt, and resolved to go and visit her tomorrow and tell her all about the wedding. The resolution cheered her. The music came to an end and Rick came back to join her just as a waltz began.

'May I have the pleasure?' he asked.

I can't stand being patronised, thought Penny, but I'll show him.

'I'd be delighted,' she said. 'But I'm not the world's best dancer.'

'You're always putting yourself down,' he commented.

Oh, yes? thought Penny. I'll get you for that.

As they moved on to the crowded dance floor, and Rick guided her into the middle, she stepped smartly and deliberately on his toe. And I hope I've ruined his Guccis, she thought.

Chapter Two

Fiona couldn't believe how lucky they'd been.

All yesterday, while she and Alastair had been driving to Scotland, the skies had been a crystal blue, and with the car's heating on, she could almost have thought it was summer. Only the dusk falling at four o'clock persuaded her otherwise. It had been dark when they'd arrived at the Loch Kyle, but the hotel had been a blaze of welcoming lights, and since it was out of season, it felt as if everything had been laid on specially for them.

Their room was wonderful: rich tartan curtains, a tartan bedspread, a mahogany mini-bar and a view across the loch with a ruined castle on the far shore. They had dined on gravad lax and venison, and had lain in each other's arms all night, revelling in the luxury of not having to make love. They had the rest of their lives for that.

Alastair had woken first in the morning, and gone to the window to pull open the curtains. Brightness flooded the room. Fiona could hardly believe it when she came to join her husband and saw all the snow. It had fallen silently during the night and now covered everything. The rest of the world had vanished, and all that was left was Alastair and Fiona, a prince and princess in an enchanted castle.

So they had risen late, had a light breakfast, and sat in the conservatory to look out over all that whiteness. Fiona had brought a novel with her to read, but found she could not concentrate. Instead she glanced idly at a copy of *Good Housekeeping*, and even then was too happy to do anything more than look at the pictures and imagine herself and Alastair living in such sophisticated interiors. They could sit together on that sofa, his arm around her; that four-poster bed would make a wonderful centrepiece for the master bedroom, and they could hide inside it, and stay there all Sunday. Perhaps she would suggest a four-poster bed? They would certainly need something like that. It would seem odd, sleeping in Margaret's. These were the matters she would need to see to when, in a fortnight's time, they arrived at Aberavon.

She was certainly very lucky because they had more than enough money with which to give Margaret's house the thorough overhaul it badly needed. It had tremendous potential; Fiona remembered seeing the little turret on the left as she'd approached the house for the first time. It was going to be like living in a castle. She imagined how it would be when she had decorated, filled the rooms with flowers, had some furniture delivered from somewhere like Edinburgh, made a number of friends in the village then stood by the window facing the distillery, waiting for them to arrive for the small dinner party she had arranged. It would happen. It would happen like that because she had imagined it so.

Since she was a child she had been able to imagine things, and make them come true. It was a skill she'd needed to develop in response to the situation at home. Whenever Rose and Harry argued, Fiona would retreat to her room and imagine the happy family that she knew she ought to belong to. And soon enough the arguments would cease, and they would be happy again, and Harry would ruefully bring a bunch of flowers home for Rose. That was romantic. She'd loved those times.

Her fantasies gave colour and substance to her everyday life, and she'd dreamed of the man who would one day claim her for his. These were intensely private dreams; Fiona could well imagine Penny's reaction if she'd heard about them. But, thought Fiona, placing her copy of *Good Housekeeping* back on the table by her side, Penny could do with learning to dream herself. She set her sights low, and Fiona could never quite understand why. Particularly when it was obvious to her that dreams did come true. She stole a glance at her new husband.

Alastair was immediately aware of her, and smiled. Fiona smiled back. It was as if they were linked in some special, secret way.

'Lunch?' he suggested.

They both looked at the clock above the door of the lounge. It was half-past one. This seemed a perfect time for lunch.

'I'd love some,' Fiona said.

Neither of them was very hungry. Lunch was going to be a mere formality. For that reason Alastair suggested they have a snack in the bar, rather than go to the restaurant. Fiona agreed readily.

The Loch Kyle had several bars, but the one Alastair selected was at the back of the hotel. It was dark and secluded, and the ubiquitous hotel tartan covered bar stools and settles. A stag's head stared out unseeing from above the fireplace. In contrast, a quiz and fruit machine stood cheek by jowl in a corner of the bar, looking awkwardly out of place. Except for a young man behind the counter polishing the glasses, the bar was empty. Fiona and Alastair took seats at the farthest end, in a cosy booth, and like children nestled up to each other. Alastair picked up a menu and together they discussed its contents.

'I'm not very hungry,' Fiona said.

'Just a sandwich?'

'That's enough for me. And something nice to drink.'

'Have a cocktail. I'll see what they do.' Alastair's thigh nudged hers deliberately. Fiona placed her hand on it, feeling the hardness of his muscles. He placed his hand over hers, pushing it down.

'I'll just have a sandwich too.' He squeezed her hand. Fiona felt deliriously happy and wondered why they were bothering to eat at all. Only mortals ate. Yet Alastair gave her hand a final squeeze and stood up to go to the bar. She watched him go.

I'm so lucky, thought Fiona. I actually know what it is to be in love, properly in love. All the lyrics of all the romantic songs she had ever heard made sense to her now. Just the sight of Alastair's long, lean body filled her with tenderness. He had his back to her, and was speaking to the barman. Lucky barman to be spoken to by Alastair! She tried to visualise his face, but as familiar as it was to her, she couldn't focus on it with her inner eye; she could not see his blue eyes, his fair brows and curly strawberry-blond hair. Thinking about his straight nose, his fine, tender mouth that kissed hers with such force, didn't help to bring his features to mind. She tried to remember the way his face lit up when he saw her unexpectedly, or the way he smiled at her sometimes, almost with embarrassment at the way his feelings got the better of him. She loved the deference with which he treated her, his old-fashioned courtesy, his concern that everything should be right for her, and the almost child-like delight he took in her. He loves me too, she thought, knowing absolutely that this was the truth. I am so lucky.

Just for a moment, Fiona remembered all that she had left behind in Manchester: the non-stop pressure at Tenterden and Bridges; the intrusive neighbours in the house next-door to hers at Greenmount – she thought with delight of the 'For Sale' sign that now stood in the front garden; her mother's fretting and frustration. But soon, when the new house was perfect, Rose and Harry, and Penny too, could come and stay with her, and learn to be happy again. And she would get a puppy, and perhaps the local vet would meet Penny and they too could fall in love, and . . .

And Alastair returned with the drinks: something exotic for her, and a whisky for him.

'A Lucky Strike,' he said, referring to her cocktail.

How appropriate, she thought.

Of course the alcohol went straight to her head. It emboldened her, and so Fiona once again placed her hand on Alastair's thigh and stroked him gently, hoping to arouse him or at least imply that she had thought of something she would like to do that afternoon.

'Enjoying yourself?' he asked ambiguously.

'Mmm.'

'So you like the hotel?'

He had asked her that question many times, only because he was confident of getting the answer 'yes'.

'It's wonderful.'

'You deserve it.'

Fiona smiled lazily like a contented cat. 'And you.'

The barman came over with the sandwiches and placed them on the table unobtrusively.

'Do you think he knows we're on honeymoon?' she asked.

'It's pretty obvious.'

'Why?' she said, placing her finger on his nose.

Alastair laughed.

'This is so good,' he said, 'it's almost frightening.'

'Frightening?'

But Alastair just shrugged. Fiona picked up his beef sandwich and brought it to his lips for him to bite. He did so, and some cress fell out on to his chin. She licked her finger to scoop it up. He bit her finger.

'You hurt me!'

He growled softly at her as he ate. Fiona, however, found she did not want her sandwich at all. Looking at Alastair was food enough. She reminded herself yet again that they were married, really married, man and wife, because it didn't seem true, not yet. She had embarked on her new life the evening of that leaving party at The Moon Under Water in Manchester when her friends had somehow got entangled with another office party, and she had met Alastair. And here they were now. She bit into her sandwich.

That was the past; she would think instead about the future.

'Can't you stay a fortnight in Aberavon?' She cajoled him now.

'Just a week. Else I lose the contract.'

'Does it matter? Can't you ring them and say you're giving it up anyway? You're bound to find work in Aberdeen. You told me you were.'

She watched Alastair swallow his sandwich and saw his Adam's apple bob as he did so.

'There could be legal problems if I just walk out. You especially should know that.'

Fiona was a solicitor, but dealt exclusively with conveyancing.

'We have enough money to compensate them if they complain.'

'Yes, but wouldn't you prefer to have the money to spend on the house?' He was replying gently, but also disagreeing with her. So Fiona backed off. Nothing was going to spoil her honeymoon.

'I suppose I only have to wait six weeks for you.'

'And I'll try to come up every weekend.'

'And it was good of the firm to give you such a large bonus for the project.'

Alastair nodded.

'I suppose if I came back to Manchester with you, your mother might not be able to move out unaided.'

'That's the whole point,' he said.

Fiona kissed him on the cheek. It was natural she should not want to start her married life without him, but she would do nothing to spoil their harmony just now. She ate some more of her turkey sandwich, and finished her cocktail. She leaned against him.

'And when I've finished the contract,' he said, 'I'll have a long holiday. Long, long, long.' He put his arm round her and with his hand pushed up the hair at the back of her head, turning her face to his. 'No need to work for a bit. We'll have other things to do.'

They kissed each other lightly.

'Then I'll enrol on a course to convert my English Law degree to Scots Law.'

'And I'll find work in Aberdeen. Or maybe even in Elgin.'

This was their long-term plan. But right now what Fiona wanted most was to kiss her husband properly, and since no one was in the bar, she put her face up to his, their mouths met and they gave themselves up to the passion of the moment. When they finally moved apart, the barman had mysteriously reappeared.

'We'd better go back to our room,' said Alastair.

They did so, his hand on the small of Fiona's back, guiding her. Their suite was not far away. Once the door was shut behind them, Fiona walked over to the window, marvelled at the whiteness outside, and closed the curtains. She turned and looked at Alastair, who had been watching her. She held him in a direct gaze, and felt her happiness grow into unmistakable sexual longing. She walked slowly towards him. And as she did so, the phone by their bed rang.

It surprised them both. They stopped what they were about to do.

'I'll get it,' Fiona said. 'Did you remember to pay the bill?'

'I gave our room number.'

'Hello?'

'Yes, this is Fiona Green— no, Fiona Gordon.' Who could be asking for her by her maiden name?

'Yes, yes. Put her through.'

One-thirty, and not half the letters read. Penny sighed audibly but no one was around to hear her as most of Features had gone to the canteen for lunch. She ran her hand through her hair and decided that the sandwich she'd eaten at her desk at twelve wasn't enough, and she would have to have the Mars bar she'd bought with it, in case she was hungry later. She had intended to start dieting again straight after the wedding, but now she could see that was unrealistic. Besides, giving up Mars bars was a serious undertaking, and she'd need several courses of therapy before she could even contemplate it.

The fact that she felt guilty as she bit into it had less to do with the calories than with the fact she'd not yet got round to seeing Lily. Yesterday she'd coped with a monumental hangover, and had fallen asleep in the middle of the afternoon, only waking when the Gladesmore residents would be having their dinner. So Penny had decided to pop in to see Lily after work on Monday. She could leave the office around four-thirty. Provided she finished getting through the letters.

Here was yet another one from some bloke whingeing that all the women he met were only after one thing – his wallet. And another one from a guy who complained he couldn't get a woman because he was out of work. And a woman who complained that she couldn't get a man because blokes were put off by her children. And here was a single mother begging Penny for some cash so her kids could get some new clothes. Freud was wrong. It wasn't sex that lay at the bottom of everything. It was money.

Just then the door to the open-plan office was pushed open and some of the men came back.

'All right, Pen?'

She made a strangulated noise as her mouth was full of Mars bar.

'What's it this week? My lesbian lover's stocking fetish?'

'No. But if you like kinky sex, there's one here from a single Agony Aunt who gets her kicks from strangling half-pissed sports writers.'

There was some uneasy laughter. Penny felt a little protective towards her correspondents, and even if some of the letters did amuse her, she would not share them with her colleagues. Especially her male colleagues. She picked up the next on blue Basildon Bond, the letters curiously flat and the 'i's dotted with circles.

Dear Penny,

I am writting to you because I don't no what to do. I saw my best friend's husband and he was out with a girl I know. I saw them kissing. But she is pregnant. I don't no wether to tell my friend. Please tell me what to do. Do not print this letter in case she finds out.

Penny licked the inside of her mouth to see if there were any stray remnants of chocolate. She felt desperately as if she needed some. Were there some mints in her handbag? She hated letters like this. For a start, she hardly understood it. Who was pregnant? The girlfriend? The wife? And there were only the bare bones of the situation. For all Penny knew, the wife could be a bitch and the husband might desperately need to escape. Or the kiss could have been a goodbye kiss. Or the start of an affair. And the writer was asking to be told what to do! That was what Penny hated most.

Although the paper seemed satisfied with her page, and she had a good track record of thank-you letters, most of the time she felt such a fraud. And a dangerous fraud at that. Who was she to know how other people should conduct their lives? If the readers of the paper knew the real Penny Green, they'd have as little confidence in her as she did. But to make the world go round, and to keep the circulation of the paper up, there had to be this other Penny Green, replete with wisdom like some latter-day oracle. If only she was that bit more certain of herself, how much easier it would be. If only . . .

And again she thought of Lily. *There* was someone with the courage of her convictions. If she'd thought her best friend's husband was having an affair, Lily would have walked straight up to him and clocked him one. Penny smiled to herself. Or she'd have gone to see the wife and marched her down to the solicitor's to get the divorce papers. Good old Lily. She wouldn't recognise a moral dilemma if she saw one walking down the road to greet her. So far as Lily was concerned, indecision was weakness. Penny remembered the story Lily told about the man who took her out one evening and made an unwanted pass at her in the front seat of his Alfa Romeo. She released the handbrake and it ran into the Volvo in front. That soon put paid to his mischief. Those were Lily's words: 'That soon put paid to his mischief.' Penny began to feel better. She began to type into her computer.

You can't let a situation like this drag on. Go and see your

*friend's husband and tell him what you saw. I know it might
seem scary, but if you can find the courage, you could help sort
out a potentially tragic situation.*

Courage, that was the word.

The phone on her desk rang.

'Penny Green?'

It was the editor.

'Hello, Brian.'

'We've got a half-page ad here from Providential Assurance.
They'd like to share your page. The copy reads "We have the
answers to your future problems".'

'But I've got seventy letters sitting in front of me!'

'I know, I know. But with the price of paper rising . . .'

Immediately Penny backed off. Did he think she was being
stroppy? Was her job at stake? And did she have any choice?

'OK, I understand. For this week, then.'

'That's good. I'm looking forward to reading your letters.'

The line went dead. Penny was furious. But not with the editor
– like everyone else in this building, money mattered most to him.
She was furious with herself. Money wasn't supposed to matter to
her. And how come the editor always reduced her to a quivering
wreck? What was wrong with her? The next man who told her
what to do would get it in the neck. The phone rang again. Penny
picked it up like an explosive device.

'It's your fiancé,' said the telephonist.

'My what?' Penny was bewildered.

'Hi,' said a male voice, intercepting. 'I have a problem.'

'Then write to the paper in the normal way,' she snapped.
'And who are you, anyway?'

The caller seemed undeterred by her brusqueness.

'Someone with two tickets for the Halle this evening, but
there's only one of me.'

The voice sounded familiar.

'It's Rick, isn't it?'

'Of course. So what's your solution?'

'You're having me on, aren't you?'

'No. I'm completely serious. What shall I do with my spare ticket?'

'Take it back to the box office.'

There was a momentary silence. Penny felt a little breathless. Had she been rude? But on the other hand, Rick had probably been put up to this. Kitty was no doubt standing there with her hand on his shoulder.

'I thought you were glad to see me at the wedding?' he said. 'I enjoyed meeting you again.'

'Sure. Me too. But let's leave it there.'

'Any reason?'

'What is this? The Spanish Inquisition?'

'No. Just a request for your company.'

He must be desperate, she thought. For one moment the idea of a night out with an attractive man appealed to her. It would certainly get the neighbours talking. Then she came to her senses, and remembered her previous resolution.

'Not tonight. I'm going to see Aunty Lily.'

'What's wrong? Don't you like me?'

He doesn't give up easily, I'll grant him that, she thought to herself. Yet his question troubled her. She had hurt him after all, and it was vitally important not to damage anyone's self-esteem, even a man like Rick Goldstone.

'Of course I like you. But I am going to see Lily, and . . .'

'And what?'

'I'm at work, Rick. I can't talk.'

And Penny replaced the receiver, feeling quite short of breath. She'd done it! She turned him down! Turned Rick Goldstone down! There was hope for her yet. It was so important to her to try to live by her principles, and one of these was that a woman had the right to say 'no'. This was exciting. She felt much, much better. With a bit of luck, he might even phone her back. The advice she was in the process of writing was right. It *was* scary to have courage, because her heart was thumping wildly. Imagine Rick Goldstone actually asking her out! Yippee! But, she told herself sternly, she wasn't pleased about that. It was the fact she'd managed to turn him down, that was far more impressive. Then the phone rang again. Taking a deep breath and crossing her fingers, Penny lifted the receiver.

'Penny Green?' Her voice was light.

It was her mother, the telephonist said.

'Oh, OK. Put her through.'

The large hand of the kitchen clock clicked into position. Rose looked up and noted that it was half-past one. Hadn't he gone yet?

That man! No sense of time. No sense, come to think of it. It took more than fifteen minutes to get to the dentist, so why was he still in the house? She could hear him moving about upstairs, and heard the floorboards creak as he walked from the bathroom to the bedroom. As if it was necessary to smarten yourself up for the dentist! Until Harry had gone, Rose knew she wouldn't be able to settle down to anything. Partly this was because she was used to being on her own. She had retired a year ago, and had now established a nice little routine for herself. There was the charity shop she helped in, her painting class, her visits to the library, and the frequent trips to get fresh bread, or fruit from the greengrocer's. At the weekend Harry took her in the car to Tesco's, though she could well have done without him. He would stand by the chilled meals picking up impossibly expensive dishes and oohing and aahing at them. Easily taken in, that was his trouble. And no idea how much these things cost. Wild salmon in orange and dill sauce! As if they were made of money. If you want salmon, she told him last Saturday, I'll get you a tin of pink. That shut him up.

1.32. Well, if he was late for the dentist it was his own fault. Rose let out her breath audibly. And then she began to worry. What if the dentist suggested he needed the crown replacing? That would be a couple of hundred at least. And where would the money come from?

At last Harry came down the stairs, dressed in pale blue

trousers and a navy sweater with an anchor motif. He dresses like a young man, Rose thought to herself, with a mixture of contempt and pleasure. She stood at the door to the kitchen watching him put on his jacket.

'Remember to go and pay the florist,' she told him.

'I know.'

'And don't forget to check the bill.' She couldn't trust him.

Harry winced and put his hand to his mouth. Rose knew this was a ploy to get her sympathy. But she wasn't so easily won over.

'Go on,' she said. 'You'll be late.'

'OK.' He unlatched the door and shut it behind him.

Rose felt her shoulders sag with a feeling akin to relief. He was out of the house. There was peace and quiet. She smiled to herself as she thought that most women dreaded the school holidays because the kids were at home; the cross she had to bear was her husband, the teacher. Despite her liking for silence, he insisted on listening to loud concertos first thing in the morning. Then there was the way he slurped his coffee. Oh, and his habit of taking off his slipper and reaching with it down his back to give himself a good scratch. Rose tensed with irritation at the thought.

But she was alone now, and need not think about him. Perhaps she would put on the radio and do a crossword. But before she could do that she re-entered the kitchen to check it was tidy (it was), glanced into the living room, which was tidy too, and then, on the dining-room table, she saw some unfinished business. Her heart sank. How could she have forgotten? She had promised herself that she would work out exactly how much this wedding had cost them. It was important to know. And besides, there were still some bills to come in. How could they budget for the rest of the month until they knew – until *she* knew – what the next batch of outgoings would be?

So reluctantly Rose sat herself down at the dining-room table and faced the page of calculations she had begun earlier. There was the caterer to be paid, and the car firm too. And what about tips? If only all these people could understand that tips were out of the question. The band's account needed settling, and the MC hadn't sent in his bill yet. She totted up the figures, praying they would come to a manageable total and knowing they wouldn't. Of course, there was Alastair's money, but it came to a pretty pass when the bridegroom had to fork out for his own wedding. It was shameful. But on the other hand, it was just as well, else Fiona would not have had the send-off she deserved. Even then, she and Harry had spent far more than they could afford.

Well, there was only one thing for it. With a glint in her eye Rose decided there would have to be some economies. The decision filled her with a sense of her own righteousness, which was immensely satisfying. Here was something she could do; she could make economies. When it came to struggling with money, she was a Mike Tyson. Round one. Newspapers were a luxury when the news was on TV, and for a few months they would stop having a take-away on Friday nights. End of round one. Round two. No new clothes for either of them, at least until the summer. The settee would not be re-covered. Rose breathed deeply as the adrenalin surged round her body. It was going to be hard, but necessary. If they could put away a hundred this month, and maybe a little more the next, then they could begin to retrench. Then she remembered Harry's crown and was nearly out for the count. She would have to tell him when he came home that times would be hard. No more CDs. No nights out. It was a lesson he needed to learn. If only he would worry about money a little more, she wouldn't have to worry about it as much as she did. Rose had won on points.

She felt cheered by her own resolution. She was in control again. It was lucky one of them had some common sense else how would they have managed? Harry was a dreamer, she told herself, not for the first time. She glanced again at the figures in front of her, and knew she could trust herself to make up the deficit. At least there was someone she could trust.

Six more years and they'd be living on a pension. Then how would they manage unless they had put some by? That's what

I'd like to know, she thought to herself, and then the nervous energy that had gripped her began to dissipate, and Rose began to relax. As she did so, she involuntarily thought of Lily. She ought to visit her, if not today then tomorrow. She had saved her some wedding cake. What she would not think about was Lily's money. Anyway, she told herself, a little ashamed, not much of it would be left. It was true that the takeover of her dry cleaning chain had left Lily with a tidy sum, but the Gladesmore fees for both herself and Kitty must have dented her savings considerably. There was every possibility that Lily would live for many, many years yet, and by that time all the money would be gone. Which is exactly, exactly as it should be, Rose concluded. She did not want Lily's money. She didn't want one penny of it.

Then the shrill ringing of the telephone shattered the silence.

It took her completely by surprise as she had been lost in thought. Now who could that be? Slightly nervous, as ever, Rose approached the telephone. Afterwards she would tell Penny that she knew what had happened before she even lifted the receiver.

It was Anne from Gladesmore. 'I'm so very sorry,' she began. Rose stood stiffly at the phone, braced for the blow. Anne told her that Lily had suffered a second, massive stroke. She had died at half-past one.

At first, tears did not come. Rose simply felt that she was alive and her sister was dead; she felt like a tree that had survived an earthquake. And then there was an exquisite relief, the end of an unbearable tension. It was all finally over, and provided she could trust one other person, no one need ever know. Slowly Rose sat down.

Then she thought of Penny, and grieved that she would have to tell her. Penny would be distressed. It was important to be strong for Penny's sake. She would ring her at the newspaper offices and ask her to come home. So Lily was dead. Thinking of her sister, she filled with pity. She'd had money, but perhaps that was all. A deep sympathy welled up in her and with it the tears.

*　　*　　*

As Rose had expected, Penny was distraught.

'I feel awful,' she said, sniffing loudly. 'I should have gone to visit her on Sunday. I was being selfish. I hate myself.'

'You couldn't have known,' Rose soothed her, brushing back the damp hair from her forehead.

'I should have known. I can't help it, that's how I feel.'

Saying that made Penny cry again. Harry, standing in front of the fireplace, was marooned in a sea of tears. He felt it was incumbent upon him to throw out a lifebelt. He was the man of the house. It was up to him to be positive.

'It's a blessing in disguise, really.'

Both women looked at him, appalled. He shifted uneasily.

'A second stroke could have left her like a vegetable. That's all I meant.'

Rose could not credit the way he could continue to look on the bright side even during a bereavement. Yet irritation at his facile optimism dried her tears.

'Lily was only sixty-four. How can this be a blessing? A blessing? Hark at him!'

Penny sat up, amazed. Her parents were arguing even now. If Lily knew, she'd be livid. And Penny smiled amid her tears. Lily would be so angry, she'd never speak to either of them again.

'And dying right after the wedding too,' Rose added, ramming home her point. 'How can that be a blessing?'

'At least Fiona doesn't know,' Harry said meekly.

'I think Fiona ought to know,' Rose said, still wishing to contradict. 'It doesn't seem right, keeping the news from her until her honeymoon is over. She'll need to send some flowers for the funeral.'

'We could send some in her name.'

Rose automatically thought of the expense, and hated herself for that. Perhaps Harry was right. She would consult Penny.

'What do you think, Penny? Should we tell her?'

Poor Fiona, Penny thought. Either her honeymoon is ruined, or the start of her married life is doubly spoiled by the news of Lily's death and the fact that no one in the family thought she was grown up enough to cope with it. Penny believed staunchly in honesty. She also suspected that, of all of them, Fiona was best insulated from the shock of Lily's death. Alastair would comfort her. She was conscious of her parents waiting for her decision.

'I think we should tell her,' Penny concluded. 'She's not a kid.'

'And there may be money for her,' Harry said, glancing quickly from wife to daughter.

Both looked daggers at him as he began to study the pattern in the carpet. Whatever they thought, it was true. Lily had had money. Money that, in all fairness, should come to them. In some respects it was a relief that she had died, and Rose, of all people, ought to know that. He guessed her tears were mostly due to shock. Surely thinking of the money would cheer her up? It was the only reason he'd mentioned it.

There was an uncomfortable silence.

'I ought to ring Fiona,' said Rose. 'She gave me an emergency number. I have it somewhere. I think it's upstairs. Penny, you know my black leather case? – the one I keep important documents in – it's in there. You wouldn't run up and get it? I need to phone Simon too, and Monty. Anne said she would leave it to me to tell the rest of the family.'

Fussing made Rose feel better. It was important to keep busy, she knew that. Not that she had any choice. There was a funeral to arrange, a notice to be put in the paper, and a hundred and one other things to do.

Penny came down with the number of the Loch Kyle Hotel.

'I'll ring if you like. She might be less upset, hearing it from me.'

Rose was grateful. 'But don't be too long,' she added automatically.

'Fiona?'

'Penny? I'm Fiona Gordon now, remember. And why are you ringing?' she sounded puzzled.

'Is Alastair with you?'

'Yes. Why? Is there some bad news?' Immediately Fiona thought of her parents and froze.

'It's Lily,' Penny said. 'She died this morning.'

Thank God, thought Fiona, it wasn't Mum or Dad. It was only Lily. Poor Lily.

'I'm sorry, Penny. What was it?'

'Another stroke.'

'Is Mum all right?'

'Coping.'

Another thought struck Fiona, most unpleasantly. 'Do you want me to come home for the funeral?' Her voice was small, disappointed.

'No, no,' Penny assured her.

'Can I speak to Mum?'

Penny passed her over.

'I'm so sorry, Mum.'

'Don't worry, Fiona. It was a blessing in disguise.'

'Are you sure you don't want us back for the funeral?'

'I'm sure. We just thought it best you should know what was happening, that's all. The last thing I want is that your honeymoon should be spoiled.'

Those were the words that echoed in Fiona's head as she replaced the receiver. Having assured her mother that she was perfectly all right, and glad to have been told about Lily, she knew it was pretence. It struck her as dreadful that Lily should choose now to die. She was as shocked and angry as a toddler who trips and is smacked in the face by the floor. And frightened, too.

'Who was that?' Alastair asked, coming to sit with her on the side of the bed.

'Penny. She rang to say my Aunty Lily's died.'

As she spoke the words, Fiona regretted being so blunt. Only a few weeks ago Alastair's father had died. He had barely recovered from one death, and now she was plunging him into another. She took his hand and squeezed it tightly, trying to reassure him.

'She'd already had one stroke. In a way we were expecting this.'

'Are you all right?'

'Yes. I think Penny will be more upset than me. She was closer to her. Lily always preferred Penny to me. She used to complain to Mum that I was too timid.'

Alastair put his arm round her and kissed her cheek.

'I know she was my aunt, but we weren't that close. It's a shock, that's all.'

'I know, I know.'

Fiona nestled closer to her husband, glad of his support.

'I feel sorry for Mum and Penny. And it's horrible that it should happen now. It's like a bad omen.'

'Don't say that!'

'I'm sorry,'

Alastair turned her face towards his and kissed her full on the lips. Fiona revelled in the feel of him, his strength, and his need for her. She gave herself up to the kiss, sensing that this was the balm she craved.

It was a kiss that seemed to have no end. In a few moments they were on the bed, still kissing, Alastair's hands roving now over her body, as if searching for something. He pushed up her sweater, and lifted it off her, and buried his head in her breasts. Fiona was surprised this was happening now, and grateful too, that she would not have to think about that phone call. It was surprisingly easy to give herself up to the moment. There was a desperation in Alastair's embrace that roused something in her. Quickly they undressed, and soon they were clinging to each other, and she arched to meet him in complete surrender. Just for one moment she opened her eyes and saw his were closed, and his brow was furrowed. He stopped for a moment as he reached his climax. She ached with pleasure at being so loved by him. He fell on her now, covering her face with kisses. She gloried in them.

Like two children sharing a guilty secret, they told each other over and over again how much in love they were. The fact

45

of Lily's death had shrunk to the size of a pea in Fiona's mind.

'I'm so lucky to have you,' she told her husband.

'That's right. You're lucky. Never say that you're not.'

Fiona knew Alastair was right. It was important to think positively. Her mother was right; Lily's death was a blessing in disguise. It must have been dreadful for her, living in that home. Fiona had visited her there a couple of times, and hated the way the residents sat on high-backed chairs staring vacantly at the television set. It had surprised her that Lily had put up with it, since she had money enough to arrange her own nursing care. She mentioned that to Alastair.

'Lily was quite wealthy, you know.'

'Was she?' Alastair turned to her, propping himself up on his side. Fair, curly hair grew on his chest, and Fiona put out her finger to touch it while she spoke.

'She owned a chain of dry cleaning shops – Colman's Cleaners. They were all over the north of England. Then she was bought out, and apparently it was a very good deal.'

'Will she be leaving your mother a lot of money?'

'I suppose so. I haven't really thought about it. Lily had no children, so I suppose Monty, Simon and Mum are her next-of-kin. I can't imagine her leaving Simon anything, though.'

'Do you know how rich she was?'

'I haven't a clue. It'll be nice for Mum – she's worried about money all her life.' Fiona suddenly felt glad. With that anxiety about money gone, her parents would stop arguing. There was a whole new future for them too.

Fiona felt restored now, and was pleased to see that Alastair also looked happier. He was lying on the bed, gazing at her fondly. She revelled in the intimacy of the moment.

'What shall we do now?' she asked him.

'I don't know. There's no chance of going for a walk.'

'I'm happy to be entirely lazy.'

'Shall I switch on TV?'

'Yes.' Fiona never watched much TV but was happy for

Alastair to do so. She turned round to the bedside table to reach for her novel. It wasn't there. Where did she have it last? She remembered looking at it in the hotel conservatory, and then she'd taken it with her to the bar. Or had she?

'Alastair, I think I've left my book in the bar.'

'In the bar?'

'I'm pretty sure. Shall I ring down and ask?'

'There might not be anyone there now. If you like, I'll put some clothes on and go take a look.'

'Would you?'

'No problem.'

She watched her husband dress swiftly, heard the rattle of change in his trouser pocket, and saw his well-proportioned chest disappear into his Aran sweater.

'Won't be long,' he said.

It was lovely to be fussed over, Fiona thought, as she watched her husband leave. The rest of her life stretched ahead of her bathed in a rosy glow. And then she thought of Lily, whom nobody ever loved like this. She must remember to send some flowers to the funeral. Wriggling further into the bed, Fiona sleepily thought to herself that at least she had made Lily's last days happier by giving her a wedding to think about. Or she hoped so.

When Alastair returned she would ask him to get back into bed with her so they could snuggle up and relax. Thinking of him made her miss him. He had been gone a long time.

Perhaps her book wasn't in the bar after all, but in the conservatory, and he had gone to look there. Perhaps it was in neither of those places. She wondered what it was that could have delayed him.

Slightly impatient now, Fiona sat up in bed. Where could he be? It wasn't the book she wanted but Alastair. Were those footsteps along the corridor? Yes. A key turned in the lock.

'Here we are,' said Alastair. He looked flushed.

Fiona took her book.

'Where was it?'

'Under the seat in the bar.'

Come back to bed,' she cajoled him.

Swiftly and silently he removed his clothes, paused to turn on the television, and then slipped under the covers next to her. She kissed him tenderly on the forehead, and they settled down comfortably together. Fiona was utterly content.

Chapter Three

Rose was still furious.

'Simon's house is three times the size of ours,' she muttered again to Penny. 'And he's perfectly well aware that the wedding has strained our resources. But would he offer his place for the funeral tea? Would he indeed! I'm surprised they've bothered to turn up at all!' She glared in the direction of her younger brother, who was inspecting the flowers with Pearl.

'Shhh,' Penny said. She rubbed at a white mark on her black jacket. 'Lily wouldn't want you arguing at her funeral.' And then she realised that Lily probably would, and smiled to herself.

'Look,' Rose said, 'there's Anne. It's good of her to come. Lily was always very fond of Anne.'

Anne's trim, petite figure made its way along the path, an umbrella shielding her from the rain. She joined Rose and Penny at the entrance to the chapel, and embraced them both. Penny smelled her fresh cologne.

'Where's Kitty?'

'She's not very well – nothing serious. Only she's taken Lily's death rather badly. We've had to give her some sedatives.'

At that moment, Harry came over to them and shook hands vigorously with Anne.

'Glad you could make it,' he said expansively. 'There's tea for everyone at our house after the service, you know.' Rose glared at him. 'A sorry business,' he added, glancing at the coffin lying in the chapel. As he did so, all their eyes were drawn to it. Monty, Sally, Simon and Pearl, however, had their backs to the coffin and were conferring quietly. Some elderly friends of

Lily's, whom Penny vaguely recognised, were standing clutching their handbags reproachfully, as if blaming Lily for letting the side down. The minister, ignored by everyone, wore the anxious expression of a tradesman when business was bad. Penny decided she didn't so much mind that Lily had to die, but that her going-off should be conducted in this highly inappropriate way. All this peace, all these hushed voices . . . it simply wasn't Lily. She'd been all noise and laughter. Lily used to sing along to her recordings of *Carmen Jones* and *West Side Story*, and laughed so loudly she could give you a headache.

The minister took his position by the coffin. The muted conversations stopped. Someone closed the chapel door. Penny moved nearer her mother and linked arms with her. The service began. Then Penny was aware of the chapel door opening once more, and a latecomer slipping through. She glanced sideways to see who it was. Rick Goldstone. What the heck was he doing here? Maybe he'd taken it on himself to be Kitty's representative, which was touching if true. Or more likely his firm of management consultants was doing a time and motion study on the undertakers. She looked at him surreptitiously again and saw him flicking through the service book, trying to find where they were. Penny asked herself what Lily would think of his appearance at her funeral. She had to admit that her aunt would be rather pleased. Rick's film-star demeanour would have appealed to her. Because he did look like a film star, it was just a matter of deciding which one. Someone with a boyish smile and eyes that laughed. Tom Cruise? She couldn't help turning her head just once more to see if she was right, only this time her glance met his. Embarrassing! Penny hoped he didn't see the blush that was stealing across her face. Perhaps he would put it down to a welter of emotion.

Emotion. She tried to concentrate on the fact of Lily's death, and failed. This panoply of doom and gloom had nothing to do with the Lily she knew. And because of that she could not feel sad. Instead she felt rebellious. The minister intoned that Lily was a loving sister, and Penny looked deliberately at Simon, who seemed to be engaged in a detailed examination of his shoes. *Never spoiled by her worldly success,* said the minister. That was true enough. Lily never lost her Cockney accent; in fact she cultivated it as a sort of trademark. And the flat she lived in was a paean to bad taste, from the gold velvet three-piece suite to the mural of a Spanish beach she had commissioned to adorn the wall. *Her warmth and affection endeared her to the residents of Gladesmore . . .*

Where did this man come from? Had he ever met Lily? Most of the Gladesmore nurses couldn't stand her. She criticised the way they handled her, and hurled abuse at anyone who mistakenly sat on her chair or switched channels when *EastEnders* was on. Most of the residents were terrified of Lily. Except Kitty, of course. Penny remembered what Anne had said about Kitty, and was sad for a moment. She would visit as soon as was reasonable. Thinking of Kitty reminded her of Rick, so she peeked at him again. He seemed to have turned in on himself, gazing unseeing at the minister. As Head Boy, he used to stand like that in school assembly, by the Headmaster on the stage, seemingly oblivious to the fact that all the fifth-year girls were ogling him.

It was an inappropriate memory, and Penny rebuked herself for it. Though the real Lily, the one who hadn't died and seemed to be with Penny at her own funeral, didn't mind. As the coffin was prepared for its journey to the grave, Simon took his place at the head of the procession. Penny knew Lily would mind that. If she could have directed her own funeral, it would have been a knees-up down at a local, with a bit of a sing-song and a few good belly laughs. Penny began to think that perhaps funerals ought to be like that. Just as you could get married anywhere these days, you ought to be allowed to get buried any way you liked. And any place you liked. Lily would be bored stiff in this cemetery. Penny smiled at the unintentional pun. Lily had been a city woman, living first in Bethnal Green, and then in Manchester. Nature meant very little to her, except for birds. Lily liked birds. She'd had a budgie called Pip whom she trained to wolf-whistle at her. She always placed a bet on the horse with a bird's name in it in the Grand National. It was a good system; she won more often than not.

The coffin was lowered. Penny only looked at it momentarily. She had the real Lily locked up inside her and wasn't letting her go. The minister read some prayers to which Penny would not listen. She noticed that the sky had cleared now, and that there was some faint birdsong from the trees. Rose looked stern, but Penny reckoned she was probably thinking about the sandwiches she had prepared, and worrying that they wouldn't stretch far enough. Harry looked sombre too. The minister closed his prayerbook. Suddenly he put his hand to his head and rubbed furiously, nose wrinkled in disgust.

'What's wrong?' Pearl asked him, as she was close by.

'A bird,' he said. 'It got me.'

Rose and Harry's house was in the centre of a short street that connected two through roads. Although freshly painted in green and cream, with a neat front garden, it nestled cheek by jowl with less tidy houses. On one side, the neighbours had converted their front garden to a car parking space, where they had left a rusting yellow Mini without a road licence. On the other side the Jordans had let their garden run riot, and it was a tangle of weeds and bushes.

Seeing the house now through her mother's eyes, Penny understood Rose's reluctance to invite the family back. She didn't mind Monty and Sally so much; their little semi in South Tottenham wasn't much better than this. Simon's house, however, was entirely different. He lived in a large, detached dwelling on the Ringley Road, with a hall just as big as the lounge and *Gone with the Wind* steps that led to a galleried first-floor landing. Simon and Pearl even had a live-in maid, and probably paid her starvation wages. They were disgusting, Penny thought to herself. And what would Rick Goldstone make of her parents' house? Rick, to her surprise, had followed them back to the house in his brand-new BMW. She'd expected him to go straight back to work; perhaps he had the day off and couldn't think of anything else to do.

Penny walked into the porch, and unlocked the door. Down the shadowy passage in front of her was the kitchen, where she could see plates of sandwiches covered in cling-film. On her left was the living room, with the tatty turquoise sofa that needed re-covering. Harry stood by the door, taking coats and ushering in the guests. Penny was aware of the almost festive sense of relief everyone exuded. The funeral was over; they had permission to be happy again.

Penny followed Rose into the kitchen where she was busily preparing tea.

'What can I do?'

'Take the cling-film off the sandwiches. Oh, and get the Madeira cake out of the pantry. It needs slicing. But not too thick. And be careful with the knife.'

Once when cutting bread Penny had sliced into her thumb. Rose had never let her forget it.

'By the way,' she added, as she swished hot water around the tea pot to warm it, 'what's Rick Goldstone doing here?'

'Search me.'

'Nice of him to come,' Rose said absently, spooning in tea.

'I can't find the Madeira.'

'Here. Let me. It's behind the biscuit tin. Is he interested in you?'

'Rick?' Penny guffawed. 'No. I can only think that having been in the States, he's lost track of his old friends over here and I'm the first he's come across.'

'Didn't you go out with him, when you were teenagers?'

'No!' Penny was emphatic. 'We were just friends. Friends,' she repeated, for her mother's edification.

'Hello!' came a voice. It was Anne. Penny looked up with some pleasure. She liked Anne who managed Gladesmore efficiently, with warmth and humour. 'I wondered if I could have a word?'

'Come in,' Rose said. 'I'm afraid there's very little room.' This was true. The table that jutted out from the wall, laden with food, took up most of the available space.

'Tell you what,' said Penny, 'I'll take the food into the lounge and you two can have a chat.'

'Be careful!' Rose enjoined her.

'It's just,' said Anne, fumbling in her attaché case, 'that I have some things for you. Some things of Lily's.'

'Oh,' said Rose. Her discomfiture made her sound ungrateful. 'I mean, thank you. It was kind of you to bother.'

'I think this might be quite important,' Anne said, bringing out a large stiff white envelope from the bag. 'Lily's will is in here.'

Rose lost colour; she turned almost as white as the envelope. She took it from Anne, and held it as if it might explode.

'I know,' Anne said reassuringly. 'It feels wrong, looking into someone else's affairs.'

'Do you know what's in the will?'

'No. Lily said nothing to me, which was as it should be. Her only words were that I should give her papers directly to you. She was closer to you than anyone else, you know that.'

'Papers?'

'There's more in there than just her will. A lot of our residents give me objects of sentimental value to look after in the safe. One chap who died last year gave me all the love letters his wife had written him.'

Rose smiled nervously, holding tightly on to the envelope.

'Well, thank you for handing these over.'

'Don't mention it.'

Penny returned at that moment and saw the envelope in her mother's hand.

'What's that?'

'Nothing,' said Rose.

'Do you mind if I go now?' Anne asked. 'Marla is coming off her shift at four and we're short-staffed this week.'

'No, no. Not at all,' Rose assured her.

'I'll see you out,' Penny offered.

Rose stood by herself in the kitchen, still gripping the envelope.

Harry, Monty and Simon stood together at the French windows overlooking the small square of garden bisected by an empty washing line. Pearl and Sally sat on the settee, Pearl's expensive grey suit contrasting with Sally's black elasticated skirt and brown cardigan. Rick stood by the wall unit, apparently examining the ornaments that Rose had chosen to display – the cut glass decanter Penny had bought them for a wedding anniversary, two silver candlesticks, and the obligatory family photographs. He turned as Penny entered, and his face brightened.

Before he could say anything, Harry saw her too.

'Penny – tell them it's true. The Astra failed its MOT on fifteen different items.'

She was glad to see the men were taking Lily's death so much to heart. Or perhaps this car talk was displacement activity.

'Yes, it's true,' she said, tight-lipped.

'We had the car made good, but I'm beginning to think I'd be better off with a new one.'

'What are you thinking of getting?' Monty asked, as he eased himself on to one of the chairs by the dining table.

'A Toyota would be nice.'

'There's nothing to compete with the smell of a new car,' Simon said.

'True,' Harry agreed.

How do you know? thought Penny. You've never had a car direct from the showroom in your life. She didn't want to listen to the men any more, and decided to join her aunts. So she perched on the side of settee, and hoped no one had noticed how badly it needed re-covering.

'I must tell you, Penny, we're having our kitchen redesigned. I was explaining to Sally, one of Geraldine's boyfriends is going to create a design.'

At the mention of Geraldine, something clicked. Perhaps Rick had thought she would be at the funeral. Now that made sense.

Poor Rick. Her cousin wouldn't be seen dead at a funeral, thought Penny.

'This time,' Pearl continued, 'I'm determined to get it absolutely right. The problem is, the kitchen is so large that I walk miles when I'm cooking. Geraldine suggests an island unit in the centre.'

'That'll cost a bit,' Penny said. She noticed that the men had finished their conversation and were listening to her.

'I know,' Pearl continued, 'but Simon told me . . .'

He shot her a warning glance. Penny realised that there was an uneasy silence. Rick stepped in.

'Talking about cars,' he said, addressing himself to Harry, 'the thing to do is to get a year-old model. Most of the depreciation happens in the first year. It makes good financial sense, and you'll get a nice motor into the bargain.'

Penny glanced at him with amusement. The Material Man, she thought.

'That might not be necessary,' Harry said.

Once again conversation stopped. Is there something going on here that I'm not aware of? Penny wondered. Then Rose came in with a tray of tea cups, and Penny realised guiltily that she should be helping her mother. She got up immediately and made her way to the kitchen.

There was that envelope on the dresser. Penny picked it up and wondered what could be inside. A death certificate? Probably. It must be painful for Rose to have to deal with all these formalities, and Penny made a mental note to offer her help. She filled another tray with cups and saucers, and walked carefully back to the living room.

Rick met her at the door and took the tray from her.

'Are you all right?' he asked.

'Yes. Fine. Well, not fine, but coping.'

'It's difficult, I know.'

'I've got to go back to get the sandwiches.'

Penny realised she was breathing rapidly. It was silly, the way Rick affected her. She'd better regain some self-control, else she'd be making a fool of herself. She took the last plate of sandwiches and brought them to the lounge, almost bumping into her mother on the way out.

'All done,' Penny said.

'I'll just tidy round,' said Rose.

Back in the kitchen, Rose pulled out the chair from under the table and sat down. She had no inclination to go and join the guests, but imagined she would not be missed for a few moments. There was the envelope on the dresser. What did you do with a will? Did a solicitor have to read and open it? Rose tried to remember what happened when her mother had died. Evie had not left a will. It hadn't mattered as there was nothing to leave.

In this case, with Lily's will, it was vital that Rose see it first. Would she have time to open it now? Almost certainly not. So she stood, took the envelope, and scurried upstairs to her bedroom. She opened her wardrobe. Down one side were open shelves, and on the lowest was the black leather case where she kept the family documents. She was about to place the envelope in there when she faltered. Should she open it now? She felt the contents. Impossible to say what was in there.

She ought to go and join the family, she knew that, or they would think something was up. Nervously Rose twisted her wedding ring around her finger. She would go downstairs, but not just yet. Not just yet.

Penny wondered if her mother was all right. She had heard her run up the stairs and she still had not come down. If she wanted time alone, that was perfectly understandable. Penny too wished she could be anywhere but in this cramped front room with her uncles and aunts, munching sandwiches and drinking tea in an unnaturally subdued fashion.

Simon dabbed at the corners of his mouth with his serviette, then crumpled it and laid it on his plate.

'That's better,' he said.

'I always say it's important to eat at a funeral,' Sally declared. 'It reminds you that you're still alive. I have to say, when Rose rang us up to say that Lily had passed away, and right after Fiona's wedding, I wasn't half shocked, I can tell you. I didn't have any supper that night, did I, Monty? I didn't. I couldn't believe she'd gone. She always liked egg sandwiches. Do you remember, Monty? Lily always liked egg sandwiches. I wouldn't be surprised if that's what killed her. All that cholesterol.'

Pearl shook her head in gentle disagreement.

'Lily was a candidate for a second stroke because of her temper. I have to tell you that Simon and I stayed away from her because whenever she saw us, she'd work herself up into such a state. She was always very highly strung. Simon and I sometimes wondered if she was really all there.' Pearl lowered her voice. 'She was irrational, you see.'

Penny felt herself bridling. She could just about handle the family not talking about Lily before the funeral tea, but badmouthing her now was taking it a little too far. Already the close proximity of her uncles and aunts was making her feel claustrophobic. Now she was irritated too. However, Monty intervened to defend Lily.

'She couldn't have been that doolally. Her business did all right for itself.'

'True, true,' Simon assented. Penny looked at him suspiciously. He was being unusually kind.

'Ah, yes,' said Pearl, reluctant to concede her point. 'Poor Lily was still relatively sane when she was running Colman's Cleaners. But it was after that. Once she'd retired, and realised there was nothing else for her. No children, you know.' Pearl lowered her voice and oozed concern. 'That's why I maintain she became slightly unbalanced. Otherwise she would never had said those things to Simon. She loved him really.'

Penny found herself gripping the edge of her chair. Ought she to stop them?

'We all felt sorry for her,' he said, as if concluding a faculty meeting. 'Now Lily was never one to mince words, and in deference to her memory I don't think we should mince ours.'

Pearl nodded heartily.

'She was a wealthy woman,' Simon continued, then stopped and took a deep breath. 'Does anyone know if she left a will?'

Monty and Sally looked at each other blankly, as if he had asked them the capital of Swaziland.

'She must have done,' Harry said. 'She was always careful about her business affairs.'

Penny could feel the tension in the room, and it made her feel ill. Their money lust was palpable. Her father spoke next.

'I expect she's left most of it to Rose. She was the only one who visited regularly. Apart from Penny, of course. Rose deserves it.'

'We could hardly come up every week from Tottenham just to see her,' Sally pointed out.

'I think you'll find,' Simon said to Harry, 'that all her family was important to Lily. Blood is thicker than water.' He sounded dangerous.

'Yes,' said Pearl. 'Lily loved Simon. She helped bring him up. He was the child she never had. Weren't you, pet? It was so sad she never married, but then she had that dreadful limp . . .'

'Do you know how she got that limp?' Penny's voice was vibrant with anger. 'It was just after the war. Uncle Simon was playing on a bombed out estate. She saw that he'd clambered up to the first floor of a ruined house, and went up after him. Then the floor collapsed. He escaped scot-free, but her right leg was smashed to pieces. What right have any of you to patronise her now? Lily would have made a dozen of you.'

Penny was shocked at her own outburst. She knew she had been rude and the thought was unbearable to her. But she'd had no choice. Now she wanted the release of a good cry, and felt the tears coming. It was essential to get out of the room. They were all so greedy . . . She fired one more parting shot.

'And I hope she's left all her bloody money to the cats' home!'

She stormed out, and Rick followed her.

'But Lily didn't like cats,' Sally protested. 'She said they gave her the evil eye. She liked birds, though. Do you remember that budgie – Pip? When I was in her flat, I used to think it was the kettle whistling. Mind you, Lily had an electric kettle, so it couldn't have been. One of those jug kettles, it was. Now I remember . . .'

Rose jumped visibly as she heard the front door slam. Who could that have been? She could frame no circumstances to fit a sudden departure. She hoped no one had gone out to look for her. She didn't want to cause any trouble. She had better return to the company.

Yet she could neither go downstairs without having opened the envelope, nor summon the courage to open it.

'Penny?' shouted Harry. No reply. 'Rose?'

'I'm coming,' she shouted.

She stood, then carefully inserted a finger into the envelope and tore it open. She pulled out a form and could see the words 'Last Will and Testament'. But that was not all. There was a building society pass book and one other document. Rose unfolded it and started at the contents. So Lily had kept it after all!

Rose's hand trembled visibly as she read the familiar words. Ought she to put this into her document case? No, someone might find it. Penny might find it. Rose moved the dressing-table chair over to the open wardrobe and, taking off her shoes, climbed on to it. On the top shelf of her wardrobe were her spare handbags; she never threw away a handbag as it might come in useful one day. She selected an anonymous-looking black bag, placed the paper back in the envelope, and put it in the bag. She returned the bag to the back of the shelf. She climbed down carefully, and wiped the marks on the chair made by her feet, afterwards slipping on her shoes again.

The will and the pass book were lying on the bed.

'Rose? Do you know where Penny's gone?' Harry's voice boomed.

'No. I'll be with you in a minute.'

Quickly, her heart pounding, Rose opened the pass book and found the final balance. There was almost four hundred thousand pounds. That much! And Lily had never said a word. Rose broke the seal of the will.

'Are you all right? Shall I come up?'

'Just a moment!'

Rose saw her own name – forty thousand pounds, what on earth would she do with that?—and then there was Fiona, who was given five thousand. A good wedding present. Here was Simon's name. Lily had left him five thousand pounds, on condition he displayed and used the furniture that she had put in store when she left for Gladesmore, the stuff she couldn't bear to throw away. He would be absolutely hor-rified. Five thousand for Monty too. There was something about a trust find for Kitty . . . And everything else to Penny. Even after death duties that would be at least a quarter of a million.

Quickly she shoved the will into the document case. Nobody need ever find out about that except for Penny. Thank God she'd had the presence of mind to open the will in private. Obviously Lily had intended her to do just that. No one must find out that Penny was so rich else there would be begging letters, and jealousy, and stalkers, and . . .

'Rose!'

'Coming!'

She shut the wardrobe doors and turned the key in the lock, patted her cheeks to bring back the colour, and made her way downstairs.

Tears stinging her eyes, Penny walked rapidly away from her parents' house. If Lily were alive, they wouldn't have spoken this way. And her father too! Standing around like a vulture, waiting to pick Lily clean. A fresh breeze played with her hair as she walked, and Penny put up the back of her hand to wipe her nose which was uncomfortably damp.

'Penny!'

She turned and saw Rick. For a moment she was furious with him too, for following her and catching her like this. She carried on walking, turning the corner to the road that led down to the canal.

'Leave me alone,' she said to him. 'I'm all right.'

'And I'm the Queen of Sheba,' he said, falling into step with her.

'I need to be alone.'

'I don't agree.'

Penny increased her pace, then slowed it again as she reached the barrier at the end of the road designed to stop the local kids from riding their bikes straight into the canal. There was a narrow opening that led on to the towpath, and she squeezed through that. Rick followed her. She realised that although the sun was shining, it was chilly, and it was foolish of her to have run out without a coat. Her black blouse didn't keep out the cold.

The towpath was empty. On the opposite bank some boats were moored, small house boats with their sides painted bright colours. The water was black and slick. The trees that grew along the path were leafless and barren. Penny walked more slowly now, her energy ebbing rapidly. They passed the back of a council estate, the flats looking like a prison camp.

'You did the right thing,' Rick said, 'standing up for Lily.'

Penny was pleased to hear that. Already she was beginning to regret her action. She had a habit, whenever anything went wrong, of blaming herself and replaying the situation in her mind over and over again. She was beginning to do that now.

'I'm not even sure that Pearl knew how Lily hurt her leg. I should never have said anything.'

'Perhaps she needed to know.'

'Yes, but I walked out. I had a temper tantrum. It shows I lost control.' Penny hugged her arms around herself to ward off the cold.

'I disagree. Lily would have been proud of you. Here, have my jacket.'

'But what about you?'

'It's OK. I've got my thermal vest on,' he said.

Penny smiled at that, and gratefully took the jacket. She stopped walking to put it on. It felt strange, but not unpleasant, wearing Rick's jacket. The day was taking on an unreal aspect. Here she was, on the towpath that led to Heydale Park, with none other than Rick Goldstone. When she was a teenager, she used to fantasise about having an opportunity to be alone with him. It was a safe fantasy because she knew it would never happen. It was almost unbelievable that it had finally come true. Penny had to remind herself that he had only followed her because he was sorry for her.

'Have you seen Kitty?' she asked him. Enough of thinking about herself.

'Yes,' Rick said, and stopped. He did not want to describe to Penny how distraught his aunt was.

'I'd like to go and see her.'

'I'll go with you,' he offered.

'OK.'

Penny laughed inwardly. A date with Rick after all these years of her dreaming about it, and to where? To an old folk's home. Some people had all the luck.

'Then afterwards I'll take you out for dinner.'

She turned and looked at him. Was this a joke?

'You look like you need a treat,' he said.

Ah! So he *was* feeling sorry for her. Penny would not be patronised.

'You don't have to,' she said, then began to search for an excuse. 'I'm on a diet.'

'Quite unnecessary,' he remarked. 'But if you insist, we'll have a salad in a wine bar.'

They reached the boathouse opposite the bridge that led to Heydale Park. It was beginning to get dark. Maybe it was going to rain again. Penny knew she ought to turn back. She heard the sound of bicycles, and in a moment two youths sped by them. Then they were alone again.

'No, it's not just that,' she said, feeling desperate. 'I have a lot of work on at the moment.'

'Why don't you want to go out with me? Don't you like me?'

The direct questions disarmed her. At all costs she must not hurt his feelings. 'Of course I like you. But . . .'

She couldn't bring herself to say the rest. *But the problem is, I like you too much. And you make me feel so inadequate.*

'But?' he persisted. 'But what?'

'I think it's better to stay just friends.'

'OK. I propose a compromise. Come out with me just as a friend.'

Penny was well and truly cornered.

'So long as you realise there's nothing in it?'

'Nothing at all.' Rick smiled that smile that made her go dizzy. 'On Saturday? I'll meet you at Gladesmore around seven.'

'Seven,' she repeated. Large drops of rain fell on her hands and face.

'We'd better run for it,' Rick remarked. He took Penny's hand, and together they hurried back along the towpath. She was moving so fast she could not think. The rain began to come down more heavily now. Only when they finally arrived back at Rose and Harry's house did they slow down. Penny was out of breath after the dash in the rain, and knew she must look dreadful, her hair plastered to her face. It brought her to her senses. Despite the dinner invitation, Rick's interest in her was not romantic; it was for old times' sake. She wasn't the sort of woman who appealed to men at first sight – or at second sight, come to think of it. He had simply been being kind.

'Thanks,' she said to him. 'You did help me. I'm feeling better now. Do you want come in for another cup of tea?'

'I'd better get back,' he said. 'But I'll see you at the weekend. Can I have my jacket?'

Penny had forgotten she was wearing it. She took it off and handed it to him.

''Bye,' he said, and gave her a brief farewell kiss.

Penny watched him get into his BMW. Yes, he was an attractive man, but not her type. And she wasn't his type, although they got on well enough. Dinner on Saturday would be fun; he was intelligent and good company. It would be all the more enjoyable because there would be nothing to it, so she wouldn't have to make an effort. She could just be herself. But there would be no harm in having a word with the Beauty Editor tomorrow, as she might have a few tips. Was it possible to lose a few pounds by Saturday? Penny told herself off; she was being very foolish. And all the more foolish because she was standing at her parents' front gate in the pouring rain without a coat. She was wet through.

She surveyed the street. It looked as if her uncles and aunts had gone; at least, their cars weren't in evidence. Taking courage from that, she walked up the path and rang the bell.

Rose opened the door.

'Where on earth have you been?'

'I'm sorry, Mum.' Penny gave her a kiss. 'I need a towel.'

Rose hurried to the kitchen and returned with one.

'That's better. I really am sorry. It was just that Pearl was saying rotten things about Lily, and I lost my cool. I'll ring her tonight and apologise. I know I was out of order. I was wrong, wasn't I?'

Penny saw that Rose didn't seem to be listening to her.

'Are you all right, Mum?'

'Yes. Your father and I would like to have a word with you.'

Penny thought she must have upset Pearl more than she'd realised. Feeling subdued and repentant, she followed her mother into the living room. There was Harry seated at the dining table, a pile of used plates to his side. The remnants of the Madeira sat in the middle of the table. Penny could not read her father's expression. He looked serious, yet he was drumming his fingers on the table with nervous energy. Rose sat down opposite him, and sensing that this was shaping up as a formal occasion, Penny sat down too, pushing a tea cup away. Whatever her parents had to say to her was so important they hadn't even cleared the table.

'I have something to tell you,' Rose said. Penny suddenly felt apprehensive. Her mother's stern demeanour made her certain it was bad news. She looked up at her father. He winked at her. Now why would he do that?

'Anne gave me Lily's will,' Rose said, looking around her, almost as if she was worried she would be overheard.

'Poor Mum. You get landed with everything.'

Rose and Harry exchanged glances.

'Would you like to tell her?' Rose asked her husband.

Harry cleared his throat. 'No, you.'

'Tell me what?' It was bad news, certainly.

Rose looked down at the table. 'Lily has left you a lot of money. We can't quite work out the exact figure because of death duties, but it'll be in the region of two hundred and fifty thousand pounds.

'A quarter of a million,' added Harry.

'I don't believe you!' was Penny's rejoinder.

'It's true.' Rose's voice held no shadow of doubt.

'Can I see the will?'

'Monty took it straight round to the solicitor's,' Harry interjected. 'But it's all in order, legally binding, that sort of thing. It was only drawn up a few weeks ago. As if she knew she was on her way out.'

'Your father's right,' Rose said. 'It is true, Penny. I'm an executor.'

'Surely her money ought to be yours?'

'No. I mean, Lily has left me some money. A lot of money. More than we need.'

So that was all right then. Penny would not think of accepting any money from Lily's estate if her mother was not provided for too.

'And Fiona?' she added.

'She has been given a lot of money. Not quite as much as

you – Lily always had a soft spot for you – but a considerable amount. Lily has been more than fair.'

'How much?' Penny was still numb, only capable of asking questions. She would assimilate all this later.

'A lot. It's best you don't compare amounts. It can only lead to rivalry.' As she spoke, Rose twisted her wedding ring repeatedly. Penny could see that this was a matter of some importance to her.

'I agree with your mother,' Harry said.

It wasn't often her parents saw eye to eye. When they did, it held the force of law. Penny decided there and then to keep quiet about her money.

'What about Monty and Simon?'

Harry laughed, and even Rose managed a smile. 'Monty's been left comfortable.'

'Good,' said Penny.

'But Simon – you'll love this – he has been given all Lily's old furniture that she put in store. There's the budgie cage, a Utility sideboard she wouldn't part with – all of it rubbish. If he finds a place for it in his house, he gets five thousand pounds, otherwise he forfeits the lot. You should have seen his face!' Harry chuckled at the memory of his brother-in-law's discomfiture.

Penny was delighted too. Then she remembered her new wealth and felt rather giddy.

'Any chance of a whisky? A stiff one?'

'Good idea, Penny.' Harry busied himself at the drinks cabinet.

'A quarter of a million,' she repeated. It had not sunk in. She felt slightly hysterical.

'You'll adjust,' said Rose.

'And what about you? If you've got as much money as me, you can afford to splash out a bit.'

'Absolutely,' said Harry, as he placed the whisky glasses on the table.

'We'll see about that,' Rose said, a warning note in her voice.

Penny was amused. Would her mother ever be able to give up her habits of economy? But what about herself? She was rich. Penny still could not absorb the fact. It was all right for Fiona; she and Alastair had moved seamlessly into the echelons of the upper-middle classes. But wealth didn't go with Penny's self-image. Penny Green was an impecunious freelance journalist who lived from hand to mouth and didn't mind about it. Her idea of extravagance was fish and chips with curry sauce on the side. All this money – whatever would she do with it? Of course, she could always give it away. Except it was Lily's money, and since Lily didn't give it to charity, Penny had no right to either. So she would just keep it. Which seemed a waste.

I'm a rich woman, Penny told herself. That ought to make me feel better about my date with Rick. No, not a date, she corrected herself. Does the knowledge of my wealth make me feel more his equal? No, not at all. She just felt doubly unworthy, doubly fraudulent. The gulf between Penny Green as she really was and all this good fortune made her want to laugh, loud and long. Except Lily had just died, and the thought that she would never see her aunt again was too unbearable to contemplate. And her aunt had loved her so much, she'd left her all this money.

She thought about Lily. When Penny was small, her aunt appeared to her almost impossibly glamorous. She dyed her hair blonde, wore orangey-red lipstick and flowery perfume. She took exotic holidays and came home with all manner of kitschy souvenirs, like that gondola that rotated to the tune of 'O Sole Mio' and that three-foot doll in Spanish national dress. Lily's shoes had impossibly high heels and she let Penny stomp around in them once when she'd come to stay the night when things were bad at home. Lily was a refuge, but more than that: she presented a completely different view of how to be a woman. Rose saw life as her adversary; she battled against it, and against her husband. When things were bad for Lily, she just put on another layer of mascara.

Like me, Penny thought, remembering Fiona's wedding. She remembered the stinging in her eyes, and thought how strange it was that she could actually feel that now. Then she realised she could feel hot tears. Penny took hold of her mother's hand, and gave herself up to the luxury of a good cry.

Chapter Four

Rose never slept well. Sleeping badly ran in the family; towards the end of her life Rose's own mother, Evie, was awake most of the night and would sometimes spend until three in the morning completing a jigsaw puzzle in the front room. That was when she was very ill. Rose was not ill, and that was something to be grateful for. Nonetheless, she could not sleep. This was one of the reasons she had her own bedroom. Her restlessness in the night would disturb Harry, and his boisterous snoring and habit of rolling over with all of the duvet disturbed her.

Rose switched on her bedside lamp and sat up, propping her back against the pillows. It was five-thirty in the morning; almost late enough to get up and brew a pot of tea. It was a tempting thought. Rose decided she would do that once she had planned her day. It was Friday so Harry was at school and she was on the afternoon rota at the shop. That meant she could pop into Spar and get the few items she needed, and they could put off going to the supermarket until next weekend. Because once the supermarket people get you inside, Rose thought, they display the food in such a way as to tempt you, and you always end up spending more than you planned. Cunning, that's what they are. Cunning. But she knew she was more cunning than they were.

And there was something else she was going to do. Something unpleasant. She had to put her foot down. Bit by bit, Rose remembered last night. Harry had come in to help her with the dishes, although he knew she didn't like anyone drying with a cloth because it spread germs. Yet he had come in, and taken the teacloth with a map of the London Underground which Sally had given them one Christmas, and begun to dry the dishes.

'I've been thinking,' he'd said.

Dangerous words. Rose was on the defensive immediately.

'That money of Lily's . . . You haven't decided what you want to do with it?'

He was humble, but it was a front. She knew him of old.

'I can't say I've given it much thought. It'll be some time before it's through.'

'But there's no harm in planning ahead.'

Rose reached for the Brillo pad to scrub the saucepan and said nothing. Let him make it clear what he means, she thought.

'If I wanted to go part-time,' he said, 'or even take early retirement . . .'

'No!' Rose said, quick as lightning. Better knock that one on the head. Imagine him under her feet from morning to night! No. As long as he was capable of going out to work, she'd be handing him his briefcase at a quarter past eight.

'Come on, Harry. You know you'd be lost without a job. And the money wouldn't stretch that far. Forty thousand is nothing these days. People earn more than that in a year. Besides, it's capital. You don't eat into your capital.'

'It's capital we didn't have a few days ago,' he commented.

Rose carefully picked up the carving knife from under the soapy water and held it still.

'All the better that we have it now,' she parried.

'At the least, we can afford a holiday.'

'What kind of holiday?'

She was still holding the carving knife.

'A decent holiday. My head of department spent the summer in Tuscany.'

'Tuscany!' Rose's voice was rich with contempt. Tuscany for the likes of them?

'Do you fancy somewhere more lively? We could take a fly/drive to the States. A few days in New York, then we could roam around.'

'At our age?'

'Speak for yourself.' He was two years younger than Rose and enjoyed reminding her of the fact. 'Or Israel. We could visit my cousin.'

'The political situation,' Rose objected.

'OK,' said Harry. Then he'd come up behind her and kissed her on the back of her neck. The shock almost paralysed her. The touch of his lips on her skin made her tingle. She didn't know whether she liked it or not. Thus it was that she felt herself being gently derailed. 'A second honeymoon,' he'd said. 'We'll spend a month in Cyprus or Crete, getting to know each other again. Evening strolls along the harbour. *Mezes* in a cafe.'

Rose pulled the plug and the water gurgled as it left the sink.

'How much do you think that would cost?'

'Hundreds at the most. Then the rest can be capital. After we've replaced the car and the settee, and seen to my tooth.'

'Hang the dishcloth on the radiator,' Rose told him.

As she said that the doorbell had rung. It was Harry's pupil. He earned a bit on the side from giving piano lessons. It provided him with a little bit of pocket money. God knew how he spent it; Rose certainly didn't.

Thinking it all over now, she could see that she had given him the impression that a holiday was a possibility. She should never have done that. Just for a moment she had let down her guard. It was that cajoling, almost flirtatious way he'd spoken to her. It had reminded her of the old days. But Rose had learned her lesson. She was foolish to have been taken in by him this time. There was no fool like an old fool.

What Harry didn't realise, she told herself, as she got out of bed and reached for her dressing gown hanging on the back of the door, was that you had to set limits on your spending. If they agreed on a holiday, then that would set a precedent. There would be no reason not to get the settee re-covered – Harry admitted that himself – and then where would they be? Back where they were before. And it wasn't just that. She sat on the bed and eased one foot into a slipper, eyeing that familiar varicose vein, which was not, thank God, getting any more prominent. It wasn't only that. To spend Lily's money on a second honeymoon – why, it would be like dancing on her grave.

That wasn't the only objection. Rose put on her other slipper, then stopped. What swept through her now was a nameless dread. Away together they would have to confront what they had become. Anything but that! Better and safer that they should continue just as they were. A holiday – a second honeymoon – was out of the question. They couldn't afford it. They really couldn't afford it. Harry would have to see that, and the sooner the better. This morning. She would make it clear this morning, before he went to work. That was the unpleasant job she had to do. That, and taking out the wheelie bin.

The ceiling vibrated as Harry walked across the landing to the bathroom. Rose glanced at the kitchen clock. He was on time. She switched on the kettle, and went to the pantry to take out the reduced-sugar jam that she spread on his toast. He complained it wasn't as sweet as the real thing, but she had the job of watching his waistline, and it was a sorry sight. Rose smiled grimly to herself.

She placed two slices of toast in the toaster and took the low-fat spread out of the fridge. She began to rehearse what she would say to him when he was munching on his breakfast.

A nice idea, Harry, about the holiday, but there are some things you have to understand. Forty thousand pounds – I know it sounds a lot of money – but forty thousand pounds isn't going to last forever. If we fritter it, it will vanish before you can say Jack Robinson. That was an expression her mother had used, and Lily had used it too. Rose wondered where it came from. *I'm not saying we'll never have a holiday, but I do think we ought to spend within our means. Lily's money gives us security, and that's what we ought to be using it for. Security. You don't know what it's like to be poor.* He didn't. That was the trouble. Harry's family was well off. Hers wasn't. He didn't know what it was like to count every penny, and never to wear new clothes. Rose always wore Lily's cast-offs, even though they never suited her. A second-hand Rose, just like the song. Second-hand in every sense.

There was a time, in the early days of their marriage, when they were both hard up. Yet even when they were facing bankruptcy, Harry always believed it would come right. It did come right in the end, but it was no thanks to him. The truth was, it was thanks to Lily. It was she who gave him that job, managing the Swinton shop. And the irony was it was Rose who'd suggested it. There was a bitter taste in her mouth. She needed to eat something. *You don't know what it's like to be poor,* she continued mentally. *Who knows what's going to happen in the future? We're not touching that money. If you want a holiday, we can always go and stay with Fiona in her nice new house. And . . .*

Thump, thump, thump as Harry came down the stairs. Rose started guiltily. The toast jumped out of the toaster and a dull thud suggested the papers had arrived. Harry went to the front door to pick them up and entered the kitchen reading the headlines. He tutted as he did so.

Rose looked at him covertly. She always had a faint sense of surprise that he was still a handsome man. She'd once believed that plainer men weathered better. But Harry was good-looking as a youngster, and even now there was something about him. His greying hair was thinning, but he had kept most of it. His eyes had stayed lively, and perhaps because he carried a bit too much flesh, he didn't have that wizened look of some men of his age. He could pass for fifty, she thought. Harry was fifty-nine.

He sat down at the table and riffled through the paper, stopping at the back pages.

'Ah ha!' he exclaimed.

Rose guessed he was reading about the football.

'Look at this! Return to New York two hundred pounds. That's nothing. For another hundred or so, we could get to the Bahamas. Katmandu, Singapore, Hong Kong . . .'

'Harry!' she said warningly.

He bit into his toast and ate as he spoke, which she disliked. She turned her face from him.

'I know, I know. Only joking. But I can get out of school at lunchtime and drop into the travel agents. We can have a look at some brochures tonight.'

'No.'

'Why not?'

Now Rose turned and looked at him directly.

'I'm not touching Lily's money.'

'But last night you—'

'Last night was last night. I've thought about this and I'm not—' She couldn't remember what it was she'd planned to say to him. 'I'm not frittering it away.'

'Frittering? A holiday isn't frittering. Everybody goes on holiday. Monty and Sally had a fortnight in Benidorm in November. Simon went to Canada.'

'Harry, you don't have to do what everybody else does.'

'Be reasonable, Rose.'

'I am reasonable. It's you who aren't being reasonable.'

Rose's heart was thumping. This was going badly wrong. She didn't want an argument. She just wanted to explain the situation to him, and to show she was simply being prudent. But if he was going to be like this . . .

'I'm a working man. I need a holiday. And now we've got forty thousand pounds.'

'She left the money to me,' Rose reminded him gently. For this was true. Harry was mentioned nowhere in the will. This was Rose's trump card, and she hadn't wanted to use it. It was just that she felt she was losing control.

'Go on holiday yourself, then,' he said.

'No, no. That wasn't what I meant. The money is for both of us. But it won't last forever. We've got to be careful. That's all I'm saying.'

'All your life you've been careful.'

'I've had cause to be.'

Now they were treading on a precipice. The air between them

vibrated with tension. They were approaching the dangerous place. Harry retreated.

'All I'm saying is that it would do us good to go on a little holiday. You only live once.'

Relief filled Rose. Harry had moved to safer ground, so she conceded a point too. 'I didn't say we wouldn't take a holiday this year. We can put some money aside each week, and then we can have a break with Monty and Sally. I've always liked Bournemouth – we could go there.'

'With Monty and Sally?'

'Or we can stay with Fiona. She'll be settled by then. If you put your piano lesson money aside, and I'm careful with the housekeeping, we'll have a bit to spend. Now look at the time, Harry. Ten past eight already. If you don't leave soon, you'll get caught in the traffic, and you know you don't like that.'

Rose made a show of adjusting her watch. She just wanted him out of the house now. She'd made her point. The money was safe. Once he was gone, she could pretend none of this had happened, and life could revert to normal. All she wanted was that life should be normal.

Harry bolted his toast, drained his coffee, and set about preparing for work. They said nothing. He took his briefcase from the stand in the hall.

''Bye,' he said, and left.

At least they were still talking, thought Rose. That was something. She had achieved that much. Most women, she thought, as she began to clear the breakfast things away, would have kicked him out years ago. She hadn't. For the sake of the children, she'd kept this marriage going. The girls had cause to be grateful. One day they might understand what she had been through. No, of course not, she would never tell them. Mind you, she'd told them over and over again that there was no point getting married until you could find a man whom you could trust. Trust was the nub of it all. Once you lost trust, you never, never, got it back. Like capital.

Alastair seemed a nice boy, and generous too. There was no

reason for history to repeat itself. Not with Fiona. She was sensible. She had her feet on the ground. As for Penny, she solved other people's problems, rather than have any of her own. And with a quarter of a million pounds, how could you have problems? Rose did not worry about Penny. She'd instilled a proper amount of caution into her. Sometimes she wondered if Penny was a little too cautious about men. All that feminism, for example – she hoped it hadn't come from her. Rose did not so much dislike men as feel disappointed in them. And what woman didn't? she said to herself, taking a J-cloth, sprinkling it with Dettox, and annihilating the germs on the kitchen table. What woman didn't?

As Harry turned the key in the ignition, the overture from *Carmen* came pounding out of the speakers. He leaned forward and turned the sound up. Then he backed carefully out of the drive, and turned his car in the direction of the main road.

Never had a man felt so misunderstood. All he had done was suggest a holiday. Most wives would jump at the chance. But Rose? A downright refusal. Last night he'd thought he'd succeeded in getting round her, but this morning she was back to her old tight-fisted self. It was almost impossible to believe.

Fancy inheriting forty thousand pounds and not wanting to spend any of it! Harry imagined himself telling this to his mates in the staff room. Everyone would sympathise with him. No one could possibly see the matter from Rose's point of view. With all that money . . . not to go on a holiday . . . when they hadn't had a decent break for years!

Anger bubbled up in his breast. It soured his good mood. Generally, of a morning, he was in a good mood. He sang on the way to school, and sometimes even carried on singing as he walked across the car park, ignoring the strange looks the fifth years gave him. This morning he didn't feel like singing and it was all that woman's fault. There was something wrong with her – there must be. She wasn't normal. This thought comforted him. Maybe Rose had some sort of obsession with money, a mental illness like clinical depression or ME. Harry was rather vague about illness. That was Rose's department. Or maybe she had a form of agoraphobia – she was frightened of going abroad.

Then Harry began to feel better. He was not an aggressive man. If he ever shouted at Rose, it was because she drove him to it. The girls understood that, because they had seen their mother in action. Left to his own devices, Harry told himself, he was a peace-loving, reasonable man. He didn't want arguments. If Rose were ill, then maybe he could get her to the doctor's and she would cheer up and agree to a holiday. Any normal woman would be delighted to go on holiday with him. He glanced at his reflection in the mirror, and liked what he saw. His pleasure at his own appearance helped him ease back into the role of genial, piano-playing, popular music teacher at Albert Road School.

I know what's wrong with Rose, he thought, approaching the school gates. She doesn't have a life. *He* had a life, a role to play in school. She had nothing except for that potty little charity shop. It was difficult for a woman when the children flew the nest. Fiona getting married had obviously made Rose depressed, and Lily's death wouldn't have helped either. Harry congratulated himself on his sensitivity. Rose was lucky to have him. Tonight he'd put his foot down and insist on a holiday. She needed a break.

Liking himself again, he made his way into school and the the shame that he felt, at having been defeated by his wife, had dwindled almost to nothing. He put it out of his mind, and tried to remember instead what it was he had planned to do with the third years after break.

No one ever listened to the Head during assembly. Harry was no exception. Today, however, he looked at the Head. He was an imposing, well set up sort of chap, with a dry sense of humour and a short way with villains. Harry rather admired him. The Head had a nice place in Cheadle; the wife was a magistrate, no less. The Head had invited the music and art departments over once, for a getting-to-know-you session. He had a conservatory, state-of-the-art, it was, and a music system that would have set him back about two or three thousand. He'd done well for himself.

Like Bobby, Harry's brother, the dentist. Dentists made quite a bit, whatever they might say. Every year Bobby went abroad twice. He said he needed it – stress, that sort of thing. Stress! Harry could tell him a thing or two about stress. His sense of injustice was swelling again. Stress! Stress was having to get thirty reluctant fourteen-year-olds to sing. Stress was all the unnecessary paperwork he ended up doing. If anyone needed two holidays a year, it was Harry. And now they had the money, Rose refused to budge. Give me strength, he almost murmured to himself.

Had he married the wrong woman? This was a serious question, and Harry gave it due thought. Certainly, he and Rose were opposites. She was quiet – withdrawn, really – and he was an extrovert. She was anxious, fretted like most women. He was easy-going. Sexually – Harry knew he shouldn't be thinking about sex in assembly, but it gave him a frisson – they were compatible. Or at least they used to be. *That* side of their marriage had been in abeyance, as it were, for some time. Which was what happened as you got older. Harry felt sad. He wasn't that old. He was fifty-nine. What was that? Look at Tina Turner – almost the same age as him.

Here he was, young, energetic, full of the joys of living, married to a woman old before her time. Harry felt as if his wife had trapped him in a net. Every time he moved, she was there with her constraints. He struggled to get free. He moved around slightly as the school muttered the Lord's Prayer. *Lead us not into temptation* . . .

Harry was free after assembly, and as he walked back to the staff room he hoped he was not on the substitution list. It was pinned up just inside the door. He scanned the names and saw he was not needed. He must have been the only person to escape. Everyone else seemed to have been used.

The Deputy Head slapped him on the shoulder.

'Bearing up?'

Harry was puzzled. Did he know about his row with Rose? Then it occurred to him this was a reference to the day he had taken off for Lily's funeral.

'I'm OK. The wife's rather down.'

'Understandable. Why don't you two plan a holiday together?'

Before Harry could respond, the Deputy Head had moved off. Quite quickly, the staff room started to empty. Lessons were beginning. Harry wished that someone was able to stay and talk. He was beginning to feel more aggrieved than ever, and although he had no intention of talking about his wife to anyone, a conversation would help him to unwind. But no one at all was left in the staff room.

Too unsettled to work, he decided to make himself a cup of tea. He walked over to the corner of the staff room where there was a facility they called the kitchen which was in fact a sink, two aluminium kettles and some open shelves with the staff mugs arranged on them. Harry picked up one of the kettles to assess how much water was left. Enough for him. He switched on the kettle, feeling lonely.

At just that moment he heard footsteps and turned with alacrity. To his pleasure it was Rita, the flute teacher. Harry had always liked Rita. Today she was wearing a checked pleated skirt and cream satin blouse. Harry noticed that her stockings were black. Typical Rita. Always a touch of the eccentric about her. Harry appreciated that. It showed she had a wild side. Unlike some. Rita's fair hair was arranged in regular waves, and her lipstick was a startling orangey-red. It reminded Harry of a person he knew, but never mind that now. Rita mixed convention with something . . . something almost sexy. Her face lit up when she saw him.

She put her hand on Harry's sleeve and moved close to him before she spoke.

'I had such a lovely time at the wedding. It was so good of you to invite me.'

The wedding? Harry was a little disorientated. Of course – she was talking about Fiona's wedding. Rita was one of the school party, and he had danced with her then. Remembering that made him faintly, but not unpleasantly, embarrassed.

'Not at all, not at all. Glad you could come. I daresay you haven't heard what happened afterwards?'

Rita hadn't heard. She encouraged him to tell her. Together they stood with their tea by a window overlooking the chemistry block, as Harry explained.

'My sister-in-law took ill and died, just two days later.'

Rita's face filled with sympathy.

'Oh, Harry! How dreadful for you!'

Yes, it was dreadful for him. He was glad that Rita could see that. He liked the way she patted him on the sleeve again.

'We've only just had the funeral. I'm a bit shell-shocked, to tell the truth.'

'Of course you are, Harry.'

Now it occurred to him how cruel Rose had been, picking an argument with him so soon after the funeral. He began to feel sorry for himself.

'You can never tell what life has to throw at you,' Rita continued, shaking her head at the randomness of fate. 'I know how I felt when he . . . But never mind about me.'

Harry remembered the staff-room gossip. Apparently Rita's husband had come home one night and told her he'd been having an affair for the past two years, and was leaving her. Here was a woman who knew a bit about trouble. Here was a woman who knew just how difficult marriage could be. He watched her lift the cup to her lips and deposit a red lipstick imprint on the side, and saw how exactly it followed the contours of her mouth. Dare he tell her a little bit about his argument this morning? If anyone would understand, it would be Rita.

'My sister-in-law dying,' he continued, 'has upset the wife a bit.'

'Of course it would!'

'So I thought about taking her on a holiday. Strange to say, she isn't too keen.'

'Why not?' Rita looked gratifyingly surprised.

'She worries about money, you see. Even though we have enough, old habits die hard. She doesn't understand that we can afford to treat ourselves. I have my work cut out to make her see that.' He laughed indulgently.

Rita looked serious, inviting more confidences.

'You wouldn't believe it, but this morning she had a go at me as I was on my way to work. Just because I suggested a holiday last night.' Harry shrugged. He decided to be magnanimous. 'It's just her nature, I suppose.'

'Some people are like that,' Rita said, consolingly.

'Marriage isn't always easy,' he reflected. It was good to talk adult to adult like this. If only Rose were as reasonable as Rita, then they would not have their difficulties. Then Harry remembered that Rita had her problems too, and here he was, selfishly harping on about his. He changed tack.

'And you?' Rita had been a sympathetic listener and he would repay the compliment. 'I hear you've been having a tough time.'

Rita gave a wan smile.

'Oh, Harry, it's sweet of you to think of me. There aren't many men as sensitive as you. I'm resigned, Harry. That's how I feel. I'm resigned. I wouldn't want him back now, not if he came on bended knees. I manage, Harry.' Once again she put her hand on his sleeve. Rita was like that. She was a tactile person. She also stood close to the person she was conversing with. Normally Harry found himself edging away from her, but he was standing right beside the sink. In any case, her closeness was comforting right now. He could feel the warmth of her body, and hear the rustle of her blouse against her slip as she raised her mug to her mouth once more. And again Harry watched the lipstick stain, and saw how it became blurred as she smeared it with a second imprint.

'It's not easy,' she said. 'Life isn't easy. But you've got to keep up appearances.'

Harry wondered if she wiped off her lipstick before she played the flute. Otherwise it would be covered in lipstick. He was

amused at the idea. He thought of the traditional depiction of
the straying husband who comes home with lipstick on his collar.
Certainly Rita wouldn't be a woman to mess around with. He
smiled to himself.

'Now that's more like it!' she said. 'Being unhappy doesn't suit
you, Harry. I always tell everyone that what I like about you is
your cheerfulness. Now you go home and tell your wife you're
taking her off to Tenerife, no questions asked!'

Yes, I might just do that, thought Harry.

Chapter Five

'You had a happy childhood, Alastair, didn't you?'

Fiona knew the answer to that question but asked it anyway. She wanted to hear her husband talk about his early days now they were close to Aberavon. She wanted to watch the hills go past out of the window and think of Alastair as a boy, stalking rabbits with his dad, or fishing in the river that occasionally flashed past them from beneath a tangle of trees.

'I did,' Alastair said.

'It must have been wonderful, growing up in the country.'

'But quiet.'

'Not that quiet.' As she said it, a large, articulated lorry clattered by on the other side of the road. Despite that, the countryside was restful to the eye, with double-fronted stone houses punctuating the roadside and untidy crows loitering with intent on the verge. North-east Scotland was much less remote than the Highland coast where they had spent their honeymoon. They had gone out in the car, once the snow had partly melted, and seen wild coasts with rocks and boulders scattered on them, as if some angry child having a tantrum, had thrown them down. But here in the north-east were signs of the sort of rural communities that Fiona had read about in the novels she enjoyed. She could see herself fitting in here very nicely.

They approached a group of large, squat buildings that reminded her for a moment of the factories she had grown up with, and then caught a glimpse of a gleaming copper still. Now she knew what she had seen.

'Your father managed a distillery like that.'

'Mmm.'

Alastair was still sensitive about his father who had died only two months ago. Fiona had met him the once when she had come up to Aberavon six weeks after meeting Alastair and was taken to the nursing home where he was being looked after. He hadn't seemed to take in the significance of who she was, and Fiona had been sad about that. She thought she had better change the subject.

'Are you glad to be coming home?'

Alastair turned his face to her and smiled. Fiona loved that special smile he gave her; no one had ever smiled at her like that before. He meant that anywhere he went with her was home, and she felt like that about him too. She loved Aberavon already, because she loved Alastair. If these fields, this air, these skies nurtured him, she knew she could be happy here.

She was lucky. How could a marriage fail to prosper in such glorious surroundings? She surveyed the sweep of hills to each side of the road and thought of her own parents. Her mother had been much on her mind lately. It had been kind of Rose to tell her about the five thousand pounds, and it was generous of Lily too. Poor Lily had never married. Rose had married, and Fiona knew, as much as she liked to pretend otherwise, that her parents had not had such an easy time. Fiona had her own theories as to why this was. First there were the money difficulties but that wasn't all; there was something else. There was a lack of kindness. Her mother was so intolerant of her father's faults, and always ready to accuse him. Fiona had often thought that if she had been her mother, she would have handled Harry differently and there would not have been all those arguments. Now was her chance to prove herself. She was married, and was not going to make the same mistakes as her mother.

They were coming into Aberavon now. The village was strung out on either side of the wide main road. There were lines of traditional stone cottages, a gaudy petrol station, a video store, several gift shops, a butcher, a newsagent. The car halted to allow a tractor to turn awkwardly into a side street, and Fiona looked into a shop selling old-fashioned women's wear: pleated skirts, little jerseys with pearl buttons, and flowery dresses that spoke of fifties respectability. She wondered if the shop ever had any customers. The car moved on and proceeded out of the village in the direction of Alastair's mother's house, which was soon to be their own.

They turned left and travelled for a while along a single-track road past inquisitive cows and a rusty-looking forest. Then Alastair took the car along a private road between two rows of tall firs, and the car crunched to a halt on the gravel in front of the house. They had arrived.

Fiona felt odd now the car was no longer in motion. She had been travelling for the best part of the day and being still seemed unnatural. She noticed a net curtain twitch at the side of the house, and in a moment the front door opened and there was Margaret, ready to greet them.

Margaret's house – my house, Fiona corrected herself – was a substantial stone residence, detached, taller than it was wide, and on the left-hand side was a small turret, covered with slate, giving the place the air of a fairy-tale castle. Fiona loved that. She was going to take photographs of the turret to send to Penny and her friends. Alastair opened the boot to begin to take out the suitcases while Fiona approached Margaret and put her arms around her to give her a kiss.

Margaret seemed surprised at that, and Fiona immediately regretted her action. She knew she ought have taken things a little more slowly.

Margaret, in a tweed skirt and brown cardigan buttoned tight, ushered them into a front room. Fiona glanced around the square hall, with a grandfather clock ticking arthritically in one corner, and caught sight of a heavily framed painting of a winter scene, with snow-topped mountains and skies as white as the land below. She hoped Margaret would take both of those with her to her new cottage.

In the front room, a table was laid out with a tempting spread. Margaret had evidently spent some time arranging sandwiches and cakes, and there were small pies, too. The room was just a shade chilly, and Fiona noticed that the open fireplace was not lit but was filled with pine cones. Above it a pair of stag's antlers were displayed. Once again Fiona imagined the room different, as she would have it. The antlers would go, most definitely, and the fire would be blazing, and she would decorate it with Victorian-style tiles, in keeping with the decor. They needed a new carpet, perhaps in a blushing pink for warmth, and a three-piece suite in a printed fabric, and a huge vase of flowers in the window. Fiona moved over to the window and pulled the net curtains to one side. Surely Margaret didn't need these? She remembered from her last visit they obscured a tremendous view for in front of her was a real mountain. Rocks like broken teeth on its summit almost scratched the clouds that hung low in the sky. A track wound its way along the lower slopes, then vanished into a forest. It was wonderful.

'Tea or coffee?' Margaret asked.

Fiona turned round.

'Coffee would be lovely,' she said.

Once they had eaten, looked after by an attentive Margaret, Fiona felt it was time to relax. She noticed that Alastair seemed a little quiet and guessed how strange it must feel, being with his mother and his wife, and strove to make it easy for him by being as pleasant as possible to Margaret.

'This is very kind, making us this delicious tea.'

'It's nae problem.'

'I do like these little pies. Did you make them yourself?'

'Och, no. They're from Walker's in the village.'

Fiona pointed to the stag's antlers.

'Are they real?'

'I really don't know,' her mother-in-law said.

'I just wondered if anyone you knew went hunting. Did your father, Alastair?'

'No.'

Fiona thought that her husband seemed rather taciturn. Was

it because she wasn't trying hard enough with his mother? She redoubled her efforts.

'I know I've said this before, but I think it's so kind of you to let us live here. It's such a wonderful house. And the view of the mountain!'

Margaret just smiled at her. Fiona realised that in her enthusiasm she had failed to ask a question that Margaret could answer. No wonder the conversation was going nowhere. So she tried again.

'What is your new house like?'

'Just a wee bungalow.'

'Won't you miss this one?' As she said that, Fiona knew it was a tactless question. Margaret had lived the best years of her life here, raising Alastair, and must still be mourning the death of her husband. Fiona watched Margaret's face anxiously.

'Och, no,' the woman said, revealing no emotion whatsoever.

These Scots are dour, she thought, and turned her face to Alastair, hoping for an encouraging smile. Yet he looked constrained, she guessed because of the presence of his mother. Fiona didn't want to be uncharitable but Margaret was a little difficult. It was a pity Fiona had never known Alastair's father. He must have been the jolly one in the family, else where would Alastair get his sense of humour? But Fiona would not be deterred. She would break down the barriers by talking honestly. That was the kind of thing Penny would do.

'I hope you won't be lonely? It must be hard for you, living alone. You can come and visit us at any time, and I shall be glad of your company when Alastair is gone.'

Margaret turned to him.

'Where are you going?'

'My contract in Manchester has a few more weeks to run.'

'You didn't say.'

'Fiona knows.'

'Yes,' she said brightly. 'I don't mind. Well, I do mind, of course, but the money will come in useful and you and I can get to know each other.' As she said this, she had the sinking feeling that Margaret didn't want to get to know her. And why hadn't Alastair told his mother he had to go back?

He got up.

'I'll take our cases up to the bedroom.'

'Shall I help you clear the tea things?' Fiona asked Margaret.

'It's nae bother.'

'You can give me a hand,' said Alastair. 'I can show you the rest of the house at the same time.'

Fiona looked directly at Margaret, seeking her permission. She nodded, so Fiona followed Alastair out to the hall where their cases were lined up. His face seemed harder than usual – there was a tightness in his expression. Fiona was just a little scared. She hoped she hadn't done anything wrong. She wanted to be reassured.

'Have I upset you?'

Alastair turned to look at her and his face immediately softened. He was beautiful, Fiona thought. Like the statue of David by Michelangelo. He had the same curly hair, the same manly body, and a beauty and concentration in his expression that made him infinitely desirable. As she thought this, Fiona understood the source of the awkwardness over tea. If you were the mother of this beautiful man, you'd never want to let him go. Margaret was jealous, that was all it was. Fiona felt reassured. She gave Alastair a brief kiss, and lifted the lightest of the cases.

'Through there,' Alastair pointed to the room opposite the dining room, 'is the lounge.' Fiona put the suitcase down and peeked in. It was full of boxes. Margaret was clearly well on in her preparations for moving. Fiona was glad.

He took two cases, and mounted the stairs. 'Mother said she'd like us to have the main bedroom. There are three others – they'll all need redecoration.'

'Good. That money of Lily's will come in useful.' Fiona followed her husband into the main bedroom. A double bed had been made up for them, with a flowery duvet and valance. Not what Fiona would have chosen. A large, old-fashioned dressing table dominated the room. From the window the mountain was visible again. Fiona walked over to look at it.

'Which mountain is that?'

Alastair came up behind her, and put his arms around her waist.

'Ben Voulin.'

Fiona twisted round and looked into his eyes.

'Are you all right?'

'Aye. I suppose I just feel a bit strange. I haven't lived here for some time, and this is my parents' old bedroom.'

Fiona imagined what it would be like sleeping in her own parents' room with Alastair and sympathised with him immediately.

'We don't have to sleep here once your mother is gone.'

'We'll try to make that as soon as possible.'

It was a relief to Fiona that apparently he found his mother difficult too. That meant she could ask him some questions.

'Why didn't she know you were going back to Manchester?'

'I told her. She forgot.'

'You said she needed me, and that's why I had to stay here. But she seems all right.'

'Aye. That's just a front. She'll be glad to have you around.'

'Does she really want to move out of this house? If I was her, I'd want to stay here, with all my memories.'

'That's precisely why she doesn't want to stay here! No, I'm only joking. The house is too big for her now, and her new bungalow is close to her sister Elspeth. She was keen for us to have the house.'

'Is it actually a present, or are we living here until we can find . . .'

'Enough questions,' he said, stopping her with a kiss. 'We've work to do. Let's unpack.'

Together they began to empty the suitcases. Fiona opened a large fitted wardrobe and was greeted by a smell of mothballs. That was another thing she would have to see to.

'Can you turn on the light, Alastair? It's getting dark.'

He did so, and the room was bathed in a soft light. Fiona drew the curtains. She glanced at her watch. Six o'clock. Time for her pill. She looked for the half-finished packet in her suitcase. Evidently it had slipped to the bottom. Or perhaps not. It was nowhere to be seen. Fiona frowned to herself. Where did she last see them? On the bedside table in her hotel room. Did she put them in the suitcase? She didn't remember. She had no spare packets with her. It had been her intention to register with a new doctor as soon as she arrived in Aberavon, and get a new prescription. One day she would have a baby, but certainly not now.

'I think I've left my pills in the hotel,' she told Alastair.

'Are you sure?'

'Pretty sure.'

'Whoops.'

She smiled ruefully.

'What shall we do?' he asked.

'No sex for at least three weeks,' she told him, then grinned to show she didn't mean it. 'No, you'll just have to get some condoms, I'm afraid.'

'At the next available opportunity,' he said, eyes upon her body.

Fiona enjoyed a frisson of sexual excitement, then remembered where she was.

'Come on,' she said. 'We'd better finish unpacking or your mother will wonder what we're up to!'

'Aye, aye, Cap'n,' said Alastair.

It had taken until today, Saturday, but finally Margaret had moved out. Fiona thought to herself, as she watched Alastair drive off with her in the front seat, that real married life was going to begin for them now. Except it wasn't, because tomorrow he was going back to Manchester.

Last night they had lain whispering in bed so that Margaret couldn't hear them. Fiona had begged Alastair to stay, or at least to let her go back with him. She had even cried a bit. She wished she hadn't; he had become very distressed, and she felt as if she had been selfish. Alastair had been patient with her and explained yet again why it made sense for them to be apart for a few weeks.

And besides, he'd said, he'd be home at the weekends. And when he'd finished his contract, they'd have more than enough money to renovate this house from top to bottom. Or even buy a new one. With my wages, and Lily's money, and the proceeds from the sale of this, we could move to Aberdeen, he'd told her. Or just outside Aberdeen. We don't have to stay here forever. Mother won't mind.

Fiona remembered that now as she turned from the window into the bare dining room. She was guiltily glad that this house was not going to be a permanent home. It *was* lovely living deep in the Spey Valley, even though it was not quite spring. But this house . . . the fact was, it was not quite her. This was a disloyal thought, and one Fiona would not have had were it not for the fact that Alastair seemed to feel uncomfortable here too. Penny's suspicions were probably right. Margaret had given them the house so she would not lose her son. But living in Aberdeen, they would only be half a day's driving distance, and there they could make a really fresh start. That, Fiona decided, was what she really wanted.

She looked up. Alastair and Margaret had forgotten to take away the antlers. How could she possibly live with those things protruding from the wall? She pulled over a chair to the fireplace and climbed on it. Just at that moment the phone rang.

Fiona jumped down from the chair and ran across the room, empty except for an elderly settee, a rocking chair, a nest of tables and the fire burning slowly in the grate. The telephone was on the window sill. Fiona picked up the receiver.

'Hello?'

'Is that you, Fiona?'

'Penny!' Fiona was delighted. She had been thinking about her sister on and off all week, and intending to ring her. Only she had decided to do so after Alastair had gone back to Manchester and she was on her own.

'So how's married life?'

'Wonderful!'

Penny gave a loud yawn over the phone, and Fiona smiled to herself.

'Where's Alastair? Have you got him cooking and cleaning like I told you?'

'I'm on my own at the moment. He's taken his mother to her new place, and then he's getting some shopping. Tonight's going to be our first night alone – and our last. Can he come and see you when he's in Manchester?'

A pause. 'Yes, of course. What's the weather like?'

'Raining quite heavily.'

'Here too.'

'Penny?'

'Yes.'

'It's a bit difficult with his mother. She's – no, she's very nice but she doesn't say much. I feel as if I'm not being very useful. I'm supposed to be here to look after her.'

'And she won't be looked after?'

Fiona laughed.

'Count your blessings,' Penny said. 'I have it on good authority from my correspondents that mothers-in-law can be a problem. The interfering type isn't just a fictional stereotype.'

'I know I'm lucky, but she doesn't talk to me. One afternoon Alastair went out with a neighbour to get some peat for the fire, and Margaret sat in the front room reading. She didn't talk to me.'

'Don't make too much of that. You've got to remember that in our family, silence was always used as a weapon. If Mum and Dad weren't speaking, it was because they were making a point. In other families, silence can be quite companionable.'

'Yes,' Fiona said eagerly, thinking what an excellent Agony Aunt her sister was, 'that's it exactly. I need to adjust to another family's ways.'

'I'm sure that's right.'

'Anyway, Alastair said that maybe we could sell up and move a bit further away. He says the house is Margaret's wedding present to us, and we're free to do what we want with it. Only she hasn't mentioned transferring the deeds of this house to our names, and unless she does, we couldn't afford anywhere else.'

'Have a word with Alastair.'

'I will. Because the truth is, I'd love to move.'

'Is village life not so idyllic?'

Fiona laughed, and decided to be disloyal. 'Down in Aberavon, nearly everyone has satellite TV and the video rental store does a roaring trade.'

'No night life?'

'There's a crowd of kids who stand outside the chippy every evening.'

'Haven't you joined the flower committee at the local church?'

'Kirk,' Fiona corrected her. 'And, no, I haven't.' She was beginning to feel uncomfortable. She had told Penny almost too much already. She didn't want to have to explain to her as well how different she felt from everyone around her. When she went into the local shops with Alastair, people were pleasant. When she went out on her own, everyone seemed to have forgotten who she was. 'If we move, we'll go to Aberdeen. There's more going on there. And then I can study Scots Law, in case I want to go back to work. It's lucky about Lily's money, isn't it? What are you going to spend yours on?' Rose had said that Lily had given Penny five thousand pounds too.

Another pause. 'Haven't thought yet. Probably a course of liposuction, a complete makeover, or a harem of males with visual handicaps. The last might be the easiest option.'

'Penny!'

'Only joking.'

'And what about Mum and Dad? How are they? Are they glad about the money?'

'Don't, please! It's all I've heard about all week. First Dad rings and slags off Mum for being a tight-fisted old bitch because she won't take him on a round-the-world cruise, and then Mum rings to complain that Dad can't understand that it seems wrong to spend Lily's money at all.'

'Who do you think is right?'

'Both of them. No, neither. Oh, I don't care!' Fiona knew she did care, and felt sorry for her.

'And how are you?'

'That's what I was going to tell you,' Penny said, her voice somewhat arch. Fiona was interested. Some juicy gossip in the offing?

'Tell me what?'

'Guess who I'm going out with tonight?'

'Oh, you've met someone. That's wonderful!' Fiona was thrilled. Penny had not been out with anyone for years, it seemed. This was excellent news. 'Who is he? Do I know him?'

'As a matter of fact, you do.'

'Who is it?' Fiona was keen to know.

'What would you say to Rick Goldstone?'

'No, really, who is it?'

'Rick Goldstone.'

'You're kidding.'

'I'm not.'

'But you had a huge crush on him! And once he rang you up but it was only to ask you for Linda's phone number.'

'Ouch,' Penny said, but she sounded amused.

'So how did this happen?'

'Since you were quite preoccupied with your own wedding at the time, you didn't notice that I whiled away some time with Rick at the reception. He came to Lily's funeral too. And then he asked me out!' Penny's voice was a parody of girlishness. Fiona knew there was a punch line coming.

'So where are you going?'

'To Gladesmore Residential Home. Motto: care, courtesy and consideration. No, it's not really a date. We're going to visit Kitty together, who's his aunt. That's all. I just thought it would amuse you.'

'Do you still fancy him?'

'Heavens, no!'

'Oh. Why don't you invite him to your house afterwards?'

'Fiona!' Penny said warningly. 'Actually, we will be going out to eat, but just as friends. Just friends.'

'But you will tell me what happens?'

'Nothing will happen. It will all be dreadfully boring, I promise you.'

'Do you want me to ring you back? We've been on the phone for ages, and you're paying for this call.'

'No. It's all right. I must go now – I have some things to do before tonight. But keep in touch, Fi.'

'I will, I promise. And look after Alastair for me.'

'I'll keep him under lock and key.'

'Ciao.'

'Ciao.'

Fiona put down the phone. She felt a great deal better. Penny always had the capacity to cheer her up. Since childhood she'd looked up to her elder sister, and instinctively believed everything she'd told her – except for one thing. It amused Fiona that someone as capable and lovely as Penny should have such a low opinion of herself. Because she did, and Fiona had never been able to work out why. It was Fiona's considered opinion that if Rick Goldstone had asked Penny out, he didn't share that low opinion. The thought of her sister involved in a romance pleased Fiona immensely, and made her smile as she eased herself back into her own life.

Like Penny, she had things she needed to do. There was some washing up in the kitchen, and she had intended to rearrange all the furniture so when Alastair came back things would look different. And they would be alone together – at last. That was something to look forward to. Come on, Alastair, she thought. Hurry up and come home.

'You'll come in for a wee while?' Margaret asked her son hopefully.

'I don't think so. Fiona's on her own, and she's waiting for me to come back.'

Alastair stood just inside the front door of Margaret's bungalow. It was one of a row of six on the main road leading into Aberavon. It had a long front garden, bigger than the house itself, which was spare and compact but ideally suited to Margaret's needs.

'Thank you for your help, Alastair.'

'It's no problem.'

'She's a lovely girl,' his mother said.

'I know.'

'Look after her.'

Alastair shot his mother a warning glance. There was absolutely no need for her to say that at all.

'Will I see you again before you go?'

'I don't think so,' he said. 'I'm off early tomorrow morning.'

'I see. Yes, it's a fair way down to Manchester. Take care.'

Take care? What did she mean by that? He itched to get away from his mother's suffocating concern. If only she knew that she made him worse rather than better. He just needed to be alone with Fiona.

'I'd better go now.' He knew he sounded gruff, and was immediately repentant. He didn't want to upset his mother. 'I'm sorry,' he said.

'I'm sorry too. I know things are different now.'

'You're right. They are.'

'Good.'

She still didn't sound as if she believed him. Swallowing his frustration, Alastair said his farewells and hurried down the path to the car, head bent against the driving rain. He fumbled with the keys and got in.

The rain drummed relentlessly on the roof of the car. Alastair felt as if he could hardly breathe. It wasn't so much the effect of the weather as the gentle, unremitting pressure from his mother, the way she stood like a moral guardian over his life. She treated him like a little boy. *Things are different now*, he had told her.

Good. What did she mean by that? What on earth did she think he'd be getting up to? He hated the way she seemed to be expecting him to turn into his father. Didn't she realise that was the last thing that was going to happen to him?

Alastair pressed his foot a few times on the accelerator, deliberately over-revving the car, to give vent to his anger. Then he was off, along the road to Aberavon. Thirty-two years old, and his mother didn't trust him. He pulled out to overtake a tractor in front of him.

As he drove, his mood changed. He remembered Fiona, waiting for him. He was lucky, he knew it. He loved her gentleness, her femininity, and burned with a sense of pride in her. He could hardly claim to deserve her, but he would do his best to protect her. In that, he would be nothing like his father. He didn't just love Fiona – he admired her too. She was practical, intelligent and competent in every way. And sexy too. Yes. He was very, very lucky. No one, he thought, as he parked the car outside McFarlane's, the grocer's, could love his wife more than he did. He would make their last evening together a memorable one.

Thinking of Fiona cheered him, as did the sunny greeting of Janice in McFarlane's. She complimented him on his pretty young wife, and asked if they'd be seeing more of him now. 'You'll have a fine job getting rid of me,' he chaffed her, and then walked round the small supermarket selecting what he needed. It was just before he lifted the lid of the freezer that the idea occurred to him. Every nerve in his body flared into life. Then the fire went out. All that was in the past.

Not *so* much in the past, a voice reminded him. There was that slight slip at the Loch Kyle, and no harm done. Anyway, you're on a lucky streak. Alastair gazed into the freezer attentively, seeing pizzas, fish fingers, frozen grey haggises frosted with ice.

Just a small amount, prompted the voice. If you can keep it small, it proves you've got it under control.

Alastair removed a pizza absently, and then selected some coleslaw, some yoghurt, a pint of milk. The buzz in his veins was familiar, and it felt good. Not that he'd decided to do anything about it yet. He was in control now. That was the point.

He asked Janice where she was going that night, joked with her about her boyfriend, held the door open for Mrs Morrison, and felt good. He deposited the shopping in its brown box in the boot of the car.

They needed a paper else they would not know what was on TV. Unaware of the rain, Alastair made his way to the newsagent's. His breathing was rapid. Your mother wouldn't like it, came the voice. Damn my mother! he thought. And felt guilty. He tried to think himself back to where he was only a couple of hours ago. He was packing a suitcase, going back to Manchester tomorrow. Six more weeks of work. No Fiona.

He pushed open the door of the newsagent's, picked up a paper – and some mints and asked for ten Instants.

'Not so good,' remarked Ken Taylor, the newsagent, referring to the weather.

'Aye,' Alastair agreed automatically. He wasn't in the mood for conversation.

A quick sprint back to the car, and once Alastair was in the driver's seat, he took a coin from his pocket and rubbed at the first scratchcard. Of course, they always gave you two of everything in order to keep you guessing. Fair enough. It was better that way. The first was a dud. He put it to the back of his pile. The second was no good too. But there were eight more. He was going to be lucky today, he was sure of it. He deserved to win. He had been good. Not the next. Nor the next. His stomach felt small, and his pulse was racing. It was good to feel so alive. Nor the next. He was ashamed. Nor the next. His hand was shaking now, and he ached with a leaden despair. Why on earth had he let himself do this? Maybe the next. Two fifties, two twenties, then a third twenty. Three twenties. He'd done it! Twenty quid, and he'd only laid out ten. He was a winner. Triumph coursed through him. Triumph, the smugness of the victor, the arrogance of the surfer who comes through successfully on the crest of the wave.

'Yes-sss!' he crooned to himself.

This money was for Fiona. She was his lucky lady. Getting out of the car again, Alastair returned to the newsagent's to collect his winnings. A slim, suggestive, twenty-pound note. Then back to the grocer's.

'Something I've forgotten, Janice,' he told her.

He glanced at the chocolates, and rejected them. Fiona rarely ate chocolates. Then he saw the single malts. Now there was an idea. A bottle of Glenfarclas would keep Fiona warm while he was away, and make a good aperitif before their dinner tonight. He exchanged his sexy, crisp twenty-pound note for the bottle. The rain outside had begun to abate now, but Alastair was oblivious to the weather.

He placed the box on the kitchen table, and brought out the bottle of Glenfarclas.

'For you,' he said to Fiona, who had followed him into the kitchen to see what he had bought.

'Whisky!' she exclaimed. 'It hasn't left you short of cash?'

Alastair shook his head, unconcerned.

'Let's have a wee dram now. We'll need something to help us pretend that this frozen pizza really *is* a pizza.'

Fiona laughed, and found two tumblers on the kitchen dresser.

'Where shall we take them? The lounge?'

'The bedroom,' he told her.

Fiona, smiling to herself, ascended the stairs. She was amused by how quickly a suggestion like this from Alastair could arouse her. On reaching the bedroom, she flung the flowery duvet off the bed. It reminded her of Margaret. She sat on the end of the bed. Alastair came to join her, opened the bottle, and poured whisky into both glasses.

Fiona sipped it, and its warmth seemed to illuminate her from within. She luxuriated in its glow. Alastair stood and faced her.

'Did your mother settle in OK?' she asked.

'Fine,' he said, contemplating his wife. Her fair hair shone in the light cast by the lampshade. It hung loose, framing her face, just the way Alastair liked it.

'Are you all right? You're not saying much.' This was a tease. Fiona's voice was affectionate.

'I'm thinking how beautiful you are,' he said.

Fiona laughed, took another sip of her whisky, and felt her legs relax, despite the fact she was taut with anticipation, waiting for Alastair to make the next move.

And he looked at her, glorying in her. He deserved her after all. He was in control. He wanted to express that sense of control, of dominance. He knew exactly what he wanted to do. He kneeled down by Fiona and reached out to stroke her soft, silken hair.

'I love you,' he told her.

'Not as much as I love you.'

Fiona drained her whisky.

'I was hoping you were going to leave some of that for me,' Alastair said. 'Come here, little Miss Greedy.'

He got up on to the bed with her, and with his mouth opened hers. His tongue played with hers, sharing the last drops of the malt. Fiona marvelled at the way his kiss melted her, and the centre of her consciousness moved from her mind to a place between her legs.

'Are you warm enough to get undressed?' he asked her.

For answer Fiona pulled her jumper over her head and unhooked her bra herself. Almost at once Alastair's head was between her breasts and he was kissing them, his mouth fixing on her nipple now, and she threw her head back with pleasure, with acceptance of him.

Now they were naked on the bed, flesh on flesh, his hand caressing and probing her. Then small screams of pleasure from Fiona told Alastair that she had reached her climax. He watched her body curve and rise and saw the flush on her cheeks. As he now prepared to enter her, she whispered to him: the condom.

Where was it? There was a new packet in his underwear drawer in the dressing table. He went to get it, opened the packet, and quickly glanced at Fiona. She wasn't watching him. Her eyes were shut. Good. Because he was feeling cheated. If only she hadn't forgotten her pills. Then this last time he could have felt her properly, felt her squeeze him, remembered the sensation of her most secret and intimate places next to him.

He held the condom tightly in his hand, told himself he was on a lucky streak. So it didn't matter if he took a risk. He got back on to the bed, and turning from Fiona, took out the condom and unrolled it so just the tip of it was on his penis. Then he kissed her, and as he did so, slowly entered her. It felt good, so good. And when he felt the condom become displaced, and all of Fiona was clutched around him, he knew nothing but joy and an electrifying excitement. Perhaps he would impregnate her. It was a gamble. Then came that moment when he almost stopped breathing, and then the spasm of release, and the knowledge that his ejaculation was inside her. And again. And again, until he was spent. He sobbed with joy. It had never, never, been as good as that before.

Fiona kissed and nibbled his shoulder. Slowly he eased himself out of her.

'Damn,' he said. 'It's gone.'

'What's gone?'

'The condom.'

'Oh my God!'

Immediately Fiona began to feel for it.

'Here. Let me.' Alastair, with his longer fingers, soon extracted it. It was still half-rolled.

'We must have been too athletic,' he joked.

'It's not funny. I could be pregnant.'

'I doubt it somehow. The condom is bound to have acted as a barrier. It's coated with spermicide. Here, let me get rid of it.'

He put on his dressing gown and ran down the stairs. He remembered the fire was lit in the lounge. He went in there and threw the condom on the fire. It gave a satisfying sizzle.

It certainly was his lucky day.

Chapter Six

These exercise videos – the sort that promise you a flatter stomach in just fifteen minutes a day – did they work if you just did them for the first fifteen minutes? There was a chance, Penny thought, which was why she extracted the tape from the bottom of the pile of videos, blew the dust off it, and inserted it into her machine. Then she drew the curtains.

The warm-up exercises were easy, and as she swung her arms and shimmied from side to side, she thought again about the evening ahead of her. It was strange, very strange, that Rick should want to give a whole night up for her. All day she'd been trying to think of a set of circumstances to explain it, and the best she came up with was that he had a problem and wanted a free consultation. Except someone as sophisticated – and, let's admit it, drop-dead gorgeous – as Rick didn't have problems, or at least should be able to solve them by himself. Which left the tantalising possibility that he actually *wanted* to spend time with her.

The lady on the video was doing something tricky with her feet now, and Penny attempted to follow, staggering across the carpet. Realising she hadn't been paying attention, she put more energy into her half-jacks, and tried to visualise the fat melting from her.

Of course, she thought, *I* could afford a personal trainer now. Penny imagined what that would be like. Your own personal slave driver. Why do some women do it? These knee-bends made her sweat. When she was jogging on the spot again she thought of Fiona, and wondered if she should contact Alastair during the next week. He was living in Fiona's old house in Greenmount. Perhaps I will, she thought, knowing she wouldn't. She couldn't begin to imagine what she could say to him. She had only ever spoken to him when Fiona was there. If he rings me, she thought, then I'll arrange something.

Down on to the floor now, and Penny watched enthralled as the woman on the video contorted herself into strange positions. She tried to copy them, but they made her back ache. She decided it was silly carrying on; the last thing she wanted to do before her date with Rick was to strain her back, and walk around like a cripple.

So Penny lay down on the floor on her back with her knees bent, and enjoyed the relaxation. I need this more, she thought. She closed her eyes and allowed herself the luxury of thinking about herself. Time out, she thought. Time to think about how she ought to conduct herself with Rick. The odd thing was, she was more concerned about this date which was not a date than she was about her inheritance. It was as if the human mind was only designed to cope with small things; she couldn't absorb the fact of her wealth, or begin to decide what to do with all the money. There was too much; it paralysed her. Perhaps she would never spend it, but just pass it on to Fiona's daughter, should she have one, who would pass it on to her niece. The Curse of the Maiden Aunts. Penny smiled to herself.

She had said nothing to anyone about the money. It was embarrassing. Like haemorrhoids. Piles. Piles of money. Penny told herself to be serious for a moment. There was no one she could talk to about it. Most certainly not Rick, in case he thought she was trying to buy him. And she'd promised her mother she'd not mention the money to Fiona, as clearly there was some inequality. Rose was right. She couldn't imagine having a conversation with her sister in which she said something like: 'I've got this much money – how much have *you* got?' like two kids counting their Smarties. People don't talk about money openly; they just imply how much they have. A bit like wearing a Wonderbra. Penny's mind was drifting and she realised she was tired. She hadn't slept well all week. It ran in the family.

She wondered how much of her reluctance to deal with her money had descended from her mother. No, it was different with Rose. By economising, she felt she was in control. It was a way of handling Harry. Typical, really, of a pre-feminist marriage. The woman allows the man to have the appearance of control, but manipulates from within. The woman realises the man is pretty hopeless, but perseveres. Penny thought of her father. Like a child, really. Lovable, but far too easy-going. She could see that now, although when she was small, he was the one who would sneak her up an ice cream when she'd been sent to her room for some misdemeanour. Marriage, she thought, closing her eyes again. Only for the foolhardy. Lily knew that, and I daresay she made other arrangements . . .

When Penny opened her eyes again she wondered why she was lying on the middle of the carpet. There was white noise on the television set. She rolled over and stopped the video, then checked her watch. A quarter past six. She had precisely three-quarters of an hour to get ready and get to Kitty's, and she hadn't even showered. Penny flew into a panic.

She ran upstairs, threw off her clothes and stepped into the shower. Frantically scrubbing herself, she noticed in passing that her stomach looked just the same as ever. She decided to give Rose the video to sell in the charity shop. She ducked her head under the shower, squeezed shampoo into her hand and rubbed her scalp furiously, even though Diana, the Beauty Editor, had told her this encouraged the sebaceous glands. Whatever they are, thought Penny.

She rubbed herself down, ran out on to the landing naked, like in some French farce, realised she hadn't drawn her bedroom curtains and so stood at the threshold of her door in indecision. Then she burst into the room, lunged at the curtains, and closed them. Her bed was a low futon, and the duvet lay in a heap. Penny didn't see the point of making a bed as you were only going to mess it up as soon as you got into it.

She opened her wardrobe, and realised she didn't have a clue what to wear. Rick had given no indication where they were going. Something neutral, then, and all-purpose. She took out a long black high-waisted dress, and wriggled into it. She glanced down. It revealed a certain amount of cleavage, and she hesitated. She didn't want to give him any unintentional messages. Or did she? No, she didn't. She took off the dress, and selected a multi-coloured Indian skirt, teamed with a navy shirt she'd bought in the market a few weeks ago but had never got round to wearing. She glanced very quickly at herself in the mirror, then discovered it was already twenty to seven.

A second-hand table under the bedroom window held Penny's make-up. At the speed of light she applied eye-shadow – plenty – kohl liner, and mascara, layer after layer. Now she would be able to face him. She plumped up her still damp hair with her hands, confident it would dry out in the car. Then she hesitated as she saw the Chanel perfume in the corner – a wedding gift from Fiona. Ought she? One didn't normally put on expensive perfume for a visit to an old people's home. If she put some on, it would be for Rick. Penny hesitated, then reprimanded herself for being so silly. Rick didn't come into it. She was visiting Kitty. She would appreciate the perfume. Old folk didn't lose their sense of smell along with their sight and hearing. So Penny sprayed herself liberally with Coco.

She grabbed her black handbag and sprinted down the stairs. She checked the lounge. It was a tip. The settee was littered with the various sections of Saturday's *Guardian* and an empty mug had rolled over on to its side. The gas fire was on a low light, so Penny bent down to turn it off. The front room needed a lot of heating as it was only divided from the back room, a combined kitchen/diner, by a bead curtain. Penny walked through there now, checking that the back door was locked. There was some washing up in the sink.

She walked into the short corridor that led to the front door, about to switch on the burglar alarm. First she kicked to one side the free paper that had arrived on her doormat, and as she did so, felt a ladder start at the toe of her tights. She cursed. It was important to stop that spreading, and the quickest thing to do was to paint it with nail varnish. Luckily there was some scarlet nail varnish in the front room. Penny applied a thick layer and waved her foot around in the air, encouraging it to dry. And then there was a ring on the doorbell.

Penny froze. The last thing she wanted was someone arriving just now, especially someone with a problem that needed solving. She realised how much she was looking forward to seeing Rick again. The bell rang a second time. She could hardly pretend to be out with all the lights blazing and her car outside the house.

'Penny?'

It was Rick. She shoved her foot back inside her shoe and went to the door.

'Hi. I thought we were meeting at Gladesmore?'

'I did say that, but then I realised we'd have two cars. I'll take you in mine. You look nice,' he said, with an appreciative smile.

He looked nice too. He wore a cream pullover and navy Armani trousers.

'But, Penny, there's something hanging off the sleeve of your shirt.'

She looked down. She'd forgotten to take the label off her shirt. She tugged at it, but it was fixed to a plastic tag and refused to be loosened.

'Here, let me.' Rick took her hand, lifted it to his mouth, and bit off the tag. He held it in his hand, and Penny realised that it read 'Salim Men's Fashion, Extra Large'.

'I'll take that,' she said. 'Right. Well, let's go!'

She picked up her bag, turned on the alarm, and stepped out on to her front path. It was dark now except for the glow from the street lamps. Penny recognised that fluttering feeling inside as excitement. Just good friends, she reminded herself.

When they arrived at Gladesmore, Kitty had finished dinner and was sitting in a high-backed chair facing the television. She wasn't watching it. She didn't notice Rick or Penny either as they made their way towards her. Penny was alarmed at the change in her. She was an old lady now. Before she used to sit at Lily's side in state, with a proud little smile. Now it was as if a light had gone out.

'Kitty!' Penny said.

She turned round and saw them both. Her expression changed from blankness to the pleasure of recognition.

'Lily!' she said.

'No, not Lily. It's Penny. Lily's niece.' Penny took Kitty's hand, its skin as fragile as crêpe paper. It was like a child's hand, soft and unsure. Rick came to kneel by her. 'It's Rick.' And then he sneezed. He had sneezed a couple of times in the car, Penny had noticed. She hoped he wasn't getting a cold. But Kitty ignored him and turned to Penny.

'I haven't told anybody,' she said.

Penny glanced at Rick, in case he knew what she was talking about. He shook his head.

'How are you, Kitty?' he asked, rather too loudly, so that all the old ladies around her turned to watch them. Or perhaps, Penny thought, they'd turned to look at him. And she couldn't blame them.

Now Kitty looked more like her own self.

'It's Rickie. You've come back from America. Did you see the Statue of Liberty?'

He sneezed. 'I certainly did.'

'We did, didn't we, Lily? We went inside it.' She smiled confidentially at Penny.

'I'm Penny,' she said again.

Kitty turned to Rick with animation. 'You must meet Penny. She's a nice girl. Very clever. Answers all the letters in the paper. They didn't give me any dinner tonight.'

'I'm sure they did,' Penny said.

Kitty paid her no attention.

'Have you been out today?' Rick asked.

'No.'

Anne heard that as she passed them by with the pill trolley.

'Nonsense! We took her to the park.'

'I didn't go to the park.'

Anne ruffled her hair affectionately and moved off, heard Rick sneeze and looked at him with concern.

'Have you got a cold?'

'No. I think it's an allergic reaction.'

Penny wondered what could be causing it. Perhaps it was the floral disinfectant they used in the home. Penny inhaled the sweet aroma. It reminded her powerfully of Lily. But the pale peach wallpaper with its bright border, the painting of a vase of sunflowers, the conservatory with its wicker chairs – all these were Lily's too, and it seemed wrong that they should go on without her. Worst of all, in the chair where Lily usually sat was another old lady, who was knitting. Lily never knitted. 'Two left hands, that's what I've got,' she used to say. Penny realised she was holding on to Kitty for her own comfort.

'Penny and I are going out tonight,' Rick informed his aunt.

Kitty didn't react. Penny tried hard to think of something to say. Yet the more she tried, the more she floundered.

'Fiona's had a lovely honeymoon, but it snowed on and off. Did you enjoy the wedding?'

Kitty looked blank, as if she didn't understand the meaning of the words. Penny could have kicked herself. Kitty, just as a child would do, had excised from her consciousness anything leading up to and including Lily's death. So as far as she was concerned, the wedding never happened.

'Mum sends her love,' Rick said, sniffing.

'They didn't give me any dinner tonight.' Kitty glared balefully at them.

'Let's see what I've got,' he said, rooting around in his pockets. He found a packet of Polos. 'Would you like these?'

Kitty's face lit up and she took them, letting go of Penny's hand. She popped one in her mouth and bit straight into it. Penny understood this too. Comfort eating. She vowed that next time she came to Gladesmore she'd buy Kitty the biggest box of Ferrero Rocher she could find. She glanced around the day room where they sat. It was light, airy and modern, and a pleasant place to be, except that everyone was old. Lily had always referred to the other residents as 'the old people', as if she wasn't one of them. And she wasn't, Penny thought.

'Have a mint, Lily.'

Kitty offered the packet to Penny. She shook her head, and whispered to Rick.

'She thinks I'm Lily.'

'I know.'

'Shall I play along with it?'

'I don't know.' He sniffed.

'Are you all right, Rick?'

'I just need to blow my nose.'

Anne reappeared with the pill trolley.

'Time for your medicine, Kitty.' She turned to Rick. 'Just some sleeping pills. The doctor recommended them.'

He stood up to speak to her privately.

'How is she?'

'Bearing up. She's still in a state of shock. We're doing what we can to bring her out of herself.'

Penny rose too.

'Shall we go?' Rick said.

Penny nodded. She was glad he'd made the suggestion first. She felt guilty at the thought of leaving Kitty, but eager to go from this place that reminded her so much of her aunt.

'We'll come again soon,' he told Kitty, who was munching her way through the Polos, and bent to kiss her.

'Give *me* a kiss!' came a sandpaper voice from the next chair. A little, wizened lady with not much hair was the petitioner. Rick gave her a kiss too, and she cackled with delight. He blushed.

'Come on,' he said to Penny.

As they got to the front door, she noticed a photograph she'd not seen before. It was obviously from Christmas as all the residents wore paper hats and there was a large decorated tree in one corner. Penny stopped to look at it more closely.

'Their Christmas party,' she said unnecessarily. Rick paused with her. Penny's eyes hungrily sought out Lily, and there she was, tucking into her Christmas dinner with steely determination. The paper hat was awry on her head. Penny felt a pricking behind her eyes, and a tingling in her nose, and tried hard to stem the tears.

'Ah-tishoo!' It was Rick. 'I'd better get outside.' Penny followed him, glad to be distracted. Rick took a few deep breaths in the night air. They stood by his car, under the mesh of branches of a large tree.

'You don't happen to have any tissues on you?'

'I'll have a look.' Penny opened her bag and peered inside. 'Sorry, no.'

Rick tried to sniff. 'Just ignore me. How do you think Kitty is?'

'Anne's right. She's in shock. She's coping by not admitting Lily's died. That's why she thought I was Lily.'

'You were close to your aunt, weren't you?'

'How did you know that?'

'I felt it, when you were looking at her picture.'

It was the wrong thing to say. This time Penny's tears refused to be beaten. She allowed herself to cry a little, and as she did so, Rick put a comforting arm around her.

'It's OK,' he said. 'Cry if you want to. Excuse me.' And then he gave an enormous sneeze.

'It's me,' Penny said in horror. 'You're allergic to me!'

She looked at him and saw that his eyes were watering too.

'Are you wearing any perfume?' he asked her.

'Yes, Coco by Chanel.'

'It's that! It's the perfume.'

'I'm sorry!' Penny cursed the vanity that had so backfired on her. 'Will you be all right?' She had forgotten her own distress.

'It'll take a while to subside. Is there any way you can have a wash?'

'Shall I go back inside and ask Anne?'

'I've got a better idea. My house isn't far from here. I'll take you back to my place.' And he sneezed.

'Ought I to sit in the back of the car?' She asked anxiously. Obviously she was going to have to keep as far away from Rick as possible.

'Yes, you'd better.' He unlocked the BMW and pushed the passenger seat forward. 'Let's get going.'

'Where do you live?' Penny shouted to him, over the noise of the engine.

'Quite near the Pack Horse, if you know it?' His nose sounded badly congested. 'It's a couple of cottages, knocked through. After three years of high-rise apartment living, I craved something on the ground.'

'So you can't have been living there long?'

'Since I got back – just a couple of months. My parents and sisters had to take my instructions about decor and furniture. I arranged the whole thing by proxy.'

'Risky. Did you like it when you saw it?'

'Yes,' he said. They turned into a narrow lane between two large houses, bumped along a pitted track, and arrived at two tiny stone-built cottages with narrow leaded windows. Penny had expected something far more pretentious.

Rick unlocked the door and switched on a light.

'You go up to the bathroom,' he said.

Penny orientated herself. The exterior of the cottage belied the luxury inside. It was beautiful. An arched hallway led to a large through lounge, with a soft grey carpet and a fireplace surrounded with pale blue tiles. An enormous off-white sofa with spoonback sides was placed at an angle in front of it. There was a large stereo system, of course, and odd, undoubtedly expensive, objects d'art on some open shelving with wiggly sides. A tall, asymmetric pot stood in a corner and a Hockney print was displayed on the wall. Penny felt hopelessly outclassed. Thank heaven she hadn't asked him in to her place.

As directed, she climbed the stairs to the first floor and looked around for the bathroom. Fortunately the door was ajar. She slipped in and closed the door behind her. Just as she'd expected. There was the jacuzzi, enthroned in the corner of the bathroom, and a full-length mirror almost opposite it. The bathroom carpet was navy, and on every available shelf there were dark-leaved plants. It was utterly decadent. The whole place was a hymn to the power of money. There must be a side of Rick, she concluded, which was very shallow.

She had still not undressed. She felt unbearably self-conscious. Then, moving out of sight of the mirror, she unbuttoned her shirt, went over to the sink, turned on the hot water and began to wash as thoroughly as she could. She guessed a shower might have been more effective, and indeed there was a shower attached to the jacuzzi – with gold fitments, naturally. But there was no way she would stand naked in Rick's bathroom.

She patted herself dry with a soft white towel, and went to pick up her shirt from where she'd discarded it on the jacuzzi step. She lifted it and put it to her face. It reeked of perfume. If she put it back on, he would be in as bad a way as ever. Penny was in a quandary.

Opening the bathroom door only slightly, and standing behind it in her skirt and bra, she shouted downstairs, 'Rick! My top smells of perfume.'

'Go into my bedroom and find something to put on,' he called to her.

She pulled a face. Arms crossed over her chest, Penny tiptoed on to the landing and tried one of the doors. It was evidently a spare bedroom. The other one was Rick's. His bed was a four-poster, with maroon curtains tied back with black sashes. One wall was all fitted wardrobes, with mirrors for front panels. Penny gasped. Deliberately not looking at herself, she opened one of the wardrobes and saw a row of suits. She opened the next and saw some shirts, investigated them and realised they would be too small. Eventually she found some casual wear, and took out a black Lacoste sports top which she thought might fit her. She wriggled into it. It was tight across her bust but otherwise decent.

She undid the top button. Penny looked around the bedroom, conscious that this was going to be the last time. It was good to see how the other half lived. Her money notwithstanding, she could not imagine herself getting used to this kind of lifestyle. And yet . . .

She kicked off her shoes and lay down on the four-poster bed. Mmm. How could Rick bear to get up in the morning? How could she bear to get up in the morning, if she was lying here with . . .

'Penny?' His voice came from just outside the bedroom. She leaped off his bed.

'I've found something. Look.'

Rick grinned at her. 'It suits you better than it suits me.'

Penny flushed self-consciously. Here they were alone at the door of Rick's bedroom, only an inch or two apart. It was essential to remind herself that they were old friends, that was all. So why did they both seem so tongue-tied?

'Right,' she said.

'Right.'

'Shall we go out to eat now or . . .' Her voice trailed away.

'Or?'

'Well, I don't know.' Penny felt fifteen again. Rick had that effect on her. Perhaps because that was when she first knew him. Penny, she exhorted herself, pull yourself together. You're an Agony Aunt, thirty-one years old, and worth a quarter of a million. The thought of her inheritance cheered her. Rick might have a wonderful house, looks, poise, charm, sophistication, but she had money. It evened things out a little.

Then he broke the tension.

'Maybe that skirt and top is an odd combination.'

She decided to get back at him for that. 'And you look awfully puffy.'

'What shall we do?' he asked her.

Penny, ever sensitive to the needs of others, realised from the tone of his voice that Rick no longer wanted to go out with her. Not surprisingly. Allergic reactions can be quite debilitating. So this was the end of her date. She was her own worst enemy, sabotaging the prospect of the best evening she'd ever had. She felt devastated by disappointment but, ever the trouper, did the decent thing.

'I'm not hungry,' she said. 'And I've been given a feature to write. If you want to take me home . . .'

'Take you home?' He sounded disappointed too. Penny's spirits soared again.

'No, I was thinking that there's an Indian restaurant near here that delivers. What do you say to a curry?'

'The hotter the better!'

'I can promise you that.' Rick grinned at her.

They had not moved from the upstairs landing. Penny savoured this moment of intimacy, then told herself that there'd been enough play-acting.

'I'm starving, Rick. Do you have a menu?'

'Downstairs,' he said, and led the way.

Returning to the lounge, she attempted to talk some sense into herself. She was not under any illusions, as Rose might say. And so she was free to appreciate the evening in a way she wouldn't if there was any chance of his making an advance. They would have a cosy evening, like brother and sister. Which in a way they were, their mothers being such old friends. Penny made a mental note not to mention this evening to Rose or she'd be getting ideas. As if!

'A chicken balti?' Rick suggested, studying the pink card in front of him.

'A vegetable one for me.'

'I'll ring straight away.'

They sat at the dining table by a French window overlooking a square, walled garden, illuminated by the light from the windows. Unusually for her, Penny had little appetite. Her vegetable curry seemed too rich tonight. She was quite happy to push it around with her fork occasionally, as she had seen Geraldine do, and just steal glances at Rick, while sipping at her wine. Bit by bit she was familiarising herself with his face, trying to account for the extraordinary effect he had on her. Was it that little cleft in his chin? The firm lines of his jaw, contrasting with those bright eyes? The way his fine, dark hair fell on to his forehead? She wished she had a camera with her.

Or rather, she wished it was possible to send messages back in time to the teenage Penny, telling her that one day Rick Goldstone would be having dinner with her in his house. She'd have never believed it. She took some more wine, and realised that neither of them had spoken for some time. Clearly it was up to her to make conversation.

'How's work?' she asked.

Rick paused while he swallowed. 'OK. Not too busy at the moment. I might have to work in London for a while.'

'What is it exactly you do?' Penny propped her chin on her hand and looked attentive. In fact she knew she wouldn't understand a word of Rick's monologue on management consultancy, but it was a wonderful excuse just to gaze at him.

'You must miss New York,' she said, when he had finished. 'It must be exciting living there.'

'It was, but I'm glad to be home.'

'Why?'

'Manchester is where I belong. It's why I've bought this house. And to be honest, I missed my family. They're not getting any younger, and it's good to have people to care about you.'

'Men don't usually talk like that.'

'Don't stereotype us. I've every sympathy with feminists, except when they use the word "men". It always ends in an unfair generalisation.'

'Stop being clever. It's true that men are reluctant to talk about feelings.'

'Not all men.'

'Well, all management consultants then.' Penny took refuge in a pleasantry.

Rick smiled at her, but his expression made her feel uncomfortable. He looked as if he were reading her. In the silence that ensued, he took the initiative.

'And what about you? Do you enjoy your job?'

'Of course. I'm lucky.'

'Lucky?'

'Writing a problem page is something lots of women would like to do, and most of them could. All it takes is some common sense and a desire to put the world to rights. Most women have both.'

'You're generalising again. I think it takes someone special to do what you do.'

Penny laughed. Rick was way out. She was only a freelance journalist after all.

'What do you want to do next?' he asked her. 'Write for a national paper?'

Penny felt the ground shaking beneath her feet. She was conscious of her money as an invisible barrier, surrounding her.

'I'm not sure. I quite like my life as it is.'

'So you'd be reluctant to make any changes?' He smiled at her almost suggestively. What was he implying? Penny wasn't sure. She noticed he had finished eating.

'I've got some ice cream in the freezer,' he told her. 'Haagen-Daz.'

'No,' Penny said quickly. 'I mean, far too many calories.'

Rick looked at her steadily.

'You're not trying to lose weight, are you?'

'Who isn't?'

'You look fine the way you are.'

Self-consciousness swept through her again. It was vital to change the subject.

'Shall we go and sit in the lounge?'

'OK,' Rick said. He stood, and waited for her. Penny also rose and began to take the plates from the table through to his kitchen – an immaculate room with light oak units and a marbled worksurface. She was conscious of Rick watching her, and prayed she wouldn't drop anything.

'How's your mother?' she asked suddenly.

'My mother? Fine. It's her wedding anniversary soon. Thirty-five years. They're having a long weekend in Venice.'

'That's nice,' Penny said, her back to him.

'And your parents?'

'OK.'

'Is your father still teaching?'

'Yes. Mum's retired.'

Penny turned round. They seemed to be on safer ground now. Rick took the bottle of wine and walked through into the lounge. Penny followed him with the glasses and watched him sit back on the settee. She decided to sit on the floor by the fire, and crossed her legs.

Rick looked at her, and laughed.

'I never thought I'd be doing this.'

'Doing what?'

'Sitting here alone with you. When I was sixteen it was my main ambition.'

Penny felt her throat constrict with shock.

'What?' That wasn't very elegant, but it was all she could say.

'Yeah. Most of the boys fancied you, but no one would ask you out.'

'They wouldn't?'

'We were frightened of you. You used to quote Germaine Greer in Debating Society. No one thought they had a chance with you.'

Penny was incredulous, but delighted. Then angry.

'Men! Frightened of women with opinions. Typical!'

'There you go again. Generalising.'

'But I don't understand. You could have had any girl you wanted at school. You never asked anyone out. We thought you were gay!'

'I'm not,' he said, and looked at her steadily once more.

'But why, then? Surely you knew you were the school heart-throb?'

'Was I?'

'You mean, you didn't know? Ask Fiona. She'll tell you how I used to go on and on about you. I even carved your name on the desk at the back of the physics lab!'

Penny grinned at him, to share the joke.

'I never took physics,' he said, his voice level.

'I shouldn't have taken it.' Penny's voice died away. 'I failed all the exams.' She placed her hands on the floor to steady herself.

'I rang you once,' Rick said. 'Do you remember?'

'Yes. You asked me for somebody else's number. I was devastated. Scarred for life.' She laughed lightly to show this was an exaggeration.

'I wanted to ask you out, but I lost my nerve.'

'You lost your nerve?'

'I was only seventeen. I was shy.' He smiled at her. 'It was the inner accountant in me.'

'I can't believe this,' said Penny. It was the truth. One of the immutable laws of nature was that men like Rick didn't fancy the likes of her. And why was he telling her this now? Because it was history, like Nell Gwynn and her oranges or the Edwardian bustle? It was history, so they were free to laugh about it. Of course. So Penny laughed.

'It's funny how much we change. I had such a crush on you! But I never told any of my friends. I never wanted you to know,' she said.

'Why?'

'There was no point.'

'I don't understand,' he said.

'I didn't think you'd ever go out with me.'

'Why not?'

'Well, look at me and look at you.'

'Penny. Why do you think so little of yourself?'

She laughed. 'I don't. I'm horribly self-centred.'

'That's not what I mean. You keep putting yourself down.'

121

Penny wasn't sure she understood what he meant.

'No,' she said carefully. 'I'm just honest.'

Rick shook his head and said nothing. Penny was impelled to defend herself.

'I get it from my mother,' she said.

'A pity. You should be more like Lily.'

'Did you know her?'

'Kitty never stopped talking about her. There was a woman who knew what she wanted. I liked her.'

Penny loved him for saying that.

'What do *you* want, Penny?'

You, she thought.

'Did you ever meet Lily?' Penny steered the conversation away from these treacherous waters.

'A few times. After I came back from New York, I went to the Home quite a bit.'

'Strange I didn't bump into you.'

'I was hoping we'd meet.'

That breathless feeling was returning.

'Penny, come here.'

She didn't. She stayed on the floor where she was safe. He came and knelt in front of her.

'Do you like me?' he asked.

She nodded, as if owning up to a misdemeanour.

'Can we be more than friends?'

She was about to say yes, and then thought better of it. She couldn't understand why he should want her. She had no confidence in her own attractiveness. He seemed to read her mind.

'You're lovely,' he told her. 'Look at yourself. You're a real woman.' He put his hands on her hips.

'I'm fat.'

'If this is fat, I like it.' He ran his hands lightly down her body.

'But I . . .'

'Go on.'

'But I'm wearing your shirt.'

'You can always take it off.'

'I taste of curry,' she said, and his face came nearer hers.

'And so do I.'

The kiss, when it came, was like no other Penny had ever experienced. It made her cling to him, as it affected her centre of balance. The feel of his face against hers was almost more than she could bear. She dared to think it had to be as good for him.

'There,' he said. 'That wasn't too bad.'

'More,' she said.

Once again she dived down into a heady darkness, in which every sensation was exquisite. Yet she never lost consciousness of who she was kissing. It was a miracle. After tonight, she would believe in anything: life on Mars, anything.

They stopped for a while.

'I didn't think this was going to happen,' she said.

'I hoped it would.'

'Yes, but let's be careful.'

'What do you mean by that?' Rick was teasing, and Penny realised her unintentional double-entendre.

'I mean that we shouldn't rush into anything. Perhaps I need time to adjust.'

'We have all the time in the world.'

She liked the way he said that. Penny took his hand, and played with his fingers.

'Kitty and Lily wanted this to happen.'

'I know.'

'That's not why you're doing this?'

'No.' He kissed her again. 'Although anything your Aunty Lily said was law.'

Penny laughed, pleased. 'Come to think of it, you're right. We have very little choice.' She kissed him, delighted at her own boldness.

'True. Else she'd take her revenge, like she did on your Uncle Simon. Did he take her furniture out of store?'

Penny laughed. 'Mum says he will.' And then she stopped. She hadn't told Rick about Uncle Simon's bequest. How did he know? Her first thought was that Geraldine had told him. Had he been seeing her too? Rick took Penny's face in his hands and turned it to him, but he could see immediately that something was wrong.

'Penny?'

'How did you know that – about Uncle Simon? Did Geraldine tell you?'

'Who's Geraldine? Oh, she's his daughter. No, Lily told me what she was going to do.'

'Oh.' Penny felt unaccountably jealous. 'So you knew about her will?'

'Yes. I witnessed it.'

'Oh.'

This was understandable. If Rick was around when Lily was playing power politics with her worldly goods, he, as an accountant, would be the obvious person to be a witness. So he would have known about Uncle Simon and also ... also ... The thought was slow in forming, but once it came there was no going back. Also, he knew about her money.

'I see,' she said, and wriggled from his embrace. 'Look, I really do have a feature to write. And I think the curry has disagreed with me. I think I'd better go home.'

'What's wrong?'

'I've just told you!' Penny spoke sharply. She walked out into the hall and took her jacket from the coat hook.

'Here we are,' she said. 'I want you to take me home.'

'But I don't understand?'

'Oh, I think you do.'

'Penny!'

She walked out of the house and stood by his car. He came out with the car keys.

'Tell me what I've done wrong.'

'Come off it. Take me to the nearest taxi rank.'

The curry really was disagreeing with her. She felt sick. They both got into the car, and Rick started the engine. He seemed quite upset. As well he might. Why stop at renovating a cottage or two once he laid his hands on her fortune? Wasn't he going to kick himself in the morning for his little slip about Simon?

'Just drop me off in the centre of Heywood,' she instructed him curtly, digging her fingernails into her palms to stop herself from crying.

'Please will you tell me what I've done?'

Penny was silent. There was a black cab in the taxi rank. She got out of the car.

''Bye,' she said. She knew he was watching her as she got into the cab, and having given instructions to the cabbie, sat back and stared straight in front of her. It was now perfectly clear what Rick had found attractive in her.

What a fool she'd been! What a complete and utter fool. As the cab set off towards Manchester, her eyes filled with tears. Never again would she let her defences down. Never, ever again.

Chapter Seven

Harry struck the final chord.

'And that's it today, Cast,' June Metcalfe, Head of Drama, said wearily. 'I've got a doctor's appointment, so we'll have to finish now. Can I just see the Munchkins?'

Harry closed the score of *The Wizard of Oz* reluctantly. He enjoyed rehearsals, and it was no hardship to him to stay late at school four nights a week as musical accompanist.

''Bye, sir!' shouted a few of the kids.

'Oh, God – look at the time! I have to be there in five minutes.' June picked up her coat and bags and, bidding Harry farewell, ran down the corridor to the main entrance. And so he was on his own.

Time for him to go, too. Only Harry wasn't ready to leave yet. Playing the piano filled him with excess energy, and now he was in the mood for a conversation or some staff camaraderie. He was niggled that June had to rush off. He picked up the music from the piano and closed it. At home, there would be no chance of a pleasant chit-chat. Rose would be deep in a book, or cleaning things in the kitchen, anything but be the sort of companion he needed.

Harry's footsteps echoed as he walked through the empty school hall. He turned into the corridor that led to the staff room. He passed a cleaner in one of the classrooms, sweeping the floor, the chairs placed on the desks. He didn't think it would be wise to interrupt her. So he ascended the steps to the staff room, and considered having a cup of tea before his homeward journey.

The staff room, as he'd suspected, was empty. Alone, Harry scratched the base of his nose, and put the score down on one of the easy chairs. Suddenly his senses were alert. He could hear something. A sort of snuffling sound. For all the world, it sounded like somebody crying. Harry listened intently. Yes; there was a sniff, a flurry of little sobs, and a sniff again. It was coming from the Ladies' cloakroom, so he hesitated. He couldn't go bursting in there. He coughed loudly, to alert whoever it was to his presence, then walked heavily in the direction of the Ladies'.

'Are you all right?' he called. He was curious to know who it could be, and glad he was there to help.

'Harry? Is that you?'

It was Rita's voice.

'Yes – it's me. What's wrong?'

A short corridor led to the Ladies', a corridor that was used by both sexes as it housed a photocopier and several stationery cupboards. Harry made his way through there, but still could not see Rita. All there was in his line of vision was a row of basins and a vending machine. He didn't think he ought to go any further. Then he heard a cubicle door open and Rita emerged, her nose red at the tip, her eyes somewhat swollen. Harry remained behind the magic line that separated the Ladies' area from the staff room proper.

'Oh, Harry. You shouldn't be seeing me like this!' Rita exclaimed, and sniffed once again, opening her handbag to fish around for some tissues. She gave her nose a little blow, then went over to the mirrors to examine her face. She extracted a powder compact from her bag and dabbed at her cheeks. Then Harry watched fascinated as she brought out her red lipstick, straightened her lips in a grimace, and painted them.

'There. That's better.'

Whatever it was, thought Harry, she was being very brave about it. She was dressed well, too, in a short, checked skirt that hugged her bottom and a cream tabard top. She was smart for a woman of her age. She hadn't let herself go. Harry wondered why her husband had left her – there seemed to him no obvious reason. Perhaps it was him she was crying about now. Harry was determined to find out, and equally determined to be of some assistance.

'Can I make you a cup of tea?' he asked.

'Oh, Harry, that would be lovely. I'm so sorry you caught me like this.'

'Don't mention it.' He scurried back to the staff room to put on the kettle.

He was pleased to be busy. He placed two teabags carefully in the staff mugs with a little bit of milk, and poured on boiling water. Then he carried them over slowly to a coffee table in the rest area of the staff room, where two easy chairs had been placed side by side. Harry was pleased with himself. He was doing well so far. One day I might take a counselling course, he thought.

Rita came in. She smiled sadly at him, and together they sat down. The easy chairs had wooden arms, which separated them. Harry lifted Rita's tea, which was in a mug with a design of a grey kitten playing with a ball of wool, and handed it to her. Their fingers touched briefly.

'You are kind, Harry. Are you sure you oughtn't to be getting home?'

He shook his head vigorously.

'Not when you're in trouble.'

Rita took a sip of her tea, and Harry watched her throat bob as she swallowed it. He saw that her hand was shaking slightly too. He felt very sorry for her.

'Is there anything I can do to help?'

'No, Harry love. There's nothing anyone can do. It's just that—' she sniffed again '—I've been on the phone to *him*.' She emphasised the 'him', so Harry knew immediately she was referring to her husband. 'I stayed late to catch him at work. I can't bear to ring him at his flat. *She* might answer the phone.' 'She', Harry assumed, was her husband's new girlfriend.

'I had to speak to him because of Stephen.'

Now who was Stephen – Rita's boyfriend? Then the mystery was explained.

'Stephen is our son. He's in his first year at uni. Oh, he's a tearaway, is Stephen. He's spent all the money I've given him, and can't get a job. Harry, he won't be able to afford to eat unless I send him something. But, honestly, I haven't got the money. I'm paid per lesson, and they've cut my hours this year.'

He nodded, encouraging her to continue.

'So I rang *him*. To ask if he had anything to spare for Stephen. And he told me he's washed his hands of him, that he should fend for himself. He said he didn't think Stephen should have gone to university in the first place. He thinks he should be out at work. In the university of life. And he was abusive, Harry. He said . . .' At the memory, Rita shook her head, and was unable to continue. Harry instinctively reached out and took her hand, to comfort her. She squeezed it, and her wedding ring cut into him.

'No, I can't tell you what he said. It destroys me, Harry. But I can survive his comments. It's Stephen I worry about. And then last evening I had to have some men round to look at the roof – there's a leak in the bathroom ceiling. And they went up on the roof, and when they were up there, they said the chimney was rotten. It's in danger of toppling over, and I—'

Rita broke off to cry. Harry squeezed her hand more tightly. She freed it so she could open her handbag for some more tissues. Pre-empting her, he handed her his handkerchief.

She took it from him, dried her eyes, blew her nose, and handed the handkerchief back.

'What will you think of me, Harry? I'm such a cry-baby.'

'I don't blame you at all.' He felt the words were inadequate. What Rita needed was practical help, the sort of help only a man could give.

'Now, listen. These roofing contractors. Hmmm.' Harry narrowed his eyes in thought. 'How sure are you that they knew their business? There are a lot of cowboys about. Were they recommended?'

Rita's eyes widened at the intelligence of his question as she tried to remember.

'Well, no. Nor recommended, exactly. I found them in the Yellow Pages. It was a boxed advertisement.'

'Ah! Just as I thought. They're out for a quick buck. Listen to this. The house next-door to ours had some men come to do the roof, and they knocked on our door to say our chimney needed replacing. They offered to do the job cheap. So I got the ladder out and went up to look myself. That chimney was rock solid. I sent the blokes packing, and our chimney's standing yet. And that was ten years ago.'

Harry was gratified to see Rita's face brighten. If only there was something else he could do.

'If it's really bothering you, I'll come round myself and take a look. I'll soon be able to tell you how much work needs doing.'

'Really, Harry? Would you?'

'Whenever you want.' He looked out of the window. It was raining.

'Not tonight, obviously. But we'll fix a date.'

'A date! That would be lovely!'

Harry expanded with pleasure. It was good to feel he was still useful. Now he ventured an opinion on Rita's husband's conduct.

'I can't understand a father who won't support his own son.'

'He's jealous of him, Harry. Stephen's a lot smarter than him. And Stephen wouldn't talk to him, after what he'd done to me. Stephen won't go round and visit him, Harry. And *he* says it's all my fault. That I've poisoned Stephen's mind. Harry, I'm beside myself. I don't sleep at night. I don't know what a night's sleep is.'

Poor Rita. She certainly had problems, he thought. This gave him an idea.

'You should write to my daughter, Penny Green. In the *Manchester Post.*' Harry was quite proud of this connection. But Rita looked a little dismayed.

'No, Harry. That's so impersonal, writing a letter to an Agony Aunt. It's not the same as being here with you. I feel you understand me.'

He did, he was sure.

'But I know what I have to do, Harry. I'm just going to have to support Stephen by getting another job myself. I've thought of doing telesales. You can do that of an evening.'

'No!' Harry was vehement. 'You shouldn't have to do that. You're a talented flautist. I should know.'

'Oh, Harry. Do you really think so?' Her face brightened again.

'I should say. One of the best.'

'Oh, Harry, you say such lovely things. You don't know how much it means to me, after all the abuse I get. And you don't know how much it destroys your self-esteem, having your marriage collapse. It makes me feel so worthless.'

'You're not worthless.' This was true. Rita was a good flautist – not as good as he'd implied but good enough to justify his statement. She was an attractive woman too – not as pretty as Rose, but on the other hand Rita looked after herself. Men appreciated things like that.

'It's kind of you to say so, Harry. But when I look in the mirror, I see this old crone.'

'No!' Harry was emphatic again. 'You're an attractive woman, Rita. Take it from me.'

She placed her hand on his, and stroked the skin on the back of it. He was startled, but enjoyed the sensation.

'Harry, you're so sweet. You're so sweet, Harry.'

The stroking continued, and he felt somewhat awkward. What if one of the cleaners were to come in?

'I try my best, Harry, and when you compliment me, it means a lot. Oh, it does. Because I get so lonely—' And she broke off, and unsuccessfully tried to stifle a sob.

So Harry put his arm around her shoulders to comfort her. The sides of the chairs were between them, creating a barrier. Nevertheless, Rita half turned towards him, to rest her head on his chest. The side of her face was warm, and slightly damp. Harry's heart pumped rapidly. He wasn't sure what to do next. Perhaps he should kiss the top of her head. Or maybe not. As it happened, Rita freed herself from him.

'That's right,' said Harry. 'Have a good cry. It'll do you good. Get it all out of your system.'

'Crying won't find me the money I need.'

'True, true. How much money do you need?'

'Stephen's asked me for three hundred pounds.'

'Now you mustn't worry.'

'Not if you say so, Harry.'

'I do.' He felt strong, dependable, heroic even. He liked the effect he had on women. He was sure he'd be able to help Rita in some way. If not financially then . . .

'Harry, I'd better go. Stephen will be ringing me this evening, and I want to be home when he does. I'll tell him not to worry too.'

'You do that.'

Rita rose, adjusted her skirt and pulled down her tabard, stretching the material over her bust. Harry got up too.

'You've made me feel so much better.' Impulsively she put her hands on the shoulders of his jacket and kissed him directly on the lips. She paused just a fraction of a second longer than was necessary, and Harry knew it was in his power to protract the contact between their two mouths. Surprise made him indecisive. He did nothing. Rita broke away, and immediately he felt guilty. Not guilty about Rose, who did not exist for him at that moment, but guilty about Rita. She would think he had rejected her, and a rejection was the last thing she needed. So he put out his hand and patted her on the cheek. She gazed into his eyes.

'You will come and see about the roof, Harry?'

'Of course. I said I would, didn't I? As soon as the weather improves. Now don't you worry.'

'Oh, I won't, Harry,' she said.

The lift doors opened and the passengers spilled out on to the ground floor, secretaries and managers. Amongst them was Alastair Gordon who looked up at the large clock above the reception desk of his office block and decided that Fiona was bound to be at home now as it was lunchtime. It was the right time to call her. However, it was out of the question to ring her at the office; phone conversations at work were easily overheard, and he needed privacy. A long-distance call to Fiona would be unwise, to say the least. But he had to speak to her. It was very, very important.

The High Street was busy; there were hungry employees in search of sandwiches, shoppers, mothers with buggies – his workplace was a little way out of the city centre. Just outside the post office Alastair found an empty call box, and to his satisfaction the phone purred as he picked it up, indicating it was working. He lined up three pound coins on the metal shelf in front of him. Alastair inserted the first of the coins and dialled Fiona's number. He held his breath between rings. Please be in, he whispered to himself. Please be in.

He was in luck. There was a click and he heard Fiona's voice quite clearly, even above the rumbling of the HGV that passed just outside.

'Fiona darling, it's me. I'm ringing from a call box.'

'Alastair! I'm so glad you've called!'

'Why, baby? Is anything wrong?'

'No, not wrong exactly. But it still hasn't come.'

'What hasn't come?'

'You know. My period.'

'Just that?' Alastair was relieved. Before he questioned her further, he would put her mind at rest. 'It's silly to worry, Fiona. You know you're not regular.'

'Yes, I know. It runs in the family. None of us are. But I've just got this feeling . . .'

'Look at all the upheaval you've had. The wedding, the move, settling in. It will have affected you.'

'Yes, I know it could be that. But something isn't right.'

'Are you feeling sick?'

'No, not sick.'

'Well, there you are. If you were—' Superstition prevented him from saying the word 'pregnant'. 'If you were, then you'd be suffering from morning sickness.'

'I suppose I would. You're right. Mum was dreadfully ill with me, and probably with Penny too. Thanks, Alastair. You've made me feel better. Being alone up here is making me obsessive.'

That was a hint that he decided to ignore.

'Have you heard from your mother? Is the money through?'

'Yes. This morning, in fact. All five thousand pounds of it. I suppose I ought to think about how we can spend it.'

'Absolutely.' Alastair was feeling more cheerful now. 'This weekend, when I come home, we'll look for furniture.'

'Yes, but when you finish in Manchester, we can have the Greenmount furniture sent up here. I'm missing it.' She laughed. 'But not so much as I'm missing you.'

'I miss you too.'

'It was snowing yesterday. There's still snow on Ben Voulin. It looks like someone's flicked a paintbrush at it and splashed it with white. And it's bitterly cold. What's the weather like down there?'

'OK. It's OK.'

'I wish I was with you.'

'Soon, soon, baby.'

'But now we have Lily's money, can't you jack in the job?'

'What would that look like on my employment record? Remember, I'm coming home for the weekend. We'll talk about it then.'

He inserted another coin in the slot.

'Fiona, listen. There's a reason I'm ringing. You know Paul and Janice – Paul who works with me? He's made an interesting suggestion.'

'Yes?'

'He wants to rent the house in Greenmount.'

'But he can't. You're living there.'

'I know. But I'm spending one and a half hours travelling each day. The house is the wrong side of Manchester for my office. If Paul and Janice rented Greenmount, I could find somewhere near here. It makes sense.'

'But we want to sell the house, not rent it.'

'Paul is quite happy to show people round. Not that there's been any interest from prospective buyers. The market's dead. We don't know how long the house will take to sell. Meanwhile we could be making something from it. And people are more likely to buy a house that's occupied by a happy couple. I think it's an excellent idea.'

'I see. I need to think about it.'

'Paul said that if the house suited them, they might end up buying.'

'What do you think, Alastair?'

'I think we ought to go for it.'

'Are you sure? Even though you'll have to move?'

'I'm sure.'

Fiona took a deep breath. 'OK, then.' She laughed. 'It feels like I've cut my moorings.'

'You did that when you married me.' Alastair laughed too.

'Anyway, we decided that we'd look for a new house, new to both of us. Do you fancy the idea of Aberdeen? Or would you prefer somewhere rural?'

'Alastair, I've just thought of something. If we rent the house, will we still be able to get my furniture sent up here when you finish in Manchester?'

'Sorry, no. We'll have to leave it in the house. Paul did make a point of saying he wanted a furnished property.'

'I'm not very happy about that.'

'I know, baby. But we'll be able to afford new furniture, with all the money I'm earning. And eventually we'll get the pieces you're fond of.'

'Are you sure this is a good idea?'

'Trust me.'

'Sorry. I'm just feeling a little strange today. A bit emotional. I'm missing you.'

'Think about where you'd like to live. Take a drive out with my mother.' Alastair put in his final coin.

'Alastair – does your mother know we're planning to move?'

'Not yet. Let's not tell her until it's more definite.'

'Because we need to clear up whether this house is a present or a loan.'

'I told you, it's a present.'

'Then why hasn't she transferred the deeds?'

'I'll have a word.'

'I'd like that.'

The flat tone of Fiona's voice disturbed him. She didn't sound happy. But it would only be temporary. Before too long she could have all her furniture back. Moreover, if what he was planning came off, he could come back to her much, much earlier than she expected. But it was to be a surprise. That was why he wasn't going to say a word.

'Fiona?'

No answer.

'Fiona? Are you all right?'

'Yes, yes. I was just watching the birds.'

'What are they doing?'

'Nothing. Alastair, come home soon.'

A rapid tone signalled the end of their conversation.

'I love you, Fiona. I'll ring you tonight.'

'Love you too. 'Bye.'

Click. He was gone. Fiona wiped the tears from her eyes. It was lunchtime, but she was not hungry. She would force herself to eat something, and then go and sleep. Then she ought to ring Margaret. Except all efforts at befriending her had failed. Their conversations were purely superficial; even Fiona's requests to hear stories of Alastair as a boy met with no success, as Margaret said she had a poor memory. Her shy, rather startled manner made Fiona feel she was intruding. She could understand why Alastair wanted the two women he loved most to love each other, but that had proved not to be the case. She felt a little guilty. Maybe she ought to try harder. But not today. Today she wasn't feeling quite herself, and almost resented Alastair for not being here.

She made her way to the bathroom, and once again looked to see if her period had arrived. It hadn't. Alastair was right. It was too early to worry. Fiona told herself this as she left the bathroom and made her way to the large, rather gloomy kitchen that was Margaret's, not hers. Come on, Fiona, she rallied herself. Pull yourself together. She attempted a smile, and opened the fridge to see what she could have for lunch.

On replacing the handset, Alastair left the booth and a man in overalls took his place. He stood at the pelican crossing with two elderly ladies, a woman with a child, and two Afro-Caribbean girls. He crossed the street to the bank, entered it, extracted his cheque-book from his pocket, and stood at the side of the bank, writing busily. He queued impatiently, glancing at the clock, seeming to weigh up some decisions in his mind.

Fiona was missing him. That much was patently obvious. He had to leave Manchester as soon as was practically possible. The problem was, they needed money. But there was a solution. Renting the Greenmount house was part of it, and Lily's money would be another. And there was another part . . . Alastair's face brightened. His way was clear. He had no option but to do what he was about to do. When the woman in front of him moved away from the cashier, Alastair took her place, handing over his cheque and receiving in exchange a sheaf of twenty-pound notes. He placed them carefully in his wallet. Outside the bank he stopped again, and inserted his cashcard into the automatic teller, waiting until one hundred pounds in twenty-pound notes shot out at him. He put these in his wallet too. Then he returned to the phone booth, which was empty again.

This time he rang his office.

'Paul? I've spoken to Fiona. You can have the house. But not the furniture. Yes, I know you wanted it. Can you make do? Good, good, that's great. And can you tell David I won't be in for the rest of the afternoon? I've got some flexitime owing me and I want to go and see about a flat. Sure. Sure. Yeah, thanks.'

Alastair replaced the receiver. He took a deep breath. Once more he waited at the pelican crossing and once more he made for the bank. But this time he walked past it, turned into the betting shop at the corner of the street, and was lost entirely from view.

'More potatoes? Please could somebody have some more potatoes, because otherwise I'm going to end up throwing them all away. Michael? Rick? Look at you – you call that an appetite? Your sisters eat more than you.'

Brenda Goldstone came round the dining table and served the remaining roast potatoes to her son.

'For me,' she said. 'Eat them for me.'

'In a few minutes,' he replied.

Michael Goldstone chuckled to himself. It was nice to see Brenda force feeding someone else for a change. He looked down, not without pride, at his little pot belly. He felt perfectly satisfied, and enjoyed listening to the banter between his wife and son. Rick hadn't been round to dinner for a couple of weekends, but finally Brenda had prevailed upon him to come over. It was just a shame the girls were out.

The grey satin-effect curtains were drawn now, and two candles in silver candlesticks were burning on the sideboard. Plates, condiments and glasses jostled for position on the heavily laden table. To Rick's left was the glass-fronted display cabinet where Brenda kept all the trophies of her family life; here were her wedding photos, baby photos of the children, a series of A-Level certificates, a number of table tennis cups, a framed graduation picture of Rick in gown and mortarboard, a set of silver wine goblets and various ornaments, all with sentimental value. Brenda was the sort of woman who liked everything to be on view, all the time.

'So where have you been for the past few weeks? You haven't been near this place. Do your father and I have leprosy?'

'I've been busy,' Rick said, putting down his knife and fork. He braced himself for the inquisition to follow, but without resentment. His mother was not so much nosy as passionately on his side in everything.

'I rang you a few times,' he said in self-defence.

'He rings me. What am I, a business acquaintance? Next time, send a fax.'

'I've been on a job in Preston, and not been getting home till late.'

'Preston? Is that such a long way?' She looked at her husband quizzically.

'An hour the M6.'

'Not so far. But don't tell me what you've been doing there, because I won't understand.' Brenda laughed with pride. 'Now, the last thing I would have imagined is that I would have a mathematical genius for a son. I could never add up. I was terrified of my Maths teacher. If we got anything wrong, it was up in front of the class with us. We had a test once—'

Rick had heard this story before, but this time he listened more carefully.

'—and I didn't understand any of the questions. I was sitting next to Rose and tried to look at her answers. She saw what I was doing and she put her arm down so I could have a peek. Just then Miss Wren walked past. Now, in those days it wasn't illegal to use the cane, and . . .'

'What was Rose Green like as a girl?' Rick asked, feigning a casual interest as he began to eat again.

'Rose? A quiet little thing. Pretty, very pretty. But she didn't seem to know it. She blushed whenever she had to answer in class. The teachers used to make a thing about her being Lily's sister, because they were so different. Now Lily . . . Why are you asking?'

Rick shrugged.

Brenda, although not good at maths, made some quick and accurate calculations.

'It's Penny, isn't it? I saw you two at the wedding.' Brenda smiled as everything fell into place. 'You've been seeing Penny Green. That's why you haven't been round. Well, what do you think of that, Michael?'

'I—' he began.

'No.' Rick was firm. 'I haven't been seeing her. That is, I saw her once. But—'

'But what? What happened?'

Rick hesitated. Since Penny's precipitate departure from his house, he had not spoken a word about her to anyone. The next day he had rung her, determined to find out why she froze him off. She had put down the phone. This had happened twice. Not wanting to be a nuisance caller, Rick had desisted.

Common sense had told him to give her up as a bad job. Yet at inconvenient moments thoughts of Penny came popping up; at work on a set of accounts, relaxing in front of the television, in the middle of the night, as he brushed his teeth in the morning. With the patience of a sleuth he had replayed their evening together again and again, trying to discover what it was that could possibly have upset her. He knew he was becoming mildly obsessed, and realised he needed to offload his preoccupation with her. This had been at the bottom of his decision to have Friday night dinner with his parents.

'I saw Penny, but it didn't work out too well.'

'You found that you didn't like her?'

'No, no. I like her very much.'

'So why aren't you going out with her?

'I wish I knew.' Rick pushed his plate away.

'What do you mean, you wish you knew?'

'We had a meal at my house, and we were getting on well. Then, for no apparent reason, she told me she must go, and now she won't speak to me.'

Michael chuckled again, this time suggestively, and Brenda glared at him. He was immediately quiet.

'More fool her,' Brenda declared. 'There are lots more fish in the sea, and a lemon and mango sorbet in the freezer.'

His mother was just a little touchy about his love life, Rick knew. She both wanted him to marry, and dreaded it. Rick understood that but he wanted to talk about Penny, and his determination was as strong as his mother's.

'We were talking at the time. I mentioned something about Lily's will, because we were there when she was drawing it up – do you remember?'

Brenda nodded.

'I think I was indiscreet, mentioning that I knew what Lily had left Simon. But I don't see why that should have upset Penny so much.'

Brenda snorted. 'Touchy, I daresay. One of the secretive sort.'

Rick shook his head. 'No, it doesn't add up. She mentioned Simon's daughter, Geraldine, and I thought perhaps that was it.'

'The jealous type? Worse still.'

'I've tried ringing her, but she won't talk to me.'

'Drop her. You don't want to get involved with a Colman.'

'You were Rose's friend,' Rick reminded her.

'Rose is different. But the rest of that family was always arguing. Lily never spoke to Simon, you know that. What you didn't know is that for years she never spoke to Harry. One day he was working for her, and the next – poof! She sacked him. Her own brother-in-law. And then Rose never spoke to Lily either. They all fly off the handle. Penny is the same. You're better off without her.'

'I'm not convinced,' Rick said.

'He likes the girl,' Michael suggested meekly.

'I don't see why talking about Lily's will should upset her so much,' Brenda deliberated aloud.

There was silence. Both men deferred to Brenda's superior mental faculties, and now she was at work on the case they fell into an expectant silence.

'Unless, of course . . .'

'Unless, what?'

'Unless she thought you were after her money.'

Rick laughed. 'Don't be so ridiculous! Penny doesn't have any money.'

'Surely Lily left her something?'

'Did she?'

'You should know. You're the one who saw the will,' Brenda reminded him.

'I didn't read it. I only knew about Simon because Lily pointed that clause out to me. She was thrilled at her own ingenuity.'

'But just suppose that Lily left Penny a decent sum of money. And Penny thought you knew that . . .'

Brenda looked jubilant, and Michael nodded wisely at her. Rick was silent as he thought this through. It made perfect sense. He wondered precisely how much money Lily *did* leave Penny.

'Was Lily rich?'

Brenda shrugged, but her eyes glinted with interest. 'Yes, but I don't know how rich. She paid Kitty's fees, and Anne tells me there's a trust fund for her now. Her dry-cleaning chain must have done very well for itself.'

Rick thought aloud. 'But even then, Penny wouldn't have been left that much. There was her mother and father, and Fiona . . .' His voice trailed away. He realised that the amount was immaterial. Someone with Penny's low opinion of herself would immediately assume that money was what made her attractive. He had only just succeeded in convincing her that he really did want her when he'd mentioned Lily's will. Anger at his own stupidity welled up in him.

'Damn!'

'Don't swear in front of your mother.'

Rick ignored his father's remark.

'You're right,' he said to Brenda.

'I know I'm right.' She was a keen reader of detective fiction, and realised now that she'd not been wasting her time.

'I'll have to ring Penny again and explain.' Rick looked at his watch. 'It's not too late now. Do you mind if I—'

'She won't believe you.'

He was already halfway out of the room, and turned back.

'Why should she?' Brenda said. 'What proof do you have?'

Rick placed his hand on the door and thought hard. He had no proof. It was his word against hers, and everything was against him. He'd appeared on the day of Lily's funeral and since then had been relentless in his pursuit of Penny. Why? He could imagine now what she would be thinking. How could he possibly like her? He just wanted her money.

How could he ever convince her otherwise, short of asking her to give it all up, which was crazy?

Rick began to understand that the only woman he had ever really wanted was effectively as out of reach as if she were married already. Another expletive rose to his lips, and he only just suppressed it. He glanced at his mother and saw that she felt sorry for him. Her sympathy made him feel worse.

'Michael, you were right. He does like her.'

Rick could not disagree.

'Shall I speak to Rose?' Brenda sounded anxious.

'No!' Rick's tone was final. 'I want to try and sort this out myself.'

Brenda and Michael exchanged glances as Rick left the room. Nothing was worse than your children refusing to let you help them. Michael put a comforting hand on his wife's shoulder.

'She'd better have him back,' Brenda said, sounding quite dangerous.

Michael wanted to reassure her, but couldn't. The only thing he knew for certain was that women always got what they wanted in the end. But what did Penny want? He eyed Rick's uneaten dinner and wondered if any was going spare. What did Penny want? That was the question.

Chapter Eight

Rose thought the ring at the door was Harry, and muttered to herself as she dried her hands on a teacloth. He never remembered his keys, and one of these days he'd come home and—

But it was Penny. This was a nice surprise. Rose opened the door happily.

'What's this in aid of?' she said, as Penny took off her coat and placed it over the banister.

'I felt like a chat. Something smells nice.'

'A chicken casserole. You can stay for dinner. Your father will be pleased to see you.'

Penny walked into the kitchen. 'I don't know. I said I'd see some friends.' She opened the fridge, and then the pantry door.

'Can I have some biscuits?'

'Of course. I'll put on the kettle.'

Penny peered into the biscuit tin, but there were none there. Seeing an unopened packet of digestives, she tore it open and helped herself to the first one.

'I've come to a decision.'

'Don't talk with your mouth full,' Rose said automatically.

'It's about my money.'

'What about your money?'

'I'm going to start spending it. Has the kettle boiled?'

'Good for you. So what's brought this on?'

'Come into the other room and I'll tell you.'

Rose showed she'd accepted Penny's invitation by taking off her apron prior to making the coffee. She glanced at the kitchen clock; if Harry were rehearsing again he wouldn't be in for an hour or so. A chat with Penny was an unexpected treat.

Penny, in black leggings and a long black sweatshirt, sat back on the settee, one leg crossed over the other. Rose thought she looked rather tired; perhaps she'd been working too hard. She took another biscuit from the tin that Rose had placed on the coffee table.

'The truth is,' said Penny, 'I had a bad experience.'

'What kind of bad experience?'

Penny twiddled with a piece of hair behind her ear as she spoke.

'I misjudged a situation. Oh, there's no point in beating about the bush. I meant to tell you this ages ago, but I suppose I was embarrassed. I should have known better.'

Rose was a little apprehensive.

'You remember Rick Goldstone was at the wedding?'

'He came to the funeral too. That was nice of him.'

Penny shot her a warning glance. 'Yes, and I thought it seemed odd at the time. He insisted on taking me out. No, don't smile like that. Wait until you hear what happened. We had a takeaway at his place, and we were getting rather friendly, and then he let it slip that he knew about my inheritance.'

'But how on earth? No one knows how much . . . Unless your father—'

'No, it's not Dad's fault. Not this time. Apparently Rick witnessed Lily's will. He told me so himself. Cool as anything. That was the worst part. He didn't even bother to keep it from me. He thought I was that desperate.'

'I hope you told him to keep it quiet?'

'I walked out on him. He was only after my money.'

Rose was incredulous. 'Not Rick? He's a nice boy. He's Brenda's son. And why shouldn't he like you? You're an attractive girl.'

'Come on, Mum, I'd love to believe I'm absolutely irresistible, but there are such things as mirrors. Don't look so upset. I'm over it now. OK, I'll admit I was a bit thrown at the time. I felt dirty – and used. Like a prostitute in reverse. I wasn't being offered money for sex, but sex for money.'

'Penny!'

'Sorry. But it helps to make a joke of it. And I don't care whose son he is, he's a bastard. If Lily knew, she'd be livid.'

'It's lucky you found out in time.'

'It sure is.'

'But I don't understand why this is going to make you spend your money?'

'It's simple. If I'm going to be taken for a ride without even having the advantages that money can bring, I'm a double fool. What's the point of being rich and not enjoying it?'

'You'll need to invest some of it, you know.'

'Whatever,' Penny said, sounding uninterested.

'But spending some would be all right, I suppose.'

'The way I feel at the moment, I'd willingly spend all of it. I feel I'm entitled to cheer myself up, after all that's happened. Which is why I've nearly finished your digestives. And why I'm going shopping.'

'So long as you don't go too mad.'

'Why don't you come with me?'

'Me?'

'You've got some money.'

'It's different for me,' Rose cut in swiftly. 'We need the money to supplement your father's pension.'

'Nonsense. Fiona and I have enough for you both. Live a little, Mum. I'm going to.'

Rose gave an odd laugh. It was meant to be ironic, but it lost confidence and petered out.

'I suppose it's a way of getting back at Rick. Childish, I know, but I've never claimed to be grown up. I want him to see me enjoying my wealth, and I want him to know that none of it's for him.'

'If he's hurt your feelings, Penny,' Rose suggested timidly, 'you're better off steering clear of him.'

'I told you, I'm over it. I'm just angry now, that's all. And I'm not going to be fooled again.'

Rose laughed. 'You're just like me.'

'I know. Two of a kind.'

'We bear grudges,' Penny admitted.

'I'll certainly have a few words to say to Brenda.'

'No! Don't. The whole sordid affair is over now. My self-esteem will recover eventually, although I'm tempted to send Rick my therapist's bill. And invoice him for the Kleenex.'

It was difficult to know how upset Penny was, Rose thought to herself. She wore her humour like armour. On her daughter's behalf, she felt a sense of outrage. Yet Penny was stolidly munching on another biscuit, and now idly turning the pages of *TV Quick* to see what was on that evening. Perhaps she was all right after all. Penny put down the magazine.

'To be honest, Rick's not the only reason. I've been thinking about Lily too, and what she would have wanted. I never saw the will. Did she say anything about us? Or why she left Fiona and me her money?'

Rose cleared her throat. 'No.'

'I thought not. It's just that, knowing Lily, I'm certain she would have wanted us to spend it. Do you remember those face creams she bought? Every week when I went to visit her, she'd bring back something new from Kendals, that rejuvenated your skin or debagged your eyes, and she'd line them all up in the bathroom. It was like a dermatalogical museum in there. She loved cocktail dresses and collected them as well. She had a craze on those executive toys and put them all over her living room. She told me she'd earned herself the right to have whatever she wanted.'

Rose was silent. Penny was talking to herself.

'It's a funny thing, because in some ways Lily was a true feminist. She revelled in being single, and wasn't uncomfortable with power. Do you remember when you were in hospital with your appendix and Lily looked after us? I was ill and couldn't go to school so she took me to the Colman's HQ and I saw her run a board meeting. Wow! But at the same time, she'd dress herself up like a dog's dinner and go out dancing, just in order to meet a man. Do you think she was a virgin?'

Rose shrugged.

'I asked her once. She said, "Mind your own business." And then she said, "Are you?" I blushed – I had a boyfriend at the time – and she told me she didn't care what I did, but it was important not to miss any opportunities. I was quite shocked by that, and never told you in case you thought Lily was a bad influence. She used to like me to tell her about my boyfriends – it was like she was living vicariously through me. More than with Fiona, but she was only little. And Lily took me to Weight Watchers with her, and I stuck to the diet religiously and became utterly obsessed while she just pigged out every weekend.' Penny laughed. Running through all these memories was bringing Lily back to life.

'Lily always wanted me to have a good time, I'm sure about that. Now I have her money, *I* think I ought to have a good time too.'

'She was fond of you,' Rose said.

'I know. Don't talk like that otherwise I'll cry again, and I've done enough crying recently. Roll on the good times! And now, Mother, what about you?'

'Me?' Rose said dismissively.

'Yes, you. Are you enjoying your newfound wealth?'

'Enjoying is hardly the—'

'I think you ought to spend some too. If Lily were here now, she'd insist on it. Join me in a spending spree!'

'What will the rest of the family think?'

'They need never know. Come on, let your hair down.'

'I can't change at my time of life. I've always been careful.'

'You should have heard the lady who rang me on Tune FM the other day. Seventy years old she was, joined a tai chi class and has now been proposed marriage by two gentlemen, one oriental.'

'What did you advise her?'

'Definitely a case for bigamy. Get it while you can, that's my motto.'

Rose pretended to be shocked, but realised to her surprise she was a little envious too.

'Use your money for something. Think what it is you really want.'

'What I want, money can't buy.'

Rose regretted saying that. It was too close to the truth. But fortunately Penny misinterpreted it.

'In that case, use the money to have a second honeymoon. This time, I think I agree with Dad. Go away and get to know each other again.' Penny paused. 'Please.'

Rose gave a dry laugh.

'No, listen to me. What chance have you two had? First there were all the money troubles, then Fiona and I came along, so you've never had the conditions for a marriage to thrive in. No wonder you're always at each other's throats. Give it a try. I'm sure it's what Lily must have wanted you to do. Why else would she leave you so much money?'

Rose felt herself growing uncomfortable. Penny presumed she knew so much about their marriage, but she knew nothing.

'Give it a go, Mum.'

'I'll think about it,' said Rose, as much to change the subject as anything else.

But she did think about it. She thought about it as she opened the oven, checked the casserole, and put the lid back on again. She thought about it as she looked at the kitchen clock once more and saw that it was a particularly long rehearsal. Just as well Penny had insisted on going, as dinner would be late tonight.

It was true she and Harry had never really had a chance. What was that old saying? 'When poverty flies in at the window, love flies out the door.' Perhaps it was money all along – or the lack of it – that had been their problem. None of the other things would have happened it hadn't been for the lack of money. And now they had money.

It was tempting to go along with what Penny had suggested. In a warm climate, sitting on a balcony overlooking an Italian bay, how could any relationship fail to thrive? The truth was, they did have the money. A thousand pounds would only make the tiniest dent in their savings now. She could afford it. An unfamiliar feeling, akin to excitement, was kindled in her at the idea.

Rose knew that at heart she was a romantic, like Fiona. Like Fiona, she had known what it was to fall in love. And it was Harry she'd fallen in love with, almost at first sight. She was repairing the hem of a skirt in the kitchen when Lily had come in, bringing him with her. He was Lily's boyfriend then – he'd come to call and take her out. Lily had introduced them, and he'd shaken hands with Rose, and right from the start – it really was right from the start – there had been a spark between them. He had shaken her hand just that bit too long, and too vigorously. He was boyish then, tall, eager, with tight curly hair like a film star, and Rose had felt quite flustered, and had blushed, and had hoped Lily didn't notice.

But it was all right. Lily lost interest in him, as she did in all of her boyfriends. The next time he called, it was to see her – Lily's sister. And Rose knew, even at the beginning, that he was the one. She felt she hadn't been truly born until then. It was one of the happiest times in her life, their courtship. And there Rose stopped remembering. Was there something that could be rekindled?

Then there was the sound of a key in the latch, the stamping of feet on the mat, and Harry's voice.

'I'm home! Just popping upstairs to the bathroom.'

He was one of those men who always had to be telling you what he was doing. Rose smiled to herself.

'Dinner's nearly ready,' she warned him.

She brought the casserole out of the oven and left it to cool while she strained the potatoes. Soon Harry came down and put his head round the kitchen door.

'What is it?'

'Chicken casserole.'

'Very good.'

'Go and lay the table and we'll eat together.'

Rose was giving him a sign. They rarely ate together. Sometimes the sight of him irritated her so much she enjoyed her food more alone, in the kitchen, skimming through the newspaper. But not tonight.

She came in holding his plate with a tea towel.

'Careful! It's hot.'

'Looks delicious.'

She returned to the kitchen for hers and brought it to the top of the table, so they were sitting at right angles to each other.

'Penny came round before,' she told him.

'Did she?' said Harry, in between mouthfuls.

'She had a bit of a story to tell. You know Rick Goldstone, Brenda's boy? The one who came to the funeral? Well, Penny is convinced he knows about her money, and has been making a play for her.'

'How did he find out about it?'

'He told her he witnessed the will.'

Harry finished the mouthful he was eating. 'Yes, but he wouldn't know exactly how much money she has, because it didn't specify it on the will. It said, "the residue to Penny" – don't you remember?'

Rose was struck silent. For once in his life, Harry was right. They'd only discovered quite how much Penny was left when they looked at the building society pass book. Penny did not know that because she had never seen the will. This put Rick's behaviour in a different light – possibly.

'But he would still know she had come into something.'

'I don't see why she should suppose he was only after her cash. For a man like Rick, there are easier ways of making money than courting a woman he doesn't like. Money doesn't come into it. There's more to life than money.'

Harry spoke with feeling. Rose liked what he said. She liked his loyalty to Penny, his sensible interpretation of the incident with Rick, which she could use to cheer Penny up. And he had given her a nice opening for what she was going to say next.

'You're right. There is more to life than money.'

Harry put down his knife and fork and looked at her.

'You were right all along,' she said. 'We ought to take a holiday – just the two of us.'

He looked completely taken aback. Rose was pleased she could have this effect on him.

'You're coming up to the Easter break. We could have two weeks somewhere. If you fancy Florida we'll look into it, although I do have a hankering for the Italian lakes.'

Harry stroked the bridge of his nose and looked unusually thoughtful.

'Easter's very soon,' he said.

'Yes, I thought we might be able to get a cancellation.'

'Ah – but if it's a cancellation, we might not get exactly what we want.'

Rose reflected how well she'd succeeded in persuading Harry that they didn't need a holiday. Life was full of ironies. He gave a little cough.

'Look, I thought about what you said, and decided *you* were right. A holiday abroad would be a bit extravagant. So I had another idea. We could each take a little bit of money and spend it on ourselves. And then in the summer, or even at Whit, we could drive up and see Fiona and stay at some hotels on the way, tour around a bit.'

Rose was pacified. He did want to go away with her; that was something. And it might be nice to have some money to spend. Scotland could be quite romantic too, as no doubt Fiona was discovering. One step at a time, she told herself.

'All right.' She gave Harry a small smile. 'We'll do that.'

Of course, Scotland would not be without its difficulties. That was something Rose admitted to herself as, later, she plunged the dishes into soapy water. She could hear the murmur of the television in the other room but did not resent doing the washing up. Harry worked long hours and when he did wash up, there were always smears of food left on the plates. If you want a job done properly, you're better off doing it yourself. Yes, Scotland was not without its difficulties.

They had been to Scotland once before. A memorable visit. For during it, Penny had been born, rather earlier than expected, and Rose had returned to England a mother. She had not been back since, although she had told Penny the story of her birth many times. *Your father and I knew we shouldn't have taken a holiday that late on, but he was in between jobs and it seemed like a good opportunity. We were staying at a small hotel in Elgin, and in the middle of the night I started with the pains. We disturbed everyone in the hotel, ringing for an ambulance. The owner kept an Alsatian who began to bark when the ambulance arrived. I'm sure you were so scared it sped up the labour. Because as soon as we arrived at the hospital, one, two, three, you were born.* That was how it was.

Rose wiped her hands on the tea towel and carefully laid it over the radiator. As she did so, it came to her that she needed to get away. In a moment of clarity, she realised that her life had shrunk to the size of her house. She travelled in well-worn grooves to the charity shop, the library, the supermarket on a Friday evening. And that was more or less it. It wasn't that she was bored; bored wasn't the word she would use. It was just that she feared this shrinkage was final. She could never imagine herself growing again, changing. Her routines had become straitjackets; her pleasures had become compulsions. Perhaps that was another reason why the visit to Scotland struck her as dangerous, and so it was all the more important she should go.

Enough introspection. Rose turned off the light in the kitchen and decided she would go and join Harry now. She could hear the television clearly; it sounded like a documentary, one of those programmes about animals, and both she and Harry enjoyed those.

She was right. There were some zebras grazing on an open plain – no doubt the lion is in wait somewhere, Rose thought – and Harry had his feet up on the pouffe, and had taken off his glasses as it was easier for him to see television without them. Carefully she came to join him on the settee. He said nothing. I daresay he's surprised, she thought, feeling somewhat bold. I don't often do this.

She glanced at him sideways, saw his grey shirt, which she had ironed for him so often, his thin, black belt, and the dark grey trousers which were just a little baggy at the knees. His hands were lying loosely in his lap. Large hands, a light covering of hair on them, masculine hands, as strong and capable now as they had ever been. Rose looked at her own hand, etched with fine lines, a gold wedding band on her finger, and in one quick movement put it over his. He started at the touch. He wasn't expecting it. But he didn't move away. They stayed like that, quite still, watching the zebra.

The camera zoomed in, the voiceover explained their eating habits, and Rose began to think that perhaps there were no lions after all. Good, she didn't like any kind of violence on the screen, even animal violence. The world was brutal enough as it was. Penny was always telling her to get a cat, but she couldn't be doing with all those dead birds. Then Harry moved his hand slightly, to squeeze hers. It was a sign and filled Rose's heart with something akin to joy.

It was all she needed; more than that, and she would have retracted. She distrusted shows of emotion. She was quite satisfied when Harry said he needed an early night, and disappeared into the shower. She followed him upstairs, knowing his bedroom would need tidying. If she collected his dirty washing now, she could let the washer run during the night.

It was strange, she thought, as she picked up his socks, how vivid the past became as you grew older. Thinking of Harry as a young man had sparked off other memories. What was it Lily had said about him? He was a loser, that was it – spineless. But she had said that out of resentment: Harry preferred her, Rose. He was a good few years younger than Lily, anyway. She only liked him because he sang; he'd been in a three-piece combo, Rose recalled. Being married to a younger man has its advantages and disadvantages, she thought, as she picked up his shirt and noticed that the front looked a little dirty. On the one hand they kept you young, but on the other they were ... restless. That was it, restless. But Harry was older now, considerably older. Penny said people changed, and she should know. Rick used to be such a nice boy, and now look. And Harry. There had been a time ... But she wasn't going to think about that now. That was the past.

She could hear the swish of the shower and remembered that when they were first married they'd had to share a bathroom with the flat below. They had come a long way since then. She remembered she used to do all the washing by hand. They had achieved a measure of prosperity after all. Here were his trousers. Really, he ought to buy himself a new pair. He certainly could, if they were each to spend a little bit of the money. Rose debated whether to throw them away.

No. Old habits won the day. She would give them a wash through. So she automatically put her hands in the pockets, to take out any loose change or paper clips which might find their way into the washing machine and do God knows what damage. But there was only his handkerchief. She pulled it out.

There was red on it. Had he hurt himself? No – that wasn't the red of blood. It was more like the red of lipstick. Perhaps he'd lent his handkerchief to a woman at work, for blotting her lips. A silly idea, Rose knew. Or was he wiping lipstick from his cheek? Or lips? Why else would there be lipstick on his handkerchief? Another woman's lipstick, from another woman's lips. Rose sat down on the side of the bed. Her legs were incapable of holding her up much longer.

There was no such thing as change. She was kidding herself. Humiliation winded her. She was always too trusting, and as for Harry ... there were no words for what he was. She felt sick. People never changed. And now the past was beginning to replay itself, all over again.

Fiona and Alastair parked the Volvo next to a small barn. A

black cow stood guard by it and eyed them malevolently, or so it seemed to Fiona, who still found the countryside rather alien.

'Will he do anything to the car?'

'She,' Alastair remarked.

Of course. Fiona looked down and saw the cow's udders. She should have realised.

'Come on,' she said.

It was a warm, sunny day. The wind that that been playing around the house aimlessly all week had suddenly vanished, as if it had an appointment elsewhere. The sky was entirely blue, blue as a summer's day, and it drew Fiona's eyes upwards and told her that all might yet be well. Alastair stood near a plan of the walk they were going to take, apparently studying it.

'It's not too far, is it?' she asked.

'An hour, an hour and a half,' he said, non-committally.

'I'm a bit tired today, that's all.'

Alastair did not seem to respond, and Fiona flinched a little. She felt guilty and foolish. If she had told him the reason why she was feeling tired, he would have reacted immediately, would have turned and told her that they weren't going on the walk at all. He would have looked at her wonderingly, as men do at women when they're confronted with the greatest mystery of all. But Fiona had chosen to bide her time. She wanted to tell Alastair when the moment was right.

When she had used the pregnancy testing kit on Tuesday afternoon, and it had proved positive, at first she had not believed it. She simply thought she had misread the instructions. So she did the test again. Once more it was positive. Fiona was shocked, yet as she paced the front room, coming to terms with the fact that she was pregnant, accepting that she was going to have a baby, she felt unaccountably pleased.

For a start, she was married. This was important. The world would approve of her and would support her. Then, she loved her husband, and the thought of a baby made up of the two of them, as sentimental as that might seem, appealed to her in her present loneliness. Even with the baby, she need not alter any

157

of her long-term plans. There would still be enough money for her to study Scots Law, and so she could finally qualify when the baby started school. At this point, she realised she had accepted that she was pregnant. It was a reality for her.

Besides, the baby would constitute a pressing reason for them to leave the backwater of Aberavon and move to somewhere with more facilities. Aberdeen sounded nice. But the truth was, even Aberdeen was a compromise. Fiona wanted to move back to Manchester where she could be near her mother. Rose knew about babies. And then she needn't study Scots Law after all, and when the baby was old enough she could go out to work, and they could afford a decent education for the child. These struck her as being somewhat disloyal thoughts, and so she gathered her courage together and told herself to decide on nothing until she had spoken to Alastair. And the telephone would not be good enough. She would wait until he came home for the weekend.

There was no choice. How could she devalue one of the most significant moments of their lives by making it the subject of a long-distance telephone call to business premises? If she told him over the phone, she would not be able to see his face. So it would have to be the weekend. Last night he'd been too tired from the journey. This morning she had held back. There was something so special about her news and the new life inside her, that she wanted to stage the moment when she told her husband. So when he suggested a walk to the Ladder Hills, she agreed, despite her unnatural tiredness, because she would have the opportunity to talk to him alone, free from interruption and in a setting that befitted her news. She had sat silently in the car, and Alastair was silent too, his face impassive, his gravity making him all the more handsome, all the more dependable.

They began to trudge along the marked path that led away from the road, towards a line of trees that fronted a small forest. Fiona placed her arm in Alastair's, feeling ever so slightly fragile. He was conscious of his wife's confiding touch. The soft pressure of her arm brought him to acute consciousness of the present, and he hated himself even more.

It was clear she knew nothing. Alastair could only imagine she hadn't checked the balance in their bank account, and that the bank hadn't written to question the size of the overdraft. He had known them to do that in the past. They were only a couple of hundred overdrawn, and that had only been for a day or two. His salary was through in a week, and if he could believe that Fiona really would not check the balance, he would not be about to tell her now. But the truth was that two appalling alternatives stood in front of him. Either he did nothing, waited, and she would discover that almost everything had gone. Or he told her now, and told her the truth. The sunshine mocked him, and the blue sky scorned him. Alastair burned in his own private hell.

The path turned, and became more uneven. Fiona and Alastair let go of each other in order to step to the side to avoid puddles of old rain. The ground was marshy. Ahead of them, Fiona noticed, was a signpost with an arrow, which pointed out the direction they were to take. The path led away from a small building to their left, and instead seemed to ascend into the hills.

'Are you sure this is the right way?' she asked.

'Quite sure.'

They reached a stile, and Alastair moved over it with speed and grace. Fiona had to think out each move carefully, placing one leg on the stile, bringing the other up to join it, and all the while conscious of the spark of life inside her, and the vital importance of not stumbling or falling. Coming down, concentrating on her feet, she felt something slimy beneath one of them, and stepped back quickly. A yellowy-green frog slid from under her trainer, and then leaped away from her in spasms.

'Alastair, did you see that?' The frog revolted her. She shuddered. She could so easily have squashed it.

'There are even more further down,' he said laconically.

Because they were talking about frogs, Fiona would not tell him yet. She would wait until they were somewhere different, away from here. And the more she refrained from telling him, the more special the baby became, and the more it seemed as if the baby was a present from her, something he'd had nothing to do with.

Now the path began a steady ascent to the hills, and Fiona looked up, a little alarmed. She neither had a head for heights, nor wished to exert herself unduly. Around her hills undulated along the horizon and she could see the ruins of old crofts, jagged walls of stone, bare outlines of ancient cottages, she could sense the shadows of earlier lives. Now she wondered how people had managed in those days, and thought what a lonely life it must have been. She imagined children playing, and then thought it might not have been so lonely after all.

'I'm warm, Alastair. Can we stop? I want to take off my jersey.'

It was surprisingly mild for the end of March. Alastair decided to pull off his jumper too, and welcomed the coolness that greeted him. He watched Fiona tie the sleeves of her pullover around her neck, making a cape of the body of the pale green sweater. He took his by the neck, and swung it over his back. He contemplated telling her now. Casually, as if it didn't matter. *When you go to the bank next week, you might find the account's rather low. I've been moving some funds around. It'll get back to its normal level in a week or two.*

But that would be foolish. His losses had been so great lately that it stood to reason that the next time he was in the casino, he'd be in line for a big win. Better not to tell her. Except, if he did tell her, and she understood, then he could ask her for more money, for a bigger stake, and could get out of this hole he was in all the more quickly. There was another alternative too. This was the most frightening of all. He could tell her the truth about himself, and ask her for help. It was frightening not because he was scared that she would leave him; they loved each other too much for that. It was frightening because she would tell him to stop gambling, and he was not sure that he could. Not yet. Perhaps she wouldn't tell him to stop. Perhaps he could encourage her to come with him to the casino, and maybe she would enjoy it too.

No. Alastair reminded himself what it was he'd planned to do in the early hours of this morning. He was going to tell Fiona everything, and make an abject confession. He would grovel. He would show her how low he was. He would demand her pity. If only there was something he could do to show her how much he hated himself.

At five o' clock that morning, he had contemplated suicide. Now, as they climbed further and further into the hills, that seemed foolish. There would be a solution after all. They were leaving their everyday lives below, like toy lives. He was almost ready to tell her now. What was money, after all? And he would have said something, he was sure of it, only when he turned to see where she was, she was some way behind. The moment passed.

Alastair's steady stride was too fast for her, and Fiona was conscious of her heart thumping painfully in her chest. She wondered whether this was because she was out of condition, or because of the baby? The incline was steep now, and she knew she would have to ask Alastair to halt.

'Can we stop?'

He turned again and saw that she was red with exertion.

'I feel a little faint,' she added.

'We'll have a rest over there.'

He pointed to a small hillock overlooking an abandoned croft, with molehills dotting the sparse vegetation. Fiona took a deep breath, gathered her strength, and climbed a little higher. Then down a slope – carefully – up again, and she was there. Gratefully she eased herself down on to the rise, stretching out her legs in front of her. Alastair was by her side. Together they surveyed the view. All around them rose other, higher hills, dark with old heather. Lines of snow were still visible on the higher slopes, in crevasses and gullies. The sky was still a brilliant, cloudless blue. Hills surrounded them on every side; it was as if they were in a basin. Nothing stirred. There were no people, no animals. Fiona imagined the moles beneath the surface and wondered what they were doing. All she could hear was the rush of wind at her ears and bursts of birdsong that she could not identify. I shall say something in a moment, she thought. But not now. Instead she thought of her baby, trying to visualise the tiny embryo latched on to her, and failing.

Alastair was fumbling for the words he needed. *There is a problem. I know I should have told you before, I know, but I thought I could handle it myself. But being away from you, I –* Shame engulfed him. He could not tell her that. Also he could not tell her that he had lost all of Lily's money. He remembered Lily. They had visited her once or twice, in the Home. She had stared at him suspiciously, as if she knew what he was like. Now he felt an irrational anger with her. If she hadn't left Fiona all that money, he wouldn't have been tempted. He glanced at his wife, and saw her eyes were shut. He could not disturb her rest, because he loved her so much. The wind played with her hair. Now she opened her eyes.

'Alastair,' she said. She was looking into the distance. 'I have something to tell you.'

So she knew all the time. She had been to the bank. Alastair's stomach jumped, but the rest of him was motionless. He waited to hear what she had to say.

'Last Tuesday I bought a pregnancy test as my period still hadn't come. And it was positive. I'm pregnant.'

He had the confusing sensation of someone who had switched channels mid-broadcast. Fiona's words did not make sense. She said she was pregnant. He turned to read the expression on her face. There was a Mona Lisa smile. Everything was all right. She knew nothing about his debts. He was safe. Instead she was going to have a baby.

'A baby,' he echoed his thought aloud.

'They normally result from a pregnancy,' she said, teasingly.

'Fiona!' He sounded amazed, delighted. She was glad she had saved her news until now. She took his hand nervously, and with her fingers played with his wedding ring, speaking softly.

'At first I didn't know what to think. It must have been the afternoon when that condom came off, but we might as well get it over and done with.' Her casual words belied her emotion. 'How do you feel?' she asked him.

Alastair shook his head to signify speechlessness. There was no way he could tell her about his troubles now.

'I know. It *is* a shock. I didn't know what to think either, in the beginning. For a while it seemed unfair as we've just got married, and now before we can get used to each other there's a baby.' Fiona moved quickly to her next point. 'I think we have to make decisions now based on the baby. We'll need money, and I don't want to be isolated up here. So I could come back to Manchester with you, and we could live in Greenmount. I can book into a local hospital and—'

'What about my mother?' he reminded her.

'I know.' Fiona felt contrite. She recognised she was being selfish. But there was the baby.

Alastair placed his hand on her stomach, against where he thought the baby might be.

'We'll see,' he said. 'Let's leave it a couple of weeks. I don't want to break the news to my mother yet.'

To her surprise, Fiona found she was crying. 'I don't want to live here any more. It's awful, being alone every evening. I wish your contract hadn't been extended. Let me go back with you on Monday?'

'Hush, hush.' He wiped her tears with his hands. 'Paul and Janice are in your house. We'll have to give them a month's notice at least.'

'But I could stay with you.'

'I only have a bedsit. We're saving money, remember?'

'Or with Mum and Dad.'

'My mother would think you were running away from her.'

This was cruel, he knew. But at all costs, Fiona must not come back to Manchester for a week or two. She must not see where he was living, and must not find out that he'd sold her furniture. It was impossible now to tell her about their financial situation. Instead it was up to him to rectify it, and there was only one way to do that. Once his salary was through, he would have a stake.

Or he could get a loan. Then, with a bit of luck – luck that was long overdue – he could sort out this mess. All he could do now was reassure Fiona.

'Just give me two more weeks,' he said, putting an arm round her shoulders. 'Two weeks. Then we'll tell Mother, I'll explain to Paul and Janice, and you can come back to Manchester, I promise. Can you last just two more weeks? Can you?' he added, addressing the baby.

'I think so,' Fiona said.

'I love you,' he whispered to her.

'But will you still love me when I start bulging?'

This was an easy question. Alastair answered in the affirmative, and pushed back her face to kiss her. Fiona saw the hills and sky wheel round her, and shut her eyes to close them out and give herself over to pure sensation. All would be well, she was sure.

Chapter Nine

Penny checked the rear-view mirror and then glanced sidelong at her mother, who was in the front seat of the Mini. Rose's face was drawn and tight, her lips pursed, almost as if in disapproval of something.

'I do need a new car, Mum,' Penny said defensively.

'I'm not saying you don't. Good luck to you.'

'So it's not that you're upset about?'

'Good heavens, no!'

So it was that Penny deduced Rose was upset about *something* and began to probe gently.

'It's not Fiona, is it? I know you're glad about the baby and everything, but it is sudden, and she's far away from home. Or maybe you feel bad about becoming a grandmother. It's a fairly major transition.'

'Stop talking to me as if I'm a problem page letter! I'm all right.'

Like hell you are, Penny thought to herself, and continued to drive in silence. Perhaps it wasn't such a good idea after all, taking her mother with her to choose a new motor. She was putting rather a dampener on the occasion. Penny waited until she turned into the main road, and then, patiently, began again.

'Is it Fiona?'

'No. She seems happy about the baby, and so I'm happy.'

'Me too. I shall be an aunty.' Penny chuckled with delight. 'Just like Lily. Excuse me while I accelerate. There's a boy racer coming up behind.'

'Penny!'

'Damn! He's gone past. But wait till I've got my new sporty model.'

Rose shook her head in disapproval, and Penny smiled. She liked winding her mother up. The main road leading into Manchester was fairly busy. Penny passed the wholesale warehouses, Carpet World and B & Q, and began to look for a car showroom. As yet she was undecided where to go. She pulled up at a queue in front of some road works.

'Perhaps it's Alastair who's upsetting you? You think he should have come to visit you. Well, I haven't seen hide nor hair of him either.'

'I expect he's been busy. Fiona says he wants to pack in the contract as soon as possible.'

'That's not what she said to me. She told me she wanted to come back to Manchester and have the baby here. I told her I thought that was a very good idea.'

Rose looked taken aback. 'Why didn't she tell me that?'

'I daresay she wanted to surprise you – when it was all definite. I've let the cat out of the bag, haven't I?'

'Never mind,' Rose said. 'I'm pleased.'

'Good. So it is Alastair who's been worrying you?'

'No. Yes. Nobody ever comes to see me.'

The car inched forward slowly.

'Is it Dad?' Penny asked.

Silence.

'Do you want to tell me about it?' She felt her stomach knot as she spoke those words.

'There's nothing to say.'

Penny thought she ought to encourage her mother to speak but dreaded hearing what she was going to say. Selfishness won.

'OK, we'll change the subject. I haven't told you about my Star Letter this weekend. This chap's a transvestite and he's been stealing his own wife's undies from off the washing line. She thinks it's a thief from outside and she's only got the police in. He doesn't know who to turn to, so he writes to me so I can splash it all over the *Manchester Post*! It's a funny old world. Ah

– Mazda! I thought they made light bulbs. But we'll have a look in here.'

Penny turned into the forecourt of the car showroom and parked her car in the MOT bay. She straightened herself as she got out of the Mini, and waited for her mother to join her. Together they made their way to the showroom, and Penny experienced the surreal but pleasurable effect of seeing shiny new cars indoors, on a marbled floor, like metal sculptures in an avant-garde gallery. She gave a low whistle.

In a small office at the rear of the showroom she saw a salesman observing them, waiting to pounce. Wanting to appear comfortable in this situation, Penny strolled over to the bright red car in front of them and opened the driver's door. Rose stood a little way behind her. Penny closed the door again and rejoined her mother.

'I don't know what to look for,' she whispered. She wished she'd stuck out the car maintenance course at the Women's Centre, but unfortunately she'd had no mechanical aptitude. The salesman walked towards them. He was young, with hair slicked back with copious quantities of gel, an eager expression and slightly receding chin.

'Can I be of any assistance?'

'Yes,' said Penny assertively. 'I want to buy a car.'

The salesman smiled, not sure if this was a joke or not.

'What sort of—'

'Four wheels, an engine . . . No, seriously, I fancy something sporty.' Penny noticed her mother backing off.

'For yourself, Madam?'

Penny sniffed the odour of sexism.

'Who else?' she countered. Lily would have been proud of her.

'Of course.' The salesman was gratifyingly deferential.

Penny moved towards the red car again and stroked its highly polished surface in the way she imagined a man might do. Cars, she knew, turned men on. Rick would no doubt be aroused by something like this. Like her, it was worth a lot of money. She peered inside but the smoked glass window prevented her from seeing the dark interior. The salesman stepped around her to open the door.

'The MX-3,' he said. 'Driver air bag included, alloy wheels, and 24-valve V-6 engine, 4-wheel, anti-lock brake system . . .'

'Yes, of course. I would expect all that,' Penny remarked loftily. Rose backed off further, looking somewhat alarmed.

'The steering gear ratio is fixed at 15:1,' said the salesman.

'I should hope so.'

'Do you have any questions, Madam?'

'Does it have a radio?'

A slight pause. 'With CD player. Four speakers . . .'

'Oh, right. Those big black boxes at the back?'

Penny walked round the car slowly, exulting in the knowledge that she could afford to buy it, yet utterly mystified by the sales jargon. With a sinking heart she realised you couldn't just buy a car like shopping at a supermarket. Or could you? It was men who created all this mystique about cars. Surely one was as good as another? She racked her brains, trying to recall the conversation of the motoring correspondent of the *Post*. Not that she spoke to him very often as he was terminally boring, though she did remember him raving about the old-style MG and saying that a Mazda MX-5 was the nearest you could get.

'Have you got an MX-5?' she asked.

'Surely,' said the salesman, and indicated to Penny and Rose that they should follow him. Rose had retreated as far as the window, and they waited while she rejoined them.

'Oh, this is a beauty!' exclaimed Penny. And meant it. Here was a car that actually appealed to her. It was a gleaming little white sports model which almost seemed to preen itself as she regarded it, like a kitten. Its soft top was pulled back to reveal two black seats and a reassuringly old-fashioned dashboard.

'The convertible top can be raised and secured quickly. It only takes a minute or two.'

Penny was not really listening. She walked slowly round the car, imagining herself at the driver's wheel, her mother next to her – Manchester's answer to Thelma and Louise. Or perhaps not. Here was freedom and glamour and power on four wheels. Wait till Rick saw her in this!

Rose approached the salesman. 'Is it safe?' she asked.

'It has high tensile steel beams,' he assured her. 'The upholstery is made of flame-retardant materials.'

Penny opened the door and sat inside. The smell of the leather seduced her. She placed her hand over the gear stick. She realised she had never driven a new car before. Not a brand-new one. Lily used to buy cars direct from the showroom. She would have loved this.

'I'll have it,' she said.

The salesman looked a little dubious.

'Would you like me to bring you details of our finance package? We have a good deal at present . . .'

Penny got out of the car.

'No, it's all right. I've got the cash.'

'He'll think you're a bank robber,' Rose whispered. 'Tell him you mean you won't need credit.'

'Sshhh!'

The salesman beamed. Penny could tell he was curious about her, and she revelled in that. Sure, it was unhealthy, but most fun was, come to think of it. For once she was determined to impress.

'I'll sign all the forms now. I'd like to have the car as soon as possible.'

The salesman led them eagerly to his little office where he offered them chairs. Rose began to explain.

'You see, what it is, my sister left her a lot of money. She had a stroke, you see, a second stroke. Now she used to own some dry-cleaning shops . . .'

Penny nudged her sharply in the ribs. She wanted nothing to spoil the delicious excitement that bubbled in her chest at the thought of buying and owning and having and driving this wonderful machine. It was all very well doing good deeds with money – already a few charities were receiving some generous cheques she had written – but *that* wasn't as exciting as *this*.

'How soon can I have it?' she asked the salesman.

'We can get it to you in under a working week,' he replied.

In the end it was Harry who accompanied her to the showroom to pick up the car. Rose told Penny that she wanted her to get used to driving it before she would go for a spin, and besides she'd had her hair set, and if Penny wanted to put the top down, her hair would blow all over the place.

'I don't have that problem,' Harry quipped, rubbing his balding head.

Rose did not look at him and did not laugh at his joke. Penny noticed, and deduced that her parents were still not speaking, or rather, Rose was not speaking to Harry. She was resigned to the fact that her father would try to put his case during the afternoon. At least her curiosity would be satisfied; she couldn't think what it was that he could have done this time.

''Bye, Mum!' Penny said brightly.

She felt traitorous as she revved up the Mini for the last time, but not very traitorous. She was as excited as a child about getting her new car. Harry, too, was full of questions about the Mazda, the cost of insurance, the sound system – his enthusiasm made Penny glad that she had brought him. He obviously understood how she felt.

When they arrived at the showroom the MX-5 was waiting for them on the forecourt and on the front seat was a bouquet of flowers. For a moment Penny wondered who they could be from, thought of Rick, reprimanded herself for being so silly – and then the salesman and his manager presented the flowers to her, compliments of the showroom. Serves you right, she told herself.

She accepted the keys, slipped into the driving seat and adjusted it until she was comfortable behind the wheel. Harry, by her side, grinned contentedly. Penny revved the engine and slowly edged the car towards the exit.

*　　　*　　　*

Harry sat on Penny's sofa, legs splayed out. A mug of tea was at his side. Penny sat on a chair close to the window, so she could keep an eye on the car which was parked in the street. If she could have brought it into the house, she would have done. For the umpteenth time that afternoon, Harry said, 'She's a beauty.'

'So exciting to drive.'

'An investment, an investment.'

Penny laughed. 'There! You're a grandfather twice over. Once when Fiona has her baby, and now with the Mazda.'

Harry looked a little uncomfortable, and hid this by lifting his mug to take a drink of tea. He realised it was empty and put it down again.

'You're as bad as Mum. Everyone's very lukewarm about Fiona's baby.'

'No, I'm delighted. But I've been thinking – the baby needn't call me Granddad. I could be Harry. That way I wouldn't feel so old.'

'You're not old,' she assured him.

'Old in experience. Is it still OK?' Harry was referring to the car.

'Fine.'

'And your mother's not talking to me again.'

'I noticed.'

'Do you know what it is?'

'No. You mean she hasn't told you, Dad?'

'No, I think I'm supposed to guess. One night we were getting along fine, and in the morning she gave me the cold shoulder.'

'You really don't know?'

Harry shook his head mournfully. 'Your mother is a difficult woman, Penny.'

She began to walk along the tightrope of her parents' marriage.

'Not really. You have your moments too.'

'But she never speaks to me. She never tells me what she wants. In a marriage there should be communication.'

'She talks to me. Mum might be a little shy, but she's not withdrawn.'

'She's forgotten how to enjoy herself. All of Lily's money is sitting in the building society, and your mother carries on collecting the money off coupons from her magazine.'

'No one changes overnight.'

'I wish you'd have a word with her.'

'No,' Penny said firmly. It was hard enough listening to her father while defending her mother. Had Rose complained about Harry, she would have supported him. It was important to be even-handed. But wearing. She looked longingly out at the Mazda. How she'd love to be in it right now, all on her own, the CD turned up high.

'You need a garage,' Harry remarked.

'I know, but it's impossible. The house is rented, so I can't build one. I'll just have to make do with the alarm and steering-wheel lock.'

'A pity.' Harry got up awkwardly, as the settee was low, and strolled out to the window.

'She's a beauty.'

'What if I was to move to somewhere with a garage?'

Harry was delighted.

'I was waiting for you to say that. This place . . .' He waved his arms about. 'This place isn't good enough for you. Especially not now. I'm sure I can smell damp. I know about these things. Get yourself somewhere nice. Have you thought about a city-centre flat? You could walk to work.'

The idea was certainly appealing.

'Money invested in property is never wasted,' he continued. 'You could afford to buy a flat outright. Then get your cousin Geraldine to come round and give it a makeover. She's an image consultant, isn't she?'

'Then I'd be buying a flat to match the car!' Penny announced.

'Why not?'

'Fiona's being much more careful than me. If she comes back to Manchester, she's going to carry on living in her little

Greenmount house. I'm surprised she doesn't want to buy a new one.'

'She's got a lot less money than you.'

'Has she?'

Harry turned so his back was towards Penny. He could have kicked himself. He'd well and truly let the cat out of the bag. He stared at the car, trying to regain his equilibrium.

'How much exactly did Fiona get?' Penny enquired.

Harry coughed. 'A bit less than you. She is the younger daughter. That's the way it goes.'

'Dad! Tell me.'

'It's not for me to say. So don't ask any more questions. Your mother will kill me. Lily liked you, all right? She probably liked you a little more than Fiona. Your mother and I were trying to keep that quiet. That's all.'

'I wish we had exactly the same.'

'But that's life. Some people are cleverer than others; some people are better looking than others; some people are richer than others.'

'It's still not fair.'

'I know.' Harry, having recovered from his unintentional slip, turned again and came to stand by Penny. 'Life is unfair. Take this woman I work with. Her husband walks out on her, her son's at university and badly in debt, and now she needs repairs to her roof, and she has nothing.'

'Poor woman,' Penny remarked.

Harry was glad to hear some sympathy for Rita.

'Not only that, the Head's cut her hours so she's earning less this year.'

'Would you like me to help her out?' Penny was glad of the opportunity to be charitable. Her self-indulgence with the car had made her feel a little guilty, not to mention what she had just found out about Fiona.

'What do you mean, help her out?'

'I could pay the roofing contractors on the quiet. She needn't know about it.'

'No, no. I'll think of something.'

'Tell me if you change your mind. Look, do you fancy a ride up the M66?'

'Now you're talking!'

At three in the morning, Penny jerked into wakefulness. She was aware that something was different. It was the car. She owned a brand-new car which was down in the street. It was an almost unbelievable fact, so unbelievable that she felt compelled to check that the car was still there. So she crept out of bed, walked over to the window and peeked through the curtains. There it was, the night turning it a pale grey. The street was silent. In the distance she could hear the rush of traffic on the main road. But that was not all. There was also the sound of laughter and footsteps, and from the alley at the back of the terrace came three black youths.

Suddenly Penny was alert. Would they notice the car? They were bound to – there was nothing else like it parked on the street. Thank God she had woken and was watching from the window. At least she would be able to give the police a detailed description. Two wore baseball caps, and the third a parka with a hood. He was the tall one. She wondered what they had been doing in the back terrace – meeting a dealer? Now they came up to the car. Penny was tense with apprehension. It was immobilised of course, but a sitting target for mindless vandalism. She held her breath.

One boy turned and looked at the Mazda; the other two ignored it. All three walked past, laughing at a joke, and the boy in the parka slapped another on the back. Soon they were lost to view.

Penny felt her heart thumping in her chest. But why? Nothing had happened. Three perfectly ordinary youths had walked along the street. They clearly had no intention of doing anything apart from getting home. And here she was, buying in to the worst racial stereotypes, all because of her MX-5. Penny was filled with self-disgust. What was she becoming? Perhaps she ought to take the car straight back to the showroom.

As she left the bedroom to go downstairs for a hot drink, she dismissed that thought as ridiculous. Instead she would compromise. She would try not to overreact like that again, and meanwhile she would look for a new flat. It was clear she had to move. If only there was someone who could help her choose a new place. She could ask none of her friends; to do so would be to parade her newfound wealth in front of them. She had been seeing far too much of her parents lately; they would not do. Perhaps she ought to give Geraldine a second chance. Penny wondered how much her dislike of her cousin was fuelled by envy – Geraldine had always been richer, more glamorous, more successful. Envy was a sin and ought to be fought. She would give Geraldine a ring in the morning and test the water. Yes, that was a good idea. She would call Geraldine, then take the car and drive on to see Kitty.

Penny edged the Mazda carefully between the two stone gateposts at the Gladesmore entrance. She was through. It was impossible not think of Lily and how delighted she would have been by this car. Impossible, also, not to think of Rick, and how he'd tried to comfort her after their joint visit to Kitty. Penny couldn't help but look to see if his car was there now. It wasn't. She was safe, but slightly disappointed.

One of the care assistants opened the door for her, and Penny inhaled the smell of disinfectant and air freshener. She walked along the high corridors leading to the day room, feeling slightly apprehensive. What if Kitty was having a bad day? What could Penny say that would cheer her? She could always take her for a spin in the Mazda. Penny smiled at the thought.

Her smile froze on her lips. There was Kitty, in her usual chair by the lampstand, and on the chair next to her was Rick. As she entered the day room he turned and saw her. There was to be no escape. He rose immediately.

'Penny!'

'Hello,' she said, as stiffly as she could manage.

'What are you doing here?'

'The same as you. Hello, Kitty.' Penny took a seat to her other side. Kitty turned to her, delighted.

'Are you Lily?' she said. Kitty looked well today; there was colour in her cheeks.

'No, it's Penny.'

'I know who you are. Rickie, this is Penny. Lily and I think you should get married.'

Penny ignored that, and noticed Rick did too.

'How are you, Kitty?'

'Rickie has come to take me out. He's come to take me on holiday.'

'I'm taking her to my parents' house for the afternoon,' he explained tersely.

Kitty held Penny's hand. 'Rickie will take you too. I'm going to have a baby.'

'That's a coincidence,' said Penny smoothly. 'Fiona's going to have a baby.'

'Lily had a baby.'

'Is Fiona pregnant?' Rick cut in. 'That's good news.'

Penny paid no attention.

'How's the food been this week, Kitty?'

'Not bad. I want ice cream.'

'Mum will have some ice cream,' Rick interposed. 'Penny, please can we talk?'

'I was going to take you out in my new car, Kitty. Perhaps another time. Do you like going out for drives?'

'Yes. Can we go now? Rickie, would you like a drive in Penny's new car?'

'Mum is expecting you at her house, but Penny is welcome to come with us.'

'No, thank you.' She rose to her feet. This was getting worse by the minute. She wanted nothing more than to be out of Gladesmore. Then it occurred to her that Kitty would think her departure abrupt, so she bent down to give her a kiss and explain that she would come back soon.

''Bye,' Penny said to Kitty. Head held high, she left the day room, and only then did her face redden with embarrassment. Luckily Kitty was living in a world of her own, otherwise she would have noticed the tension between her two visitors. Rick seemed angry, not glad, to see her, but surely she was the one who had the right to be angry? He was nothing but a gold-digger.

She reached the Mazda, and put her hand in her pocket for the keys. Wrong pocket. She searched in the other one. No keys there either. Penny frowned. Her denim jacket pockets were empty too. She cursed to herself. The car was locked, so obviously she'd had the keys on arriving at Gladesmore. She looked on the tarmac of the car park. They were not there.

With mounting humiliation, Penny realised that she had no choice but to go back into the day room and search for them. Taking a deep breath, she rang on the doorbell and once again entered the Home.

Rick was still in the day room. As he saw her he rose, held out his hand, and from his fingers dangled her keys.

'Thank you,' she said.

He put them behind his back.

'Rick!'

'Not until you agree to talk.'

A gentleman with a tremor was listening to them.

'Talk to him,' he suggested.

'Why aren't they talking?' asked a woman on his right in a pink cardigan.

'I expect they've had an argument,' replied the gentleman.

'That's Penny Green!' exclaimed another lady. 'She does the problems in the paper.'

The lady in the pink cardigan spoke next. 'Then she ought to be able to sort out her own problems. Let's watch her and see what she's going to do.' The palsied gentleman nodded. 'When I was in Mesopotamia,' he added, 'I were kicked wi' a mule.'

'Back soon, Kitty,' Rick said and, leading Penny by the elbow, took her out of the room.

Once more they were in the car park.

'Where's your car?' asked Penny.

'I'm in my parents' – mine's being serviced today. Is this yours?' He was looking at the Mazda.

'It might be.'

'Nice one, Penny.' There was a pause. 'Look, we can't talk here. Let's go for a walk in the park.' Rick put her car keys in the inner pocket of his jacket. Penny felt she had no choice.

They walked through the gates and along a diagonal path between two grassy areas, where a puppy was running around excitedly, his owners watching. In the distance was a bank of daffodils and early tulips, and a playground where a child in a brightly coloured anorak sat poised at the top of the slide. Penny could hear the far-off chimes of an ice-cream van.

'Although I witnessed Lily's will,' Rick said, his voice hard and definite, 'I didn't read any of it. I only knew about Simon because Lily told me. It never occurred to me to think that you'd inherited any money. I just want you to know that.'

She stayed silent. He would say that, wouldn't he?

'Look, if it helps, I have plenty of money of my own. Why should I want yours too?'

Penny stopped walking suddenly.

'Because Lily left me a quarter of a million pounds.' *That* shut him up. She looked at him to see how he took that. It was a test. To pass, he was supposed to be surprised. Only he didn't seem to be. His mouth was set firm.

'I didn't realise,' he said.

'I find that hard to believe.'

'Practise on this! Try believing that I spent the evening with you because I like you! You're funny, you're intelligent, you're sexy, and I want to be with you because for some reason I feel I know you better than I've ever known anyone. Only you don't seem to know me very well.'

Fortunately they were approaching an empty bench. Shock and anger prevented Penny from walking any further. How dare he shout at her like that! But he'd said she was sexy . . . She was thrilled by that, and furious at herself for being thrilled. It was a line; of course it was a line.

'I admit I don't know you well,' she said. 'But I don't see how anyone could witness a will without snooping into the contents. I just don't believe you're being honest.'

'How much of the will did you take in when you saw it for the first time?'

'I haven't seen it. It was taken straight to the solicitor's.'

'You haven't seen it? Why?'

It was a relief for Penny to talk about this. It had been preying on her mind.

'I don't know, but I think, from something my father said, that it was because Fiona was left less than me. I've only just found that out. I'm annoyed with Lily. I always suspected she liked me more, but she should have dealt fairly with Fiona.'

'Your aunt had a mind of her own.'

'I know.'

'You couldn't shift her easily.'

'Mmm.'

'Like you.'

'I suppose.'

'I didn't know you'd inherited any money, let alone a quarter of a million. I'm very glad for you. And I still want to go out with you.'

Penny swallowed hard. She was at a loss as to what to say next. Supposing it was true, that Rick really didn't know what she was worth? This was good news indeed. But she had just shot herself in the foot. He knew now. How could she ever believe he wanted her for herself, despite the things he had said? Words were cheap. He'd said she was like Lily: stubborn and dictatorial. He was wrong. She was like her mother. She did not know how to trust.

'I wasn't after your money,' he persisted.

'Prove it.'

'Prove it?' He put his hands on her shoulders and looked her directly in the eyes. She averted her gaze but, feeling the ridiculousness of this, turned unsmiling towards him. He moved closer to her and kissed her hard, insistently, one hand moving to the back of her head and cradling it gently, supporting it as the weight of his kiss, and her yielding, made her neck arch with pleasure. Penny closed her eyes. All was soft and dark and liquid.

Then she came to, and pushed him away.

'Will that do?' he asked.

Penny lowered her eyes. It would not do. It could not do. What she had learned from that kiss was not that he wanted her – she'd learned that *she* wanted *him*. She was the one who'd experienced that abandonment, that deep excitement. How did she know what he was feeling? Pride at a plot well hatched? How could you ever know what someone else was thinking?

'You still don't believe me,' he said. 'Well, OK. I'll prove it.' He got up. 'Kitty's waiting to go to my parents. I'll see you around.' From his jacket pocket he took her car keys and placed them beside her on the park bench. Then he walked back in the direction of the gate. Penny watched him go, in a turmoil. It all seemed worse than ever now. What right did she have to ask him for proof? Their relationship was not a court of law. Yet without it, she knew she would question his attachment to her. Because, thought Penny, quite consciously, I don't see why anyone would want to become attached to me.

You're always putting yourself down, Rick had said to her. Perhaps he was right. Take away the work she did solving problems and what was she? Nothing. Nobody. She had no real sense of her own identity. And for the life of her, she couldn't think why that was.

Dear Penny, she addressed herself, *I'm a thirty-one-year-old woman, good job, lots of dosh, single, but suffer from crashingly low self-esteem. I guess I get it from my mother, but that's irrelevant. Tell me, what can I do about it?*

Dear Penny, came the reply, *Search me! But here's an idea. Start by behaving 'as if'. Treat yourself as if you're worth something. Then you'll begin to believe it, and maybe begin to believe that others will find you loveable too.*

A bit cliched, Penny thought, but I might as well give it a try.

Rick helped Kitty on to an armchair where the rests would give her support. The colour in her cheeks was a little hectic, but she was wearing a secret, sly smile. She looked much happier than she had for some time.

Brenda came to sit by her sister, pulling Kitty's skirt down over her thin knees where it had ridden up. Kitty leaned over to her sister confidentially.

'I'm going to have a baby.'

'You can't have a baby, Kitty. Do you mean that somebody you know is going to have a baby?' Brenda was impatient with her senility.

'Yes. Lily is having a baby.'

'You don't mean Lily, you know.'

'Penny is having a baby.'

Brenda glanced at Rick, horrified.

He laughed. 'No, I'm not such a quick worker. But her sister's pregnant.'

'That must be it,' Brenda said to herself.

'We're going to go on holiday to Spain and we'll have the babies there.' Kitty looked down and patted her stomach proudly.

At that moment Michael emerged from the kitchen with the tea things. Kitty watched him happily. Everyone was relieved. Brenda got up and busied herself at the table.

'Here we are, Kitty. Tea with lots of milk, as you like it. And I've got you some fig rolls and you can have as many as you like. I'm sure they don't feed her enough at that home, Rick. You should see them at mealtimes, standing over them like hawks.' She stood by Kitty with the biscuit plate. 'That's right, Kitty. You take as many as you want. What do you think, Rick, Michael? Is she looking a lot thinner to you? Around the cheeks?'

Brenda found the situation easier if she could talk about Kitty as if she weren't there.

'Was she all right in the car?'

'Fine,' Rick confirmed.

Kitty bit into a fig roll, unconcerned about the crumbs that fell from her mouth as she did so. Her face assumed a vacant expression. Eating something sweet satisfied all her senses.

'You were right,' Rick said to his mother. 'She did think I was after her money. Penny, I mean. She came to the Home when I was there.'

Brenda put down her cup of tea.

'Did you talk to her?'

'Yes, but I'm still not sure she believed me. Did you know Lily left her a quarter of a million?'

'Oh my God! Michael, did you hear that?'

'But keep it quiet, Mum. I'm not sure I should have told you. You can see why she suspected me.' Rick's pride was partly assuaged by the size of Penny's legacy.

'Now I knew Lily was rich, but not that rich. Maybe she made some good investments after the takeover. A quarter of a million! No wonder I've seen nothing of Rose recently. How much money did *she* get?' Both Rick and Brenda looked across to Kitty, whose eyes were half closed with the bliss of consuming fig rolls.

'That's the strange thing. It appears that Penny probably received far more than anybody else. Lily liked her.'

'You can say that again! Mind you, in a funny kind of way Penny deserves it. Lily could have just as easily married Harry, and then Penny wouldn't have been born.'

Rick's head hurt as he tried to make out the logic of this.

'Did you say Lily nearly married Harry?'

Brenda realised she was guilty of an exaggeration, so back-tracked a little.

'It was Lily who first discovered Harry. He was the singer in a band that used to perform at functions. A bit of a ladies' man, he was, according to Kitty. Lily walked right up to Harry at the end of a dance, after "God Save the Queen", and asked him out. Do you remember telling me that, Kitty?'

She was deep into a fifth fig roll and did not respond.

'What do they call them now? Yes – that's it – he was her trophy boyfriend. But Lily would never go out with anyone for long; she worked every hour God sent at that dry cleaners. It was my guess she didn't want anyone to get too close to her. You know that limp she had? It wasn't due to the stroke; she'd had it since she was young, after a bad accident. It affected her. She lost her confidence. I know that seems ridiculous when you apply it to Lily, but I'm sure I'm right. She used to flirt something rotten with the boys, then back off. They all thought of her as good for a laugh.' Brenda paused for breath. 'But to my mind, she didn't want to get close to anyone. She couldn't believe that anyone could love her. So Harry went off with Rose, and she never had a steady. For all her front, Lily was as pure as the driven snow. Wouldn't let anyone get near her, in any way. She was frightened of men. Now I wouldn't be surprised . . .'

'So Rose stole Harry from Lily?' Rick was interested.

'I wouldn't say she stole him. No, I wouldn't say that. I had the impression Lily finished with him. There were no sour grapes. Lily was good to both of them. Harry was always in and out of work. It was a mixture of bad luck and big ideas. He wanted to go on the stage, in the musicals, but never passed an audition. Rose ended up supporting them both, and then her mother was ill and she had to give up work to nurse her. Lily had her own empire to run by then so she gave Harry a job, managing one of the shops, and paid him a pretty decent salary, by all accounts. That was around the time I was pregnant with you. I remember meeting Rose in the baker's where her mother used to work. She'd been married some time, but there was no baby. I didn't want to ask her if she was having trouble – it's not like me to be tactless – but you could see by the way she looked at me that she was jealous.'

'But she must have had Penny soon after.'

'Don't rush me! Harry was away from home a lot – he travelled for Lily. She was a woman alone, and in those days you didn't . . . Now I remember! That was it! That was the time when Rose fell with Penny. Because I remember thinking that it was him being away from home that made her pregnant. And her mother was very ill at the time. Rose had her work cut out, pregnant and looking after her mother. I rarely saw her then. And all that hard work, lifting her mother, turning her in the night – it brought on a premature labour. Penny came when they were on holiday in Scotland. I can remember seeing her in the pram some time afterwards. She was a tiny thing, pretty as a picture. You were on reins, because you insisted on running everywhere and you wouldn't stay in the pushchair. Do you recall that, Kitty? Rickie not staying in the pushchair?'

Kitty nodded perspicaciously, and helped herself to another fig roll. She was going to have a baby. The nurse had come to her in the middle of the night and told her she was going to have a baby. The nurse had said that she wasn't to tell anyone, ever. Kitty thought that now she had told someone, they would take the baby away from her, but that was all right. She would just have another one. The fig rolls were soft and sweet and crumbly. She would have another one.

Rick decided against opening another can of lager, and closed his fridge resolutely. He had drunk enough tonight. The game of squash had ended in the sports club bar, and the exercise, coupled with ice cold lager, should have been enough to put him straight to sleep.

However, he was not ready to go to bed. His mind was racing. There was far too much to think about. Until now, he had not had the chance to sit down and piece it all together. So he returned to the fridge, opened it again, removed a can of Budweiser and carried it back to the lounge, not bothering with a glass.

So that was why Lily had left Penny so much money. She was fond of her, yes, of course she was, but Lily had obviously seen herself as a provider for Harry and Rose. She found Rose a husband, found the husband a job, and now she'd provided the girls with a fortune. Except from what Penny had said, the bulk of the money had been left to her? Why?

It was a recent will. Maybe Fiona had done something to disqualify herself. Was that something marrying Alastair? He was Scottish, and Penny had been born in Scotland . . . Rick swung his legs on to the settee. Everything was connected but nothing made sense. Irrationally he felt that if he could understand why Lily had favoured Penny, he could begin to find some sort of proof.

OK. So perhaps Lily was angry with Fiona for getting married at all. Maybe Penny inherited because she stayed single. But in that case, why did Lily always tease him about Penny, evidently wanting them to get together? A dead end.

Lily loved Penny. Maybe that was enough. A shame she wasn't allowed to see Lily's will. *Why* wasn't she? Perhaps she wasn't left the money after all, and it was a gift from her parents. Lily left her fortune to Harry and Rose because she was indebted to them in some way. And whatever it was, it had to do with Penny. He drained the can of lager, and as he did so, a stupendous idea occurred to him. No, it couldn't be. His mother had said that Lily was as pure as the driven snow. But she and Kitty went on all those foreign holidays. Now why would she do that? Lily had loved Spain, and she'd loved the Spaniards. Did she love *a* Spaniard? And was Penny the result? *The Spaniard that blighted my life*, Rick hummed to himself.

He thought of Penny's dark eyes, brown irises flecked with black, and what he sensed was a passionate nature. Crazily, he hoped his supposition was true. If it was, he would be able to show her he loved her no matter who she was.

Rick Goldstone, he told himself, you're mad. Completely mad. Penny is not the offspring of a dry-cleaning tycoon and an oversexed Spaniard. She's ordinary Penny Green, Harry and Rose's girl. He tipped the Bud back and caught the few last drops before squeezing the can so it collapsed in the middle. Just as well you're off to London for a couple of weeks; you need cooling off time, a chance to regain your sanity, he chided himself.

But then, he thought, when I come back, I might just dig around a little bit more. Yes, I might do just that.

Chapter Ten

Rita's house was the third along a red-brick terrace off Haslam Road. The front door opened straight on to the pavement; there was no garden. The door was painted olive green and boasted a gilt knocker. Harry stood in front of it, deliberating for a while.

He decided not to knock. Instead he turned, crossed the road, and looked up at the roof, screwing up his eyes against the sunlight as part of an unconscious pose; if Rita should happen to be looking out of a window, he wanted to appear professional. The chimney seemed sound enough to him. From further along the street came a harassed young mother, pushing a double buggy containing a large baby and angry-looking toddler. Harry nodded to her as she passed, and her look in response was one of exasperation and helplessness. Impulsively he wished there was something he could do. But no. He was here to help Rita.

There had been no hardship in giving up his Sunday afternoon to come round and look at her roof. He had told Rose where he was going, what he was doing, and when he expected to be back. She had cleared her throat as if she were going to say something, thought better of it, and stopped. Harry decided to take that as assent. Anyway, there was absolutely no reason for him to feel guilty. Far from it. If anything, he felt aggrieved. Rose had the power to stop him going to Rita's; not only that, she could have come with him and had a cup of tea with Rita while he climbed the ladder and mounted the roof. If Rose was as friendly as he was, that's what she'd have done.

But these were maudlin thoughts. He was here to inspect Rita's chimney, and couldn't do that properly from the other side of the street. As he recrossed the road, he thought to himself that Rita really was hard-up; the terrace was cramped, shabby – the sort of place that belonged to the Salford of the thirties, and that he'd mistakenly thought had all been torn down. Still, he told himself, they do have character. Picking up the gilt knocker, Harry rapped vigorously.

Almost immediately Rita opened the door, face lit up with gratitude. She eagerly ushered him into her living room – there was no hall. Rita's hair was soft and fluffy today; she wore paisley-patterned leggings in blues and reds, with a long black sweater over them. There seemed something less defined about her, it occurred to Harry. Then he realised she wasn't wearing her lipstick.

He looked appreciatively round the living room.

'Very nice,' he said, half from politeness and half from conviction.

To either side of a small fireplace with a coal-effect gas fire were shelves of books, mainly musical. There was a music stand in one corner, and near it, on an occasional table, lay Rita's flute. The armchairs were chintzy and pretty, and festoons of net curtains hung over the windows.

'Very nice,' said Harry.

'I'm so glad you like it. I do my best, Harry, with it being such a small house. But can I get you something? Something to drink? I can't tell you how glad I am you've come, Harry. Now what would you like?'

Rita seemed nervous and even more vulnerable than ever, despite being in her own home. To put her at her ease, Harry sat down in one of the chintzy armchairs, and stretched out his legs.

'Cup of tea?' he suggested.

'Come on now, Harry. That's not very wicked! Can't I tempt you with some brandy? Or a spot of whisky?'

Harry never drank in the afternoons. In fact, he rarely drank in the evenings. About to decline, he was once more aware of the need not to disappoint Rita.

'Just a small whisky,' he said. 'But not too much. You don't want me to be falling off the ladder.'

Rita gave a fluttery giggle at his joke, and moved over to a silver tray with bottles on it. Her back towards him, she poured out two drinks. Harry saw the way her sweater curved round her bottom, and noticed that she wasn't wearing any shoes. Rita turned and handed him a glass. She took the armchair opposite his, sat down, and crossed her legs. Harry's eyes were drawn to the shapeliness of her thighs. That made her seem much younger. Rose never wore anything like leggings.

'Now you enjoy your whisky, and don't feel there's any rush to get up on the roof. I've borrowed Wilson's ladder from next door – it's one of those extendable ones. And, oh, Harry, I can't tell you how grateful I am! It's such a load off my mind. I actually slept last night.'

'How's your son – Stephen?'

'My Stephen?' Rita gave a little pout with her lips. 'Well, not so good. He's got exams coming up, but he's not working, Harry. He's not working. He says what's the point, when he's in so much debt? Says he needs to get a job, but there's nothing available. And if he does get a job, then he won't have the time to revise. I read a dreadful article in a magazine about students who turn to drug-dealing to get them through their degrees. Oh, Harry, I don't know.'

He pretended he had an itch or an irritation just below his shoulder and put his hand inside his jacket to rub his chest. In fact he was checking to see that the envelope containing the three hundred pounds he had taken out of the bank was still secure. He felt its reassuring presence. If he wanted to, he could offer Rita the money. He wasn't sure he wanted to, but having the money gave him a choice. It was Penny's idea, of course. He wouldn't have brought the money if she hadn't suggested that the decent thing to do was to help Rita out. He took a sip of the whisky, and resisted the impulse to cough.

'*He* wrote me a letter the other day,' Rita said, and Harry realised she was talking about her husband again. '*He* explained that his new woman needed some private hospital treatment, and that was why he had no spare cash. Oh, the NHS was always good enough for me, Harry!'

'The NHS,' he repeated. 'Badly underfunded, that's what it is.'

'Like me,' said Rita, and laughed a little at her joke.

'If I were Prime Minister, I'd double the nurses' salaries.'

'I'm sure you would, Harry. That would be just like you. You're such a kind man.'

He looked down and flexed his knuckles. Her compliments pleased him, but he wasn't sure how he was meant to react.

'Harry, do you play on the lottery?'

'I'm in the syndicate at school. But not on my own. The wife's agin that sort of thing.'

'Oh. Well, that's very odd. I hope you don't mind me saying this, but there are rumours about you. Somebody – I'd better not say who – somebody said you'd won the lottery.'

He guffawed. 'Nonsense. Ha, ha! The way these things get out of proportion. No. We just inherited a little bit of money, that's all.'

'I thought it was just a rumour,' said Rita.

Harry felt awkward. He had money; Rita had none. She knew that. He wanted this conversation to end.

'Shall I make a start on the chimney?'

'Of course! The ladder's out in the back yard, through the kitchen.' She rose, inserted her feet into a pair of fluffy lime slippers, and Harry got up and followed her through a pretty, clean kitchen to a small yard where an extendable ladder stood propped against one wall. Immediately he set about lengthening it.

'It's so nice to have a man in the house again,' she breathed.

Harry caught her words and liked them, although he knew he shouldn't. The ladder was stiff, and proving hard work. He was getting hot and sweaty. He didn't particularly want Rita to see him like this so decided to remove his jacket and asked her to hold it for him. Eagerly she took it.

Eventually the ladder was propped against the side of the house, its final rung only a short step away from the roof. Harry prepared to ascend.

'Shall I hold it steady?' Rita asked.

'Good idea.'

'I'll just pop your jacket in the kitchen.'

Rita vanished from the garden with his jacket. Harry decided not to wait for her and to try to ascend the ladder. The first few rungs were simple enough. He debated whether to try to get to the roof before Rita returned. He reached her bedroom window and peered in, feeling rather like a peeping tom. There was a pink quilt on her bed and an exercise bike in one corner. At that moment, Rita re-entered the yard.

'Here I am,' she said brightly. She came and held both props of the ladder as firmly as she could. Rung by rung, Harry rose higher and higher, out of her reach. Rita clung desperately to the ladder as it wobbled and shook.

'Almost there,' came Harry's voice.

Then the ladder shook even more as he heaved his weight from the top of it on to the roof and Rita was left forlornly in the garden. Where she stood, the flags were cracked and a few stray weeds raised their cocky heads. There was the sound of a cat scrabbling in the coal shed. Rita craned her head back, watching him.

Feet in the guttering, he held desperately on to the coping at the apex of the roof. He felt surprisingly insecure, all the more so because he was aware that Rita was watching him, and thought he ought to act the role of hero; indeed, he *wanted* to act the role of hero. Yet now he became aware that he could easily fall off. Carefully, he edged himself nearer the chimney. He knew he was not nervous of heights, as long as he didn't look down. He cursed himself for having had that whisky. Another crab-like step to the side, and he was next to the chimney. Harry stopped to look at the panoramic view of Salford's back yards and alleys. Then he turned his attention to the chimney.

He saw it immediately. There was an unmistakable crack

191

running along the base of it. Harry wasn't precisely sure what this portended. He was less of an expert on masonry than he had suggested to Rita. Anyone, he thought, could see whether a chimney was sound or not. Now Harry found himself in the embarrassing position of not being sure. This crack that wove around the base of the chimney could have been there for ages. On the other hand, it could mean that one more autumn gale and the whole thing would collapse.

He cursed silently. What on earth was he going to tell Rita? The whole point of this visit was to reassure her. The last thing he wanted to do was climb down the ladder and tell her that she needed to lay out a few hundred on a new chimney. Besides, he wasn't absolutely sure that she *did* need a new chimney. A gust of wind played with his remaining hair. For a passing moment he felt a complete fool. Then he remembered the money in his jacket pocket. That changed everything. No one was a fool with three hundred pounds to spend. He could still make everything all right.

He began to edge back to the ladder. He would think of something to say – something that was kind, even if it wasn't entirely true. His feet found the rungs of the ladder, and he began to ease his body back down to solid ground where he greeted Rita.

'Windy up there,' he remarked.

'Poor Harry! Come straight in and let me warm you up with another whisky.'

She bustled in ahead of him, and he followed her once again, noticing his jacket and deciding to leave it there for a while. He needed a comfortable sit down. He returned to the lounge and took the armchair that he'd been sitting in before. He knew he shouldn't have another whisky but it seemed to be what Rita expected him to do. This time she had poured herself a large glass too, and rather than sit opposite him, came to the foot of his armchair and sat on the carpet on his left side. She seemed rather like a child, down there like that. Harry thought this made what he had to say all the more difficult.

'Was it all right?'

'The chimney? Oh, just the usual wear and tear.'

'Do I need a new one?'

'Hard to say. No – no, I shouldn't think so. These things are built to last a lifetime. Don't worry about it. That chimney's rock solid!'

'Harry, thank you. You are a love.'

'No need to worry at all. These roofing contractors – out for a quick buck. Good brick, that's what your chimney's made out of – good brick!' he said emphatically. Then he looked at her coal-effect gas fire. 'Look,' he said, 'you must have had that put in fairly recently.'

'My Caress?' asked Rita.

Harry wondered if he'd heard her correctly. Was it the whisky that had made him redden?

'The Caress is the name of the fire,' she explained.

'Same as I was saying, the bloke who installed it must have checked your flue and seen the chimney.'

'I wasn't in when it was installed. *He* saw to it.'

'They'd have found any problem with the chimney then.'

'Are you cold, Harry? Shall I put the fire on?'

'No, no. The whisky's doing a grand job of warming me up.'

'I'm quite warm too, Harry.' Rita now placed her hand on his knee. Then withdrew it again. He was glad. The festoons of her net curtains only reached three quarters of the way down the window. Someone might see.

Harry felt nicely relaxed. The whisky had made him feel expansive and powerful, and he had succeeded in convincing himself that Rita's chimney was fine. He looked forward to a pleasant half an hour or so. It was good to be with a woman who talked to him. There was silence as Harry decided what to choose to talk about. He obviously couldn't talk about Rose, Penny's new car was interesting but tactless in this situation, and he didn't feel like discussing Fiona either. As thrilled as he was that she was having a baby, pride forbade him from letting

Rita know he was ancient enough to be a grandfather. So the obvious thing to do was to talk about Rita herself.

'Are you feeling any happier than when we had our little chat?' he asked her kindly.

'My problems haven't gone away, Harry, but I think I'm coping rather better. I'm advertising. I'm going to see if I can give some private lessons.'

He glanced over at her flute by the music stand.

'It's all I've got left,' Rita said, rather pathetically.

'You've got me,' said Harry. He thought of the three hundred pounds in the kitchen. It would be a simple matter to give it to Rita. On the other hand, Rose would be furious. But then, she seemed to be furious with him at the moment for no reason, so he may as well give her one. He imagined Rita's gratitude as he handed over the envelope. And Penny would approve.

'Harry, love – I am rather warm. Do you mind if I pop upstairs and change?'

'Make yourself at home,' he said, and instantly realised what a daft comment that was. He attributed it to the whisky. Rita got up, opening a door by the kitchen that Harry had thought led to a pantry but in fact hid a flight of stairs. She stepped lightly up them.

Now he rose too, and began to pace Rita's tiny living room. It was certainly true that she had fallen on hard times. Her house oozed a faded middle-class gentility, from the yellowing nets to the chintzy armchairs. She was a flautist, too. It wasn't fair. Perhaps he would take her to a concert at the new Bridgewater Hall, to cheer her up, if Rose didn't mind. Rose didn't care for music much. Nor did she care for him, he thought, hurt. If he was enjoying feeling needed by Rita, what was the harm in that? Yes, he would give her the money – soon.

When Rita came down the stairs, Harry saw that she had exchanged her sweater for a black t-shirt. He saw her nipples protruding through it, and couldn't help but wonder if she was wearing a brassiere. Probably not, he thought. She was small-busted and maybe didn't need one. Harry felt guilty for thinking about Rita's breasts, but it was a pleasant sort of guilt. Thought is not a crime.

'I'm in the mood for some Tchaikovsky,' Rita said, and moved over to a small music centre by the television. As a familiar symphony began, thankfully the noise of the TV set next-door was drowned. Now Rita moved over to the curtains, and drew them. The room suddenly became shadowy and shady.

'I don't like prying eyes,' she said. 'The kids down the road like to play postman's knock if they know I'm in, Harry.'

As she brushed against him, Harry smelled something that reminded him of floral air freshener. Then he realised it was Rita's perfume. She hadn't been wearing it before. Obviously she had put some on upstairs. What did that mean? He glanced at her face and saw that she still hadn't applied any lipstick.

'You seem tense, Harry.'

'No, no, not at all.' Had she guessed about the chimney?

'Did you know I can give massage?'

'Can you?'

'I took a course, Harry. Now I think you deserve a shoulder massage, after all your hard work.'

Rita went into the kitchen, brought a wooden chair, and instructed him to sit in it.

'I can't massage you with your jumper on.'

Harry took it off.

'Oh, dear! You're wearing a shirt too. Look, if you don't mind, I think I need to have your bare skin. I like to rub in baby oil.'

No one had ever given Harry a massage before. A massage was supposed to reduce stress. In the half-light of the shadowy room, he stood, removed his shirt, and sat down on the chair, feeling exposed. He knew his tummy was a touch too fleshy and round. Rita stood by him with a bottle of Johnson's Baby Oil, and poured some on to her hands.

Then she walked round the back of the chair and, in time to the music, proceeded to rub oil into Harry's skin, moulding her hands to his back, pressing into his muscles. Her fingers worked his flesh expertly, and Harry had to admit he was enjoying himself.

'I didn't know you could do this.'

'I'm a woman of many talents, Harry.'

He didn't respond, enjoying the sensation of her fingers probing his muscles, massaging his neck, moving softly up to his scalp. It was good to be touched by a woman. He felt warm and loved again. He accepted the gift of Rita's hands impersonally, and as he relaxed, began to feel somewhat sleepy. Usually Sunday afternoon was when he had his nap. Now Rita's fingers moved down his chest, lower, lower . . . and stopped.

'I'll have to come round the other side, Harry.'

'Fine, fine.'

Rita glided round the chair and, now facing Harry, placed her hands on his shoulders again, repeating the same kneading movements. He couldn't help but glance at her face and when he did, saw that she was looking directly at him. He quickly averted his gaze.

'I can't quite get a grip, Harry. Put your legs together and let me just perch on your lap.'

In a moment, she was straddling his legs. Her face was directly in line with his, the aroma of her perfume was stronger than ever and he could hear her soft, sensual sighs as she continued to press her fingers into his shoulders, and wriggle nearer and nearer him.

'I'm hot, Harry.'

Then, so suddenly that he could not prevent it happening, she lifted her t-shirt over her head and stood naked from the waist up, her two tiny breasts with their dark brown nipples demanding his attention. Before Harry had time to analyse his amazement, and decide how much of it was shock and how much delight, Rita wriggled even closer to him and squeezed him tightly.

'Oh, Harry!' she sighed.

He felt as if he been lassooed. It was difficult to breathe. Harry shifted back slightly, and as he did so, the chair they were sitting on overbalanced and he found himself lying on the floor with

Rita on top of him. Once again she pressed herself against him, and this time gave him a long, probing kiss. Harry lay there, entirely passive, his mind spinning, unable to decide what to do next.

'Oh, Harry!' Rita said again, coming up for air.

Now her hand was straying down his chest and poking between his skin and the belt of his trousers. Harry knew he was entirely limp, and for some reason visions of the cracked chimney came to haunt him. Gently he removed her hand.

'Shall I unfasten your belt, Harry?'

'No,' he said, guided by his better angel. 'Can I sit up for a while? I think I might have ricked my back.'

He brought himself to the vertical, his eyes on a line with Rita's flute. He reached round to his back and began to rub it. He averted his eyes from Rita, scared to think what she might take off next. When eventually he dared to look at her, he saw she was covering her breasts with her hands. Then she turned her back to him, reached for her t-shirt and pulled it over her head. Slowly Harry stood and began to dress. When he had finished, he looked at Rita. Just as he had feared, there were tears in her eyes.

'I'm sorry, Harry,' she sniffed. 'I – I hope I didn't hurt you?'

'Not at all!' he said gamely.

'Don't you . . .' Rita swallowed hard. 'Don't you find me attractive?'

'Yes, yes, of course I do. Any man would. But, Rita – I'm a married man. I—' Harry shrugged, as if to say he couldn't help rejecting her. Nevertheless, he felt ashamed and deceitful. Rose was an excuse at that moment, and he knew it.

'But I thought you came here to—'

'To look at your chimney.'

From his jacket he took the envelope with the three hundred pounds.

'Look, Rita, I'm not so sure about your chimney. Take this, and get someone reliable to look at it. Don't worry about paying it back – there's plenty more where that came from.'

'But, Harry, I couldn't,' she stuttered. 'I mean, I haven't done anything for it!'

'I didn't expect you to do anything.'

There was a long, almost tangible pause.

'Better be off,' he said with forced cheerfulness.

'Expecting a phone call from my younger daughter. She's having a baby. I'm going to be a grandfather!'

And with that, he opened the front door and departed.

Slowly Rita retreated into the shadow of her front room, holding tightly on to the envelope. She knew it wasn't sealed. She opened it and took out a wad of twenty-pound notes. She licked her finger and counted them. One, two, three ... fifteen. That was three hundred pounds. Enough for a new chimney, or if she risked the chimney's not collapsing, she could send it to Stephen. Or possibly splash out on some new clothes. Still holding the money, she picked up the chair that had fallen over and sat on it.

Was it so very bad, what she had done? It wasn't as if she was one of those girls who paraded themselves down on Minshull Street, with their thigh-high boots, tiny skirts and challenging faces. No, it hadn't been like that at all.

For a start, she really was fond of Harry. He was kind and strong – such a nice man. And he liked her, she was sure of it. He had stroked her face so tenderly, that afternoon in the staff room. From hints he had given, she'd guessed there were problems with his wife. Marriage wasn't a bed of roses, that was for sure. If two people could find some happiness in the twilight of their lives, what was wrong with that?

That really was all that was in her mind until she'd hung his jacket over the back of the chair, and the envelope had drawn attention to itself. Anyone would have had a quick peek. It was obvious the money was for her. It was equally obvious what he'd expected her to do for it. And he was a lovely man, with kind eyes and that cuddly tummy. She could have done it. Would have done it, except for that silly accident with the chair.

Three hundred pounds. She stroked the notes gently, her hand moving up and down over their crisp surface. Up and down. Up and down.

Sitting in the front seat of his car, Harry tried to calm his rapid breathing. What a narrow escape! Now he lifted his hand to his mouth and blew into it, to see if his breath smelled of whisky. Hard to say. Then he twisted round to sniff at his shoulders, to see if he could smell the Baby Oil. What about Rita's perfume? Did that cling to him? He wondered if he could go straight to the bathroom when he got home, to shower. How ridiculous to feel so guilty when he had done nothing. Nothing except try to help a lady in distress.

Which is only good manners, Harry told himself. He remembered how, as a little boy, he'd gone into the classroom in advance of the pretty new teacher, against the rules, because he had seen a rude word chalked on the blackboard and had wanted to erase it so she wouldn't see it. That was what he had been brought up to do. Be kind to ladies.

And then there was the other time . . . Quickly Harry turned the key in the ignition, to prevent himself from thinking of the other time. Only he revved too hard, and the engine overheated. Against his wishes, memories of the other time came slowly back. The other woman, who had shown him that she was lonely. Her desire for him. Her ample body and its irresistible appeal. The heat of the moment, and the embarrassment, and the shame. The red velvet drapes of the hotel room and the bottle of champagne, half-empty, in the ice bucket. The unaccustomed luxury, and the shame. Like Rita, he had been prepared to sell himself too.

Harry felt sick, and perhaps, he thought, was going to be sick. Once again he turned the key in the ignition, but this time his foot was much gentler on the accelerator, and the engine caught. As he drove, he tried to steady his mind again, thinking of what was for dinner, of tomorrow's lessons of how long it was until the car was due for its service. And of Rose, his safe place. Thank God he had Rose. From now on, he would do nothing to disappoint her. He was so thankful to have a wife like Rose.

The suitcase that she had thought to have taken to Fiona's now lay open and empty on her bed. With her accustomed care Rose filled it with a selection of tops, skirts, slips, her hairbrushes and all the other objects that were an intimate part of her daily routine. She paused. Then she took the chair from the dressing table and moved it to the wardrobe. She climbed on to it, and reaching to the back of the top shelf, withdrew a plain black handbag. She opened it and took out the envelope she had placed in it on the day of Lily's funeral.

Wherever she was going, the envelope had to go, too. She could not risk leaving it. It felt like dynamite in her hand. For safety's sake, she put it back in the handbag and stepped down from the chair, placing the bag in the centre of the suitcase guiltily, as if someone might be watching her.

It surprised her how little there was to take. All these years, and now her children had gone, there was nothing left for her. Unlike Harry, she had no treasured records, books or other possessions. What books she enjoyed, she had borrowed from the library, and ornaments were something she could well do without while the girls needed school uniform. There was nothing she regretted leaving.

It was better like this. Rose didn't want a scene. If Harry pleaded with her to stay, she couldn't be sure of not giving in to him. She had done, once before. Earlier today, standing by the linen cupboard, folding towels, Rose had seen her husband place the envelope she had given him with his three hundred pounds into his jacket pocket. She had wondered why he had not put it in his dressing-table drawer. Then he had told her where he was going. To that other woman! So he was being brazen now. That was what had decided her. Leopards don't change their spots. If he couldn't change, then she would have to.

Penny had changed. She was having no trouble spending her money on herself, Rose thought acidly, as she carefully placed a sundress in the suitcase. Rose was part condemnatory, part envious. Penny was moving now; she'd found a posh apartment in a converted warehouse somewhere in town, with a health club in the basement and concierge service. Very nice for her. Fiona was having a baby, and could talk of nothing else. Rose felt appalled at her lack of response to Fiona's excited babble about blood tests and foetal development.

She locked the suitcase. She hoped that when she had done that, she would be able to decide where it was she would go. The important thing was to be out of the house before Harry got back. She could be mysterious too. Her movements, as she closed wardrobe doors and straightened her bedspread, were orderly and methodical. However, her mind was paralysed with panic and indecision. Would Penny take her in? Would she want to live with this new Penny who was spending like there was no tomorrow? Ought she to go instead to Monty and Sally in London, pretending there was nothing wrong? Should she take the holiday of which Harry had deprived her?

She pushed the suitcase along the landing, and gingerly lifted it down the staircase. It was heavy. In a moment of resolution, she lifted the telephone receiver and dialled the number of the local taxi rank. She took her coat from the hall cupboard. Rose felt remote from the house now, it had nothing to say to her.

She left the brief note on the kitchen table, and as she did so, picked up the newspaper with the uncompleted crossword, to finish later. There was a ring at the doorbell and a paunchy Cypriot stood there, stubbing out a cigarette on her drive. It seemed an appropriate gesture, Rose thought. He carried her suitcase over to his Vauxhall Estate, and she watched as he swung it into the boot where there was a tangle of jump leads and a battery recharger. She sat herself in the back of the car, trying not to inhale the acrid cigarette smoke and the smell of disinfectant.

'Where to again?' asked the driver.

* * *

Rose and Harry's house was empty. Not the slightest drift of air disturbed the stillness. The short note lay unread on the table. Time had taken a rest.

Then the shrill ringing of the telephone shattered the silence. In even bursts it continued to ring. And ring. And ring. It echoed through the house and was lost in the blanket of silence.

And Fiona sat at the other end, and wept.

Chapter Eleven

Fiona replaced the receiver. Perhaps it was as well her parents were out. She needed to calm herself before she was ready to talk to them. Calm? What was that?

The last time there'd been the illusion of peace was yesterday, when she had awoken from an afternoon nap to hear the sound of Douglas's mower on the front lawn. Douglas was a local odd job man who had worked occasionally for Margaret and was now working for Fiona. He was a burly, elderly Scotsman, a roll-up always hanging from his lips, with a slow, ponderous way of talking, as if each word needed great deliberation. Once he had invited Fiona into his tiny cottage, where there was a fridge in the sitting room and several pairs of wellington boots warming in front of the fire. The stench had made her quite faint.

As a gardener, Fiona found him an embarrassment. He insisted on passing the time of day with her when he came to attend to things and his small talk was almost entirely to do with the weather, when he wasn't gossiping about the affairs of the villagers. His accent also took some deciphering. On hearing him in the garden Fiona had summoned all her politeness, swung her legs off the settee, stood up, and waited for him to notice her through the window and wave, which he did do, almost immediately.

A few minutes later, when she was in the kitchen making tea, Douglas's silhouette appeared at the back door and she automatically got down a second mug.

He received his tea gratefully.

'Aye,' he said. 'I like a good cup of tea.'

Fiona smiled, but briefly, so as not to invite further confidences.

'That's good tea,' he said ruminatively. 'Wind's getting up a bit. There'll be rain before evening.'

Fiona glanced at the sky.

'It feels chilly,' she said.

'How's wee Alastair?'

'Fine. He's not coming home this weekend. He's busy at work.' Fiona had accepted this now, although they had almost argued about it last night.

Douglas shook his head slowly, and pursed his lips. Fiona thought he was disagreeing with her, but then decided that his dour expression was meant to convey sympathy. After another brief silence, Douglas spoke again. He was evidently feeling voluble.

'Wee Alastair. He was a bonny lad.'

Fiona nodded in assent.

'A bonny lad. And his mother, a fine woman.'

'She is.'

Douglas shook his head again.

'Aye. Now, the father. There was a pity.'

Fiona agreed. It was always sad when someone died early, and she had often regretted that she had never come to know Alastair's father.

'Aye, but it was just as well, some say.'

'Why? Was Alastair's father very ill before he died?' Fiona was curious; Alastair had said little about that final illness.

Douglas's watery blue eyes lit up with the discovery that pretty young Fiona seemed not to know about the Gordons. He loved nothing more than telling a good story.

'You didnae know that your husband's father used to drink? Aye, Graeme liked his dram, but it didn't like him. They had to call in the minister on more than one occasion.' Douglas stopped to inhale at his cigarette.

'The minister? What for?'

Douglas shrugged, suddenly wondering if he had said too

much. After all, Margaret Gordon was one of his employers. On the other hand, what he was about to tell Fiona was common knowledge in the village, and if Alastair hadn't told her, someone ought to.

'The drink made Graeme ugly,' Douglas said, coughing to clear the phlegm from his chest. 'Beat his wife, and the child didnae escape either.' He saw the look of horror on Fiona's face. 'But that was – oh – nigh on twenty years ago. They sent him away, to get him to stop. He did for a while, but it poisoned his liver. Aye, the drink poisoned his liver. And there's plenty more folk hereabout who don't know when to stop drinking. Nae worry, it's all in the past.'

'Yes,' said Fiona, numb with disbelief.

Feeling awkward, as if he had overstepped the mark, Douglas began to retreat, murmuring about another job over in Craigellachie. He handed his mug to Fiona and departed.

At first she believed none of it. Something sly in Douglas's manner predisposed her to think he was exaggerating, or even lying, for conscious dramatic effect. Life in Aberavon was so tedious that the locals had to do something to amuse themselves, and perhaps that something was telling stories.

Or perhaps that something was drinking. Fiona tried to remember whether Alastair had ever spoken about his father drinking. But all she could recall were tales of fishing with his father, and shooting the occasional rabbit. Douglas had clearly been telling malicious lies. If there had been trouble with his father, Alastair would not have kept it secret. Alastair told her everything.

Douglas said that Graeme had beaten his wife, and Alastair too. It was inconceivable that her husband would keep that back from her. Inconceivable. Pointless to give these lurid allegations any more credence. Especially when you considered Alastair. It's common knowledge, Fiona decided, as she prepared for bed, that history, in these cases, repeats itself. If Graeme drank, then Alastair would too. Yet Alastair consumed no more alcohol than she did. If Graeme was abusive to women, then his son would be abusive to women. And no one, thought Fiona proudly, could treat her with more tenderness than Alastair.

Relieved at having proved Douglas wrong, she pulled back the duvet and got into bed. The obvious explanation – she could see it now – was that Douglas held some sort of grudge against Graeme. His slanderous tale was a way of settling old scores. So much for village life! Fiona couldn't wait to get back to Manchester. And there was only one week to go. With that comforting thought, she fell fast asleep.

As Douglas had predicted, the wind was up and blew vigorously around the corners of the house, whistling in derision, troubling the tangled branches of the trees and bringing with it the morning rain.

The rain did not deflect Fiona's purpose. Today she intended to go shopping in Elgin. Not boring old food shopping, but baby shopping. Although she did not need to go into maternity clothes yet, her skirts were getting a little tight around the waist. At least she would see what styles were available.

As she drove through roads lined with tall Scots pine, and past rolling hills with square new forests on their sides, like dark handkerchiefs laid out to dry, Fiona was quite cheerful again, and more certain than ever that Douglas's gossip was nine-tenths exaggeration. No doubt Graeme had on more than one occasion drunk more than was good for him, and perhaps Margaret had taken fright. She smiled to herself. There were no such skeletons in her cupboards.

Elgin itself completed the job of bringing her back to reality. She drove past Dr Gray's, the hospital where she would have been giving birth to her baby, had she been staying in Aberavon. She noticed the imposing building opposite it with its row of darkened stone urns on the portico, and its brash red double doors. That, Margaret had told her, was Maryhill, the old maternity hospital, where she had been confined with Alastair. Fiona wondered if it was where Penny was born too. It was strange to think that her parents had been here. For that reason, or perhaps because of the traffic, the shops, and one or two cafe-bars, Fiona preferred Elgin to anywhere else in the area.

The town was busy, as people were shopping for the weekend. Fiona made her way to the baby section in Boots and happily examined sterilisers and plastic bibs, Babygros and disposable nappies. She hoped that someone would look at her and guess she was expecting. She stuck out her stomach just a little and then smiled at her childishness. Of course it was far too early to buy anything for the baby. Not only that, but she'd be better off waiting until she returned to Manchester to buy maternity clothes. The selection would be so much more up-to-date.

Fiona left Boots and strolled across the pedestrianised area to Ryman's. She was attracted by the idea of buying some magazines about pregnancy and having a baby. In the store she was spoiled for choice, but finally selected two which had features on maternity wear, and health care for the expectant mother.

When she paid for them at the till, she realised she was low on cash. Remembering that her bank was a few doors away, she resolved to go there next.

There was a short queue outside the two cashcard machines. Fiona waited until a young man vacated the one on the right. She inserted her card, selected the amount of money she wanted, and waited. There was a pause. Then a message appeared on the screen. The bank would be keeping her card, and was unable to give her cash today.

Annoyed, she jabbed at some of the buttons. Nothing happened. The machine reverted to asking the next customer to insert his card. Fiona felt herself redden. This was silly. There had to be a mistake. All of Lily's money was in their joint account, and Alastair's wages had only been paid in recently

She walked straight in to the bank and rang the bell at the enquiries desk. A dark-haired woman with a neat cravat and name badge came forward.

'Can I help you?'

'Yes. Your cashcard machine's just swallowed my card and won't give it back.' Fiona smiled good-naturedly. There was no point getting angry with the cashier, who was an innocent party.

'I'm afraid there's little I can do,' said the cashier, looking concerned.

'But there has to be. Without my cashcard I can't write cheques or take out money. I must have it back.'

'I'm afraid I don't have the authority to open the machine.'

Fiona's irritation was mounting.

'Can I speak to the manager, please?'

The cashier went away, and Fiona was aware that a couple of other people had come to stand behind her in the queue. When the cashier returned she brought a fair-haired, rather portly man with her.

'Your cash machine has swallowed my card and I need it,' Fiona said, raising her voice.

'Have you been having trouble with your card recently?' he enquired.

'No. Not at all. And I'm not overdrawn, nor have I been.' Fiona tapped her foot impatiently on the floor. Why was everyone being so stupid?

'If you don't mind waiting a moment,' said the manager, 'I'll check the computer. Do you have your cheque-book with you?'

Fiona handed him her cheque-book, which had the details of her account. She told herself to be patient; all this stress was bound to be bad for the baby. Even if the card was irretrievable, the bank manager would surely let her withdraw some money to tide her over until she received a new card. He returned to the desk.

'I'm sorry—' he glanced at her cheque-book' – Mrs Gordon. I'm afraid you do seem to be overdrawn. Just a little over three thousand pounds.' He handed her a computer print-out. 'I'm afraid there's nothing we can do.'

'But this is wrong! You've made a mistake.' Fiona felt as if she was living through a nightmare.

'I see, Mrs Gordon, that your account is a joint account.'

What was he implying? That Alastair had taken out all their money? This was getting more and more ridiculous. Fiona tried to salvage what dignity she had left.

'I shall speak to my husband immediately, and when the error is cleared up, we shall be changing banks.' She marched out, face burning with humiliation.

She did not have enough money to ring Alastair from a call box. Fiona ran to the car park, and immediately set off home. It was vital she get back as quickly as possible, so she could ring Alastair during working hours. The flat he was living in did not have a phone. Gradually her speed crept up to sixty miles an hour as she neared Aberavon.

Alastair was not at work. They told her he had left early; the man she spoke to seemed to think he was going up to Fiona for the weekend. She thanked him, and replaced the receiver. It wasn't true. They had planned to spend this weekend apart. Obviously this man knew little of their situation. She would have to speak to someone who did.

She sat drumming her fingers on the side of the settee. Who could she call? Paul and Janice? They were in the process of moving out of her house in Greenmount; for all she knew, Alastair could be there helping them. In fact, that was highly likely. She knew Alastair felt bad about having to give them notice.

She dialled the number of her house in Greenmount. As she waited for a reply she tried to decide exactly what to say to Paul or Janice, if they should answer. Pride dictated that they should not know there was anything wrong. Her heart was beating rapidly. It was Janice who answered the phone.

'Hi. It's Fiona.'

'Fiona! How lovely to hear from you.'

'Everything all right?'

'Fantastic. We love it here. I'm so glad we're going to do it all without an estate agent. Much simpler, don't you think?'

'Do what?'

'The sale of the house. Alastair said you were happy for it to go ahead. You are, aren't you?'

'I didn't know . . . yes, yes, of course.' Fiona took a deep breath to still her pounding heart. How could she ask Janice now for Alastair's whereabouts? She decided to stall for a moment.

'By the way, I was worried the washing machine might be playing up. If it does, tell me, because it's still under guarantee.'

'The washing machine?'

'The washing machine – in the utility room.'

'But we haven't got a washing machine. Alastair took it with all of the other furniture.'

Suddenly everything went out of focus. Fiona felt very, very sick. Nevertheless, she was surprised to hear how cool and self-possessed she sounded.

'Of course. That's silly of me. I'm so forgetful, I'll lose my head one of these days. Have you seen him today?'

'We haven't seen him since we agreed the sale. He's at the other end of town now.'

'Right. Oh, no – there's a pot about to boil over. I must go. I'll see you when we're in Manchester.'

Fiona replaced the receiver and realised she was shaking badly. She stilled her quivering hand by raising it and putting her fingers in her mouth. She was an intelligent, rational woman, and the only possible explanation for the events of the day occurred to her in all their starkness.

Alastair had sold her furniture, and not told her about it. He was preparing to sell her house, too, without having sought her permission. Therefore the bank might very well be right, and all the money might be gone. They were deeply in debt, and Alastair had not told her about that either. Even the house she was living in was not hers, but Margaret's.

She rose from the settee. Her legs felt unsteady. She had to decide what to do next. Her nausea had returned, and with it an irresistible urge to open her bowels. The feeling came as a relief. She had to attend to herself; she need not think about this bizarre new situation.

Fear had brought this on, thought Fiona, as she pulled toilet paper from the roll to wipe herself. She did so, and then saw the blood. Where had that come from? She wiped herself again. There really was blood. For one moment she thought, Well, it's only my period, and then she thought she shouldn't be having a period because she was pregnant.

Then she guessed she was having a miscarriage.

'Please, God, no!'

Terrified, she made her way back to the settee, where she put up her legs, just in case that would help. Because the most important thing of all was that she shouldn't lose her baby. The baby was all she had left.

What should she do now? Fiona didn't know. She stared up at the antlers above the fireplace. She had never been in this situation before. She would ring her mother. Her mother would tell her what she had to do. Fiona reached for the phone, and listened to the steady double ring, and waited, and waited. Was that dampness she felt between her legs, blood? The phone rang, and rang, and rang. There was no reply.

After an infinity, she replaced the receiver. And only then did she start to weep.

The doctor was very kind. His soft brown eyes and youthful optimism reminded her somehow of Alastair.

'I'd advise complete bed-rest,' he said. 'Your bleeding seems to be quite light. It could easily be caused by a slight separation of the placenta from the uterus.'

'What will happen?' Fiona asked him.

'There's every chance it will grow back, and you can have a perfectly normal pregnancy.' The doctor smiled at her again. He felt much sympathy for this pretty English girl. He himself had only been a father for two months.

'But remember, if there's an increase in bleeding, or any pain, ring the clinic immediately.'

These words chilled Fiona. As the doctor spoke them, they

sounded like a prediction rather than a possible line of development. If only he could assure her that everything would be fine.

'Will you be able to stay with her?' The doctor addressed these words to Margaret Gordon, who was standing a little way away from them, hands clasped tensely together in front of her.

'Of course, Doctor.'

'That's good. Now, with a bit of luck, I won't need to see you again – at least until your next ante-natal check.'

'But I'm going to be having my baby in Manchester.'

'I'm afraid you won't be able to go anywhere for a while, Mrs Gordon.'

Until the doctor said this, Fiona had not thought about how this threatened miscarriage would upset her plans. She was well and truly stuck here now. Yet dismay at this thought was lightened by the doctor's optimism. He said she might not lose the baby. She would hang on to that.

Margaret took him to the front door, and watched him climb into his Range Rover. She waited for a moment, then closed the door and returned to Fiona, who was lying on the settee, the duvet from the double bed around her. The vision of her white face above the brightly coloured duvet stunned Margaret again. Not for the first time she felt a spasm of guilt.

'He says I might not lose the baby,' Fiona said.

'That's right.' Margaret perched on the edge of the cane armchair.

'We'd better find Alastair.'

'We had.'

'I can ring Penny. She'll go to his flat and find him.'

'I'm sure he'll come home as soon as he hears the news.'

These brief exchanges between the women bobbed up and down on a sea of silence. For when Margaret had arrived in answer to Fiona's frantic phone call, she had blurted out that her account was overdrawn, that Alastair had sold her furniture, and that she had begun to bleed. All those words had tumbled out, then the doctor arrived and the opportunity to talk of Alastair was lost. Now there was the opportunity, neither woman was prepared to begin.

In the end it was Fiona who possessed more courage. For she had the baby to think about, and needed to know everything, because she had to remain in control for the baby's sake.

'Has Alastair had difficulties with money before?' she asked Margaret, in a small voice.

'Yes.'

'What sort of difficulties?'

Margaret tried to look her daughter-in-law in the face, but the effort was too much for her. Instead her eyes strayed to Ben Voulin, its canopy of dark rainclouds giving it a menacing air. She clasped her hands in her lap more tightly than ever.

'There have been episodes when—' Margaret could not find a euphemism – he's gambled. It started when he was a student. We brought it under control then. There have been other times.' Now she spoke more rapidly. 'But after he met you, I was sure it was all over. I've never known him so happy. He told me, the first time he came to Aberavon after meeting you, that he wanted to keep straight now. I felt he was telling the truth. I was so thrilled when you married.'

'Nobody told me,' said Fiona.

'Alastair needed a fresh start. I truly believed this was the new beginning he needed. I thought if he told you the truth, you might not have him.'

Fiona was silent

'I never expected him to go back to his old ways. I can only think that he couldn't take the separation from you. He's so very fond of you, Fiona. He should have given up his job when he got married. I wanted him to. That's why I gave you this house. I thought he would be better off away from temptation.'

'I understand now. You didn't put the house in his name because you were frightened he'd lose that too?'

Margaret was silent.

Fiona's face was stony. 'You should have told me.'

Margaret knew she could never explain to her young daughter-in-law why she could not have told her. Guilt and shame stopped her mouth. It was her fault Alastair gambled. The dark memories of the boy's misery haunted her. It was Graeme's fault too, she knew that, but it was her fault as well. In some way, she deserved it all. She hung her head.

Fiona licked her dry lips. Alastair had lost all her money, Lily's money, her savings; he'd sold her furniture and promised her house to Paul and Janice. She had no employment. A baby was on the way. This was the fate of all her dreams. Why didn't she see it coming? There must have been clues, had she been perceptive enough to see them.

But there was no point in blaming herself. She had to decide what to do now. Assuming she kept the baby – as she was determined to – should she leave her husband and start afresh, or pick up the pieces of her marriage? What sort of marriage was it? In the few months they had been together, she had lost everything. Everything except Alastair himself. Part of her, that was soft and supple before, now hardened to the texture of steel.

'You should have told me,' she repeated.

'I'm sorry.'

'Gambling is really an illness, isn't it?' said Fiona, thinking aloud. 'In a way, he can't help it.' Now it occurred to her that all that Douglas had told her was true. Alastair was not the only addict in the family. To think of Alastair as an addict gave her a sharp physical pain. Then she thought of Penny and her agony column. Her sister had often written about addiction, and knew places where addicts could receive help. Ought she to confide in Penny?

Margaret rose.

'I'll find you something to eat,' she said. 'You must eat. I know you won't be hungry, but there's the baby . . .'

Fiona sat deliberating. If she told Penny, then Rose and Harry would know too. She would be an object of pity. She couldn't stand the thought of that. Telling Penny would be a last resort.

214

If only she could see Alastair, she was sure she would know what it was she ought to do. Besides, her last conversation with Penny had been difficult. Her sister had seemed distant, and when Fiona had begged her to describe her new car, she'd brushed it aside. Perhaps she already knew more about Alastair and felt guilty for not telling Fiona.

But the most important thing, she thought to herself calmly, as Margaret pottered around in her kitchen, was to find Alastair. That, at least, she could get Penny to do for her. Her threatened miscarriage would provide excellent cover, so they would not even have to talk about the other thing. Fiona picked up the receiver and dialled her sister's number.

Penny was on her knees by the cupboard under the kitchen sink, stretching to bring a saucepan without a handle from its dark recesses, when the telephone rang.

'Damn!' she exclaimed. If only she could be allowed to get on with her packing, she'd be through it in no time. She scrambled to an upright position and pushed the beaded curtain aside to reach the phone.

'Penny Green.'

'It's me, Fiona. I wonder if you could do something for me? It's just that I need to get in touch with Alastair rather urgently and—'

'Is something wrong?'

'I've had a little bit of bleeding, and I've been prescribed bed-rest.'

'Oh, Fiona!'

'Don't start feeling sorry for me otherwise I'll go all weepy on you. Only Alastair doesn't know yet, he's left work and his new flat doesn't have a phone. 87b Latham Street. You couldn't just pop over there?'

'Immediately.'

'That's great.'

'Just because you're bleeding, it doesn't mean you're going to lose the baby, Fi.'

'I know. I've seen the doctor.'

'The important thing is to rest and not to worry. You mustn't worry. I'll get Alastair now, and then I'll ring.'

Penny grabbed her coat, set the alarm and was off. She liked to be active in a crisis. Poor Fiona. Penny could imagine what she'd be going through, and all alone too. The sooner she got back to Manchester, the better. She started the engine. Luckily she knew where Latham Street was. It was a rundown main road that bisected one of the routes into town, not somewhere she would choose to live. She was surprised that Alastair had ended up there, although she was aware they had been renting out Fiona's house. Still, it would only be temporary.

The afternoon was ending as Penny found a space for her Mazda opposite a newsagent's on Latham Road. She started to look for 87b. It sounded like a flat. She strolled along the line of shops, past a Pakistani grocer's where tables in front of the shop displayed an exotic array of vegetables. She walked past a launderette, an optician's with metal shutters fixed firmly down, and came to a side road that intersected the street. Across the main road was a Netto supermarket, and a small block of dilapidated flats.

Penny felt increasingly uncomfortable. First, she hated to break the news to Alastair that Fiona was having a threatened miscarriage. Then, she was disturbed by this decidedly seedy place where he had chosen to live. Also she felt her own changed response to these surroundings. The Penny of even a few months ago would have felt angry that there was money to be spent on sports stadiums and Olympic bids, but nothing with which to renovate slums. Now she merely felt thankful that when her mission was over she could go home and continue with her preparations to move to a swanky new apartment. Her father was right: life certainly wasn't fair.

Across the side road was a barber's shop, and looking into the window Penny could see the interior clearly. There was a line of white basins, men sitting on one side reading newspapers, and a tall barber in a short-sleeved shirt intently cropping the hair of a white youth. She stopped outside the front door. This was number 87.

She hesitated to enter this all-male enclave, but knew she had to do it. As she expected, her presence stopped all proceedings. There was silence except for the jingle of Piccadilly radio in the background. The barber and his customers looked at her with undisguised curiosity.

'I'm looking for Alastair Gordon,' Penny explained.

'You can't get to his flat this way,' the barber told her. 'Go round the back. Second floor.'

Penny knew what the men were thinking. That she was some woman of his.

'I'm his sister-in-law,' she explained icily. Seeing the ironic smile on the barber's face, she wished she hadn't said that. The shorn youth on the chair grinned at her.

Penny walked round the back of the shop, past a low stone wall, and opened a gate that led to a small back yard where an old mattress lay twisted, its metal interior rusted and open to view. An open plastic dustbin gave off an unpleasantly sweet aroma. A door painted only with undercoat stood ajar, and Penny pushed it fully open.

In front of her were some bare wooden stairs. She mounted them with growing distaste, arrived at the first-floor landing and ascended again, until she reached two rooms. One was a bathroom. The other door was locked. Summoning all her courage, she rapped loudly at it. There was no reply.

She waited and knocked again. The complete absence of sound in the building confirmed her suspicions that Alastair was not there. Penny felt frustrated and ill at ease. After a time she came down the stairs, still undecided about what to do next. As she reached the door to the yard, it opened in front of her, she stepped back and came face to face with Alastair.

She jumped, and so did he.

'Penny!' cried Alastair.

'Yes. Fiona sent me round. She said you don't have a phone here.' Penny looked around the dark, dank hallway.

'Is there any reason?' Alastair's heart was pumping loudly. Penny registered the alarm on his face and softened to see it. That he cared for her sister was more than evident.

'I'm afraid there is. Fiona's started bleeding. Not too badly, the doctor said. You'd better ring her.'

'Will she lose the baby?'

'Not necessarily. She's having bed-rest.'

'I'll get straight up there. Are you sure she's all right?'

'Yes, I'm sure.'

Alastair looked at his watch.

'I think it's too late to get the train.'

'Can't you drive?'

'Fiona has the car.'

'Of course. I know, why don't you rent a car? Salford Car Hire's just down the road.'

There was an embarrassing silence during which Penny understood that Alastair did not have the money to rent a car. That was why he was living in a slum.

'I'll treat you,' she said. 'Have you got your driving licence?'

'Upstairs. Just hang on, and I'll be with you.'

Alastair flew up the stairs. Penny's mouth set in a grim expression. Something was wrong, and it wasn't just the threatened miscarriage. Did Fiona know Alastair was living like this? Ought she to tell her? The answer to both of those questions was a resounding 'no'. The last thing Fiona needed right now was anything else to worry about.

Alastair stood anxiously in the foyer of Salford Car Hire as Penny wrote a cheque at the desk. Understanding little about women's problems, he had no way of knowing the seriousness of this bleeding. But it sounded bad. In a way, he had been expecting it. He hadn't been too lucky lately. He had been hoping to use the weekend to straighten himself out. Now that wasn't to be. At least there was no indication that Fiona knew about their money difficulties. Did Penny?

He glanced at her, Fiona's elder sister. She wasn't like his wife at all. She looked a strong kind of woman, he thought. It was good of her to fork out for the car. She obviously cared about Fiona. Yet she frightened him; she looked at him as if she could read him like a book. As if she suspected something. He decided to try to bluff his way out of this awkward situation.

She came back with the car keys.

'This is good of you, Penny,' he said. 'I'm just a bit short of funds right now.'

'I see.'

'Let me tell you how it is. I stood security for a loan for a friend, and he went bankrupt. I'm just trying to recoup my losses, save a bit of money.' He put a hand on her sleeve. 'Please don't tell Fiona. I'll speak to her myself, when she's out of the woods.'

'OK. But mind you do. The car's outside.'

Alastair made his way to the Sierra in the forecourt, put his case in the boot, got into the car and waved goodbye to Penny. She waved back to him, deep in thought.

When Alastair arrived at the house at midnight, there was still a light shining in their bedroom window. Hastily he unlocked the door, threw his case in the hall, took the stairs two at a time, and opened the bedroom door. Fiona had just woken from a doze. Sleepily she put out her arms to greet him and he came to her. They embraced for long time.

Then Alastair sat on the side of the bed, holding Fiona's hand.

'So there has been more bleeding?' He knew this as he had rung her from the service station.

'Yes, but only a little. It's not got any worse. I'm going to keep this baby,' she told him. Her determination was impressive.

'You must rest,' he said. 'I'm here to look after you now.'

'I know. Come to bed.'

Fiona decided to leave it until the morning before she spoke to him. It would do neither of them any good to have a scene at this time of night. So she waited for her husband to come to join her, and cradle her tenderly in his arms. Whatever difficult decision she would have to take in the morning, she wanted a night of peace first. For the baby's sake.

In the morning, there was no more bleeding. A wave of optimism buoyed Fiona's spirits. She made her way downstairs to the settee, despite Alastair's protests. She was not ill; she refused to lie in bed all day.

Alastair, still in his dressing gown, brought the duvet to her. Fiona cocooned herself in it.

'Come back here for a moment, Alastair.' She took a deep breath. She was ready now, to talk about the other thing.

Her husband turned from his way to the kitchen and smiled at her, wrapped in the duvet like a brightly coloured chrysalis.

'I know all about the money,' she said to him, quite calmly.

He stood entirely still. Not a muscle, not a hair on his body, moved.

'We're approximately three thousand pounds overdrawn, Lily's money has gone, and my furniture too. You're hoping to sell the house aren't you? Is that all?'

Alastair waited. This calmness was a front. The axe was about to descend. He said nothing.

'I asked you, is that all?'

He might as well tell her the truth. 'There are another couple of loans.' The pain of saying this in front of her was torture to him.

'I trusted you,' she said.

This was a living hell. He felt steeped in sin.

'I don't see how a marriage can survive without trust.'

So it was all over. He had lost her. He was alone in a void and knew he would not be able to bear it.

'In future, Alastair, you must always tell me the truth. If you do, we can get through this.'

He stood before her, head bowed, like a convict condemned to death.

'Alastair. Come to me. I said it was all right.'

It was all right! He was reprieved! He'd never loved his wife as much as he did at this moment. Slowly he approached the settee and knelt by her, burying his head in the duvet, ashamed to look at her, wanting the comfort of her nearness.

'Hush,' she said.

She seemed tranquil, as if she didn't mind. Alastair could not believe it. He thought that as soon as he began to speak, she would scream at him, hurl abuse at him.

'Please say something, Alastair. It's all right. I just want you to be honest.'

He heard the word 'honest', but it meant nothing to him. His head was full of strategy. If he told her everything, he might not be able to gamble again. But if he told her everything, she would help him cope with his losses. She might know where they could get hold of some more money. Fiona stroked the top of his head gently, and the touch reminded him painfully of his mother's touch, soothing him when she herself was in pain, and how desperately, then, he'd wanted everything to be all right. Just like now. He would have done anything to erase the nightmare of the last few weeks.

'Tell me how much we owe?'

'There's the overdraft. And a friend lent me a few thousand. I think that's all.'

That was more or less as Fiona had expected.

'OK. I want you to promise me you'll stop gambling. Where do you gamble?'

She was genuinely curious. Gambling was an activity that had played no part in her life.

'The usual places. Casinos, bookies.'

Fiona shuddered. She had never even been inside a book-maker's, and couldn't understand how her husband could be attracted to such a sordid world.

'Promise me you'll stop?'

'I promise.' Alastair meant it absolutely.

'If we let the sale of the house in Greenmount go through, then we can pay off your debts and start afresh. When the doctor says I can get up again, we can live in your flat.'

'No! No – you wouldn't like that. We'll tell Paul and Janice we've changed our minds.'

'But we must pay off the debts.'

'Then you'll have to stay here.'

'I know.' Fiona felt the disappointment like a lead weight. But it was the least of all the evils.

'I'll have to stay in Manchester. I need to earn some money.'

'I understand. I don't mind – so long as you stop gambling.'

'I will, Fiona. I promise.'

It was true. He was heartily ashamed of himself. And yet, he couldn't believe his luck. He had dreaded the day she would find out about his problems, and now it had come, and everything was going to be all right. Deep down he had always believed he was lucky. Luck wasn't always there at the gaming tables, he knew that now. But he was lucky in his wife.

'Alastair, look at me.'

He raised his head and did as he was told.

'Why do you gamble? I want to understand.'

Alastair wanted to tell the truth. How empty the nights seemed, how he felt he deserved some activity and excitement. How he was drawn towards the promise of riches, and even got a charge from that gutted feeling of seeing his chips swept away. How life held meaning when he gambled. How it was the most intense experience he ever felt. But the words would not come.

'I don't know. I hate myself for doing it, for hurting you.' That was true. He hated himself now with a viciousness that frightened him.

'Then think of me when you want to gamble again. I know you can stop. I believe in you.'

These were comforting words. Alastair held on to Fiona's hands very tightly.

'Everything will be different now,' he told her. 'Trust me.' As he spoke these words, Alastair knew they were true. He felt a rush of exultation. He suddenly lifted the duvet and a rush of cold air attacked Fiona's stomach.

'And you too!' Alastair announced to his offspring. 'I promise

222

you too. Now you stay where you are and don't go giving your mother any more frights. We'll have trouble with this one.' He winked at Fiona.

She felt tears of gratitude and relief swell in her. Everything was going to be all right. Trust bred trust. She would keep her baby, and she would keep her husband. As she imagined it, so it would be.

Alastair's heart was lighter than it had been for ages. The sword of Damocles had fallen, but it had missed him. Now he would certainly give up the casinos, the bookies, the lottery tickets and the card sessions. He had a little space to tie up a few loose ends, and see if he couldn't salvage something. Fiona would not regret trusting him. No one, but no one, knew just how much he loved his wife. Now, he was going to prove it to her.

Chapter Twelve

When Penny arrived home from seeing off Alastair, she found her mother standing by her front door. She guessed immediately that Rose had heard the news about Fiona's miscarriage and had come to discuss it. So Penny hurried out of her car and began to talk as she walked up the drive.

'Alastair's on his way to Scotland,' she panted, 'and Fiona says there's not been much more bleeding.'

Penny noticed that her mother seemed bemused, and then saw the large suitcase by Rose's side.

'Are you going there too?' she enquired. 'There won't be a train until the morning?'

'I don't know what you're talking about, Penny, but can you tell me inside? I've been here for at least an hour.'

Once inside, Penny began straight away.

'Haven't you heard? Fiona's started bleeding. She's scared she's going to lose the baby. I've just been to Alastair's to tell him. He's on his way up there. Do you know, he's living—' Penny broke off. She could see she was going too quickly for her mother, who was now looking frighteningly pale.

'Now – don't worry. Alastair rang her again, and she said it was only very light, and the doctor said she just needed plenty bed-rest. I spoke to her – she seemed quite composed. If you like, you can get on the phone yourself and have a word. It'll put your mind at rest.'

'I will, later.'

Penny was taken aback by this. Something was evidently up.

'Why have you come round here with your suitcase?'

There was a pause.

'I've left your father.'

'Oh my God!'

Penny's first impulse was to laugh, which she succeeded in suppressing. She could not believe that her mother would actually do this – for years she had threatened to walk out on him, for years she had told Penny how much easier her life would have been without him, and even Harry himself had voiced the odd complaint. But that was how it always was, and that was how it was always going to be. Rose wasn't meant to *leave* Harry.

'You've left him?' Penny was certain that her mother would qualify her statement. Obviously she had left him for an evening, even overnight, but . . .

'I've had enough.'

'Right.'

Neither Penny nor Rose had sat down. They stood on either side of the large blue suitcase, facing each other. Penny decided she had better get her mother into the living room, despite the mess with all the boxes, because Geraldine had said she would call and the hall would soon be very crowded with the three of them. So Penny took her into the kitchen and sat her at the table.

'When you say you've left him, what exactly do you mean?'

'I was hoping I could stay here,' Rose said, in a tiny voice. At the last moment, her courage had failed her. She'd found she could not go as far as London.

'But I'm moving very shortly,' said Penny.

Would Rose expect to move into the penthouse apartment with her? That was definitely not on, Penny decided, and was instantly riven with guilt. She took a seat opposite, her face full of concern.

'You'd better tell me all about it.'

'I would have struggled on. At my age, I thought I had little choice. But your father's started to see another woman.'

'Another woman!' Penny was astonished. Fathers didn't do

things like that. She couldn't begin to think of her father as a man who would be attracted to women, or to whom women could be attracted. Harry was her *father*, for goodness' sake. 'You must be wrong. I mean, how do you know there's another woman?'

'The usual signs. Lipstick on a handkerchief—'

'Hardly conclusive.'

'And he asked me for money.'

'But that doesn't mean—'

'No, listen. I gave him three hundred pounds. He said he wanted to have some money to spend. This afternoon he took it to her house. He was quite open about where he was going.'

'No. I don't believe you.'

'You'd better believe me. I don't know how deep in he is, Penny. I do know the woman – one of the music teachers. She was at Fiona's wedding. I daresay it started then.'

'No. You've made a mistake. You've been brooding too much. There really isn't enough evidence.'

'Listen, Penny, I know. This isn't the first time.'

She was suddenly cold. This was something she had never suspected. She had believed her parents' arguments were caused by over-familiarity, differences in temperament, but not this. Penny felt as if she had been shaken like a glass snowstorm, and as the pieces settled, a whole new world was formed.

'Have you spoken to him? Have you told him you've gone?' Penny asked her.

'I left him a note.'

'Just a note. I see.' Penny drew a deep breath. It was surprisingly easy to solve other people's problems on a weekly basis, but this one was beyond her. Her father's apparent philandering shocked her profoundly; she was equally shocked by her mother's decision to go. She felt as if someone had cleft her with an axe.

'I think you need to speak to Dad.'

Rose's face brimmed with contempt.

'Look, Mum, you're angry like this because you've been

bottling it all up. Maybe he isn't having an affair. Maybe you've imagined it.' Penny was desperate.

'Do me a favour!'

'I mean, if it is true, then it's horrible.' The thought of her father with another woman made Penny feel physically sick. Now she sided with her mother. Yet it was wrong to take sides, she knew that. It was dreadful to be in distress and not to be able to turn to her parents, as they were the cause of it. In the past, when Rose and Harry had argued, there was always Lily, even if she did seem to revel secretly in the situation. Penny felt that she was close to tears, and wasn't sure whether they were for Lily, her parents, or herself.

'Penny, don't upset yourself.' Rose's voice was soothing now. 'There really is no need. You father and I can look after ourselves.'

That was just what Penny seriously doubted. She summoned all her strength. She knew it was up to her to sort out her parents.

'I've been thinking, you can stay here. I'm still obliged to pay three months' rent. You can stay here, and I'll move into my new flat.'

Rose thought for a moment. 'That's not a bad idea.'

'But you must speak to Dad,' Penny insisted. Rose's face hardened.

'I'm not letting you stay here unless you do. I'm going to tell him where you are.'

Rose gave an expressive sniff, indicating her disgust at the prospect, but her assent too.

'Now take your suitcase upstairs, because Geraldine's coming soon.'

'Your cousin Geraldine?'

'Yes. Dad suggested I contact her. The new flat isn't furnished, and she does image consultancy work. On places as well as people.'

'I thought you didn't care for your cousin that much?'

Penny shrugged uncomfortably.

'She was very nice when I rang her. Look, I haven't offered you a drink. Some tea?'

'That would be lovely.'

Rose watched Penny busy herself at the draining board and thought how lucky it was that Lily had left her so much money. Rose experienced a slight thrill at her own newfound independence too. She had never lived entirely alone before. There was her mother first, then Harry, and then the girls. Now there was only herself to consider. She felt as if she was on the brink of a new adventure. She was glad to be away. And yet something was disturbing her. What was it?

'Geraldine said she'd help me take some things to the flat, some boxes and stuff, and then she'd have a recce of the layout. Will you be OK by yourself?' asked Penny.

'Absolutely,' Rose confirmed. Now she knew what it was that had bothered her. Fiona. The bleeding could very well be the start of a miscarriage. She felt a rush of sympathy for her daughter. As soon as possible she'd find out how she was, and tell her to rest as much as possible. Yet Rose knew that a baby that wasn't all right would be aborted. A baby that was meant to survive would survive. Look at Penny.

And she did, as Penny set the drinks down on the table.

Penny had only just finished changing when she heard the sounds of a car coming to a halt, followed by a loud rap on the door. Quickly she ran her fingers through her hair, looked in the mirror, grimaced, ran her fingers through her hair again, and then gave up, knowing she would be hopelessly outclassed by Geraldine.

As indeed she was. As Penny came down the stairs she could see Geraldine at the open door, talking to her mother. Geraldine's rich brown hair was sleek and well-cut, her skin bronze, earrings platinum. Her cream suit was Versace, although Penny did not recognise it as such. She only saw in Geraldine a figure to whom, despite all her money, she could never hope to aspire. Some things came with breeding. Penny was brought up in a small terraced house and went to the local comp; Geraldine was a grammar school girl who had been fed aspiration with her cornflakes. Penny hardly understood why she had invited Geraldine to advise her about the flat. She hoped it wasn't because she wanted to impress her. That would be base. No, it wasn't that; it was because her money had freed her from the sort of inverse prejudice she'd carried around most of her life. Just because her cousin exuded wealth, it shouldn't prevent her from being likeable. Penny was generous enough to give her a second chance.

'Penny – hi! You look great. I've got a taxi outside. I was telling Aunty Rose she looks younger every time I see her. Do you have the keys? I'm so looking forward to this!'

Penny glanced quickly at her mother who seemed reasonably composed.

'Will you be OK, Mum?'

'I'll be fine. I think I'll give Fiona a ring now.'

Penny took her leave, and hurried down the front path with her cousin. As she entered the black cab, she felt a delicious spurt of guilt. She was leaving her mother and all her mother's problems behind, as it would be wrong to speak of them to her cousin.

'How is Fiona?' Geraldine asked, getting out a mirror from her handbag and checking her lipstick.

'Having bed-rest. She's been bleeding slightly.'

'Oh, no! How dreadful! Will she be all right?'

Geraldine was all concern. Penny was touched.

'We hope so. Alastair's on his way up to her.'

'Poor Fiona. How frightening!'

'It's the uncertainty,' Penny added.

'That jacket really suits you,' Geraldine said. 'Next?'

'Well, I'm not sure what to get next.'

'No – I mean, is it from Next?'

Penny laughed and blushed. 'No. British Home Stores. But I am hoping to get some new things shortly.'

'Good for you, Penny. I can't wait to see this flat. I've heard so much about the block. *Everyone* wants to live there.'

'Really?' Penny was not surprised. It was her cousin's business, after all, knowing what was fashionable and what wasn't.

'You must be doing very well on the paper to afford a penthouse apartment at Wharfside.'

'Not exactly.' This was awkward. Why was money so embarrassing to talk about? It was worse than sex. Penny flushed. 'Aunty Lily left me some money.'

'I thought so. But don't feel bad about it. Dad did tell me you've been left something, and to be honest, you and Fiona were much closer to Aunty Lily than I was. I hardly knew her. I think it's perfectly fair and I'm very happy for you, Penny. And Dad has enough anyway.'

Penny was relieved by Geraldine's generosity. 'Thanks. That's big of you.'

'Are you going to carry on working?'

'Yes, definitely. My job's important to me.'

Geraldine nodded, and they were quiet for a few moments as the taxi careered round a corner and turned into Deansgate.

'It was good to see your mother,' Geraldine said at last. 'Is she waiting for you to get back?'

'Yes. She's staying with me. Helping me move.'

'That's lovely. My mother would be afraid to get her hands dirty. Aunty Rose is so sweet. And so is your father. I love his sense of humour. My parents are always at each other's throats. They can't even bear to say good morning to each other sometimes.'

Penny appreciated Geraldine's openness. She felt better hearing that all parents argued. It meant she was able to put the business with her mother into perspective. Harry and Rose were bound to get together again, so she was foolish to worry.

'Tell me about Fiona,' Geraldine said suddenly. 'Did she inherit money too?'

'Some,' Penny said.

'As much as you?'

'I don't think so. Mum and Dad have been rather coy about it. They think we ought not to know exact amounts.'

'I understand that. It's so easy for people to get envious about money. I see it all the time with my clients. There's so much jealousy among top wage earners. The more money, the worse it gets. But you and I know there's more to life than cash flow.'

'Absolutely.'

'Oh, look! We're here. Penny – you have the most splendid view of the Bridgewater Hall. And the Time Tower too. Did you know it lights up in different colours for every day of the year?'

While Geraldine was effusing, the taxi drew to a halt outside the entrance to the apartment block with its red canopy stretching out into the street. Penny glanced at the taxi meter and was momentarily alarmed by the amount, then remembered she could well afford it.

'I'll pay,' she said to Geraldine.

'You're sweet,' her cousin said.

A uniformed concierge sat behind a marbled desk, and Penny introduced herself. He was all affability. The women waited by the floor-to-ceiling mirrors for the lift that would take them to Penny's flat. Self-conscious before her reflection, Penny turned away from it to face Geraldine.

'I'm renting for a year,' she said, excited now and therefore garrulous. 'It's an experiment – I've never lived in an apartment block before. Certainly not a posh one like this. Here's the lift.'

They walked into a spacious lift with a plush carpet and large mirrors, multiplying the images of Penny in her black jacket and glamorous Geraldine in her Versace suit. The lift purred to a halt at the eighth floor. Penny unlocked an unassuming door and they were both suddenly in a surprisingly large room, seeming all the more large because it was entirely empty. Penny switched on the lights.

'Oh, Penny,' breathed Geraldine.

Both women looked around them. The large, double-glazed windows overlooked the city of Manchester. A wooden parquet floor absorbed the warmth of the lights and shone in greeting.

A wide mock fireplace was set into the wall opposite. Otherwise the room was empty.

'There's a bedroom through there,' Penny said, pointing to the right, 'and a bathroom ensuite, although I don't know why because it's only a one-bedroomed flat, and there's another bathroom over there.' She pointed to the left. 'And the kitchen's through there. Otherwise this is meant to be a multi-purpose room, and so I was sort of hoping to have a work area for my word processor, and an eating area – I'll need a dining table and chairs – and then a sort of lounge area.'

Geraldine walked to the window and looked out over the curved roof of the G-Mex exhibition complex, the Bridgewater Hall and the Midland Hotel. Penny came to join her. She felt as if she owned it all. Now this was good for her ailing self-esteem! Then she turned and looked into the flat again.

'Penny,' Geraldine said, 'this place is going to be absolutely fantastic!'

Penny smiled to herself. She was in complete agreement. Up here, she felt different. The height of the apartment, its lack of clutter, were a blessed relief to her. It was easy to suppose, just for a moment, in Geraldine's words, that she *deserved* this. It felt so natural being here. The complications of her life fell away like burrs that had lost their grip. She could even cope with her estrangement from Rick. Or could she? But, no – just like Scarlett O'Hara, she would think about that tomorrow.

'Surprise!' Geraldine announced, and brought from a large bag she had been carrying with her all evening, a bottle of Moët and two plastic glasses.

'Sorry about the awful glasses but I was worried they'd smash or something. But congratulations, Penny. To you and your new life.'

Geraldine untwisted the wire and slowly pushed the cork out of the bottle. It exploded with a whoosh, and her jacket was sprayed with the foam.

'It's all over you,' Penny remarked, horrified.

'Never mind,' Geraldine said gamely. 'I'll pop it into the dry cleaner's tomorrow. I'm not due to see a client until Monday. It's important to have one really good suit. I've got to create an impression.'

They drank the champagne, and Penny believed she was beginning to understand Geraldine a little better now. She had confused the image – glamorous, sophisticated Geraldine – with the real woman. Her image was merely her work identity, as false as Penny's own Agony Aunt persona. This was a wonderful discovery. Penny much preferred to like people than not.

'There's nowhere to sit down,' she said.

'We'll sit on the floor.'

Their backs propped against the wall, the bottle of champagne between them, Penny and Geraldine surveyed the room.

'I like your idea of having different functional areas in the room. The fireplace will have to be the focus for leisure, and your workstation will need to go by a window. Where is the telephone socket?' Geraldine got to her feet and began to move round the room, looking for the telephone and electricity sockets. Penny watched her. It was a luxury to have someone else help you make decisions. Her father had been correct. There was no one else who could have helped her. At least something was going right. Penny took a large gulp of the wine and got up to accompany Geraldine. Together they discussed styles, colourways, textures.

'Of course I'll go shopping with you. They know me well at Kendals. But we must keep our options open. We must go to Tetrad in Preston – their sofas are out of this world. But look, Penny. You mustn't let me force you into anything you don't like. This is your apartment, and it must reflect your tastes. I'm not the sort of image consultant who tries to reshape people into the style I think they ought to have. I'm here to bring the essential *you* out, and help you find expression through the objects around you.'

Penny liked the sound of that. She felt a little light-headed. The champagne had affected her, as she had not had time to eat, and the discussions were now beginning to weary her. She wanted to sit again, relax, and drink some more.

Geraldine sensed this, and made the suggestion before Penny could voice it.

'But you must be tired now. Me too. What say we finish this bottle, then go and have some food?'

'Sounds good to me.'

Geraldine grinned at Penny in happy complicity. At that moment, Penny liked her very much indeed. She was the only person Penny could think of right now who was being kind to her, who was making no demands.

Geraldine privately thought that Penny could do without dinner, as she'd put on quite a bit of weight, and she wasn't exactly sylph-like to begin with. Penny, however, could afford to be self-indulgent in every sense of the word. And if Geraldine played her cards right, so could she.

The Colour Bar was a basement in Floyd Street. Penny remembered it as an off-the-wall antiques business, but obviously the owner had moved on to more lucrative things. As she and Geraldine walked down the stairs there was the thump of bass notes from a Wurlitzer juke box, and the buzz of animated conversation. Penny had the odd sensation of realising she was where it was happening. While Geraldine collared a waiter to arrange a table, she looked around her at the stark, minimalist decor and the old posters on the wall encouraging the clientele to 'Dig for Victory' and warning them that 'Careless Talk Costs Lives'.

Over in the far corner Penny thought she recognised someone. A presenter for Granada TV, she was certain. And with him were two notorious drag queens who hung out wherever the action was. So I've arrived, she decided, but through no merit of my own. She didn't feel so much out of place, but as if she was an onlooker. She wondered if Geraldine felt like that too.

Her cousin returned, and together they waited while the waiter cleared a table in the centre of the room. Meanwhile Penny regarded the menu written with coloured chalk on a blackboard above the bar.

'The olive and feta cheese salad is fabulous,' Geraldine whispered.

Actually Penny was attracted by the vegetable lasagne and chips, but realised that a woman couldn't be seen stuffing herself in a place like this.

'Great!' she said. 'And by the way, it's my treat.'

'No, I can't have that. It was my suggestion we go out for dinner.'

'Ah, but you forget,' said Penny waggishly, 'I'm employing you.'

Geraldine graciously conceded defeat.

Penny ordered another bottle of champagne. 'Do you come here often?' she whispered to her cousin.

'From time to time. A number of my clients hang out here. George, the owner, lives with a record producer whose ex-wife is a friend of . . .' Geraldine mouthed the name of an infamous Manchester celebrity. Penny was feeling quite excited. 'George has been known to turn people away, if he doesn't think they fit.'

That made Penny feel she'd had a narrow escape. And yet, with her money, and even her position on the newspaper, she wasn't out of place at all. Then why did she feel such a fraud? She would ask Geraldine.

'Why do I feel such a fraud in places like this?'

'It's not you, Penny. It's everyone else. You're the only *real* person here. Look over there – at that woman with the cropped blonde hair. I know her. Wouldn't you kill to have a figure like hers? Silicone implants. And the guy in the corner with his hair in a pony tail – he's working his way round all the women who will go to bed with him, and claims it's all research for the prize-winning novel he's going to write one day. He's on the social.'

All this was making Penny feel much better.

'And don't tell me – all the best-looking men are gay?'

'Or celibate. That's the latest thing.'

'Now that's me,' Penny laughed. 'I'm celibate.'

Their salads arrived. An ebony-skinned waiter placed the plates in front of them.

'By choice?' enquired Geraldine, as she watched Penny eat.

Penny savoured an olive then quickly swallowed it.

'Kind of. Well, no. I did go out with Rick Goldstone. You remember Rick – he was at Fiona's wedding?' Penny knew she was boasting, but in this setting it seemed acceptable.

'He's gorgeous, Penny. Lucky you. What happened?'

'I got rid,' she said cavalierly. 'I guessed he was only after my money.'

Geraldine was horrified. 'How rotten for you! But I'm not surprised. Not that I'm suggesting a man wouldn't want you anyway. But those good-lookers think they can get away with anything. And money is such a turn-on to a certain sort of person. I see it all the time.'

'He did say it wasn't my money he was after,' Penny said lamely.

'How did you catch him out?'

'It was when he said he witnessed Lily's will.'

Geraldine exhaled sharply. 'That was bold of him.'

Penny drained her glass. Recently she had been wondering whether she had been too harsh on Rick. Hearing Geraldine now, she was sure she'd done the right thing in rejecting him, and was beginning to feel rather sorry for herself.

'That's the problem with men. The good-looking ones are bastards, and the bad-looking ones – well, they're bastards too.'

'But surely, Penny, Rick's quite well off himself? I remember the way he was dressed at the wedding. Why would he want your money?'

Penny thought that was kind of Geraldine. She was a good friend. She owed it to her to explain.

'Do you know exactly how much I've got? Lily left me a quarter of a million.'

Geraldine's eyes widened fractionally. Penny wondered if she should have said anything. But all this secrecy about her money was getting her down. Besides, her cousin was used to money and would not be too affected.

'How wonderful!' she breathed. 'Who needs men when you have a quarter of a million?'

'Who indeed?'

'I bet that's why Aunty Lily never married.'

'You could be right there. Instead she used to go on all these holidays with Kitty. Maybe I should do that. You must come with me. I'll pay.' After three quarters of a bottle of champagne, this seemed like a good idea.

'That would be terrific,' Geraldine said. 'Where shall we go?'

'Lily went to Spain a lot. Torremolinos.'

Geraldine looked doubtful. 'The West Indies are where people are going now. You could do with the break, Penny. All this business with poor Aunty Lily dying and Rick and everything, not to mention the toll it must take on you, solving everybody else's problems – if anyone needs a break, you do.'

Put like that, Penny saw the sense of it. Yet Geraldine had also succeeded in reminding her of her mother at home, waiting for her. The thought was a sobering one.

'But there's my mother. And Fiona.'

Geraldine shook her head fondly. 'Forget about other people. Put yourself first for a change. You are harsh on yourself, Penny. Don't be.'

This was almost what Rick said. She was always putting herself down.

'Do you think I put myself down?'

'I do, rather. We must do something about that. I know a chap at the Oliver and Jo Salon who could soon sort out your hair. And your make-up – it's deliciously camp but just a bit sixties. Honestly, Penny, you've *so* much good raw material. I'd love to get to work on you. And have you thought of trying a body wrap? You can lose seven pounds at one sitting.'

'You're on,' said Penny.

Chapter Thirteen

When the banging started on Penny's door, Rose was in the kitchen, kneeling on the kitchen floor, a basin of soapy water by her side. She heard the noise and stopped what she was doing. At first she thought someone was trying to break in. She glanced at the heavy saucepan by her side, wondering how effective it would be as a weapon. Then the banging stopped. Rose stayed motionless. It started again. This time, she realised that the source of the noise was someone knocking repeatedly on the front door.

Perhaps she would not have answered it had the caller not been so persistent. Whoever it was obviously wanted Penny, not her. No one in the world knew where she was. Gathering this welcome anonymity around her like a cloak, Rose got to her feet and walked through the hall to the front door. She turned the key in the lock, and opened the door. It was Harry.

'So you're here,' he said. He started to walk in, but Rose barred his way.

'How did you know?' she countered, stalling a little.

'I didn't. I thought Penny would help me find you.'

Rose did not move.

'Let me in,' Harry begged. 'I can't talk to you like this.'

'There's nothing to say.'

'Is Penny there?'

'She's out.'

'If you don't let me in, I'll make a scene.'

Rose believed him. Angry at being out-manoeuvred she stood aside and let Harry enter, drawing her body in so they would not

239

touch. Once the door was closed and they were alone, adrenalin flowed through her, making her feel slightly nauseous.

Harry did not move from the hall.

'What did you mean by that note?'

'It was clear enough.'

'But you're wrong. There was nothing between me and Rita. It was your imagination.'

'My imagination, was it? So I imagined the three hundred pounds that disappeared from your wardrobe? So I imagined the lipstick stains? What do you think I am, an idiot?'

'OK, OK. I know what it looks like. The money was for her chimney. Penny said I should help her out.'

Rose felt sick. 'That's not true. I've been speaking to Penny and she said nothing about a chimney. You're lying, Harry.'

The fact that he was speechless made Rose all the more confident that she was right.

'Three hundred pounds. I gave it to you to spend on yourself, and you spent it on some floozy.'

'Rita isn't a floozy.' But Harry did not look particularly convinced. 'Her husband walked out on her, and left her with nothing. This was charity.'

'Charity!'

'Yes, charity. Not that you'd know much about that.'

'What are you saying?'

He took a step back.

'You know what I'm saying.'

Rose was livid. 'That I'm tight with money? That I hold you back? Well, here's a golden opportunity. You're on your own. Now you can spend all you like. Go back to your Rita. Tell her you're a free man. Because, Harry, I've had enough. I don't want you any more. I've had it up to here. Go on – go!'

As Rose gave herself up to the luxury of anger, she experienced an exquisite release. For years she had held herself in, scared of losing him. Now, as she gave vent to this volcanic, elemental wrath, she felt free for the first time.

'Go!' she repeated, but was glad to see he did not. Instead he stubbornly stood his ground.

'You don't know what you're talking about. I'm not having an affair with Rita. Though if I was, nobody would be surprised.'

'And just what do you mean by that?'

'When was the last time we . . .' He did not finish the sentence, but she knew what he meant.

'Do you ever make me want to?'

'I shouldn't have to. Let yourself go, Rose.'

'I suppose Rita let herself go?'

'Forget about bloody Rita! For the last time, nothing happened. Why don't you trust me?'

'Trust you!' The walls of Penny's hallway seemed to sway slightly. Now they were coming to it. Perhaps it was right that they should. 'I can tell you why I don't trust you. Do you want to hear?'

'That was years ago.' His voice was low and toneless.

'To me it feels like yesterday. I don't think you ever truly understood how I felt. I can still remember the look on your face when I found out. You couldn't meet my eyes. I don't think you've ever admitted to me that you knew how much you hurt me. You had nothing to say, except that you felt sorry for her. You felt sorry for *her*, but not for *me*. I was your wife, Harry, but you felt sorry for *her*.'

'We weren't ever going to talk about that again. You promised.'

Rose felt uncomfortable. Harry was right; she had broken a promise, and, of all places, in Penny's house. She was gripped with a foolish fantasy that the walls would absorb what she had just said. She dropped her voice.

'I couldn't help it. I thought it had started all over again.'

'At my age?'

Rose was determined not to be fooled again.

'You're right. I can't trust you.'

'So you're not coming home?'

The question was phrased in the negative, and so she answered in the negative.

'No.'

Slowly Harry turned, opened the door and walked out into the night air, defeated. His pathetic air tugged at her heartstrings and she would have called him back but pride forbade it. How would he cope without her? He never knew when the dustbin men were due; he never noticed when they ran out of margarine. Perhaps she ought to write him a list of the jobs that needed doing.

No, that was silly. He would have to fend for himself. It would do him good. She should have left him years ago. Rose walked back into Penny's front room, filled with packing cases, unplugged table lamps, piles of books and rolled up posters. She eased herself down on to the low settee. Her thoughts were a jumble, just like the room. She was right to have confronted him, and yet something in the way he spoke had convinced her he was telling the truth about Rita. There had been no affair. It was ironic that she should throw him out now, when she should have thrown him out *then*.

But when? At what point was a marriage over? Rose thought back to the early days, to the poverty. Yet that had not really been a problem. She'd been no stranger to poverty. She simply coped as best she could – with the inadequate bathroom down the hall, the stringent budgeting, the relentless office work. She knew it was not Harry's fault that he failed to make it as a singer. The real suffering began when she suspected she might not be able to have children. Her broodiness became obsessive, all-powerful. Everything else in her life was overshadowed by it – her mother's illness, their financial worries. None of them mattered because if she had a baby, she would be happy. It was all she wanted, and it was such a small thing. Everybody had babies. Everybody except her.

Month after month she waited, and nothing happened. Her longing for a child was an intense private grief. Once she tried to speak to Lily about it; her sister never understood. She told Rose that she'd been a fool not to think there would be difficulties. Neither of them had had regular periods; Lily hardly ever menstruated. Harry was more sympathetic but was convinced she was bound to conceive eventually. She could not bring herself to visit the doctor; they were for people who were sick, and she was not sick. She thought that if she gave up her job and rested she might fall pregnant, but they could not do that because they were too hard up. And so it was that she was trapped.

That was when it happened; that was when Harry betrayed her. While she was in the throes of despair, he let himself be tempted. That was when she should have left him, but she wanted the baby. And when it came, it was too late. Once again Rose felt the shock of discovering what it was that Harry had done. She remembered how he sobbed and pleaded with her. His eyes were wet with tears, and she couldn't stand it because she loved him then. So she took him back.

Maybe this time she would have taken him back too. Like the last time, it was probably not his fault. No doubt he was led on. Only this time there was one significant difference. When Rose realised what it was, the tears started to her eyes. This time, she wasn't sure if she still loved him.

Harry got into his car and stared through the window, seeing nothing. The unfairness of it hit him smack between the eyes. He had done nothing, and she had thrown him out. It would have been laughable if it had happened to someone else but it wasn't, because it had happened to him. Well, it would serve her bloody well right if he went straight back to Rita. What was the point of being punished for a crime you didn't commit? Yes, he was furious. Women – he hated them all!

In a gesture of bravado he revved the engine again and again, making the engine roar his fury. Stupid woman – she refused to listen to him. Never gave him a chance. Now it was too late. With a surge of determination he released the handbrake and was off into the centre of town.

Yes, he was furious. It wasn't so much that he would be in

the house alone tonight; Rose had been so distant it had often felt as if he was living alone. It wasn't that. But had she thought how awkward it would be for him at school? She was retired and didn't have this problem. But when he went back to school he would be in the embarrassing position of having to explain – or hide – the fact she had left him. It was shameful. And his brothers would have to know too. And what would they think? Rose had been very, very selfish.

Harry slowed the car. He would have to think of ways to explain all this to the rest of the world. He could say that Rose was having a holiday with Penny. Or better still, he could tell everyone that she was having a nervous breakdown. These days they called it clinical depression. The idea had its attractions. He would explain that she had been acting out of character, and everyone would be impressed with how sympathetic and understanding he was. In fact, for all he knew she *could* be having a nervous breakdown. That would explain everything – her melodramatic gesture of leaving him, her low spirits. Yes, as soon as she came round a bit, he'd get her to go to the doctor. He would help her get better. As he became the rescuer, Harry's anger subsided. He could almost have patted himself on the back for being such a reasonable sort of chap. She was *unreasonable*, but he was reasonable. When Penny came home, she would sort Rose out.

Harry hummed a tune in the car, and smiled at its appropriateness: 'Always Look on the Bright Side of Life'. He was a man on his own now, and could do the sort of things that a married man couldn't – for one night at least. It was at that point that he spotted a pub, a fairly savoury sort of pub with modern decor, a blackboard outside advertising a snug and a large-screen Sky Sports channel. He decided there and then to stop for a drink. He turned into the small car park, resolved to make the best of this messy situation. And, moreover, if Rose thought he was such a moral reprobate, he might as well start acting like one.

The pub was respectable enough. Its interior walls were of bare red brick and it was empty, the TV playing to no one in particular. Harry ordered a beer and stood at the bar to drink it. He didn't much like beer but now its creamy richness soothed him and restored him to a sense of his own masculinity. As he drank, the alcohol anaesthetised any last traces of anger. He was ready now to think over what had just happened.

It was just that Rose had got the wrong end of the stick. When Penny got home and explained that, there would be a phone call, he would be summoned back and there would be a glorious, emotional reconciliation. So it was just as well they were apart tonight. Rose needed time to cool down. He needed a night alone too, after all that had happened.

It was then that he saw the woman. She was by herself, that was the first thing he noticed, and she was blonde – that was the second. Dyed blonde – Harry could tell that because the roots were showing. There were lines around her eyes, and the drink in front of her was a half pint of something or other and it was a delicate shade of pink. Cider and blackcurrant? Harry stole a glance at her again, curious. She was looking at him. There was something hopeless in her expression. He looked away.

Ought he to approach her? Perhaps she was in trouble. At the prospect of being able to be of some assistance his pride, almost mortally damaged before, was restored. He drained his pint, feeling slightly light-headed, and ordered another while debating what to do. The woman was very clearly watching him. There was an indefinable link between them. She wore a light black cotton jacket that had seen better days. He wondered if he should offer to buy her a drink.

Now Rose's words returned to haunt him. *I can tell you why I don't trust you.* They made him hesitate. Suddenly he was able to see himself as Rose saw him. To every woman he met, he tried to give something of himself. Was that bad? Harry didn't know the answer to that. He sipped at his pint.

The other woman had been a dyed blonde too, but then most women were in those days. Rose said he'd felt sorry for her, and that was certainly true, although he was also aware that she had used him. Had Rita used him too? He would not think about that. Instead his mind strayed back to the other woman. Rose hadn't mentioned that episode for years. Neither of them was ever supposed to talk about it. The understanding was that it had been excised from their minds and from their relationship. There were some very good reasons why that had to be so. Tonight Rose had lifted the taboo. Given permission to think about the other woman Harry did so, beer gently loosening the mental strait-jacket he had been in all these years.

All they had intended was to eat together. It was a business trip that had lasted longer than anticipated, and so they were staying on a Friday night when the hotel held its regular dinner-dance. He didn't object to the enforced intimacy; she was good company, laughed a lot, and enjoyed spending her money. Tonight she seemed to want to spend it on him. He had no problem with that. They each had a sirloin and some rosé wine, a little too sweet for him but she liked her wine sweet. Funny how no one went out for steaks any more. He hadn't had one in years.

As soon as they finished eating, the band began to play. It seemed impolite not to ask her to dance. She was all too willing, and he moved her around the dance floor carefully while she complained to him that the singer was flat. It was true; he was. So Harry sang along to the tune, in her ear, and she smiled appreciatively, and his vanity was flattered. Of course the words were romantic – all songs were romantic then.

When there was a smoochy number, they smooched. It was all play-acting with him and her. They knew each other too well for anything else. They danced together closely, the taffeta of her dress rustling against his suit, and the talcumy smell of her perfume reminded him of her femininity. She wore Coty's L'Aimant. Appropriate.

After the dancing was over, they had coffee and liqueurs. She was more subdued now, and as he looked at her he could see the way her blue eyeshadow had settled in the creases of her eyelids and this made him feel sorry for her, although he did not know why. A strand of her yellow hair was damp with sweat, and the skin above the neckline of her dress was pink. It was precisely because she was not attractive to him that he was so attentive to her. That was something Rose never understood. It was something he'd never understood himself until now.

Then what happened? They talked. Harry didn't talk about himself; that was not what women wanted to hear. Besides, it was good to forget about home. Rose was still not pregnant, and had been bothering him about going to the doctor. He would not have minded her going to the doctor, but a friend had told him the doctor would want to see him too. Harry did not like doctors. Especially did not like the thought of what the friend said the doctor would do. He would try to find out if there was anything wrong with Harry.

That Rose's infertility could be his fault, Harry could not admit. His friend had jokingly suggested he should give his equipment a dry run on somebody else. Harry was shocked at the idea, but like all bad ideas, it stayed in his mind. Did it influence him that night? He was never sure.

It was the woman – she was the one who had started the intimate conversation. It was she who said that she had never had a boyfriend who had lasted longer than three months. Nobody loved her. That was why, she told him, she was still a virgin. That had surprised him. He couldn't believe that – not for a moment. He wondered whether she was having him on, or whether she was making an advance. Why tell him otherwise? *I'm sure it's not all it's cracked up to be,* she told him. He assured her otherwise. She laughed, and he laughed. Both of them had had too much to drink.

Then what? She told him it was her birthday. September the thirteenth. He was upset because he did not know and had bought her nothing. She told him it didn't matter; he insisted that it did, called a waiter over, and ordered a bottle of champagne. He could ill afford it but would worry about that the next day. The waiter told them the bar was closing, and asked if they would like the drink delivered to their room? It was the woman who nodded. So it was her fault.

Her room was like his, small but select with heavy red velvet curtains that separated the two of them from the rest of the world. Her things were laid out on the mahogany dressing table. The waiter wheeled in a trolley with the champagne in a bucket. Since there was only one chair, they had to sit together on the bed.

What they were doing did not seem so wrong. He and Lily were old friends. She was his sister-in-law. He poured the champagne, they clinked their glasses, and he toasted her. They drank, their arms entwined. What else did he remember? The lamp by her bedside table, a red velvet lamp with little gold tassels. There was a painting above her bed of sheep, little cream slugs with black faces. She put the bedside lamp on and he stood up to turn the off main light. He sensed that she wanted the intimacy of the lamplight, and guessed that she thought she would look better in its velvety softness. She was right, she did.

It was the alcohol's fault. They shouldn't have drunk the champagne. That was what made everything seem so unreal. It was the room's fault. They were distanced from everyone and everything, marooned in a hotel in West Yorkshire, just the two of them. No one would ever find out what took place in that room that night. So what did it matter what they did?

What he did was to switch on the radio. It buzzed and crackled and muttered at them in obscure foreign languages that ebbed and flowed as he moved the dial. Then he found Luxembourg. There was a ballad playing; without either of them suggesting it they rose to dance, except there wasn't much room to dance, so they both swayed slightly to the music, cheek to cheek. It was then that Lily stopped being Lily and was just a woman. It must have been then, because Harry thought it would be all right to move his face so his lips were against hers, and he could give her a butterfly kiss. What was a kiss? He had kissed her before.

At any time she could have stopped him – at any time. When his hand moved round her back and found the zip of her dress, she could have stopped him. When he pulled the zip down, revealing her full cleavage, she could have stopped him. But she didn't. She kicked her dress to one side and continued to dance with him in her slip. Harry pressed himself to her, and knew she could feel his hardness. Still she didn't stop him.

As he stroked her thighs, and felt the tops of her stockings, she lost her identity for him, and then certainly she was just a woman, a woman who was not his wife, a woman who just wanted sex, not a baby. He discarded his jacket and unbuttoned his shirt. Did he undress her? Did she take her own clothes off? Harry could not remember. It all happened very quickly. In a few moments they were on top of her bed, almost naked, and Lily had switched off the bedside lamp. They were in complete darkness.

That made it easier still. He was a man, she was a woman. There were to do what men and women did. He unhooked her brassiere and curved his hands around her heavy breasts, burying his head between them, enclosing himself, inhaling her perfume. As he reached down to unhook her suspenders she put out a hand to stop him. She was always shy of her leg. So he stroked the smooth nylon of her stocking, moving his hand upward to the soft, bare skin at the very top of her thigh.

It was almost impossible for him to hold back. Guilt rode him with sharp spurs; the urgency was unbearable. He stroked the top of her thigh again, waiting for a sign that he should go further. But her muscles were tense and he realised she was completely immobile. He knew then that she was scared. To reassure and encourage her, he took her hand and placed it on his penis. She grasped it and her fingernails dug into him. The pain was exquisite. Now with his fingers he began to work at her, feeling her moistness, gratified by this sign of her arousal.

More than anything now, he wanted to enter her. He felt as if he could not hold on any longer. Yet Lily just lay there, waiting for him. He understood now that it was true, what she had said before; she really was a virgin. But it was too late. So gently, gently he opened her and pushed himself inside her tightness, and thrust, just once, twice, and came. As he did so, he realised he had used no contraception, and in his anxiety he pulled out of her. His climax was not over and his semen shot on to her thigh. She seemed to flinch at its wetness.

Of course he apologised – for his clumsy performance, for his eagerness, for everything.

'Is that all?' she asked him.

'I'm sorry.'

'I'm all sticky.'

'You'd better go and have a wash.'

Without turning on the lamp, she moved over to the hand basin turned on the tap and started dabbing at her thigh. His passion ebbed with the running water. What had he done? The horror of it hit him hard. The pipes in the bedroom gurgled. That was Lily, naked, washing his semen off her leg. He lay naked on her bed. This should never have happened. Quickly he reached for his clothes, putting them on as speedily as possible. He was thoroughly ashamed of himself. Neither of them spoke. There was just the sound of splashing as Lily washed, and the rush of running water. And the click of the door softly opening, and the snick of the catch as it fell back into place.

He never should have done it. That was why Rose couldn't trust him now. She had cause. Despite the beer, Harry was now entirely sober. He had done a dreadful thing, and it felt as if he had never been truly sorry until now. It had been his fault after all. When the woman opposite him moved from her seat to the bar, ostensibly to get another drink, and stood close by him, Harry moved away from her. Never, never again.

Except it was too late, because Rose had finally left him. Rose had left him, and he could think of no way of getting her back.

Chapter Fourteen

Penny pushed her hand through her hair and felt how sticky it was, sticky with sweat from the effort of the removal. She decided that as soon as she finished emptying all the boxes that were scattered around her new apartment, she'd jump into the shower. That was a necessity as Geraldine was coming round shortly, and bringing someone with her.

What else was there to do? Not a lot. Penny had been frantically busy all day, arranging her cups, plates and saucers in the immaculate kitchen, hanging a few familiar posters on the walls, arranging ornaments, finding homes for books and CDs – it was heavy, backbreaking work, and every bit as effective as the bodywrap she had tried three days earlier at Geraldine's insistence. Quite honestly she had felt like a trout about to go into the oven. That experience, she decided, was not to be repeated.

Penny surveyed her flat. There was an uncomfortable tension between the odds and ends she'd brought from her old home – the cane magazine rack, the fourteen-inch television – and the splendour of her new surroundings. Maybe Geraldine was right after all. She would have to change herself to go with the flat.

The haircut hadn't been too bad. It was fun, being made a fuss of, and having a young male assistant give her a scalp massage. It had amused her to watch the senior stylist play with her hair as if he were creating a work of art. He spun her round on the chair like potter's clay. Afterwards she had watched with alarm as more and more of her hair fell on to the floor. 'It'll be easy to manage,' he assured her. In the end Penny concluded that the hair she had been left with did look very nice; the only problem was, there wasn't enough of it. Geraldine said she looked wonderful, and Geraldine should know. Penny felt she'd been scalped.

Just one box to go. It was the miscellaneous box, and Penny had been flinging things into it right up to the last moment. Her black handbag lay at the top. She'd found it in her bedroom, underneath the bed, though what it was doing there, she couldn't imagine. She had half a mind to throw it away, as it was horribly like one of her mother's. She had an unfortunate habit of choosing things that were similar to Rose's. Hopefully Geraldine would cure her of that.

They had gone shopping to an exclusive outlet in an old factory where two earnest, slim young girls were producing fashions for more generous figures. Penny obligingly tried on a number. The long shift dresses, in black, grey, and peach, made her look as if she'd walked out of a Wagnerian production. Geraldine exclaimed that she looked incredibly sophisticated and Penny could just about imagine wearing one to a posh occasion. She admitted she did feel comfortable in a dress that hid all her bulges and bought the three.

She had already hung them up in her wardrobe and they looked perfectly at home there, perhaps more so than Penny herself. Now she stood by the door and was able to see the whole of her open-plan living area. The L-shaped cream leather settee placed in front of the fireplace, looked straight out of the pages of *Good Housekeeping*. In front of it was a Chinese rug that blushed with self-consciousness at the amount on its price tag. Just beyond the settee was the door that led to the compact, gleaming kitchen, whose purity had been sullied by Penny's old coffee mugs on the mug tree, and her stained saucepans on the saucepan rack. Immediately opposite her was the bedroom, and she thought with pleasure of the king-sized bed the delivery men had assembled there that afternoon. She had decided against buying a water bed. What if it sprung a leak? Her workstation, with computer, fax machine and what passed for a filing system, was placed by one of the two extensive uncurtained windows. Outside Penny could see that evening was drawing in; streaks of darker cloud gave substance and texture to the ultramarine sky. On the shelves between the two windows were her books, a colourful assortment of paperbacks, and her CD collection. Then there was a space; the dining table and chairs had not arrived yet. Penny was looking forward to seeing the tall, curved backs of the six chairs she and Geraldine had selected.

Her eyes came back to her settee, the assortment of ornaments and knick-knacks that were ranged on a shelf over the fire, a triangular multi-coloured candle too pretty to burn, a pot-bellied, bronze buddha, a porcelain pot pourri bowl without any pot pourri. By the side of the settee was the one remaining box to be emptied. Then the move would be complete.

It seemed a shame to disturb it, Penny's last link with her past. When it was unpacked, she would have transformed herself completely into the New Penny. And she had better get a move on, because Geraldine was due very shortly with the person whom she had been begging Penny to meet. Good-looking, experienced, reliable, a man who got results. Someone who Geraldine promised could turn Penny's life around . . . a personal trainer. He would escort her to the gym downstairs, and show her how to work out. Hard.

Yet Geraldine had been so good to her, it would be churlish of her to refuse. So Penny obligingly went through to the bathroom for a shower. It took her some time to find the right switch to get the thing to work; it was as bad as staying in a hotel. Finally a jet of satisfyingly hot water gushed out, and she began to wash away the grime of the day. This felt good.

It seemed a shame, Penny thought, to go down to the gym and get sweaty all over again. She quailed a little at the humiliation involved. She was totally unfit and knew it. Geraldine had told her that was nothing to be ashamed of; a few weeks intensive training would soon put it right. Before this intensive training actually started, it had seemed like a good idea. Now it did not. Penny began to wonder what excuses she could come up with. Could she say her period had just started? That usually scared men off. Or should she say that she was just too tired?

The door to her bedroom stood ajar. Stepping out of the shower, she accidentally caught sight of herself in the mirror. Penny grimaced. No wonder Geraldine was determined to help her! Though the funny thing was, since Geraldine had taken her in hand, Penny had been feeling worse about herself, not better. Her cousin's message was clear: in her natural state she would not do.

Suddenly Penny felt mutinous. She didn't have to wear those silly dresses or that minimising bra. And she certainly didn't have to meet the personal trainer. She was a big girl, in every sense of the word, and could make up her own mind. She smiled to herself, towelled herself dry, and deliberately put on her oldest jeans and a Chicago Bulls sweatshirt. She certainly did not want to go out that evening. She was going to stay in, finish her unpacking, and then if she was hungry later, she'd find the nearest takeaway and celebrate her arrival here in the only way she knew how. And if she spilt some chow mein on her new settee, well, it was hers.

Secure in her decision, Penny walked over to the window overlooking the entrance to the apartment block. There was Geraldine now, arm in arm with a tall man in a tracksuit. Was that the personal trainer? At all costs, Penny decided, she would not let them in.

There was a buzz on the intercom. She picked up the phone.

'It's me. We're here, Penny.'

'Oh, hi, Geraldine. Listen – I've not finished unpacking yet. I can't possibly let anybody come up. Can we call off tonight?'

A pause. 'Oh, but Penny, I've got Ryan with me and he'll expect to be paid.'

'That's OK. I'm happy to pay.'

'Shall I arrange to call with him tomorrow?'

'Ah – no. I just need some more time to think about it. OK?' Another pause.

'I'd decide quickly, if I were you, or someone else will snap Ryan up. He has very little free time.'

'Well, in that case, I'll give him a miss.'

'Penny, love, for your own sake—'

'For my own sake, I think I'll have an evening in.'

She replaced the receiver. Not for the first time, she began to feel uneasy about Geraldine. But that was something she would think about later. The packing case with the handbag on top was demanding to be emptied. She would do that first.

Geraldine turned to her escort.

'Damn!' she said.

'I told you you shouldn't have charged commission on top of my fee.'

'Damn, damn, damn!'

Ryan put an arm around her. 'I feel like some exercise. Coming back to my place?'

'Push off,' said Geraldine. She wasn't in the mood for him right now. Besides, a client of hers had issued an invitation to cocktails in the Midland. Geraldine knew it was advantageous to be there, and the hotel was only a short walk away.

'I've a business appointment. I'll give you a ring tomorrow.

He shrugged. 'As you like. I'm doing nothing all day.'

Geraldine gave him a brief kiss and walked off briskly. It was so annoying that Penny had refused to see Ryan. He was getting just a little tedious now, and she wanted to pass him on. As good as he was in bed, his conversation was pretty limited. He wasn't really right for her, although he would have done for Penny. Frankly, it was what her cousin needed. Geraldine was not too happy about the way she had been dismissed tonight. She was a little anxious that she was losing her grip on Penny. She didn't like the way Penny had laughed at her haircut or begun to hum the 'Ride of the Valkyries' in the Big 'n' Beautiful Salon. And Penny had no right to refuse her entry tonight. It was humiliating. Geraldine did not like to be humiliated.

Penny walked over to her CD player, selected some John Lee Hooker, and when his charcoal voice started singing the blues, walked over to the final box and eased herself down on the floor by it. She lifted up her old black handbag and wondered if she'd left anything inside it. She was about to open it when something else caught her attention. It was Lily's photograph album.

Some weeks ago Rose had given it to her when she had collected a number of Lily's possessions from Gladesmore. At the time Penny had felt unable to look at it, but now, insulated by her new surroundings, she realised she was strong enough.

But first she invoked her aunt who, after all, had paid for this flat. Lily Colman, who wore a thick orangey-red lipstick and caked her face with powder, and always wore perfume – Coty's L'Aimant. That wasn't the only smell Penny associated with Lily. She'd bleached her hair – the sharp smell of ammonia permeated her bathroom. Lily was a real-life Diana Dors. She'd taught her budgie Pip to wolf-whistle at her, and had told Penny her first dirty joke before Rose had deigned to explain to her the facts of life. Penny was baffled for weeks. Lily went dancing, had boyfriends, but fought shy of intimacy. With her, however, independence was a conscious, brave choice.

I suppose I shall have to choose independence now, Penny thought. Rick had not got back to her. Clearly that scene in the park had been their finale. She had gone too far. Thinking about it still pained her. How could she expect him to prove that her money wasn't important? Penny understood then that she wasn't a realist after all, but was living in a fairy tale. Rick wasn't a Prince Charming who needed to prove his devotion. There were no longer any dragons to slay. He was an ordinary bloke, and she had given him the boot. He had his pride too.

Except he wasn't an ordinary bloke. He was Rick Goldstone and she was in love with him but had effectively dismissed him. She was insane! But was it too late? Perhaps not. Certainly it was up to her to make the first move. So she jumped up and went to her desk, where there was a pile of change of address cards. She took one and addressed it to Rick. 'I'd love to see you,' she wrote, 'very soon', and felt her heart beating rapidly as she penned the words. This was much better for the cardio-vascular system than a work out with a personal trainer. Tomorrow she would jog down to the post office and post it.

Feeling happier, Penny returned to the box, almost tripping over the black handbag, sat down cross-legged and picked up the photograph album. She lifted it to her face and sniffed its cover. The plastic smell seemed to evoke her aunt. Then she opened its pages. Here was Lily again: playing with little Spanish children on the beach at Torremolinos, sitting with Kitty eating tapas, Lily and Kitty sunbathing, a straw hat with a floppy brim hiding Kitty's features and a towel hiding Lily's legs; she was self-conscious about her scar to the last. Here was Lily in a Spanish bar, the waiter grinning as she held aloft a glass of Sangria. Here was one Penny did not recognise. It was not of Lily and Kitty, but Lily and Rose. Lily looked fatter than ever – no wonder she'd never shown Penny this picture before. Both were standing on what seemed to be a windswept beach. Lily wore her characteristic grin. Rose, as usual, looked uncertain. The black and white photo seemed to bulge a bit. There seemed to be something behind it. Penny removed the picture from its mountings, and found, to her surprise, a lock of hair stuck fast to the back of the picture with sellotape. Penny frowned to herself? Whose was it? Some secret lover no one ever knew about? Penny certainly hoped so.

She smiled to herself as she closed the album. Lily certainly knew how to have fun. Perhaps that was what she ought to do now. But with or without Geraldine?

It was a difficult question to answer, and rather than think it through, Penny decided to go to the kitchen for a coffee. She hadn't had any all day as she was so hot earlier she'd just been drinking Coke. She rose, walked to the kitchen and switched on the light. She spooned some coffee into her On The Far Side mug, and wondered where she'd put her sweeteners.

Then she remembered: she'd run out, and hadn't bothered to buy any more because of the move. She hated coffee without sweeteners, so began to think whether she had another supply. She felt in her jeans pocket. Nothing. There weren't any in the rucksack she'd brought here. Then she smiled as it occurred to her that there might very well be some in that old black handbag. She'd known it would come in useful.

Penny returned to the living area, picked up the bag and opened it. It was empty. Just as she was about to close it again she noticed there was a zipped compartment. It was perfectly possible she could have left some sweeteners there. So she unzipped it. No sweeteners, just a plain white envelope. Curious, as she didn't remember leaving an envelope in her handbag, she opened it.

It was a birth certificate. She was surprised to see it was *her* birth certificate. Except it didn't make sense. Rose's name was nowhere to be seen, and Lily's name was there instead, where it said 'mother'. The registrar had made a mistake. But what was a spoiled birth certificate doing in her old handbag? Penny's mind moved slowly. This wasn't *her* handbag, now she came to think of it. It was her mother's.

Her mother had moved into her house, and it was Rose who had placed this bag under her bed. She obviously didn't want Penny to find it. She didn't want Penny to find it because it held her real birth certificate. Rose wasn't her real mother. Lily was. She was Lily's daughter. Penny grew pale, the room seemed to sway, her legs felt suddenly weak, and she sat down slowly on the floor.

I'm Lily's daughter, she thought, I'm Lily's daughter.

The casino was only half-full as it was still quite early. At some tables there was no play at all. Bored croupiers stood idly by, occasionally smiling at each other; there was soft muzak in the background, a distant clattering of plates and muted conversation from the restaurant.

A few youths watched the stud poker, reluctant as yet to place a bet. At another table, two elderly women of Middle Eastern origin, dressed in gaudy blouses over their black leggings, were playing roulette with innocent relish while their escort, a dark-skinned, bewhiskered man in a shiny brown suit, looked on indulgently. At the next table a Chinese man sat, immobile as a lizard, his chips piled in front of him. Next to him was Alastair.

As far as it was possible for a man to live in the present, Alastair was wholly, most vividly, alive at that moment. The game had him in its grip. He knew it was possible to master the game; he'd done it once or twice. You needed a system; he had a system. You needed a clear head; his head was clear. He had never felt more certain than now that his luck was in. He still had one quarter of his stake money left, and not having had his number come up for the last few spins, knew he was due for a massive win.

The blond croupier in his dress suit spun the wheel. Alastair was conscious of the clunkety-clunk of the wooden ball as it came to rest in a niche by a number. The croupier placed the glass marker on 36. So it was 36. Alastair registered that. With his next stake, he always covered the number that had just won; it was part of his system. And now, with dexterous, practised movements, he covered the blue baize with his red chips, some straight ups, some splits, some corners. It looked good. He was in control of the board; his chips were everywhere. There was a tingling of excitement in his veins, he waited for the croupier to announce, 'No more bets, please', and, his face inscrutable, he saw the numbers on the roulette wheel break into a blur of colour, slow down. He saw the ball come to rest, and the marker placed on 16. He'd covered it in a split. The croupier cleared the board, and pushed two piles of chips towards Alastair.

This was good. It was a good evening. There was nothing wrong with being in the casino. Nothing at all. It was a place to have fun. He was having fun. When he was back in Aberavon, and out of the mess he was presently in, he would take Fiona to a casino in Aberdeen and show her why it was he found it all so satisfying. She would like it too. It pleased him, that picture of Fiona and himself at the tables together. It wasn't as if a casino was in any way sordid or unsavoury. He knew pubs that were far, far worse. He took in the tasteful decor around him, the diamond pattern on the frieze that ran around the wall, the artistic prints of racehorses, the plush armchairs, the lights of the fruit machine.

Then he turned his attention back to the table. Once again he covered the baize with his chips, this time tangling with the Chinese player who was stretching over and placing his chips according to his own system. The croupier spun the wheel and put down the marker. Yes! Alastair had won again, with a straight up. He wanted to punch the air in exultation. He was first past the post, he'd made it to the top, he was a winner. Four piles of chips were pushed in his direction. To Alastair this was better than the best sex. He felt pure, justified, insanely happy.

He covered the table again; again the wheel spun. This time he'd missed it. You win some, you lose some. He had plenty of chips left. No problem. More cautious next time, he ventured fewer chips. A mistake. He lost them all. A dull ache spread from the pit of his stomach and made his limbs heavy He needed to win again to take away the pain. So recklessly he covered the table. A chain of expletives exploded silently in his mind. All his chips were gone.

The words were the same ones those men had used when they broke into his room that afternoon. Two men whose hair had been cropped so close there seemed to be none of it; men who reeked of stale beer and cheap aftershave. One of them had trashed his room, tipping everything out of cupboards and drawers, looking for money and valuables. The other held him in an arm lock. He watched, impotent, as his framed picture of Fiona was hurled down and trampled on; as the man urinated on his bed.

He had to repay the loan in twenty-four hours or they would be back. Which was why he had borrowed the money from work, and come to the casino tonight. It was the only way he knew to get cash quickly. The game was a drug to him, a pleasure-inducing narcotic, a world in miniature whose triumphs and vicissitudes were so intense they blocked out everything else. The game was an anaesthetic. It desensitised him. Stopped him thinking about his betrayal of Fiona, of his unborn baby, of his disgusting, dirty, snivelling little self. He hated no one as much as he hated himself.

And he lost again. He handed the croupier a fifty-pound note. Got to keep playing. Got no choice. The red chips were everywhere. A small win. His luck was turning. A trickle of sweat made its way down the side of his brow. Another win on a split. Alastair began to breathe again. Of course it would be all right. He was wrong to doubt himself. But this would be the last time. After tonight, he'd never enter a casino again. He would confess to Fiona. All he wanted was to win one more time. Just one more time. So he played the board again.

Geraldine, her client and her client's friends stood outside the Midland Hotel, still undecided.

'We could go to a club?' one of them said.

Another grimaced. 'I've got a headache.'

'A wine bar?'

'Something more exciting than that,' said Tara, the client, whose birthday it was.

Naturally Tara's word was law.

'A casino?' suggested one of the girls. 'I belong to a casino. It's a laugh.'

Tara looked interested.

'What a super idea!' said Geraldine.

She was mildly curious. It was the first time she had been to a casino. Those sort of places held little attraction for her. She could not see the point of risking money. Yet a sort of glamour adhered to the idea of a casino, and she did not object to sampling its delights.

As she came down the stairs, the casino's interior disappointed her. It looked for all the world like an upmarket pub, with the same muted colours, the same odour of cigarette smoke. Except, in the casino itself, no one was drinking. Instead they grouped themselves around the tables, playing stud poker, blackjack, roulette. Most of the clientele, Geraldine noticed, were foreign and rather seedy. She was disappointed. She had imagined herself hanging on the arm of some tall, dark James Bond lookalike, admiring his skill at predicting the cards. Yet there was no excitement visible. No available men visible, either. Geraldine decided to write off the evening.

She followed her friends to a table where there were spaces. She stood and watched them purchase some chips, declining to join in and instead watching. Secretly she thought her friends rather silly. The chain of casinos was bigger and richer than they were; her friends were bound to lose their money. She noticed that their alcohol-induced giggles made them look rather out of place. A keen observer of manners and mores, Geraldine could see that the confirmed gamblers here were impassive and above all serious. They didn't look as if they were having fun at all. They looked as if they were at work. Which, in a way, they were. Making money. Just as she made money, as an insurance broker made money, as a lawyer made money. Just making a living was a gamble these days.

Geraldine, however, was convinced that she knew how to win. That city centre showroom she'd visited earlier in the day was just what she needed. Despite Penny's awkwardness tonight, she was sure she could get her to make an investment in it. She knew precisely what she was going to say to her tomorrow. She was a cow, though. Enough thinking about Penny; it spoiled her equilibrium. Geraldine turned to look at the gamblers. She was a winner already. It was why she didn't bother with the chips.

Through force of habit, Geraldine studied the room, grimacing at the tawdry little yellow-fringed lamps that hung over the tables, the ornate gold fittings, and searching for some appetising male flesh. The sort of men she liked would not come to places like this. As she scanned the room she saw a face that seemed familiar to her. She came back to peruse it. Yes, he was startlingly familiar. For a few moments she could not place him. He did not notice her gaze as his face was creased with concentration. From where did she know him? She thought of her business contacts, her friends, and for one dreadful moment thought she might have been to bed with him. Geraldine bit her lip. It wasn't like her to forget a face.

For some reason she associated him with Penny. Now why would that be? She took all of him in. Fair, almost ginger, curly hair, strong jaw – attractive in his own way. Registering that made her all the more determined to remember where she'd seen him before. Leaving her friends, she walked round the tables and came to rest a few feet from him. She watched as the croupier cleared the baize of chips. No emotion showed on the player's face. She watched him push his remaining chips on to the table, and saw the wedding ring on his finger.

Wedding ring. Wedding. It was the prompt she needed. Surely this was Fiona's husband? Or at least his identical twin. Geraldine was intrigued. She remembered Penny having said something or other about her brother-in-law – what was his name? – working in Manchester. Alastair. That was it. Alastair. She remembered the menu card on the table where she'd sat with Penny and Rick months ago.

She advanced and placed one manicured hand on his sleeve. 'Alastair!'

He seemed to start involuntarily, and faced her with alarm.

'It's Geraldine – Fiona's cousin.'

Now he frowned. Evidently he still could not place her.

'I don't expect you'll remember me. We met at your wedding.'

'Fiona's cousin,' he repeated. He had a charming Scottish accent. Geraldine knew she had got the right man.

'I've never been here before,' she continued gaily. 'Are you a regular?'

He gripped the table for support. What was this bloody woman doing here? Had Fiona sent her as a spy? Would she tell his wife what a mess he was in? Yet at the same time he was glad to have someone to talk to, someone to cling to. All of his money had gone. He was not ready to face the consequences of that yet. He could not leave the casino. It was possible that this woman would lend him some money. It was an idea. It was a good idea. He tried to smile at her.

'I come here from time to time,' he said.

'It's . . .' Geraldine made a little gesture, to indicate she was trying to find the correct words. 'It's not like I imagined it would be.'

'How did you imagine it?'

'I suppose I've seen too many movies.'

'Would you like a drink?'

'That would be lovely!'

Alastair knew he had some loose change, enough for a drink for both of them. He led this cousin (who'd surely been sent to save him) towards the bar, and asked her what she would like.

'Dry white,' she told him. He ordered a beer for himself. They sat at a side table.

'How's Fiona?' Geraldine asked. 'Penny said she was having some trouble with the pregnancy?'

'Aye. But she's holding on. She had a scan, and it seems to be all right.'

'Oh, good!'

Geraldine looked wealthy, he thought to himself. If she didn't have cash on her, she would be bound to have a cashcard, and he knew where the nearest hole in the wall was situated. He decided it would be politic to make himself as pleasant as possible.

Geraldine stole a glance at him again. She liked his fierce blue eyes and thick lashes. Just the type to sweep a woman off her feet, she thought to herself, remembering him with Fiona at their wedding. She wondered whether her cousin knew where he was, or whether he was deceiving her. The thought added spice to the situation. Surely a little flirtation was permissible in a case like this?

She lifted her hand and placed it once more on Alastair's sleeve.

'I'm glad you're here,' she said. 'I've come with friends – there they are – but they're just a little too over-excited tonight.' Geraldine raised her hand to push her glossy hair behind her ear.

'It can get exciting,' Alastair conceded, and coughed a little. 'I'm glad you're here too,' he said.

Geraldine was gratified. Perhaps this rather pathetic girls' night out would turn out to be something more interesting.

'I've never really spoken to you before,' she said, giving him a sly smile. 'It's hardly good manners to approach the groom on his wedding day just because you think he's good-looking.'

'Thank you,' said Alastair absently. 'Would you like me to show you how to play?'

'Play what?'

'Roulette. It's the easiest.'

'Can't I just watch you? I'd love you to show me what to do.'

'Ah! Slight problem there,' he confessed. 'I was on my way out. I've spent up for the evening.'

He's a quick worker, thought Geraldine, anticipating an invitation elsewhere. A consciousness that this man was her cousin's husband troubled her; she would make sure things didn't go too far. But the last thing she wanted to do was rob herself of a good time. The rumour was, as she remembered it from gossip at the wedding, that this Alastair was loaded. Didn't his mother buy him and Fiona a house to live in?

'So shall we move on somewhere else?' she asked her escort.

'No.' He paused. 'Tell you what, if you can lend me some money I'll play with that.'

Geraldine was suspicious.

'Lend you some money?'

'Sure. Say around fifty. I can repay you with my winnings.'

Oh, can you? she thought. As she began to adjust her mental picture of Alastair from wealthy Scottish laird to compulsive gambler, she played for time.

'Me? I'm the last person to lend you money. I'm always on my uppers. My clients never pay me until the last possible minute.'

Alastair looked gloomy. Geraldine knew she was right. Then a wicked thought occurred to her. Revenge was sweet.

'Why don't you speak to Penny?'

'Penny?'

265

'Miss Moneybags,' Geraldine trilled. 'Didn't you know about her fortune?'

'She inherited some money, I know.'

'Yes, and she's just moved to Wharfside, that new development opposite the Bridgewater Hall. The rents are sky-high. But with a quarter of a million, you can afford to throw a bit away.'

This is as good as playing roulette, Geraldine thought to herself.

'A quarter of a million?' repeated Alastair.

'As I live and breathe.'

He was a fool, an utter, complete, glorious fool! All the time there'd been more than enough money to repay his debts, to make it up to Fiona, to give him a clean start, to pay back into the account at work. Of course, he should have realised! The way she'd thought nothing of hiring a car for him. Penny was family. She would help him. Alastair glanced covertly at his watch. It was only ten; he could call on her now. How quickly could he get away from this woman?

'Well, well, well,' he said, and paused. 'Look, it was wrong of me to ask you for a loan. I'll have to go because I promised I'd ring Fiona tonight. It was a pleasure meeting you, Geraldine. A pleasure. I'm sure we'll see each other again.' Alastair shook her hand cordially.

Ringing Fiona, are you? Geraldine thought, as she watched him walk briskly out of the casino. Pull the other one!

Rose turned the Yale key in the lock and heard the satisfying click as it connected. She took the chain from where it hung loose and inserted it into the bracket. You could never be too careful, she thought to herself. She did not want to admit that she was just that little bit more nervous without another person in the house. She turned, walked a few steps down the hall, and went into Penny's lounge – now her lounge – to take the library book she was reading to bed with her. There were her reading glasses on top of it. She would need those too.

She picked up the glasses, her book, and went into the kitchen for a glass of water. Her brown handbag was beside the kettle, and she took that upstairs too. She walked into Penny's bedroom, as she had decided to sleep there now Penny had gone. The spare room adjoined a baby's bedroom next-door, and the crying had disturbed her. She placed her book, glasses, and water by the side of the bed, and turned to put her handbag on the dressing table. Her handbag . . . That reminded her to check on the other one. She kneeled to look under the bed, where she had secreted the bag earlier in the day. It was hidden well. She couldn't see it.

Rose reached under the bed and moved her hand around. The bag was evidently out of reach. She bent as low as possible and peered underneath. The bag wasn't there. Impossible. She straightened herself and moved to the other side. Maybe the light was playing tricks. Still the bag was not there. Rose felt nervous. Was she becoming forgetful? Had she put it somewhere else, and not under the bed at all? She opened the wardrobe, and pulled out all the side drawers. The bag wasn't there. She looked at the foot of the wardrobe. There it was! She *was* a silly! She picked it up and smiled with relief. Just to be sure, she opened it and unzipped the side compartment. The birth certificate was gone.

Fear clutched her. Who could have taken it? A thief? Penny? She looked at the bag again. The label inside said 'Brenton'. Hers was a Dolcis bag. This wasn't her bag – it was Penny's. And Penny had her bag – with the birth certificate inside. Rose's stomach somersaulted. Penny was in possession of her birth certificate! At all costs, she must get it back. Now. There was every chance Penny hadn't seen it yet. What ought she to do? Go to Penny's flat now? Would she suspect something? Rose was caught in a whirlwind of panic.

She took a few deep breaths. She couldn't possibly turn up at the new flat in what was effectively the middle of the night or Penny certainly would think something was up. She must calm herself and decide on a sensible course of action. Perhaps Penny hadn't even unpacked yet. Knowing her daughter, that was quite likely. All might not be lost. She would ring her and reassure herself that the handbag lay undiscovered, and would tell Penny not to touch a thing until she arrived early in the morning to help her unpack.

She stood at the telephone and slowly and deliberately pressed the digits that would connect her with Penny. To begin with she would ask if the move went smoothly, and if she had settled in. The phone rang six times. Then stopped.

'Hello?' Penny's voice sounded normal.

'It's only me,' Rose said, her usual introduction.

Penny prayed that what she had just seen was not true. She hoped her mother would be able to explain it away, as she had all the gremlins of childhood. She was glad Rose had rung.

'Guess what? I've got a birth certificate here, Mum. It looks like it's mine, but . . .'

Penny waited to be interrupted. Instead there was silence. It told her everything she needed to know.

'So *Lily* was my real mother?'

'Yes, but I can explain—'

'Lily was my mother, and you never told me?'

'I wanted to, but—'

'You let Lily die without telling me?' No reply from Rose now. 'You knew this and never told me? That's not right. You lied to me!' Her voice had an increasingly hysterical edge. 'But how come Dad is down as my father? I don't understand!'

'He *is* your father.'

'Oh my God – this is disgusting!'

'Penny, calm down.'

'I'm sorry, I can't talk to you any more.'

There was a loud click and the absent tone of the idle receiver.

Rose thought her legs would not be able to bear her up much longer. This was far worse than she had ever imagined. Yet there was only one other person who could help her now, and who had a right to know.

Once again she pressed a set of familiar digits on Penny's phone. This time a male voice replied.

'Harry . . .'

Chapter Fifteen

Alastair approached the concierge.

'I'm looking for Penny Green,' he said. 'I believe she's just moved here? I'm her brother-in-law, Alastair Gordon.'

He waited as the concierge gave him the once over.

'Eighth floor. Number two.'

'Thanks. That's great.'

Alastair walked over and pressed the control panel. The lift arrived in a moment. It swept him smoothly upwards and gently came to a halt at the eighth floor.

There was Penny's door, almost opposite. A thin line of light at its base indicated she was in. Alastair mouthed a silent prayer of gratitude. He knocked sharply on the door. No reply. He took a comb from his pocket and ran it through his hair. He knocked again, more loudly. Still no response. Alastair was very still, listening for any sounds that might indicate Penny's presence. Were those footsteps? He knocked again. Almost immediately the door was opened and there was Penny, ashen-faced.

Alastair's first thought was that somehow she had heard the truth about him – Geraldine had rung her, warned her he was coming. Yet almost instantly he dismissed that. Penny looked ill, worn. Did she have the 'flu?

'Alastair,' she said tonelessly.

'Can I come in?'

Penny stood aside, so that he could enter. Alastair looked around him and suppressed a whistle. The spacious, elegant apartment with its white walls, its expensive rug, its panoramic view, was altogether spectacular. Then he turned his attention back to Penny.

'Are you feeling all right?'

For reply, she just shrugged.

Now Alastair wondered whether she might have had a shock. He hoped it had nothing to do with Fiona. He hadn't contacted her for a while.

'Is something wrong?'

Penny did not know why her brother-in-law had called. It didn't matter. Nothing made sense any more. She alternated between bouts of acceptance and sheer outrage. For a few seconds she was Penny, everything was normal, and then she remembered what she had just seen and her world spun out of control.

'Penny – you're not all right.'

'I suppose I'm not.'

'Can I do anything, get you anything?'

'Were you sent to me?'

'Sent to you? No.'

'Why are you here?'

That was a question he couldn't answer yet.

'I thought I'd visit you.'

It was half-past ten at night, and that was a strange time to visit, Penny thought. Yet she could not be bothered to find out why he had turned up. She glanced at the settee, and saw her birth certificate lying there. Alastair's eyes followed her gaze.

'What's wrong?' His curiosity was roused. He was beginning to adjust to this unexpected situation. He had visualised coming here to find Penny revelling in her wealth and eager to dispense cash to him. Yet she looked as if a bomb had dropped. Something was up. Human sympathy welled up in him. Penny looked very poorly indeed.

'Tell me what's wrong?' he urged her, taking her by the arm towards the settee. She felt lifeless to him. 'Can I help you?' He noticed that the paper on the settee was a birth certificate.

Penny sat down next to it. Again her eyes travelled to it. She made no attempt to hide it from Alastair so he read it, and she watched him. The throb of music from the flat downstairs came to a sudden halt.

'I didn't know you were Lily's daughter,' he said.

'Nor did I, until half an hour ago.'

Alastair sat down by Penny and picked up the certificate. He read it again, taking in the careful copperplate of the registrar, reading the details of Lily's occupation, Harry's occupation.

'I don't understand,' he said.

What was the point of keeping it all secret now? In her despair and disorientation, Penny was utterly candid. Alastair was not Alastair just then; he was another human being, a witness to what had just occurred.

'Look, Lily was my mother. It says so on my birth certificate. I found it in my mother's handbag, which I took instead of mine. It was a mix-up, you see. Just like my father got mixed up, apparently.' Penny felt the bile come up in her throat. 'So that's why Lily left me all her money – because I'm her daughter. And all I gave her in return was a lock of hair. So, you see, I'm only your half-sister-in-law.' She recognised her desire to laugh as dangerously hysterical.

Alastair frowned. He couldn't take it all in.

'Are you sure somebody isn't playing a prank on you?'

'A prank? Call it that, then. A prank. A trick. Who tricked who? Lily was my mother, and she gave me to my mother . . . to Rose . . . to my aunt.'

'Calm down, Penny.' Alastair took her hand. Her pulse was racing. 'You're not making sense.'

'Yes, I am. Everything makes sense, now. The money, the lack of trust. You see, I've only ever seen my short birth certificate before. It's all you need for a passport. It doesn't say who your parents are. It said I was born in Elgin.'

'I know Elgin!' he said.

'Yes. The story was that I was premature. I came when they were on holiday. But Lily was on that holiday. I have a picture. Do you want to see it? It's my moth – Rose and Lily, on a beach.

Lily hadn't put on weight. She was pregnant – with me. So she must have had me and then handed me over to Rose. And now she's dead. My real mother's dead.'

'Are you sure all this is true?'

Penny was silent. Alastair looked around him, at the opulence of their surroundings, and saw the evidence.

'She left me a fortune. How much did she leave Fiona?'

'Five thousand pounds.'

'There you are. You see, Fiona wasn't her daughter.'

'So you're half-sisters?' Alastair was fumbling for the right response.

Penny nodded and seemed to sag.

'You must be in shock. Can I get you a drink? Do you have any whisky?'

'No.'

'Some tea. I'll make you a cup of tea.' Alastair squeezed her hand and made his way to the kitchen. A mug of coffee with coffee granules in it stood on the work surface. He opened cupboards to look for the tea and could find none. So he took another mug for himself and switched on the kettle. What he had just heard had winded him too. He could hardly imagine how Penny must feel. His heart went out to her.

Alastair returned with two black coffees.

'I think you should speak to your parents and find out more,' he told her. 'It might help you come to terms with it.'

'I don't want to know any more. It's all too obvious. My father was sleeping with both of them. God knows how long it was going on for.' A disgust so strong she could taste it welled up in Penny. The thought of her father making love to Lily revolted her. Rose was right. He was a monster. As she thought that Rose was right, and felt that familiar shift of allegiance to her mother, a new realisation struck her. For all these years, her mother – who was not her mother – had lied to her. Rose had never told her whose daughter she really was. Their relationship was built on foundations of dishonesty.

And then there was Lily, her real mother. Why did she hand

her over? Penny wondered if she was so unloveable that even her own mother couldn't bear to handle her. Only Lily had gone, and now it was too late for explanations. A new grief, stronger, more bitter, more agonising than birth pangs, robbed her of breath. Her mother was dead. Penny had no one who was for her. That thought, that first surge of self-pity, unlocked the tears. With a sharp cry, Penny began to sob.

Alastair held her, unable to express the pity he felt.

'Shhh, shhh.'

He rocked her, like a baby. She cried with howls of rage, like a wild animal.

'Shhh, shhh.'

Her prostration and desperation were dreadful to see. Her tears were damp on his face. Yet, as he held on to her, he knew he had been here before. He knew how Penny felt. Why was this so familiar to him? When had he, too, cried aloud with fear and disbelief and sobbed just like this, except there had been no one to hold him?

He had hidden behind the armchair, the green armchair with its little antimacassar embroidered by his grandmother, and heard the blows, his mother's uneven breathing, the shuffling of feet, and could not bear to look. They did not know he was behind the armchair. He had been playing with his Dinky cars; he'd hidden so she would not put him to bed, so he could stay up and protect her. But he could not protect her. Utterly impotent, Alastair sat behind the armchair and heard the cruel words, flinched from every blow.

Only later he had held his mother, tightly, to stop her sobs, as he was doing with Penny now, and through the corner of his eye had seen the swelling on her face. His mother had clung to him, and the fierceness of her embrace frightened him. He was a failure. His mother had been hurt again. And here he was, unable to help this woman who had been wounded too. Now the dampness Alastair felt were his own tears that burned him as they fell.

'I feel as if I'm no one,' Penny said. 'I have no parents.'

'You're lucky,' he said.

'I'm glad you're here.' Penny tried to smile at him. 'It helps, having someone to talk to.'

It was strange. After each bout of crying, when she felt emptied of all tears and all emotion and that she had reached the bottom of the pit, she began to feel better, safe in the way that only a person who has lost everything can be safe. There was no more to lose. At these times, she was able to pay attention to Alastair, who had sat with her all night, bringing her tissues, drinks, and listening to her. She felt a pathetic gratitude towards him.

Alastair watched her. Penny's eyes were red from weeping; there was an ugly beauty about her puckered up face, and her raw, open distress. Her timid smile made her even more of an object of pity to him.

'I don't know what I'm going to say to them when I see them again. I don't know if I'll even be able to see them again. I feel like I've been robbed. But also I can't bear to think of my father. I don't understand – I mean, what could have induced him? They were sisters. Alastair – I've been thinking about this. Perhaps because Rose was finding it hard to conceive, Lily had a baby for her? And that's why they went all the way to Scotland to have me – to keep it from the family? But in that case, why did they have to keep it secret? Because they didn't want me to know I'm a bastard? *They're* the bastards.' Penny began to laugh. As Alastair guessed it would, the laughter ended in a new bout of tears.

'I'm sorry, I'm so sorry . . .'

'No problem.'

'You go around for thirty years thinking you're one person, and then you discover you're another. I just can't get my head round that.'

Alastair nodded.

'I can't get over my disgust. It's like – your parents are sacred to you. Most kids can't even bear to think of their parents having a sex life, but my father was having it off with both of them. I feel sick again.' Penny put her hand to her mouth. 'No, it's all right.

I'll be OK. But there can be no excuse for adultery. None. "Thou shalt not commit adultery." Is there a commandment against lying too? If not, there should be. He lied to my mum, and then they both lied to me. Now I don't feel I can trust either of them. I don't care whose fault it was – I blame them all. I don't want anything to do with them!'

'I understand.'

'They disgust me.'

'At least you're an adult now. You can cope.'

'An adult? Ha! Who's an adult? You might be. I feel as if I've never grown up, as if everything's a sham – my job this flat, all of it a pretence. I'm still a kid. That's why this hurts so much. With your parents, you're always a kid. There's a part of you that never grows up.'

Alastair heard those words, and they settled in his mind. He did not understand all of what Penny had been saying, but he had enough natural sensitivity to let her talk and grieve in her own way. He simply listened. Yet as he did so, he felt that in some subtle way he was being tutored. Never had he witnessed such extreme emotion so precisely articulated. Penny could explain what she felt. He envied her deeply. He felt as strongly as she did but his feelings terrified him. They arrived unannounced and took him over with unstoppable force.

'I feel now as if, not knowing who my parents are, I don't know who *I* am.'

'Lily was your mother.'

'My birth mother. But I have two mothers – both of whom lied to me. Alastair – never, never lie to your children!'

'I've lied to Fiona.'

'What do you mean?'

He wanted to talk now. Penny had created a climate where talking seemed possible.

'I have a problem too. I gamble.'

Penny sniffed loudly to clear her blocked nose. She thought of Alastair's living quarters and realised he was telling the truth. The shock of this new discovery made her forget her own predicament.

'Do you gamble a lot?'

'Yes.'

'And Fiona doesn't know you gamble?'

'She knows, but she thinks I've stopped. I haven't.'

'Are you in trouble?'

'Yes.'

'So you came to see me to ask me for money?'

'Yes.'

'You can have it. You can have as much as you want. More. You can have it all.'

'No. I don't want you to give me anything. I just need a loan that can clear my debts and help me to stop.' It was agony for him to appear so unable to help himself. Penny's intuition helped her to see that.

'Of course I knew you meant a loan. But, Alastair, it's not going to be easy for you to stop.'

'I know.'

This new revelation, that her brother-in-law was a gambler, came as a relief. Penny had dealt on her problem page with similar cases. Switching to her professional self helped her to regain the dignity she'd just abandoned.

'How long have you been gambling?' she asked him.

The sound of the word 'gambling' pierced him each time Penny uttered it. It was a word he rarely used about his own activities. Yet he tried to answer her question honestly.

'I have periods of it. When I was unhappy at university, it started. Again when I was working in London. After the wedding, when I was without Fiona.'

Each phrase cost Alastair immense effort, as if he was lifting off heavy armour. Yet now he could see the pattern. When he was unhappy, he gambled. When his life was careering out of control, he chose the only way he knew to control it.

'Was your father a gambler?' she asked him.

Alastair took a long, slow breath.

'No. But he used to drink too much.' And then he stopped. He was not ready to tell the rest. He couldn't do what Penny could do. Yet the memories were there, crowding in his head, begging to be released. When his father drank too much, he beat his mother. He slapped her once, hard, leaving a red mark. His father's red fist and muscular fingers like snakes. Waking in the morning, praying that today would be a good day. He knew if the cows in the field opposite were lying, not standing, he would be safe. With a breathless excitement he would open the curtain. They were lying. Relief flooded him.

'They say the children of alcholics can have problems.'

'In the end the minister came and they took my father away, to some clinic.' Alastair remembered the curiosity of the neighbours, and the shame, the abject humiliation, he had felt. His mother went on as if nothing untoward had happened. He learned it was important to say nothing. That was how you survived.

'I knew that was where he went, though my mother said nothing to me,' Alastair admitted.

'Like my mother.'

'Like your mother. Then when my father came back, he'd stopped drinking, more or less. We all had to pretend to be a normal family. They did it for my sake, I think. I haven't told Fiona this.' How could he? He loved her far too much.

'So when she married you, she didn't know about your gambling?'

'She didn't.'

'Poor Fiona,' Penny said. How ironic that both of them should have been in the dark. Penny and Fiona, who'd felt so capable and independent and sure of themselves.

Alastair hung his head.

'And poor you.' Penny moved closer to him, and took his hand. 'Nothing's quite as it seems, is it?'

'I love her very much. I didn't want this to happen.' Tears pricked at the back of his eyes, but would not fall.

'We're both going to help you,' Penny said. Her own self-pity had evaporated. 'Please tell me about your debts.'

Now it was impossible to lie. So Alastair explained his predicament honestly, but in his mind it was as if he was talking about somebody else.

'We have an overdraft and I've spent Lily's money – your mother's money. I sold Fiona's furniture and I was planning to sell her house. She knows about that now. She thinks the sale will cover my debts. I'm not sure it will. I borrowed some money from a man in a pub; he sent some blokes round to threaten me. I owe ten thousand to him. I took a blank cheque from the office – that's another few thousand. I need to return that tomorrow.'

For the first time Penny was deeply, unutterably glad that she had Lily's money. She knew just how difficult it was for a gambler to stop; at the same time, Alastair's immediate problems could be solved, because he only needed money. Unfortunately her own problems were beyond that sort of help. But Penny would do what she could for Alastair.

'I can go to the building society in the morning. Then what will you do?'

'I want to see Fiona.'

'Yes. You should.' Penny wondered how her sister was coping with the knowledge of Alastair's debts. It was the most dreadful mess.

'Come to Aberavon with me,' he said.

'To Fiona?'

'To Fiona.'

'I can't,' Penny said.

'Why?'

'I lied to her too.'

'You?' Alastair was puzzled.

'My mother – Rose – told me not to tell her about the size of my inheritance. She thought it would be difficult for Fiona to accept. What crap! It was to keep the secret of my birth completely safe. So how did you find out I had so much money?'

'From Geraldine. She came into the casino.'

'She told you?' Penny was appalled.

'I asked her for a loan, you see.'

'You'd be lucky!' Penny laughed bitterly. The thought of her cousin sickened her. She could see now that Geraldine's infatuation with her had in fact been an infatuation with her money. Penny realised she had been wholly taken in. Geraldine was simply after her money. Then a thought struck her. If she'd been wrong about Geraldine, she could be wrong about Rick. But what would Rick think when he discovered who she really was? Lily's daughter. An unwanted, illegitimate baby, the product of adultery. How could he possibly want her now?

'Come back to Aberavon with me,' Alastair persisted. 'Then you can talk to Fiona yourself.'

Penny thought about his proposal. It was tempting. She could not face her parents, and needed to forget about Rick.

Fiona, the only innocent party, had like her been the victim of a deception. She would be able to communicate properly with Fiona. She could think of no one else she wished to be with more. Besides, Aberavon was a long, long way from Manchester.

'How far is Elgin from where you live?'

'Twenty minutes.'

'Take me there. I want to see where I was born.'

'Maryhill it would have been. It's where I was born too.'

Penny smiled at her brother-in-law, a measure of just how much they had in common.

'I'm Scottish too.'

'I suppose you are.' Alastair grinned at her.

Penny consulted her watch. It was two-thirty in the morning.

'We'll have to wait until the building society is open. I think we ought to settle your debts before we go. And I need to contact the paper and tell them I'm having a holiday. Then we'll set off as soon as we can.'

Alastair could not speak. The shame he felt at having to accept so much money, and his gratitude, choked any attempt at words. Penny, however, was feeling better. Having decided upon a plan of action, she felt partly restored to normality. Thinking about the opening times of the bank, the amount of petrol in the Mazda, what clothes she needed to take with her – all this diverted her mind from the one dreadful fact that was threatening to swallow her whole.

'You'd better sleep here tonight, Alastair.' She looked at her cream leather settee. It had lost its newness entirely. 'You can sleep on the settee.'

'Thank you.'

They both stood and faced each other.

'Goodnight,' she said.

'Goodnight.'

Impulsively Penny put her arms round Alastair and hugged him. He held her tightly. They were lucky to have found each other.

Chapter Sixteen

Rose jerked awake. Where was she? In a large bed – Penny's bed – with Harry beside her. In less than a second she was totally alert and lay in the bed completely still but with every nerve taut.

She was surprised she had slept at all, but dimly remembered a feeling of complete exhaustion. She had let Harry lead her up the stairs and had not objected when he'd got into bed with her and held her, quite tenderly. It had comforted her. Perhaps it was why she'd fallen asleep.

There was a translucence in the room that showed it was dawn. Rose was pleased. She could get up, have a drink, and compose herself. Carefully, so as not to disturb Harry who was lying with the duvet only covering one shoulder, she slipped out of the bed, tiptoed into the other bedroom for a dressing gown, and made her way down the stairs. Their mugs from the night before were still in the sink.

Rose rinsed them and looked into Penny's back yard. She watched a small tortoiseshell cat edge along the wall then jump down. It was strange that life was carrying on as normal, after all that had happened. The calmness of the world around her soothed her. She wondered how Penny had coped last night. Penny had no one; at least Rose had Harry. She accepted that the events of the last twelve hours had brought her back to him, but it didn't feel wholesome to her. It was as if the secret which had threatened to choke and destroy their marriage like a poisonous creeper had also bound them together. There never would be an escape for her.

The sky outside was clear and blue. Rose had often tried

to imagine the day she could finally tell Penny about the circumstances of her birth, but in this fantasy Penny accepted it all bravely and said how glad she was to have had two mothers. Rose had never anticipated she would be speaking about it to Penny on the telephone, or that her daughter would sound so accusing.

Rose sat down at the kitchen table with some coffee. Later on, when Harry was up, they would go and see her together and everyone would talk. It was still possible it would turn out all right. Harry said so. He said that Penny just needed time to adjust. It was a shock, after all.

Rose knew all about shocks. It was possible to get over them. She did.

The first shock happened on the day she'd arranged to meet Lily for lunch in town. They went to the basement at Lewis's. Lily ordered an orange squash and a toasted teacake, and only picked at that. It wasn't like her, so Rose knew something was up.

'Are you trying to lose weight?' she enquired.

'I'm pregnant,' Lily said, and Rose thought it was a joke. Then she looked into Lily's eyes and saw the desperation there. Rose could not believe the irony. Here she was, beside herself because she was unable to conceive, and Lily was pregnant.

'But Lily – you're never regular. You hardly ever have the curse. How do you know you're pregnant?'

'I've been to the doctor.'

'But—'

'Yes, I thought I was safe too. It was why I didn't bother telling him to use one of those French letter things.'

'Who was he – who is the father?'

Lily swept her arm in front of her dismissively. From that Rose learned that he didn't matter; the man was not the issue.

'What are you going to do about the baby?' she continued.

Their food lay untouched on the plates before them.

Lily shrugged.

'Don't get rid of it – it's not right. And it's dangerous. Do you remember what happened to Gloria? She had to have her womb removed in the end.'

'I don't want an abortion. I'm scared.'

Rose was surprised to hear Lily said that. Her sister was never scared.

'So you're going to have the baby?'

'Yes.' Lily sounded stubborn, mulish almost, back to her old self.

'You'll have it adopted?' This struck Rose as the only other alternative.

'No. I'll raise it myself. I've enough money.'

Rose was shocked. Did Lily realise what a stigma this would be for the child? It was thoroughly selfish of her. But Rose was jealous too, bitterly jealous. *She* wanted a baby. It wasn't fair.

'It's not fair. It's not fair on the child. It would suffer.' I am suffering, Rose thought. 'Anyway, there's Mum to think of. The shock might kill her – you bringing up an illegitimate baby.'

Lily blanched. Her mother was sacred to her. She worshipped her like no one else.

'What can I do?' Her voice trembled.

'I don't know.'

They were silent for a few moments.

'Rose, would *you* have the baby?'

'Me?'

'If you and Harry brought it up, then Mum need never know. And if she thought you were having a baby, she'd be determined to live to see it.'

Rose tried to absorb this idea. Could she bring up Lily's baby? A newborn baby who would never know who her true mother was? She trembled with apprehension and excitement.

'I'll need to think about it,' she said.

'Rose – before you do, I think there's just one other thing you need to know. About the father . . .' Lily was no longer looking at her. Her eyes were focussed in the distance. Rose wondered what was wrong with the father? For one moment she thought he might be coloured. That would never do.

'It's someone you know, Rose.'

In a way, that was a relief. It made it better. Rose looked at her sister's face for a clue and saw she was looking attentively at the door. She had recognised someone coming into the cafe. Rose followed her gaze. It was Harry. What was he doing here?

Even then, she was not prepared for the second shock when it came.

He took a seat between them, and held Rose's hand.

'I'm sorry, Rose. I'm really, really sorry.'

Sorry? What for? Lily looked more scared than ever.

'It was my fault,' she said.

'It was just the once,' said Harry. 'We never meant it to happen.'

Rose disengaged her hand from Harry's and with the other slapped him hard round the face. All the customers were stunned into silence. She got up, pushing her chair violently to one side, and left the store.

For days, weeks, there were tears, recriminations, sleepless nights. Yet never in that time did she say she was leaving him. If she did, her mother would find out everything and she was so ill. And that wasn't all. Rose knew that if she didn't look after Lily's baby, a stranger would have to. And the baby would be Harry's baby, and she was Harry's wife.

Bit by bit she accepted the inevitable, but not without a struggle that left a residue of bitterness like a stone in her stomach. The deception was surprisingly easy to manage. Since Lily was always overweight and carried at the back, no one realised the true state of affairs. Rose simply went into maternity clothes at the appropriate time and bravely accepted everyone's congratulations. Her mother was thrilled and rallied somewhat.

They chose north-east Scotland for the birth because it was as far away as they could get while remaining in a country where people spoke English. Rose, Harry and Lily stayed in a hotel between Elgin and Lossiemouth, and walked on the windswept beach every day. When Lily started with her pains, Rose accompanied her to the maternity hospital. She was there when Penny was born. Her eyes were open immediately. Two bright brown eyes, like shiny pennies. It was Lily who noticed that, Lily who named her. Rose recalled the rush of love she'd felt for the baby, and the tenderness that welled up in her. This was the baby she'd craved after all. She ached with envy when Lily fed her; Lily insisted it would be good for Penny. Rose was worried she would change her mind and keep her child.

She didn't. Rose tried to imagine the effort of will it cost Lily to give up the child. She was not there at the time. She arrived at the hospital one morning, and Lily had discharged herself. The midwife, who knew about them, explained that her sister had taken a train to Edinburgh. Kitty was meeting her there, and they were going for a holiday to Spain. Rose took the motherless baby from the crib, wrapped in her white shawl, knitted by Lily, and held her close. She looked into her eyes, and saw how the baby met her gaze, steadily, unflinchingly. Rose knew then that everything was going to be all right.

None of this was Penny's fault. If anything, she loved Penny more because she was deceived too. There was a bond between them. What had loosened was the bond between her and Harry. How could you trust a man who slept with your sister?

The kitchen door opened. Harry stood there.

'I didn't bring my shaving things with me,' he said ruefully. 'Do I look too bad?'

Thinking of the past had temporarily disarmed her. Rose found she could not meet her husband's eyes.

'Well?'

She gave him a quick glance.

'You'll do.'

'Do you want another coffee?'

'I'm all right,' Rose said, and got up to take her coffee through into the lounge. She did not want to be with him.

'Is something wrong?' he asked her.

She paused by the beaded curtain.

'You know, I still don't understand. I don't understand how you could have done it.'

'Done what?'

He was so dense at times.

'Slept with Lily.'

Harry seemed to shrink. 'I told you. She wanted me to. She'd never had a man before.'

'So you obliged.'

'I had to. She'd given us so much. She was my boss, she paid our rent. She bought that house for us afterwards.'

'You sound like a male prostitute.' She spat out that last word.

'It wasn't like that. I felt sorry for her.'

'And you fancied her too.'

'I didn't.'

'You're asking me to believe you slept with a woman you didn't find attractive?' Rose took a deep breath and continued. 'You know, that was the worst part, knowing that you'd risk losing me to have her. I was always second fiddle to Lily. Even when we were courting, I felt you were her cast off. And then you went to bed with her. That proved it. And the dreadful thing is that I still feel second best. I always will.'

'You're not,' Harry said. His voice shook. 'I didn't love Lily. I love you.'

'Too late. You should have thought about that the night she seduced you. I loved you once, but you've strangled that love. All these years I've had to keep your secret. In everything I've said, I've had to be careful. Careful with words, just like I've had to be careful with money. What kind of life has it been for me, Harry?'

'And what kind of life do you think it's been for me?'

'For you?' Rose was incredulous.

'You've never let me off the hook. You've never stopped punishing me. Even prisoners with a life sentence get out of jail eventually. You're mean, Rose.'

'So you've said, many times.'

'Not just with money, you're mean with me. I've told you, I'm sorry!'

Harry shouted those words until they almost rocked the thick walls of Penny's house. Rose was alarmed. Would the neighbours hear? She felt contrite. Only it was true. She had never been able to forgive him. Now she had forgotten how to forgive.

'I might be mean but you're too generous, Harry. Too generous with yourself.' She spoke mildly. It was a climb-down.

There was a silence that was almost tangible. The absence of words seemed to draw them together. Rose recognised that she ought to forgive him, and she would, as best she could. Things being as they were, she had no choice. They needed to visit Penny together. She decided then that she would go back to her husband. When he came towards her and put his arms around her, she submitted to his embrace and rested her head on his chest. She could hear his heart beating. It made her realise that he was mortal. One day it would stop beating. Hers would stop beating. They were both mortal, both human, both fallible. Only Harry was more fallible than most.

Rose sighed deeply.

'Come on,' she said. 'There are things to do before we visit Penny. And you need a shave.'

'Shall I pop out and buy a razor?'

'Huh! Anyone would think we were made of money. We'll go home first and you can shave there. You need a change of clothes as well.' She wriggled free from his arms. 'Let's get a move on!'

Everyone in the room was singing. In the middle, sitting on a wooden chair, was Trevor with his acoustic guitar, producing a series of chords that were barely audible above the raucous sounds of 'She'll Be Coming Round the Mountains When She Comes!' Every so often Trevor would catch the eye of one of the old ladies, and wink at her. He enjoyed seeing the response. Some of them were flustered; one of them once hoisted up her skirt to let him see her leg. So what? He knew they all enjoyed a bit of flirting. You were never too old for that.

Rick watched all this from the doorway, surprised to see how much Kitty seemed to be enjoying herself. She sang as loudly as any of the residents, performing with brio even if her voice was a little cracked. Rick considered that music had an uplifting effect on most people, and that the long-term memories of the Gladesmore residents were probably much more trustworthy than their short-term memories. Hence they were word perfect with every song. As crude as this particular form of therapy might be, it seemed to work. He wondered if he should join in himself. He wasn't getting any younger.

Trevor came to the end of the song, and the residents delightedly clapped themselves. One old lady began to sing 'Silent Night', but since it was nowhere near Christmas, Trevor decided to ignore that. He tried to think of something more seasonal. Something summery. He had it.

> Oh this year I'm off to sunny Spain,
> Y Viva España . . .

A popular choice. One by one the residents caught the tune, and grinned happily at Trevor, like children in a kindergarten, eager to please their teacher. Once again, Kitty's voice rose above the others. Rick was surprised and pleased. He'd not seen her so cheerful for ages. Anne came up to join him.

'She likes the singing, does our Kitty.'

'Shall I audition her for *Top of the Pops*?' he remarked.

'I'm encouraged by her progress recently. She's been talking to me about Lily.'

'Is that progress?'

'Yes. She talks about her now as if she knows she's died. I think much of her confusion was caused by the shock of the death. Oh dear, look, Vera's trying to take her blouse off. Excuse me.'

Rick watched in amusement as Anne tried to recover Vera's dignity and blouse. He was glad he'd come to Gladesmore this morning, although his reasons for the visit didn't really bear close examination. He wanted to talk seriously to Kitty. More than anyone, she would know about Lily's past. She would be able to confirm his suspicions. Watching her now, he smiled at his own foolishness. Mildly senile Kitty was hardly the world's most reliable witness.

'Y Viva Espanā' drew to a close. After another rapturous round of applause, Trevor signalled to Anne that he'd had enough. He got up from his chair and lifted the guitar so he could get free of the shoulder strap.

'Leave 'em wanting more,' he said to Anne.

The residents watched Trevor go through to the hallway. Kitty was still humming to herself as Rick approached her. As she saw him, she sang the refrain of the song again.

'Well done, Kitty,' he said, taking a chair and placing it opposite her. 'You were the best of the lot of them.'

Kitty grinned at him, convinced she deserved the praise.

'I like Spain,' she said. 'It's very hot there. You have to wear a sun hat. I had a straw hat.'

'I'm sure it suited you. Tell me about Spain?'

'I went to Spain with Lily. On an aeroplane. She bought us tickets in the first class. It was very hot when we got there and I wanted to see a toreador.'

'Did you?' said Rick. 'Did Lily know the toreador? Was he a friend of hers?'

'He was a toreador, with a little red cloak. *I* wanted to see the toreador, not Lily. Lily didn't want to see the toreador because she'd just had a baby. She wasn't feeling well. She kept crying, so I tried to cheer her up. I said, it wasn't as if she'd lost the baby. She could still see it.'

'Tell me about the baby?' Rick said. He was listening intently.

'I said to Lily, "You can still see the baby, because Rose has the baby. Rose will look after the baby for you," I said to her. "And you can see the baby when you get home." I said to her, "You must forget about the baby now, and go and see the toreadors." That was what I said to her.'

'How did Rose get the baby? Did she come to Spain?'

'No. Lily was on holiday in Scotland and I walked up the Golden Mile. That was in Blackpool. I like Blackpool.'

'Did Rose bring up Lily's baby?'

'Yes, but you mustn't tell anyone because I promised Lily I wouldn't tell. She will be be very angry with me if I tell. Promise you won't tell?' Kitty looked worried.

'I won't tell.'

'Penny is Lily's baby. Lily said nobody must ever know. I'm only telling you because you married her. I was at your wedding. And because you're a good boy. You come to see me a lot and Penny comes to see me. They didn't give me any breakfast this morning. And if I don't scrub the floor they're not going to give me any supper. I don't like red cabbage.'

'I'll see Anne about that. They mustn't make you scrub the floor. Kitty, can I ask you another question?'

'Twenty-four,' she said. 'Six fours are twenty-four.'

'Kitty, who was Penny's father?'

'I mustn't tell anyone that.'

'Was he Spanish?'

'Harry wasn't Spanish. He was born in Higher Broughton. It was a nice area then. I wouldn't go there now.'

'No, you mustn't. I have to leave you now. I have an appointment. I'll be back to see you very soon.'

'Give me a kiss.'

Rick kissed her, left the day room and walked down the corridor in the direction of Anne's office, planning to get into the fresh air where he could think. However, she was there to waylay him.

'We've not seen you for a bit,' she said, hoping to start a conversation. Rick Goldstone was one of her favourite visitors. His good humour and Tom Cruise looks appealed to her.

'No. I've been in London.'

'We've not seen your girlfriend either.'

'Girlfriend? Oh, you mean Penny.'

'Tell me something,' Anne continued. 'She wasn't really Lily's *daughter*, was she? Kitty does go on about it so. Or was it just Lily's wishful thinking? Mind you, she never said anything to me.'

'Wishful thinking,' Rick said. 'Look, do me a favour, Anne. I've remembered something important I have to see to. Can you explain to Kitty that I've had to go? I left rather abruptly. And tell her from me she doesn't have to scrub the floor for her dinner.'

Anne laughed. 'So she's been trying that one on again?'

'I must go, Anne. See you soon.'

Rick got straight into his car and started up the engine. Everything that Kitty said made perfect sense to him. Of course Penny was Lily's daughter. They even looked alike. He was crazy not to have seen it before. They were the same build and had the same face, pugnacious and determined. But that vulnerability, that hesitancy that Penny had – she got that from her father.

He checked he was not over the speed limit. Lily was blonde but she'd dyed her hair. Rick remembered seeing a line of dark auburn where she parted it – it was the same colour as Penny's hair. Most of Lily's fortune had gone to Penny, and that was why Rose and Harry had hushed it up.

What was also clear to him now was that Penny knew nothing of any of this. Was it his place to tell her? No, but he wondered how much longer it would stay secret. Now Kitty's tongue was loosened, she'd speak to anyone. Anne knew; it was just a matter of time before his mother knew – and that was as good as publishing the whole affair in the *Manchester Post*.

Finally he fought his way through the traffic in the city centre. He had to get to Penny. He hadn't decided yet what he was going to say but would find some words. He thought of Harry and Rose, and felt pity. It was easy to slip, and the consequences are sometimes far, far greater than the slip itself.

Here he was in Penny's road. Her white Mazda was not visible. She was probably working from the office. It was foolish of him not to have realised that. Rick sat drumming his fists on the steering wheel, debating what to do next.

At that moment Penny's door opened and Rose appeared. Immediately Rick got out of his car.

'Hi! Is Penny in?'

Rose looked behind her, then walked towards him.

'Hello, Rick. Didn't you know she's moved?'

'No. To where?'

'The Wharfside apartments in town.'

'Really? Is she working today?'

'No. I don't think so.'

'I think I'll pop down there, then.'

'No ... no. Harry and I are just on our way there. That is, after we've been home for a few things. She rang us, you see. She's not been feeling well. I'll give her your good wishes.' Rose turned back again. 'Harry?'

'Thanks, Rose,' said Rick. 'See you around.'

He got back in his car. The Wharfside apartments. He was impressed. He turned on the ignition and drove straight into town.

Rick walked into the lobby of the Wharfside and saw the concierge behind the desk.

'Good afternoon. I'm looking for a Penny Green, who's moved in here recently?'

'Oh, aye. The eighth floor. First on the left.

'Shall I go straight up?'

'You can do that, but you won't find her there. She's gone away for a holiday.'

'But her parents told me she was here.'

'It were all a bit sudden.' The concierge leaned over to Rick confidentially. He was intrigued by Penny. Last night a Scotsman had arrived very late, according to Bill, and they'd left together this morning. 'She were escorted by a Scottish gentleman. Her young man, was it?'

'Scottish? That could be her brother-in-law. How did she look to you?

'Aye. Now you come to mention it, she were a bit pale. She looked a bit red round the eyes. Bad news, is it?'

'Yes. Bad news. Can I use your phone?'

The concierge pushed one over. Rick got out his Filofax and looked up the Greens' number. He dialled quickly.

'Harry? Hello, it's Rick. I'm calling from the Wharfside. Penny's gone. I think she's on her way to Fiona's. I'm going straight there. Do you fancy a lift? . . . Fine. Give me about an hour. See you later.'

Chapter Seventeen

It was the middle of the afternoon before Penny and Alastair were ready to leave for Aberavon. Their business had taken longer than they had anticipated. There had been visits to the building society, to Alastair's bed-sit and then to his office, to the newspaper, and lastly Alastair had knocked on the side door of a run-down pub in Lower Broughton, had disappeared for a few minutes, and had re-emerged safely into the sunlight.

Penny tried to eat the egg and tomato sandwich that he had bought for her from the petrol station forecourt, but the moist bread and salty egg and the sweetness of the tomato made her feel ill. She was keen to get on the road. The noise of the city was inside her head, and she knew she had to get away.

Only the speed of the Mazda on the road gave her any relief. Penny accelerated as she drove on to the slip road of the M61, quickly moved out on to the fast lane and put her foot down with determination. Alastair made some desultory conversation, to which Penny paid scant attention. Later he suggested some music, but she felt she could not bear to listen. Any music would mock the way she felt.

Instead she took comfort from the ribbon of motorway stretching ahead and the discipline of driving, overtaking, moving back to the slow lane, watching the traffic ahead. Now the hills of the Lake District lay to either side of the road, their contours like sleeping giants. Penny could see shoulders, massive limbs, and knees drawn up to chests. She pushed down her foot more heavily as the motorway climbed even higher.

'Shall we try to ring Fiona again from the service station?' Alastair asked.

They had been ringing her all morning; there had been no reply.

'If you like,' Penny answered.

Alastair looked at her covertly. It was impossible to see how Penny was feeling as the sunglasses she was wearing reflected the windscreen and turned into a rainbow spectrum of colour. Penny's lips were tight and her face was still.

He didn't know whether she had managed to sleep at all last night. The last thing he remembered, as he'd pulled the blanket around him on the settee, was the sound of her in the bathroom. Then the flat was radiant with sunlight and Penny was sitting at her workstation, drinking coffee, gazing out of the window. That was when he had woken, and soon she had been all activity, packing, tidying the flat, as if nothing had happened at all last night.

Alastair had been reluctant to talk to her as freely as he had a few hours previously. There had been something almost shameful about their intimacy, and like Penny he preferred to get on with life now rather than refer to the past. Moreover, he was filled with the joy of owing no money and wanted to revel in that. And he had given in his notice at work, and was free to stay with Fiona for a while. He felt so lucky. Not just lucky but full of gratitude. It was a gratitude that could not be expressed in words alone; it was a gratitude that demanded action. Penny was in his trust, and he would look after her. Looking after her was also a way of coping with his own dented pride; she was in a worse state than him, and he had the capacity to care for her.

The words that described the facts ran like a mantra through Penny's head. *Lily is my mother. Rose is not my mother, but she brought me up, knowing I wasn't hers. They all lied to me.* She had to repeat the words like that, hammer them home, so she could believe them. What else had Rose lied about? Perhaps she'd never truly loved Penny. How can you love a child who isn't your own? Her presence must have been a constant reproach to both her parents. No wonder there were such frequent arguments. No wonder she'd always felt so guilty. Her parents' difficulties were her fault after all. A red Escort raced up behind her and overtook. Was she going too slowly? She put her foot down and settled into a steady eighty.

She passed the exit for Wigton. The road still stretched ahead. The other cars on the road did not seem real to her, and Penny could almost believe she was sitting at a computer screen, on a driving simulation programme. She was in a trance. The road came at her too quickly, like a road in a cartoon. If she shut her eyes for just a moment, she would feel better. So she shut her eyes, and enjoyed a moment of semi-oblivion. Then she was awake again, in a state of terror.

'Penny! What's wrong?'

'Nothing. I just shut my eyes for a moment.'

'You can't do that. Look, there's a service station ahead. We'd better stop. You can have a sleep.'

'But we'll be late.'

'If you carry on driving like that, we'll be dead.'

Penny shrugged. Yet as they approached the next service station, she pulled in.

'I think I feel better now,' she told Alastair. It was the truth. The fresh air revived her. 'If I can just have lots of coffee, I'll be fine. I want to keep moving.'

'I'd advise you to have a sleep.'

'I can't sleep in the car when it's not moving. All I need is coffee. Honest.'

They entered the service station. Groups of people stood in the lobby, some playing on games machines while others just seemed to be waiting for the sake of it. Penny made her way to the Ladies', with its uniform rank of cubicles, and washed her hands, splashed cold water on her face, then dared to look in the mirror. Her face was white, her eyes swollen, her hair lay flat on her head. She felt an instinctive revulsion at herself. No wonder no one wanted her. She thought how fragile were the little edifices we build around ourselves, those structures comprised of jobs, of rank, of self-importance. They can all be swept away. She was just this rather fat, white-looking woman with painfully short hair, ordinary, ugly. She turned her face away and left the Ladies'.

Alastair was waiting for her, and together they walked into the cafeteria.

'I tried ringing Fiona again. She's still not in. She could be at my mother's. I don't want to ring her there. We'll try again later. Now I think we should have something to eat.'

Penny's stomach heaved at the thought of food. Alastair went to get a plate of chips. She wondered how he could.

The fussiness of the coffee annoyed her. It was in a little tarnished silver pot, and she had to pour it into her fat little cup with its red ring round the rim. The sweeteners came in a little paper packet. The coffee was bitter but not hot and she was able to drink it at once.

She could not look at Alastair, picking at his thick chips like brown slugs. The smell of the sauce he'd put on them offended her. She gazed round at the other customers as she forced herself to drink her coffee. They all revolted her. Each person seemed bizarre: the man in a a black suit with a head shaped like a dome, the child with buck teeth sitting behind a gigantic paper cup of cola, the two obese women who leaned heavily on the table, having finished their meal. A waitress with hair the texture of burned straw wiped the table next to them with a cloth that was probably replete with germs. There was no beauty left in the world.

'Penny? Are you OK?' Alastair's voice broke into her reverie.

'Yes. Fine,' she said, dully.

'Come on. We're making progress.'

'Are we halfway there?'

'Oh, no. Not as much as that.' He consulted his watch. 'I'd say about a quarter of the way.'

Penny's heart sank. She finished her coffee.

'Shall I drive?' he asked.

Penny paused. It was an idea.

'You can't. You're not on the insurance.'

'Does it matter?'

Penny thought about that.

'Yes. It does. But don't worry, I feel a lot better now. The coffee is working. Let's get going.'

'Shall we listen to the radio?' Penny suggested.

'Aye. We'll do that.'

The news was on. Penny's attention wandered from items on the single European currency to the two lorries bunched up ahead blocking two lanes, then back to a bulletin on the golf, then off again to a line of slow-moving vehicles. It was a relief not to have to think.

Alastair toyed with the idea of not ringing Fiona at all. Imagine her surprise when she opened the door to him. Why spoil that by a phone call, and the long explanation of why he was bringing Penny? First he would greet his wife, and then he would tell her the reasons for their journey.

Penny took in the flat, anaemic green hills to either side of them, and told herself that this must be the Lowlands of Scotland. She recalled what little she knew about them. She tried to picture Edinburgh to her right. She had never been to Edinburgh but always watched the highlights of the Festival on TV.

'I think we ought to give Fiona a surprise.'

Alastair's voice jolted Penny back to reality. She had been in the past. Now she was dragged into the present. She hated him.

'If you like.'

'It will be easier to tell her everything when we see her.'

'Yes. All right.'

The A74 became motorway again. All three lanes were empty. Once again the road mesmerised Penny. She put her foot down on the accelerator. She saw a Discovery ahead, and decided she'd catch it up. Steadily she increased her speed. It was coming closer. Closer still. She would get as near to it as she could, and then overtake. There was a spare wheel on the back, and just one person driving, and—

'Penny!'

She swerved into the fast lane. The Discovery honked loudly at her. Penny's heart thumped loudly in her chest in a frenzy of fear and embarrassment.

'Are you sure you're in a fit state to drive?'

'Yes, I bloody well am!'

Alastair said no more. A tear trickled down the side of her face nearest him. He waited a little then spoke again.

'It's already six o'clock. We've another four hours to go, at least. Either you let me drive or we stop. You're not safe.'

Penny didn't reply.

'Did you sleep last night?'

She shook her head.

'I want you to take the next exit, and we'll find a hotel. Since Fiona isn't expecting us, we may as well arrive tomorrow. I want you to get a good night's sleep.

'All right.'

In fact Penny found she didn't care. She didn't know what she wanted any more. They might just as well stay in a hotel.

They followed the sign to the Grant Hotel, which led them up a steep incline, and then discovered themselves in front of what looked like a large stone castle. At each corner there were turrets, and a circular set of stone steps led to an imposing entrance. The hotel had been extended at some time in the past, and newer wings were attached to each side.

'They'll be bound to have room for us here,' Alastair said.

Penny sat in the Mazda while he went in to make enquiries. She felt quite calm. So what if her mother wasn't her mother, and her real mother had died without acknowledging her? She was an actor in a play. So she could switch off from time to time and feel nothing, like actors did. As she did now. A squirrel undulated in front of the stationary car, and Penny watched it move and stop, move and stop.

Alastair appeared again.

'They can put us up,' he said. 'Let's get the luggage out of the boot.'

Mechanically Penny got out of the car, and stood by as Alastair brought out their two suitcases. She took hers, and followed him up the steps into the hotel. The lobby was enormous, and Penny's eyes were drawn to the high ceiling where the plaster was grimy and cracked. Alastair had left her and gone to the reception desk, waiting for the manager who had just disappeared.

He wondered what to do about rooms. He felt responsible for Penny. Felt he ought to stay close to her. She was still in a very volatile state. His problems might be over; hers weren't. It crossed his mind that they could share a twin-bedded room and that way he could make sure she slept. Or ought they to respect the proprieties and take two singles?

The manager came out of his office. He was a dark-haired man, of middle height, and wore a pair of black-rimmed spectacles which made him look oddly dated.

'A double room?' he asked.

'Do you have two singles adjoining?' It was a good compromise.

'I'm afraid not. But I can give you two doubles adjoining. We're not so busy right now. The cost will be the same.'

Alastair called Penny over to sign the register. When the formalities were completed, they followed the manager along a corridor, up some stairs and through a fire door to the hotel extension. Right at the end of the next corridor, the manager stopped and indicated their rooms.

'Here we are.'

Penny unlocked her door and walked in. She deposited her suitcase and stood there alone, listening as Alastair was shown the room next to hers. She heard the manager ask if they wanted to eat. She looked around her room. A double bed with a paisley bedspread faced the large double window. A mahogany wardrobe stood to one side. On the other side was a door that she imagined led to a bathroom.

Alastair came in.

'This is fine. What do you want to do? Have a rest, or would you like to eat?'

'I don't mind.'

'I think you ought to eat. You've had nothing all day.'

'All right, then.'

'Why don't you change, and I'll meet you in fifteen minutes?'

'OK.'

Penny had not changed. Alastair did not comment but led the way back downstairs, through the warren of staircases and corridors, down to the lobby. He found the restaurant, another large, empty room with an enormous tartan drape hanging on one wall. He and Penny sat at a table and the manager appeared again. Alastair wondered if he was the only other person there. He handed them a typed menu, offering a plain three-course meal.

Penny took a few spoonfuls of the Cullen skink, and made a face.

'It's an acquired taste,' Alastair conceded. 'It's made of smoked fish.'

'A soup made from smoked fish?' Penny sounded dubious. She put down her spoon.

Her salmon steak sat in the middle of her plate. She had ordered it because it was the only non-meat dish on the menu. Now it had arrived, she felt she couldn't eat that either. It pleased her to think she need not eat again. She would become very thin.

'Won't you even have some vegetables?' Alastair asked.

For reply, Penny sipped her wine. 'I'll just have this.'

It was a silent meal. Alastair felt it would be insensitive to talk about himself, his feelings for Fiona and improved prospects; it would be equally foolish to refer to the source of Penny's misery. It was her right to choose to remain silent, and she had chosen to remain silent. He hoped the healing process was taking place even now. When she got to Aberavon, she would have Fiona to talk to. Women were better at these sort of things. His role was clear. He was in charge of her physical welfare; it was his responsibility to get Penny safely to her sister.

So he tried to persuade her to have some dessert. Penny shook her head. Alastair decided he would forego his, too. He consulted his wristwatch and saw that it was only nine o'clock, too early for bed.

'What would you like to do now?' he asked Penny.

'Shall I go to sleep?'

'Of course. I just wondered if you wanted to go for a walk, perhaps?'

'I don't have the energy for that. You can go.'

'No,' he said. 'I'm staying by you. Do you want to watch some television? I noticed a TV lounge on the way here.'

'OK.'

The TV lounge was square, with velvet curtains the colour of mustard. The television was enormous, as if it had taken steroids. Around the room were a selection of ugly and ill-assorted armchairs, none of which looked very comfortable. Penny sat down on the edge of one. A pile of magazines lay next to it on a stained coffee table. Alastair switched on the television, and there was some detective programme. A middle-aged man slowly deliberated on the motives of a suspect, listened to by an attentive junior. Penny doubted that she had sufficient concentration to follow what was going on. Instead she picked up a magazine.

It was one of those little tabloid magazines whose shout lines seem more appropriate to the hoardings outside a freak show. *I was anorexic, then bulimic! My son was born with thirteen fingers! I married a contract killer!* Penny was sickened. All these bizarre lives paraded for entertainment. Why did people allow themselves to be written about like that? Did it help them? Maybe she ought to try it. *I had two mothers, and they never told me!* She laughed to herself, and felt even more sick. Alastair turned round.

'What's funny?'

'Nothing,' she said.

Alastair hoped the laughter was a sign that Penny was feeling better.

'I think I'll go and have a shower.'

'Good idea. It'll help you sleep.' Alastair had no idea whether this was true or not, but it might be. He was feeling quite tired himself. 'I'll be making tracks soon,' he added.

'OK. See you later, maybe.'

Penny found her way back to her room. There was an uncanny silence everywhere. She was so used to the noise of the city that silence oppressed her; it was a blanket that suffocated. There was no television in her room, but there was a radio alarm clock. She tried each of the pre-set stations until she found Radio Four and turned it down so that it provided a comforting murmur of voices. Then she closed the curtains, opened her suitcase to find her washing things, and went into the bathroom.

It was tiny. A toilet faced a shower cubicle, and there was a sink in between. On top of the cistern was a knitted yellow dog holding the spare toilet roll. Penny went back outside into her bedroom to remove her clothes and returned to the shower, carrying her towelling robe.

She opened the doors and stepped into the shower. She stood under the running water and let it trickle all over her. As she washed herself mechanically she thought that there was very little point. She would never be clean again, never pure again. She was a mess, right from the beginning. She put her face up to the shower, wanting the warm water to blot her out. She washed her hair too, washed every part of her, hopelessly, desperately. Then she stepped out of the shower, put on her robe, and re-entered her bedroom.

Penny sat on the edge of her double bed. Now she ought to go to sleep. But she felt so lonely. The radio jabbered on by her side. She wanted to talk to someone. Like the mariner with his albatross, her burden was too heavy for her. She had to share it. But no one was with her. She began to piece together her thoughts by herself.

Her father, Penny decided, was beneath contempt. He had

crashed from his pedestal and was lying, a shattered icon, at her feet. Rose was a coward and a liar. And Lily?

Penny did not know what to think about Lily. Lily was her natural mother, but now she was dead. She had vanished. She had evaded her daughter during her life, and now had succeeded in evading her forever. It crashed across Penny's mind that she ought to visit a medium, and find her mother, and ask her why? Then she despised herself for her desperation and credulity. She would never understand why her mother bore her and then gave her away.

Above all, Penny wanted to think well of Lily. All her life she had defended her when the rest of the family reviled her for her sharp tongue and home truths. Yet for all her apparent honesty, Lily had lived a lie. Perhaps it cost her a great effort. Perhaps she was forced to give up her baby. Perhaps she was a martyr, and martyrdom embittered her.

Lily a martyr? It was too convenient. It just didn't fit. But if she wasn't a martyr, if she wasn't a victim, then she chose to sleep with Harry, and chose to give her baby away. In which case Penny ought to despise her. Her mother was a bitch. But knowing that, she could not go on living. To go on living, she needed to believe in her real mother. It was an impossible conundrum.

Alastair passed by Penny's door, stopped, heard the soft sounds of the radio, and was reassured. He unlocked his door. In his room, he was conscious of Penny next-door, and once again blessed her for freeing him. As he prepared for bed, he reaffirmed to himself that he would never gamble again. This time he had learned his lesson. From now on, he would be good. Back in Aberavon, he would seek professional help. And he would be busy enough, shortly, being a father himself.

Joy bounded in him. He had Fiona, his baby, and a new beginning. He felt guilty again, thinking of Penny next-door and her private agony. He wished there was more he could do for her. He stepped into his bathroom to clean his teeth.

Penny was still sitting on the edge of her bed. She had not changed position. Now she was trying to talk sense to herself.

Come on, girl, she said. *It's not as if anyone's dying. People have much worse things to put up with. You're a victim of too much love, that's what you are.*

Too much love? Penny argued with herself. So much love that my own mother didn't want me? She was able to give me away. Now she knew she was approaching the thing she could least bear to think about. She believed she had come to terms with much of her situation: her father was disgusting – she would have to live with that; Rose lied – we all do. But at least Rose took her. What she could not bear to admit was that Lily, her birth mother, didn't want her. She preferred her money, her shops, took one look at her blood-stained, mewling little daughter, and rejected her.

Penny dug viciously at her arm with her nails, wanting to inflict on herself the pain she felt. But her nails were bitten to the quick, and it didn't hurt enough. She was sure that if she was able to feel real pain, the dreadful pressure of her self-disgust would be relieved. She wanted to wear the injury she felt. More than that, she knew the pain would provide her with a climax, an end point to her suffering. She looked around the bedroom for something sharp. She saw a glass on the bedside table and wondered about smashing it, and using the broken glass to slash at her arms and make her blood flow. Or were there some scissors in her handbag? Her bag was on the floor and she opened it. There was nothing, nothing sharp, except for a red biro. In her desperation she seized it, and jabbed at her arm, scoring her flesh with streaks of red ink, which mocked the blood that would not come. She dug harder, breaking the surface of the skin. But still no blood. She was even a failure at trying to harm herself. Penny howled in despair.

Alastair heard her, and started. He jumped out of bed, not caring that he was only wearing his pyjama bottoms, and in a moment was at Penny's door. He tried it. It was not locked and as he came in he saw Penny trying to stab her arm with something.

'No!' he exclaimed, took both her hands and saw the biro. He took it from her.

'What on earth are you trying to do?'

'I wanted to hurt myself,' she said.

'You'll have to find something better than a biro,' he said, trying to defuse the situation, shocked at the weals on Penny's arm.

Surprisingly, she found she was able to be humorous too.

'Well, I'm a writer,' she said. 'What do you expect me to use?'

Alastair laughed, and put a friendly arm around her.

'Come on,' he said. 'I thought you were beginning to feel better.'

'No,' Penny said. 'No, I'm not. It's you who feels better. Not me.'

Alastair squeezed her. Her white towelling robe was soft and smelled fresh, as did Penny. She felt comfortable to him. He could not equate her soft femininity with her violent attack on herself.

'You mustn't hurt yourself,' he said to her.

'I had to. I wanted to hurt.'

'I know,' he said.

'You don't know.'

'I do.' He thought of the times he'd deliberately thrown away his stake money on a bad bet; of the times he'd forced himself to drink until he was sick. He needed to punish himself. But Penny did not need to. She had done nothing wrong.

'You've done nothing wrong.'

'I know I did nothing wrong. I *am* wrong. All wrong. So wrong my mother gave me away. She would have kept me if she'd loved me.'

'It wasn't so easy in those days.'

'That's the point. I feel as if, had I been more loveable, she would have loved me so much, she wouldn't have given me away.'

'Nonsense.'

Penny was silent. It wasn't nonsense. She realised now that she'd always had a deep belief that she was unloveable. It was a belief nurtured by her parents' arguments when she was young, fostered by her own rejection of her body as being too large and somehow wrong; the belief informed her relationships with men, and most of all her relationship with Rick – she could not believe he desired her; it dictated her choice of career – she would make people love her by her actions, not herself. In the last twenty-four hours, Penny had discovered the roots and extent of her unloveability. Her own mother had given her away. Alastair whispered to her.

'You are loveable.'

His words were meaningless.

'Look at me. I've lost all my wife's money. I've messed up my life. This is what you call unloveable.'

'No,' Penny said. 'It's different for you. You can change your situation. I can't. There's something fundamentally wrong with me.'

'What's wrong with you?'

'Everything.' Penny knew she was being childish, but couldn't help it.

'Penny. Look at me.' Alastair took his arm from her waist and cupped her face with his hands. He would find something kind to say to her, and it would be true.

'You have lovely eyes. I've never seen eyes like them. Do you know, you have black flecks in your irises? You're very pretty.' It was true. Looking at her face now, he could see that. He remembered the body he had just been holding. 'You have a lovely figure. You're a very attractive woman.'

These words slipped into Penny's consciousness. Alastair spoke them as if he meant them. For that moment, she believed him. She looked at him and saw that he was attractive too. She had always known he was good-looking, but now that his attention was turned on her, she felt the full force of his sexuality. Something in her responded to him.

Alastair brought his face close to hers and kissed her tenderly, on the lips, as a seal. He knew he should show her that she was loveable. He owed it to her. Anything that he could do to make her feel better, he would do. He understood her. They had been through a great deal together. He felt he was unloveable too. He wanted her to prove to him that he could be loved. So he kissed her.

Alastair dropped his hands from Penny's face, and her face felt cold now. She wanted him to bring his hands back, and touch her once more. Just once more. And she wanted him to speak to her as he had just done. She dared to look at him again. Now she was aware he was naked from the waist up. How she wanted to rest her head against the firmness, the masculine solidity, of his chest. Instead she placed her hand on his shoulder.

'Thank you,' she said. Then, 'Kiss me again.'

Alastair did so. This time he kissed her for a longer time. She was soft and yielding and warm in his arms. He heard the radio in the background. He revelled in the sense that he was helping Penny. He had found a way to make her feel better. He brought his hand round to the back of her head, and ruffled her hair.

'You're lovely,' he told her. 'Lovely and soft and sexy.'

Penny felt weak with desire. She could sit up no longer. As she fell back on to the bed, she brought Alastair with her. Her bathrobe fell open, and she could feel his bare flesh on hers.

'Penny,' he said, in his Scottish accent.

Her arms were round him tightly, and they were kissing hungrily, eating and drinking each other, seeking reassurance, seeking to have their existence affirmed. I need this, thought Penny, and I don't care. It's what I want.

And Alastair, without thinking, moved his hand to Penny's breast and caressed it, amazed at its fullness and her satin flesh, and the hardness of her nipple. He stopped kissing her, raised himself slightly, and gazed at her.

'You're so beautiful,' he said, and was silent for a moment.

And the pips went for the Ten o'clock News.

One, two, three, four, five, and the final pip.

As it sounded, Penny realised she was lying stark naked on a bed and Fiona's husband was looking at her. She was as horrified as if she was a witness to the infidelity, rather than a participant. Like a diver who had touched bottom, she began to surface again.

'No,' she said, sat up, and gathered her robe about her again.

Alastair looked at her and saw she wasn't Fiona. What the hell had he been doing?

A woman read the news and there was a new initiative for peace in the Middle East.

'Penny, I'm so sorry. I'm so sorry.'

'Don't be. It was my fault too.'

'I don't know what happened.'

'You wanted to comfort me, I guess. And I want someone to love me. But not you.'

It was Rick she wanted. She knew that now. Yet he seemed further away from her than ever. She looked at Alastair again and saw his distress. She knew she had to reassure him.

'I know you meant well, Alastair.'

Now, like a man stepping back from the brink of a precipice, he began to see what it was he had been of the verge of doing. He had almost been unfaithful to Fiona. He loved his wife more than he loved himself, and yet he would have been unfaithful to her – with her sister. He had escaped from the gambling trap, and walked straight into this. What kind of pervert was he? He didn't deserve trust. He would never get better.

It was as if Penny could read his mind.

'I encouraged you,' she said. 'Don't blame yourself. You just wanted to make me feel better. Look – I do feel better. And we stopped. It's all right. It really is all right.'

'Fiona must never know about this.'

'Another lie,' Penny murmured.

There was silence. Lies breed lies, she thought. Ought she to tell her sister what had happened? The answer was clear.

'I won't tell Fiona,' she said. To do so would be an act of cruel destruction. It was wrong.

Alastair swallowed hard.

'Thank you.'

'Look. Go back to your room now. We both need to be alone.'
She smiled at him, watched him rise from the bed and go.

Alastair walked into his room absolutely sober. He could see
that it was not going to be so easy to change. It occurred to him
now that his desire to be cured instantly from his gambling was
in itself a symptom of his illness; there were no magic solutions.
He would be tempted to slip again, and he had been tempted
just now. Any change would only happen slowly. He would
have to have the patience to wait for it. Could he trust his wife
to understand that? Could he trust himself?

Penny sat on the end of her bed, folded her hands in her lap, and
wondered why it was she did not feel as disgusted with herself as
she ought to. She lifted the inside of her arm, looked at it, saw the
weals, and wondered how on earth she could ever have wanted
to do that.

Somehow, she had recovered her equilibrium. Whatever had
taken place between her and Alastair had achieved that; what
they had done was entirely wrong, and yet it had been necessary.
No, she did not want him. She wanted Rick. She knew that now.
Alastair had helped her see it.

It seemed odd to her that something good could come out of
something bad. The world was not supposed to work like that.

Penny knew she had been bad. Like her father, she had let her
desire get the better of her. Like Rose, she was prepared to lie.
Like Lily, she took what she wanted and disregarded the risk.

Lily, with her scarred leg, her dyed hair, her crude manner,
who had never believed in her own attractiveness, had needed
Harry. Maybe she'd wanted a baby too.

I am like both my mothers, Penny told herself. I am as weak as
my father. I am as strong as Lily. And I can survive, like Rose.

She switched off the radio, and luxuriated in the silence. At
that moment there was nothing she had to do. Tomorrow life
would begin again, and she was under no illusions. It would not
be easy. She would have to face Fiona. Finally she would have to
speak to her parents.

But that was in the future. Penny rose, walked over to her window, and opened the curtains. Outside it was dark, but the night seemed almost transparent. The ghosts of hills billowed in front of her. Two or three lights shone far off, from distant farms.

Penny knew she ought to sleep, but she was not quite ready. There was still so much thinking to do. And besides, she was ravenously hungry.

Chapter Eighteen

'We must be nearly there now.'

'Just a wee bit further.'

What struck Penny about the Grampian countryside was the scale of it. The hills to either side of the road seemed vast to her, sweeping with a grand indifference into the distance. There were hardly any houses. It was as if people didn't seem to matter here. And there was so much sky. Penny realised she had never really looked at the sky before, and could see how, above her, it was bright, vibrant blue, yet as it curved down to the horizon it became watery and pale. It was a warm day, and sitting in the car, she didn't need her jacket. She just wore jeans and the black Lacoste sports top.

'That's the Avon,' Alastair said, indicating a broad river, edged with cream-coloured boulders that ran by the side of the road.

'Nice,' Penny said.

Funny to think that she was born near here, she thought. And now Fiona was living here. She wondered how it would be when she saw her sister. She had spoken to Fiona briefly on the phone this morning. Fiona seemed not in the least surprised they were coming. Typical of her, Penny thought. She always took what was thrown at her, just like her mum.

'Take the next left,' Alastair told her.

Penny did so, and found herself on the sort of single-track road with the occasional sign denoting a passing place which she had begun to associate with the Scottish countryside. Cows stood around in the fields, looking as if they had forgotten what it was they were thinking about.

'You turn right up here, and the house is at the end of the drive.'

Penny was faced by a large, double-fronted stone house with small fir trees in rows to either side. Someone was at the front window. Fiona? They got out of the Mazda and Alastair went to the boot to fetch their cases. Penny walked up to the door and as she did so it opened. It was Rose.

Penny stood stock-still. She was not prepared for this.

'Fiona's at your mother's,' Rose said to Alastair.

'I'll walk over there, shall I?'

'Could you?'

Alastair dropped the cases in the small hall, and with long strides set off down the path.

'You'd better come in,' Rose said to Penny.

Penny took refuge in small-talk.

'It's a lovely house,' she said. 'A terrific view.' She indicated the window where Ben Voulin was clearly visible, even to the rocks like broken teeth on its summit.

Rose said nothing. It was a questing silence and made Penny feel unaccountably guilty. She regretted the way she had spoken to her mother on the phone. Perhaps an apology would be as good a start as any.

'I didn't mean the things I said to you the other night. I'm sorry if I was rude.'

Rose was still silent. That was ominous.

'How did you know I was coming here?' Penny asked.

'The caretaker at your flat said Alastair had been to see you.'

'So you drove all the way here?'

Penny turned now and looked at Rose, standing erect in her pale green jersey top, her old brown skirt, tensed as if waiting to receive a blow. To Penny, she seemed to have dwindled in size. She seemed somehow smaller than Penny remembered her. She saw the fine lines around the outside of her mother's eyes, and took in her guarded, vulnerable expression. Penny ached with love for her. Rose was her mother, after all.

'Don't look like that,' she said. 'It hurts me.'

Rose still waited.

'Mum, why don't you say something!'

'I'm sorry,' said Rose.

'Tell me what happened? Right from the beginning. I need to know everything. Please.'

Rose sat down in an armchair and clasped her hands in her lap like a penitent schoolgirl

'You're just as much my daughter as Fiona,' she said.

'But I'm not,' Penny said. 'Apparently I was Lily's daughter.' Her tone was teasing.

'Yes, I know. But I was there when you were born. Right from when you were born. I was the one who took you home from the hospital.

'You must have hated me. You must have felt so resentful—'

'No! I didn't hate you. It wasn't like that at all. It was different. I wanted you. I thought you were the only baby I would ever have. I even felt as if you belonged to me more than you belonged to her, to Lily. You cried a lot, sometimes you would seem to cry for no reason. You cried my sadness for me. I used to think you knew what I was going through, and that he'd wronged both of us.'

'You thought Dad had wronged both of us?'

Rose nodded and continued, 'I was so close to you, closer perhaps than a mother ought to be to a child. But I couldn't help it. You seemed so bright. When you were a baby I could talk to you, and I imagined you understood me. No wonder you talked early. You were a companion to me, Penny. You prattled at me, and I listened to everything you said. Everything seemed dark unless you were around. I'm sure it was because of the happiness you brought me that I conceived Fiona. And when I was pregnant with her, my mother died. You were only two. I left you with Harry while Lily and I went to the funeral. She was in a dreadful state. I know why. Our mother never knew that she was a mother, too. So, Penny, don't think for a moment that Lily didn't love you.

317

She adored you, knew when you took your first step, when you began to talk. She taught you to read when I was busy with Fiona.'

'She bought me lots of books. There was one with a story about a stone dog, which turned into a real dog in the middle of the night.'

'She taught you to type.'

'I know. I used to play at being her secretary. She brought me an old Remington from her head office.'

'The truth was, she never let you go,' Rose said.

Penny's eyes filled with tears. She loved Rose for telling her that. Admired her mother's generosity.

'She never let you go. I always felt as if I was the inferior mother. Not surprisingly. I had to do all the dirty work – protecting you from Lily's desire to spoil you, and your father's habit of indulging your every whim.'

Penny let slip a small smile. Her mother was sounding like herself again. She could never talk about Harry without a tinge of bitterness.

'But I'm not complaining. You were a joy to me. Both of you. I loved you both in quite different ways. Fiona was my baby, and I protected her. But in some ways you and I were closer. You were my friend.'

'But why did you never tell me the truth? I grew up never knowing who my real mother was. Surely there was a point at which you could have said something?'

'When? That's what I'd like to know. When? On your tenth birthday? On your sixteenth? When you left home? There was never a time I could tell you. Telling you that you weren't my daughter would have been rejecting you. I never wanted to do that. I could never tell you. In the end I realised that some lies are for the good.'

'I know. I understand what you must have been through,' Penny said.

'You can't understand. How can you? I loved someone who could never be mine. Not truly.'

318

'Who do you mean? Who did you love who was never yours? Are you talking about me or Dad?'

Rose realised she meant both of them.

Penny continued, 'Whatever you think, you are my mother. You made me your daughter. You know that. So you must mean it's Dad you think didn't love you?'

Rose felt as if an open wound was being probed, mercilessly, by a surgeon who despised anaesthetic.

'You're like me,' Penny went on remorselessly. 'You don't believe anyone can love you, I can see that now. And Dad was unfaithful to you. That proved it, as far as you were concerned. Did it last long, his affair?'

Rose shook her head.

'Please tell me what happened. If you won't, no one will.'

Rose found she could not look at Penny as she spoke. 'Dad was out of work. We were very hard up. Lily found him a job managing one of her shops. Harry was very grateful; myself, I was surprised. I never thought she liked him very much. She used to complain about his habit of wanting to give everybody credit. We were trying for a baby around that time, and I didn't seem able to conceive.'

She laughed bitterly. 'It was my fault. Lily had to go to look at some new machinery over in Yorkshire. I didn't like the thought of her travelling and staying in a hotel by herself. Not in those days. A woman alone was an invitation to all comers. So I insisted Harry go with her.' Rose lowered her voice. 'He said it happened then.'

'So he only slept with her the once?'

'Yes. Yes, I'm certain of that.'

'Were there other women? Did Dad have a roving eye?'

Rose shook her head again. The question was immaterial; Harry had ruined her peace of mind. Nevertheless, she had to admit, there were never any other women.

'So on one occasion only he slept with Lily?'

Rose could not look at her implacable daughter.

'Mum,' Penny said, 'why haven't you forgiven him yet?'

Rose could not speak. She raised her hand in a hopeless attempt to stop Penny from saying any more.

'If it helps,' she persisted, 'I don't mind about having two mothers. It's fine by me. Most people only have one person to blame all their failings on. I have two. Three, if you count Dad. Sorry, I don't mean to be flippant. He made a mistake. Are you surprised? You know what he's like, just the same as I do. It sounds like Lily led him on.'

'Penny, you don't understand. He let me down. I trusted him and he let me down.'

'I trusted you. But you never told me the truth about my birth until I found it out for myself. I could say that you let me down.'

'I couldn't help it!'

'Neither could Dad.'

A light was breaking in on a dark place in Rose's heart. She continued to struggle against Penny, but revelled in her own inevitable defeat.

'We wouldn't have stayed together if it hadn't been for you and Fiona,' she said.

'So if Lily had had a miscarriage, would you have left Dad?'

The brightness made Rose honest.

'No.'

'Because you loved him.'

She was silent. Only this time there was a different quality to her silence. It was brimming with new possibilities.

'Oh, Mum, what on earth have you done with your life?'

Penny's tears were for her mother, not for herself. She cried for all the years her mother had needed her husband, and kept him at arm's length, and tried instead to get her love from a child. She cried for the pointless waste of it all.

Rose took her hand, and stroked it gently.

'Shhh, shhh,'

Rose began to wonder if it was too late. Was it possible to unlearn distrust? Her husband was with Fiona at the moment. She had refused to let him come to the house to meet Penny. Why? She knew it was the old resentment that had made her exclude him. Perhaps she had shut him out long enough now. If she could open herself up just a little ...

And here was Penny crying, when she had suffered enough. Again she stroked her daughter's hand.

'It will be all right,' Rose told her. 'Don't cry. Everything will be all right. Hush, hush. It will be all right.'

When Fiona arrived, Rose and Penny were drinking tea quite serenely.

'I'm pleased you're here, Fiona,' Rose said, 'because I wanted to ask your permission before I started cleaning out the kitchen. What have you been doing to that oven?'

Fiona and Penny grinned at each other.

'I think we'd better leave you to it, Mum. I was hoping you'd come shopping with me, Penny. I need some things from the village. There'll be seven of us for dinner tonight.'

'Seven?' said Penny.

'Yes. I was counting the baby.'

'Eating for two, are we?' Penny looked at Fiona critically. 'Yes – I can see the bump!' She hugged her sister impulsively.

'Off with you both,' Rose insisted.

Penny took her denim jacket from the back of the chair and joined Fiona in her car. Here was another interview she was dreading. It was impossible to know how much Alastair had told her. Gamblers were notorious for being profligate with their money but economical with the truth.

'I know everything,' said Fiona, as Penny turned into the main road leading to the village.

'Congratulations. Omniscience is pretty rare. I think there's only you and God who qualify.'

'Be serious, Penny. I mean, Mum and Dad told me about Lily. I was just so amazed. But it was funny how it all seemed to make sense. How do you feel?'

'Better than I did. But I don't think I could handle any more revelations right now. You're not going to spring any surprises on me, are you?'

Fiona blushed but Penny did not notice. Fiona covered her confusion by continuing to talk.

'I think Lily must have wanted you to find out the truth. I think that's why she left you so much in her will.'

'She left me a quarter of a million.'

'I know. Mum told me that too.'

'I should have told you. I feel dreadful that I didn't. I'm sure the money's changed me for the worse. I believe no one ought to have that much money – especially me.'

Fiona laughed. 'Look. There's a car park on the left. We can go and look at the Avon before we go into the village. I know a lovely walk by the river.'

So Penny parked and followed Fiona down a path lined with firs on one side, and the river curved to meet them in a wide meander. The path was cool and quiet apart from intermittent birdsong.

'So the shopping's not particularly urgent?' Penny suggested.

'No,' said Fiona.

When they came to a bench overlooking the river, Fiona asked if they could sit there for a while, as she was a little tired. Penny made no objection. The water of the river rippled past them in a gentle sussuration. A heron stalked the other bank, its eyes fixed on the surface of the water.

'I brought you here to say thank you,' Fiona said.

'For what?' Penny looked at her in surprise.

'For paying off Alastair's debts. That's right, isn't it?'

'Oh, that.' Penny felt awkward.

'We want to repay the money eventually.'

'It's not necessary.'

'I think Alastair needs to.'

Penny understood that but privately resolved to give the money to charity.

'Look, Pen. Is there anything else to find out? Alastair's lied to me before, and you must promise to tell me if there are any other debts – anything – that you think I should know about?'

Penny paused. 'Nothing.'

'Help me, Penny. I don't know what to do. What if it starts again? He says he's going to stop, but that only means he wants to, not that he will. I'm not that naive. But what do I do?'

'I don't think *you* can do anything. But he'd better get some professional help. There are groups that have a high success rate. But I only know of ones in Manchester.'

'That's OK. We're moving back very soon.'

'To your house in Greenmount?'

'No. We need to sell it to Paul and Janice to cover our debts. But we do have somewhere to live.' Fiona looked down at the footpath.

Penny thought of Alastair's flat and shuddered. Her sister couldn't possibly live there.

'Look, I'll pay your rent. Get somewhere nice.'

'No – it's all been arranged.'

Penny was a little hurt. If money was good for anything, at least it enabled you to play Lady Bountiful.

'Alastair told me he wants to get help. That's a good sign, isn't it?'

'Very much so.'

'He had a rotten childhood.'

'I'm not surprised. Addicts often do.'

'I still love him,' Fiona insisted.

'That's good,' Penny said. 'Hold on to that.'

A couple in stout walking boots trudged past them, nodding their heads in greeting. Penny and Fiona waited until they were out of earshot and the heron swooped across the river, meeting mid-flight with another heron. Penny continued.

'I have a hunch he'll be all right. But it might not be easy. Or even straightforward.'

'I know. But I'm not wrong to hope, am I?'

'There's nothing wrong with hope.'

'I'm looking forward to making a fresh start,' Fiona said.

'Neither of you is working. You'll be hard up.'

'Well, we—' Fiona interrupted her.

'What will you do for money? No, don't answer that. I want

to give you some more. Quite a lot, actually. It's not making me particularly happy, and you need it more than I do. Don't tell me you're too proud to accept it – it's not charity. Look at it this way – you'll be helping me. And there's your baby to think of. Lily would want her money to help a baby.' Penny felt herself redden. 'Fiona, this isn't negotiable. I'm going to force you to take the money. It's not a loan, and I'm not being a philanthropist. My problem is I'm hopelessly common. Wealth just doesn't suit me. So you'd be doing me a favour. I refuse to leave it all to charity when I die. Instead I'm going to be a fairy-godmother aunty instead, like Lily was.'

'Can I say something now?' her sister asked.

'If you must. I was enjoying myself.'

'I really appreciate what you're offering. But in fact we have a financial adviser who's helping us. He thinks he knows of a firm that could use someone with Alastair's skills, and his office needs someone to cover a maternity leave. That's why we can afford to go back to Manchester and pay rent on his – on a house he knows about.'

'A financial adviser?' Penny queried, annoyed. Her attempts at philanthropy seemed doomed to failure. 'That was quick work. A financial adviser who finds jobs and accommodation?'

'Friend of the family,' said Fiona.

She's certainly resourceful, Penny thought to herself, with some admiration. It made her feel rather old to discover that her little sister was so capable of looking after herself. Some financial adviser, too. Suddenly Penny went cold.

'This house – don't tell me – I'm psychic! It's a converted double cottage, not far from Heywood? Two-bedroomed, small walled garden, ideal for a baby.'

'Oh dear,' Fiona said. 'I've left my purse in the car. I'd better go and get it. Even in the country you can't be too careful.'

'Fiona – come back!'

Too late. She had gone. Penny was baffled. How had Rick got himself mixed up in all of this? How did he know about Fiona's troubles?

She had to find out. Penny got up to follow her sister. As she did so, she saw another figure making his way along the river bank. She knew immediately who it was. Rick Goldstone. She sat down again and gripped the side of the bench. He came to join her.

'You're still wearing my top,' he said.

'You've come all the way here to get it back? You must be desperate.'

'I am.'

More than anything Penny wanted to touch him. His hands were lying loosely on his lap, and the urge to reach out and make contact was almost unbearable. Yet it was too soon. She would have loved to gaze into his face, but there was something he had to know first.

'I've found out certain things about my parents,' she said, not wanting to look at him.

'Kitty told me. You're Lily's daughter.'

'How long have you known that?'

'Since yesterday. Though I'd guessed some time ago. And last night your parents filled me in on the circumstances. It doesn't make any difference, Penny.'

'So my parents brought you here?' she asked.

'You mean, did I not come of my own accord?'

Penny was silent.

'Do you like me, Penny?'

Surely he knew the answer to that? And then it occurred to her that maybe he didn't. Perhaps he wasn't as super-confident as she imagined him to be. Perhaps he was more like her than she dared to think. So she said, 'Yes.'

'A lot?'

'Yes, a lot.'

'Do you know that I like you too?'

She nodded dumbly.

'Well, that's OK then.' He took her hands and held them tight. She wondered if he could feel them trembling.

'Kiss me,' he said.

Slowly Penny moved towards him, and as her mouth met his a sense of joy overwhelmed her. She kissed him because she loved him. Money had nothing to do with it. Or rather, he was her fortune, and she was ready to claim him as hers.

'There,' she said, regaining her composure. 'That's what I think of you. And you didn't need to prove a thing to me.'

She buried her head in his chest, utterly content. Rick ran his fingers through her hair.

'What did you have done to this?' he asked.

'Oh, another of my many mistakes. I'm good at making mistakes. I misjudged you too. I'm sorry.' She took a deep breath. 'And I pretended to myself that I didn't love you. But I do.' There. She had risked everything.

She disappeared for a while, and emerged breathless from Rick's embrace.

'Only, where are you going to live now? You've let your cottage to Fiona and Alastair, haven't you?' She looked at him, her eyes shining.

'It's OK. I can move back in with my parents. They've kept my old bedroom pretty much as a shrine to me.'

'Sounds dreadful. I'd hate to live with my parents again. Look, Rick, I've got an idea. Why don't you take my flat? I'm living in the Wharfside now. Please. Oh – but you said you didn't like apartment living?'

Penny's fingers were intertwined with his. Neither could bear to let the other go.

'True. I don't much care for apartments. You're surrounded by people, but still end up feeling lonely. That's the only problem. What do you think I can do about that?'

Penny looked up at him and met his eyes fully. He was so beautiful to her. She drank him in like champagne.

'I suppose you should get a flatmate.'

'And you've become rather dependent on my wardrobe of late.'

'True. I have.' They smiled at each other, unable to conceal their joy.

'All right,' Penny said. 'I'll stay on as your flatmate.'

'No,' Rick said suddenly. 'It wouldn't work.'

'What do you mean?'

'Come on. What would people think? There's your parents, my parents, your readers on the paper, and Aunty Kitty. I don't think she'd like the thought of us living in sin.'

Penny held his hand tightly.

'This is a problem,' she said.

'A problem indeed. You're the Agony Aunt. What do you suggest?'

'I don't know.'

'For Kitty's sake, we could pretend to be married.'

'No,' said Penny, drawing closer to him. 'I think there's been too much pretending.'

'Surely you're not suggesting we might get married for real?'

Penny hid her head in his chest again.

'It's up to you,' she murmured.

'Good, because I've been under the impression we've been engaged since Fiona's wedding. You can't disappoint me now. And Kitty seems to think we're already married. She told me so yesterday.'

'Ah well, we can't disappoint Kitty,' Penny said slyly.

'Or Lily,' Rick added.

Their lips met again in a kiss, and they were oblivious to Fiona honking the horn of the car, to the salmon that leapt at that moment from the river, to everything.

And Penny reflected that her mother had got her way after all.